BEFORE NOON

BEFORE
NOON

A NOVEL
IN THREE PARTS
BY
RAMON J. SENDER

UNIVERSITY OF NEW MEXICO PRESS
ALBUQUERQUE

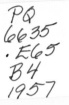

The first part of *Before Noon* was published with the title *Crónica del Alba* in Spanish in 1942 (Editorial Nuevo Mundo, Mexico City). In 1943 Doubleday Doran, New York, published an American translation followed by the edition of Jonathan Cape in London, and the Italian and Danish editions. The Italian edition (Longanesi, Milan), as well as the English, have had the good fortune of several reprintings. Appleton-Century-Crofts, New York, has published more than ten successive printings in Spanish for American university use. The second part was published in Spanish in Mexico City with the title *Hipogrifo Violento*, by Collección Aquellare, in 1954. The third part, entitled *La Quinta Julieta*, was published in 1957. These two parts are translated for the first time into English and give an original and unpublished character to the whole book.

The quotations from *Life Is a Dream* by Pedro Calderón de la Barca are from Denis Florence MacCarthy's translation in *The Chief European Dramatists*, edited by Brander Matthews, by permission of Houghton Mifflin Co., Boston.

COMPOSED, PRINTED, AND BOUND AT
THE UNIVERSITY OF NEW MEXICO PRINTING PLANT
ALBUQUERQUE, NEW MEXICO, U.S.A.

LIBRARY OF CONGRESS CATALOG CARD No. 57-14518

TO MY SISTER
CARMEN
AND HER HUSBAND
PEPE AYALA

THE PARTS OF THE NOVEL

I

Chronicle of Dawn

translated from the Spanish

by WILLARD R. TRASK

Unlikely As It May Seem

CHRONICLE OF DAWN was written in the concentration camp at Argelès. The author was a Spanish officer on the General Staff of the Forty-second Army Corps. Had I not seen it done, I could not have believed that a style so serene and cold, so "objective," was possible under those cruel conditions. The real author, José—Pepe—Garcés, was a great friend of mine. I also know Valentina V. and Don Arturo and all Pepe's family, and I knew some of the other characters, like Don Joaquín A., who died a natural death. The accessory figures and part of the setting of the narrative are unknown to me, because my acquaintance with the others was later, in the city. Pepe Garcés entered France among the remnants of the Republican Army. From his normal position as a healthy, intelligent and honest man of thirty-five, a gentleman after the Spanish fashion—which is to say that he made dignity a kind of religion—he found himself changed into a refugee under suspicion, subjected to the rifle-butts of Pétain's Senegalese Negroes. Like many others, he was herded along in this fashion to a bleak corner of a countryside open to the February ocean. He was shut up in an immense enclosure surrounded by a wire fence. There we met. He had given the few things he had brought with him—a blanket, a tin cup, a penknife—to the first who had asked for them. He never went to the place where food was distributed and consequently ate only when someone brought him food and managed to persuade him that he had more than enough. The only thing he owned in the world was a book. It was not a historical treatise, or a novel, or a religious book. It was a technical manual of fortification. As long as the central region—Madrid and Valencia—resisted, which is to say during the first four weeks of our life in the concentration camp, he continued to read his book, making sketches, filling the gaps in his knowledge. "Ah," he used to say, "they are resisting in the Centre, and one day we shall be sent for."

He made a dugout in the earth, like a moderate-sized tomb, close to mine, and there he remained with his book, day and night. This refuge would have protected us from the rough weather if it had not rained so constantly. But after the first rain it was never dry again. And we had to sleep there. At night the wet ground froze.

Pepe Garcés never went out except to go to the entrance of the camp, where the dead were laid (thirty or forty every day). He would come back taciturn. "We must take as good care of our health as possible," he would say, "because we shall be needed." And he opened his book again.

The day that we knew Madrid and Valencia had surrendered he went down to the seashore and threw his book into the water. He returned to his dugout and tried to sleep. I gave him my blanket as I had done before. When he woke up he was another man. It was hard to believe that he could look any worse than he had, but Pepe Garcés had collapsed. The fluid that sustained his nerves had gone with the manual of fortification and with the hope of returning to the fight. He was a dead man.

"All useless!" he said, pacing back and forth.

He did not know what went on around him. When he heard that someone had left camp and he was asked if he would like to leave, he shrugged his shoulders:

"What for?"

One day he began talking to me about far-off things. The village, his family, Valentina. Since I knew them, I listened at first. He talked particularly about an old peasant woman who lived in his home until his mother died. They called her "Aunt Ignacia." His chief anxiety in those days was whether Aunt Ignacia had died before the beginning of the war or not. The idea that such a pure and simple being had known so much suffering unbalanced him. "You do not know," he said, "the impression she made on me the last time I saw her. I was twenty-eight, a grown man, and I had gone to the village on business connected with the estate. It had been many years since any of my family had gone there. I stayed with some relatives, and when Aunt Ignacia heard of it she came to see me. Her husband had died many years before, and her face was as wrinkled as a walnut. She embraced me and kissed me and then sat down in a chair and looked at me. She looked at me and cried and said nothing. For two hours. When I left, she was still sitting there crying, with her hands folded in her lap." My friend repeated: "Oh, if only she died before the war, if only she died without knowing so much hatred!" My friend had seen her in 1930. She was so frail that perhaps she could not have survived for six more years.

"Do you think that she died during those six years?"

His mania for talking of those days and those people was a defense and a flight. I talked too. I allowed myself to be influenced by what Pepe said, without despairing. My one idea was to get out of the camp. When I wanted to unite my friend's fate to mine in my plans for freedom, he looked at me wonderingly and said:

"Go away from here? What for?"

And he went to the entrance of the camp to look at the day's dead. "Those men," he said to me once, "those men have gone out by the only gate worthy of us."

I never argued with him. As soon as I was in the camp I had decided to conserve my energy in every possible direction. Physical energy, moral energy, intellectual energy. My friend did exactly the contrary. He walked up and down, grew excited when he talked of anything at all, and, although he was beginning to cough and had fever in the afternoon, he still would eat only a small part of what I brought him. The rest, he shared. He used to look around and say disconsolately: "Oh, what hungry faces!" But he did not see his own.

I succeeded in leaving the camp and made an effort to secure his release, but I was always stopped by his own refusal. I went to see him and brought him food and tobacco, which he immediately gave to some peasants from his province, keeping nothing for himself but a package of cigarettes. The second time I went I found him in such a condition that I was surprised to see him up at all.

"No such thing," he answered my alarm. "I am better than ever. I've made a hut with your blanket and I am sheltered from wind and rain."

He asked for writing paper, notebooks, and pencils. And later for candle ends too. In addition, I brought him an electric flashlight and some calcium tablets. The time we were together he spent talking to me about his mother, Aunt Ignacia, and Valentina, who had been his first and great love. I listened and was as much interested as he was. When I spoke of the possibility of getting him released, he flooded me with further reminiscences of his childhood, of his early youth. I thought of the most absurd procedures, even of having him declared insane, to obtain his release. No matter how—once he was out, I would take charge of him and see that he was properly cared for. But he was not insane, he was the most reasonable man in the world, although when he talked he was always fired by a sort of idyllic enthusiasm.

When everything had been arranged for his release, he said:

"It will be useless. I am grateful to you, but you are wasting your time. I shall not leave here except to go to Spain."

"To Spain?"

"Others have been released from here and taken to Spain."

"Who had them released? The Fascist police. And they took them to Spain to shoot them."

"Obviously."

"Why obviously?"

"We lost and we must pay. Our war was an undertaking to win or die."

My efforts were unavailing. All that I was able to do was to continue bringing him calcium tablets, notebooks (which he used up in surprising quantities), and pencils. It pleased him, and, since he had been taking the calcium, he seemed, if not better, to have paused in the descent to ruin. I tried more and more arguments to convince him, but the two serious attempts I had made through the British and American committees, he himself transferred to other internees, who obtained their liberty by this extraordinary chance. "They have children," he said.

"But why aren't you willing to leave? What madness is this?" I cried.

Seeing me so excited, my friend exaggerated his own calm:

"It is useless. I don't want to drag out my life somewhere. If I get out, do you know what I will be? At best, a deceived hero. Everyone deceived us. The fact is that the generation now in power everywhere is a corrupt generation, a generation of liars. Few of us will live until the succeeding generation, our generation, takes command of things. Few will live until then because the war undermined our health. But even if we live, it is not certain that the rising generation is not contaminated. It seems that to reach the level of power, you have to lose everything first."

Lowering his voice as though he were telling me a great secret, he added:

"They believe in nothing. That is what makes them liars. What is a man without faith to say? You know what they say in our country when they condemn a man. They don't say, 'He's a thief' or 'a criminal,' even though he may be one. Those things are not so important. The serious thing is when they say, 'He is a man without substance,' or 'of no substance.' In a man, substance is faith. There lies the whole question."

"Leave this place, and there will be at least one man of faith in the world."

"What for? The air I breathe, the ground I walk on, will all be borrowed. And to live by borrowing from men without faith—I can't believe in that. No, no. Our war was a war for life or death. The vanquished must pay. And you," he added, "who were like me, do not deceive yourself."

"I?"

"Yes. There is a great cataclysm coming. You will pay too. All the nations will enter a war which began among ourselves. Our own problems will be exactly repeated on a world scale. And from the coming tension, the faith of mankind will arise once more, and in the face of danger the best will be reinstated in their own lost substance. But while things are being readjusted again, you others will be dragged down by the cataclysm. The enraged and terrified liars will attack you and destroy you because you are now the weakest among men of faith. But you," he conceded, "are under an obligation to save yourself, even among them, among the liars."

"I?"

"Yes, because you have sons. Do what you can. Bring them through, so that they will be men as we were."

The discussion was difficult because his arguments were much stronger than mine. I felt them within me each time I thought of his obstinacy. So I changed the subject and began to talk to him again about our childhood. He at once gave himself up to his memories. It was as if, instead of living ahead—refusing to go forward in life—he had begun a retrograde motion. Every new remembrance of people and things he had known filled him with delight. And he revealed something else to me:

"I am writing all this."

I told him that I should like to read it. It ought to be good, because Pepe had always had a discriminating fondness for poetry.

"It distracts me," he added, "but besides . . . besides, it helps me to remain a man of substance."

He had said it with noble humor under his tramp's beard. I gave him more notebooks and pencils. My friend was surprised by his own memory. "I do not remember names or faces or occurrences of the two years before the war, but my childhood and my school days I remember very well, and when I write about that period, names and colors and even poems come back to me."

He took some loose sheets from his pocket. "This is the poem I dedicated to Valentina, composed to a popular song." My friend identified another sheet. "This is the love *romancillo* I wrote in my peacock days— unripe melancholy trying to be mature. And this, this is a sonnet to her. I wrote it yesterday. And this one to the shepherds at home. I wrote it yesterday too." I asked him to lend them to me until my next visit. The song was graceful. It brought back the sunshine of childhood and made me smile with ineffable delight.

PEPE'S SONG TO VALENTINA

All in my father's garden
There grows a little vine.
Tell no one, no one, no one!
Let it be yours and mine.
*   'Twas you, 'twas you*
I saw beneath the yew!
I knew, I knew
How fair and firm you grew.
For you, for you
Turtledove and turtle true.

All by the garden fishpond
Bend down your face to see
It will be you, it will not be you
And a fish in every tree.
*   'Twas you, 'twas you*
That made the reeds so bold,
I knew, I knew
Because you shook with cold.

Play till time for bed
All in the ring
Of cinnamon-bread.

All in my father's garden
Tall grows the tree
Full of empty nests
Only for me.

Come, girl, and play
Play till time for bed
All in the ring
Of cinnamon-bread.

'Twas you, 'twas you
With the lemon-flower spray,
I knew, I knew
That you would cry all day.

Where are you, Valentina?
"Where would you have her be?
She's gone to gather shells
At the bottom of the sea."

Dindle and dandle!
Here comes the notary
Bringing his candle.

It produced, perhaps, as much emotion in me as in him. Reading it, the song kindled in the air. To think of such things in the midst of such suffering was a kind of pleasantry of God's. Pepe had given me a *romancillo* too. It belonged to the age which is already adolescent in sexual impatience and melancholy. I did not intend to publish it, but here it is:

ROMANCE TO VALENTINA

(When they were both in Boarding School)

Beloved of my waking,
Beloved of my dreaming,
Here in the peace of the window
There waves a rustic curtain
While from the distant pastures
A pastoral clamour rises,
Behind the flock in motion
Rises a cloud of incense
And in the crystal evening

Sounds all the vale of Vero.
Come to the solanar
And there we two will temper
The hours in good romance
With the wind for diapason
Because this wind from Sobrarbe
Will set your hair on fire
Will chant his ancient ballad
With the rhyme-words of my kisses
Then if it so befall us
Before the stars bring evening
Will make you even fairer
Will make my thoughts lie quiet.

Although it has a certain country fragrance, the melancholy seems affected. But in the following sonnets there is poetic talent, a talent which he never began to cultivate "professionally," we might say, if poetry ever becomes a profession. But these qualities in him were mere trifles beside his prodigious strength of character.

SONNET TO THE SHEPHERDS OF SANCHO GARCÉS

These mountain shepherds, leaving to the care
Of dogs their cabins, put their sandals on
And to the confines of themselves have gone
Thus shod; God's praise in hymns they did declare
Under the auspices of dead kings mourned
They congregated in an oak tree's shade
Their crooks in sceptres flowered; they obeyed
And from God's praises to God's laws they turned.
All through the mountain peaks the tempest rolled
From the horizons dropping hail to fold
In storm Guatizalema's either side
Lightning descended even on the oak
In a golden cross, whereat the new king spoke:
Kneel down, kneel down, for this shall be our sign.

I was not surprised that he could write such serene verses in those surroundings, since I had seen him wake under the frost of dawn disturbed at the idea that Aunt Ignacia should have known the horrors of war. But these things sustained life in him much better than my calcium tablets. Alas, there was no sustaining it longer than the time he needed to transfer the last of his memories to paper!

SONNET TO VALENTINA

Evening in the garden of my sisters
Kindled to flame by a boreal breeze
Diana of broken marble and falconry
Stark naked in an intimacy of frogs.
Pentecosts of the wind in the bell-towers
The azure rooster scratching at his comb
Flowers and fruit in the forgotten basket
And a trembling in your two early hands.
You were not you but your conjecture
Barely raised from the waist
Two leaves of henbane in your hair.
I leaned against your blond knee
"Look at me now no more, for such are dreams"
And you closed your eyelids of rain.

My friend continued to write his recollections, interspersing them with poems which I did not know and which, because they were sometimes written on loose sheets instead of in his notebooks, have been lost. After I read the last sonnet I asked him a stupid question:

"Blond knee?"

"Yes."

"Valentina?"

"Oh, she was very dark, but her knee, her arms, her throat under her first-communion chain, were blonde."

My friend died in the concentration camp at Argelès on November 18th, 1939, aged thirty-five. When he had finished writing his recollections—the things that seemed most interesting to him at that "midday" of his thirty-five years—there were no calcium tablets that could keep him alive. He died on my blanket, under a rainy sky. Without suffering, failing quietly. When he died, rain was falling. Drops trembled in the beards of war veterans. Perhaps from the rain. Before he died, my friend smiled and said:

"I am leaving by the only door worthy of us."

His manuscripts were all given to me. In the first notebook I found the following annotation: "If you use any of this and publish the first narrative, do what you can to send a copy to Valentina V. I know that she is alive, and you can get her address from the R. M.'s, who live at 72 Coso Bajo, Zaragoza."

These are the first three notebooks. I give them as they were, under what seems to me—after hearing my friend speak of the "midday" of his life—to be the most appropriate title.

Here Begins the Book Which Is Called Chronicle of Dawn

For the first time in my life, men have confined me to a limited space. My feet cannot go where they will nor my hands do what they want to. Yet there is a way to escape from all this. Only, dreaming is not enough. It is necessary to write. If I write down my recollections, I feel that I am adding something material and mechanical to recollection and to thought. I shall start with the period of my childhood when my memories begin to be continuous. I shall go on until I have told everything, down to today.

I shall make no digressions. That is why I allow myself to make them now, before I begin. Once I have begun I shall only relate facts. Setting down one memory after another, as I might lay one brick after another to build myself a shelter against wind and rain. Perhaps that is what, really, I am setting out to do.

‡ 1 ‡

When I became ten years old I thought I had entered the period of responsibilities. I began to take less part in street fights, in our gang wars. I had a gang of my own in our town—eight or ten boys who fought under my orders wherever the enemy showed himself. The most blood-thirsty of the enemy gangs was led by Colaso, and his most dangerous henchman was Carrasco, who lived in the house next to mine. However, I had seen nothing of either of them for three months. This change was caused partly by my introduction to regular studies and partly by my parents' making it more and more difficult for me to have a "private life." I had to study—and it was no longer a question of primary school, but of serious professors who lived in the capital, and before whom I should have to present myself to be tested in such arduous subjects as geometry, history, and Latin. All this impressed me considerably. My father regarded it as a matter of great importance. That didn't make me work any harder; it only made me uneasy.

To study, I had to stay at home, and this change in my existence made the details of our family life stand out in clearer relief. My room was at the top of the house, and beside it there were two large storerooms through which I could get out on to the tiled roof of the second story. The doors of these storerooms were kept locked so that we children should not get in, but I went in and out easily, and left them locked behind me. The way I could manage old locks surprises me even yet.

To study my geometry, I used to rise at dawn, let myself into the storerooms, and then climb out on the roof. It was not a very good place to study, and I ran some risk, because the tiles were covered with hoarfrost and sloped steeply. The first time, my boots slipped, I fell, and started sliding. I should have been killed on the flagstones of the inner court if there had not been a chimney in the way directly below the window. After that I learned to slide down to the chimney on two rows of tiles. Once there, I turned round, settled down comfortably in the sun, and opened my books. I read through my lessons, but I paid more attention to the cats and the sparrows. The cats came to know me, and we ended by being good friends. But the sparrows could not get used to me—at least not then.

Naturally, I knew our house cats and could tell them apart from those of the neighborhood. We had one light-red cat that no one in the family liked. He was the victim of a proverb which, in his case, seemed to me wholly unjust. When anyone wanted to say something disagreeable about a man or woman with light-red hair he would wink one eye and recite, "Nor dog nor cat that color!" My family's dislike of the light-red cat proceeded from this prejudice, and the poor beast bore it stoically. Realizing that I was the only one who liked him, he showered me with attentions. He used to wait for me on the roof-tree—cats always like the highest places they can find. When he heard me opening the window he came picking his way down the tiles, avoiding the places where the hoarfrost lay. I slid down the tiles like a mechanical doll until I bumped into the chimney, and he came up and put his wet paws on my open book, making a mark beside a Latin declension or a triangle, depending upon whether I was studying Latin or geometry, then he strutted back and forth, rubbing his back on my chin and his tail on my nose. The other cats gathered around and looked at my cat admiringly, and I kept watch on their movements. I called to them caressingly and held out my closed hand as if I had something to give them, and when I was sure that they wouldn't make friends I took my slingshot out of my pocket and hurled little volleys of grapeshot at them—sometimes with good effect. Then they went away, but showed no signs of fright.

From my post on the tiles I could see the tower of the Convent of Santa Clara where it rose above the housetops, wide and square and covered with Moorish arabesques. Between the tower and my lookout there were many roofs—reddish or black or shades of green—and between them here and there the thin pillars of a *solana*, hung with drying clothes. And every day invariably, as soon as I had greeted the cat, the little bell in the tower began ringing, turning over and over in a sort of sonorous alarm. "The nuns are leaving their cells to go to chapel," I would say. And it served as a warning, because the chaplain of the convent was my tutor. He was named Don Joaquín A., and he lived at the foot of the tower. He was fifty years of age, rough and melancholy in appearance. My father said that he had been a priest of note but that because of an accident—he had broken a leg and limped considerably, though it was not an ignoble limp—he had had to renounce his ambitions and retire to this secondary post. His house contained several rooms, with glass doors opening on to a terrace entirely covered with flowers. The terrace ended in a small balcony which overlooked the little Plaza of Santa Clara; the side toward the entrance-court of the convent was filled by a long balustrade. The pavement, the walls, the pillars of the convent portico, and the stairway were all of brick, to which the years had given a dusty color. A few straggling weeds grew in the crevices. There was a bell in the court, which rang whenever anyone opened the gate. The convent belonged to a cloistered order, which means that the nuns never went outside it nor did anyone from the outside world ever go in, least of all persons of the opposite sex. In the morning—which was the time I went there—the portico was full of sunlight. In the afternoon, and even more at twilight, I would have had no doubt that ghosts haunted it. The chaplain, with his rough and melancholy manner, was a man to get on well with them.

To reach the convent I didn't really have to go out in the street. At least not by the front door. I went down into the inner court by the open stairway from the kitchen, from the court I went to an empty stable (it was always empty—a wonderful place for us to play in), from there to a poultry yard full of geese and hens (the roofs of their shelters peopled with pigeons), and from there to an alley paved with wide uneven flag-stones which ran right to the Plaza of Santa Clara. This alleyway—Nun's Alley—was flanked on one side by small houses held together, God knows how, by worm-eaten wooden balconies. In one of these houses lived a woman named—like the Plaza and the convent—Clara. She was the bishop's sister (my father, to lessen the offensive relationship, said she was his "cousin"). She was some forty-eight years of age and received a monthly pension from her brother which was paid over to her by my mother. The bishop's entire family spent the better part of their lives trying to convince Clara that she ought to enter the convent but she laughed at them all and answered roguishly, "Yes, a nun, a nun! The kind that live two in a cell!" She spent her pension on clothes, especially underwear, and she always had a flower in her hair. When she went out it was to buy sweets at the confectioner's and wine at the tavern. Her dresses were ugly, almost in rags, and if one of her neighbors made a remark she pulled up her skirt and proudly showed her starched petti-coats covered with lace. When she called at our house to get her pension she never came inside, but we children used to run to the door to see her.

Every day when I passed her house in winter time, she would grumble from her balcony, "Poor child, with his legs blue with cold! With what they steal from me they could make him long trousers!"

Sometimes in spring, her grudge against the bishop would grow stronger. "A nun, a nun!" she would say. "Some day I'll catch my brother under a hedge!" This threat translated itself for me into an amusing scene: the poor old bishop whom everybody venerated ("a saint," my father used to say) fighting with his sister at a crossroad.

I was quite well advanced in Latin. While this was my first year of geometry it was my third of Latin, for my father was a victim of the cultured delusion that unless you know Latin you can never know Spanish. But there was a difference, because now I was studying for the examinations, which meant that it was in deadly earnest. My tutor was terribly exacting, because what he wanted was that "when I went up to be examined, I should know more Latin than the professor." He meant the lay professor at the Institute. He believed that only priests really know Latin.

On this particular day we were studying Seneca's 114th Epistle on the "causes of corruption in eloquence," where he writes: *"Multi ex alieno saeculo petunt verba: duodecim tabulas loquuntur."* Mosén Joaquín asked me to explain to him why Seneca wrote *"duodecim tabulas"* instead of "*sermonem duodecim tabularum.*" I didn't know, and although Mosén Joaquín realized that he had asked too much of me, he was not in a very good humor when we turned to geometry. That proved to be my undoing. As so many times before, the cats were to blame. The open book still showed their damp paw-prints, looking like rough sketches of clover leaves.

At the end of the lesson Mosén Joaquín said: "I refuse to take the blame for your faults, and if you fail at the end of the course your father must know that the responsibility was yours and not mine." It was a fact that I had not learned my geometry lessons for several weeks. He had come to realize that I was being obstinate about it, and he wanted to put a stop to it. He looked at me, undecided. Then he shut his eyes as if he were making a great decision, muttered, "I'm sorry," and made a cabalistic sign in my little oilcloth-covered notebook. I had to leave the notebook open at my father's place at table every day at dinner time. Ordinarily, I understood the meaning of the marks my tutor put in it, but today I could make nothing of it. There was a queer scrawl and a figure 20. I reached home extremely curious. It was noon, but my father was not in. My brothers and sisters, most of them younger than I, were playing up and down the halls. Their nurses and wet nurses were working in the kitchen, along with the famous Aunt Ignacia—who was not our aunt but who, having seen our mother born, was almost as important a person in our household as she. In the dining room, which opened on to a small inner court, the table stood glittering with glass and silver. The dining room had a large fireplace, framed in light carved wood; a fire of logs was burning in it. The fireplace was directly behind my father's chair; across from it was a balcony, beyond which you could see the gallery opposite, full of sunlight. Beside my father's plate stood a glass siphon covered with metal mesh, with an arrangement for inserting a lead capsule of carbonic-acid gas; this manufactured the soda which diluted our wine. Once empty, the lead capsules became mine.

My brothers and sisters began coming in. The little ones tried to put on their bibs themselves—to do so, they hung them over their shoulders, tied the strings under their chins, and, when they were tied, turned the bibs around to the front. Aunt Ignacia ate with the maids in the kitchen, and that day we had looked in because she was eating with an enormous ladle, and calling out, to make us laugh, "My mouth is as small as an angel's, so I eat with a coffee spoon." The maids had already eaten, but Aunt Ignacia used to dine at the same time as ourselves or after us. Her

husband almost never came to the house. He was a laborer. But one day
when Aunt Ignacia was quarreling with the woman who made our
bread they got so angry that the woman, who envied her, told her that
she had "a face like a carnival mask," and Aunt Ignacia answered, "I
may have a face like a carnival mask, but I married the handsomest man
in this town." From that time on, Aunt Ignacia's husband seemed to me
a sort of mythical being—"the handsomest man in this town." I had never
heard of "handsome men." My elder sister, who was three years older
than I, told me that he really was.

The peculiar scribble in my notebook had a fatal effect. What happened had never happened before. It was quite true that I was behind
in geometry—the course was going on, and I had not mastered even the
first ten lessons. My tutor had seen that I was regularly neglecting both
geometry and history, and had made up his mind to condemn me to a
whipping of twenty strokes. When my father looked at my notebook he
ordered me to leave the table and wait for him in my room. He shook his
head despairingly. His eyebrows, his nostrols, and his short-clipped
moustache were all expressive of energy. "You are setting out to be a
shame and a disgrace to us. But you shall not be, because I am your
father and I won't tolerate it." I was standing beside him, motionless.
My little sisters—especially Maruja, who had reasons for bearing me a
grudge—kept staring at me with a sickening, I'm-better-than-you expression. "I'll get you," I said to myself, humiliated, "I'll get you, you harpy."
My father hesitated between putting another capsule into the siphon and
continued his scolding. "Is this the example you give your brothers and
sisters? Is this the way you repay your father's trust?" What kind of an
example could I give Maruja? I'd give her a good slap, that's what I'd
give her! My mother interrupted gently, telling me to go to my room.
But my father had not finished. "Can't you even look ashamed? No—you
have no shame. Look at him, how coolly he listens! You're cynical—
stupid and cynical. And you'll grow more so every day. But I"—and he
raised a threatening hand—"I'll find a way to stop it. If I don't stop it,
God will call me to account, and I'm not going to tell Him that you were
the stronger and I couldn't control you. I shall find a way to stop it, no
matter what it costs."

The reprimand was more dramatic than ever before. I had made up
my mind not to listen, but I did not dare leave the room until I was told
to. I thought of indifferent things. Across the thought, for example, of
my bird snares in the yard, my father's voice would float, solemn and

persistent. "The shame of the family, a disgrace to every one of us—if you don't pass in the Institute I'll apprentice you to a shoemaker." Instead of indifferent things, I began to think of the things that moved me most. Of Valentina. I was in love with Valentina, the notary's youngest daughter. My father's words could not penetrate her image. Valentina had deep eyes which were too big for her face, her two short braids were drawn over the top of her head, and at the place where they came together her mother always put a little bunch of artificial flowers, yellow and green and red. And when I spoke to her she stood first on one foot and then on the other and sometimes scratched one leg with the other shoe, though there was nothing for her to scratch. On that image my father foundered. His voice rang false, and the more impressive he tried to be, the more artificial and meaningless he sounded.

As always when my father scolded me, the light-red cat came and jumped up on my shoulder. My father shouted, holding the siphon capsule in his hand; the cat purred, passing from one shoulder to the other by way of my back or my chest, and rubbing himself against my chin and the back of my head as he went. Maruja continued making a great show of eating nicely to please Father. Concha, amused by the cat, concealed a tolerant smile behind her grown-up's napkin.

My mother got up, came to my side, and took me by the arm. That meant that my father's anger had reached its climax. She led me out and went with me up to my room; she continued to scold me, but in gentle tones. "Your father isn't well, you mustn't upset him." Terribly offended by having been made to leave the table and humiliated at the threat of a whipping, I thought: "Good! He isn't well? Good! If he dies, so much the better! I wish he would die and we were poor and I had to look after mother. Then they'd see who I am!" But when I said so to my mother in measured terms, she became frightened.

"My son," she said, taking me perfectly seriously, "at present your role in life is to obey."

"To obey?"

"Yes indeed. You were born. And having been born and being in this life, there is nothing for it but to obey."

"Well, if I'd known that, I wouldn't have been born!"

I was engrossed in the thought of the whipping. My father wanted to settle the account before he began his dinner, and I could hear him coming up the stairs. Before he entered, my mother kissed me and went out. I could hear them arguing in low tones in the hallway. My mother's kiss incited me to heroic measures. I would lock the door, or go out on the roof where my father couldn't come after me, or defend myself with my air rifle. But my father was already in the room, and in his hand he held a whip. Once again I took refuge in the thought of Valentina; but if her image was stronger than any injury, it had no real efficacy against physical pain. The idea of being chastised in my naked flesh, with my trousers pulled down, was so humiliating that the thought of Valentina only increased my shame. My father began to whip me with some force. I bore it without moving an eyelash.

At last he asked me, "Have you anything to say?"

"Yes. It was supposed to be twenty and you've only given me eighteen."

My father went out and slammed the door behind him, muttering, "You may be a tramp, but I'll straighten you out!" When I was left alone I began to have a tremendous desire to be a "tramp." Really to be one, to justify myself for all this in some way that would utterly disgrace my father and send my mother crying into a corner. These ideas evaporated a little later when I heard everyone getting ready to go out and my mother and Aunt Ignacia appeared, the latter with a tray of dinner to which my mother, by way of an extra dessert, had added some of the sweets that the nuns of Santa Clara occasionally sent her. Mother stole a glance at me, trying to hide her uneasy curiosity. Aunt Ignacia joked, "Here comes the condemned man's last dinner."

And she told a story. Aunt Ignacia's stories were in a peculiar vein which was usually not appropriate to the situation. But at the end of them someone would speak some highly expressive phrase which she would repeat, imitating accent and gestures in such a way that there was nothing to do but burst out laughing. This time, the allusion to my situation as a "condemned man" brought to her mind a story of a hanging. Mother didn't listen to her, and I didn't listen to Mother, who was sighing. All my attention was given to Aunt Ignacia.

"And then they put the noose round his neck and fastened the rope to the gallows. And the criminal said to the hangman, 'For God's sake, don't pull it so tight, or I'll choke.'"

The "for God's sake," which was forbidden in our house, but which was overlooked when Aunt Ignacia said it because she was Aunt Ignacia, made me burst out laughing. It was a sort of revenge. Aunt Ignacia, in the depth of her simplicity, understood that. But the story was not finished. The hangman answered the criminal:

"That's just what you're here for, my man."

I devoured my dinner. The end of the story did not make me laugh as much as the "for God's sake," pronounced with such a rustic air, had done. Besides, the poor criminal who could not conceive that they meant to kill him caused me pain. Mother watched me eating, and sighed. I asked her if I might go out to play, and she said it would be better if I stayed in the house and that I could play if any of my friends came.

"What this little boy wants," said Aunt Ignacia, "is something I know."

"What?" I asked.

"That's a secret."

"How do you mean?"

Aunt Ignacia screwed up her face like a circus clown's and, hunching up her shoulders and dropping her hands in her lap, repeated, "It's a secret, a great big secret."

I laughed again. My mother went out; she was smiling too. When she was gone, Aunt Ignacia wiped my mouth and said:

"Valentina is coming."

Then she said I ought to be ashamed of myself, and told me another story. This one was about a hanging too. Each of Aunt Ignacia's stories had a title; this one was called "Justice in Almudébar, or He Who Owes Not Pays." It was about a tailor who was going to be hanged in the plaza of Almudébar for having committed a murder. When he was standing on the scaffold and they asked him if he had anything to say, he turned to the audience and said: "Except for my crime, I have always been a good neighbor and on good terms with everyone, and besides I am the only tailor in Almudébar. When I am gone, who will make clothes for you as well as I did? On the other hand, you have two blacksmiths here, and one is quite enough for the trade in the place." And the people began to say that he was right, and they caught one of the blacksmiths, who was in the square, and they hanged him and let the tailor go.

Again I couldn't laugh at the end as I had laughed when she raised her voice in imitation of the condemned man's speech. The blacksmith at the end caused me great pain. Aunt Ignacia concluded:

"You must begin to behave better, or else . . ."

"Or else what?"

"Someone will get spanked."

That offended me. It called back the humiliation of my whipping, those blows which had established between my father and myself the relation of criminal and executioner. And my skin was smarting where I had been struck. Aunt Ignacia gathered up the dinner dishes and went away.

Valentina was coming.

The wardrobe was open, and there hung my clothes. There was my green velveteen suit, which looked like velvet. It was my favorite, a "hunting" jacket with four pockets and a belt, which came down almost to my knees and left room for barely two inches of trousers to show. In the darkness of the wardrobe it looked black; between the lapels the thin silver chain of my watch shone dimly. Even when I didn't wear the jacket, I went every night to wind the watch and look at the time. I took the jacket down and put it on my bed. The watch was thin, and had a cover that opened by a spring. The cover was engraved with oak leaves and acorns, leaving a little space bare with room for a shield in which were my initials. The numbers on the dial were yellow. My elder sister said they were amber, they had a soft brilliance, it seemed as if there were a light inside them. The trademark was composed of three initials, m. z. a.—Madrid, Zaragoza, Alicante—and someone had convinced me that the trains ran in accordance with my watch. I was very fond of this suit, but it had a dressed-up look so that when I wore it I was obliged to scrub my knees with soap and water and sometimes with a stiff brush or even with pumice. I made my toilet as well as I could, put on white socks and patent-leather shoes, combed my hair, using plenty of soap to hold down my curls, looked at my watch, and went downstairs.

I have said before that Valentina was a brunette. Her father, the notary, was named Don Arturo V. He was a friend of my father's and had another daughter, two years older than Valentina, named Pilar, a blonde beauty in the standardized American manner. Her pale golden hair and white skin, and a look of passivity which was her habitual expression, made me dislike her intensely. Valentina had big eyes and a little pouting mouth, her face was a perfect oval, the color of her skin, light olive. They were both pretty, each in her way, but I, who adored Valentina, naturally felt obliged to detest Pilar. They were both studying the piano, and on gala occasions they would play charming sonatas for four hands. Don Arturo was very fat and dark and had the appearance of a patriarch. His wife was much more bourgeois-looking.

I loved Valentina, but until that evening I had not told her so. Fortunately, she arrived before my brothers and sisters had come back from their excursion. I was especially glad that Maruja was not there, because

I was afraid that she would make me ridiculous by telling about my whipping. I listened for sounds on the stairs. I knew that Valentina would not come in until someone went downstairs to receive her, because we had a ferocious mastiff chained in the court. He had never shown any signs of disliking Valentina; even so, she was right to be afraid of him. I went downstairs twice in error. The first time I found a beggar sitting in the street by the door, a contented-looking man with rosy cheeks; his thick eyebrows and his beard were beginning to turn white. From under his cloak he produced some empty tin cans into which he carefully packed scraps of food. In one of the cans I recognized something that I had left on my plate, and experienced a momentary anguish linked with a feeling of security. Yet that beggar, who studied neither Latin nor geometry and whose father had been dead for years, was a fortunate being.

Valentina appeared at last, running down the street; when she saw me at the door she stopped. Then she came walking along, wearing a faraway smile; suddenly she changed her mind and started running again. When she arrived she began blaming her sister Pilar. She said she had wanted to come sooner, but they had made her practice her music. I thought this was a good opportunity to look at my watch and tell Valentina that the figures on its face were amber. Though she perfectly well knew it, she thought it was her part to ask me if it had been a present for my first communion. I told her that it was, and that the chain was silver too. Then we ran in through the door. Every two steps Valentina hopped twice on one foot, which made the artificial flowers in her hair dance gaily. When we came where the dog was I told her she mustn't be afraid. He was lying down; I went up to him, sat on his ribs, opened his mouth, put my clenched fist into it, and said, "These dogs are perfectly gentle."

Valentina looked at my knees, and I thought I had done well to wash them. Upstairs, panting with impatience and fatigue, she told me that her sister went too fast on purpose when they were playing the Bertini sonata so that she couldn't keep up with her and would make a show of herself. I asked her if she wanted me to kill her sister, but Valentina answered solemnly:

"Leave her alone. It's better to let her live and have everybody see what a fool she is."

Valentina's two little ears showed in front of her braids, which were wound over the top of her head. Her black hair was parted from the nape of her neck, exactly over the clasp of a gold chain from which hung a medal the size of a centime representing the Virgin of Sancho Garcés Abarca. On the back of the medal were engraved her initials and the date of her first communion. I was going to ask her if it had been a present; but these were questions that we asked each other rather too often, so I stopped. One of the things that troubled Valentina was that her parents called her sister by a pet name: Pili. I said that that very day I would name one of our old cats Pili and the whole family would call her that and when everyone had taken to using the name we would invite Pilar to visit us and I would call the cat so that everyone would hear. Valentina giggled.

We were now in the downstairs part of the house, and I kept calling, "Pili!" For some reason, the cat came, which filled us with delight. Meanwhile, we were making our way to the gallery. As we went, I put my open hand against Valentina's ear and followed its outlines as if I were sketching it with my palm, pressing down and lessening the pressure at the same time.

"That does the same as a sea shell," I said.

And I added that Pilar's ears would grow every day until they were as big as an elephant's. Valentina remembered that her mother had told her one day that she had very pretty ears, and then felt obliged to explain to me how she washed them and how she always used a thin towel to wipe them because you couldn't do it with a bath towel.

"Who do they like better, Pilar or you?"

Valentina said that no one at home liked her. Wtih a superior air I asked her if her father had ever beaten her. She said no, but that her mother had sometimes boxed her ears. I didn't think that her mother was an enemy worthy of me, so I only made a face and clicked my tongue. But Valentina added that her mother had never hurt her, and that sometimes it was her own fault because she liked to make her angry. It was clear that she was on the point of asking me the same question, but she stopped, no doubt because she thought it unnecessary. Then she burst out laughing. She made fun of herself:

"What a fool I am!"

"Why?"

"I was going to ask you if you had ever been beaten."

Me? Who would beat me? And what for? Just then I had some difficulty in sitting down. At once I said to Valentina, over-eagerly:

"When Maruja arrives, don't talk to her."

"She always comes and pulls up my dress," said Valentina, "to see what I have on underneath, and then she tells me what she is going to wear on Sunday."

I turned pale with anger. Pulling up her dress was something that couldn't be done, or at least could be done only under a definite risk, that of going to hell or falling asleep for ever in the woodshed among the rats. Sometimes when I was playing with Valentina I saw part of her thighs, but I knew very well that you don't pull up a girl's skirt. What I saw when my eyes, without my wanting them to, fell on Valentina's thighs was an intimate white garment with little strips of lace, and I received the impression that the parts of her body which I could not see were made not of flesh but of some precious and inanimate material. Since I had owned the watch, I liked to think that they were of amber. Neither could I imagine (if I had ever even thought of it) that Valentina had physical needs like other people. I knew that she sometimes disappeared into the bathroom with one of my sisters, but the bathroom, for children, is the place for secrets and confidences because it is the only place where they are allowed to lock themselves in.

I hated Maruja, but I had not succeeded in communicating my hate to Valentina. At first this annoyed me. But I soon understood that Valentina was so good that she was incapable of hating anyone. Perhaps, on mature reflection, she did not even hate her sister Pilar. She came and went with the little roses in her hair, smiled when I looked at her, and washed her ears every morning by a method of her own. But today I saw her as a stronger being than usual. I was compelled to it by the idea that I had been whipped. That lowered me so much in my own eyes that Valentina grew and grew. Besides, I was sure that Maruja would tell her as soon as she arrived. Maruja, with her barely eight years, had the gift of perfidy. I had come to fear her bickering weakness.

But I had been whipped. The afternoon was passing, and my brothers and sisters would be coming back. The first thing they would do would be to ask me, "Have you had dinner?" That would certainly make Valentina wonder. Then, perhaps, "Aren't you allowed to go out and play?" That was less revealing, but Maruja would seize any opportunity to show me up. In spite of my romantic clothes, I felt weak and dispirited. No one could feel anything about the blows I had received but an ugly, animal pity. Anyone knows that a father might strike his son, but I was a free entity in the world and no father on earth had a right to lay hands on me. Moving closer to Valentina, I said:

"They say I am your sweetheart."

"Do you want to be?" she asked.

"I do, yes. How about you?"

"That doesn't matter. If you want to be, we are. What do we have to do?"

"Don't talk to my brothers and sisters. Go right back home now."

"The maid is coming for me at six," she said, not understanding.

"I will take you home. I don't want you to be with my sisters, because all they do is talk nonsense. I'll take you home."

I stood up and took her hand.

"If I am your sweetheart," she said very seriously, "I have to do whatever you tell me. If you tell me to come, I'll come. If you tell me to kiss you, I'll kiss you."

"No, no, not that," I said, blushing terribly; but realizing that I was being stupid, I kissed her on the cheek. Then I took her hand and we started toward the street.

"Now we'll go to your house."

She was my sweetheart and had to obey me, but she wanted to tell me something and said nothing. She liked being in my house, with me, and the fact that I was sending her back to her own, where Pilar ruled, was inexplicable. When we were in the street, hand in hand and side by side, we felt contented again. We had not gone far before we encountered Enriqueta, the mayor's daughter. She was twelve years old, and I had hated her since the year before. Enriqueta was a little harpy. With all the knowledge she had acquired from nursemaids, she led on small boys of her own age, which aroused my hatred. I had listened to the confidences of older boys, who presented things in an ugly and dirty light; but these confidences, in which I did not in the least believe, remained completely apart from my understanding of love. Seeing Enriqueta at that moment, I pretended to be preoccupied, but she looked at us with ironic disdain. I wanted to say something definite against Enriqueta to my sweetheart, but it seemed as though anything I might say would offend Valentina more than it would hurt Enriqueta.

"If you see Enriqueta again," I said, "don't look at her."

Valentina did not understand.

"How can I do that? If I see her, it's because I've looked at her."

But she gave the answer herself. "I see her from far away and know it's she. And when she passes me I turn my face away slowly, like this, and look at the wall."

She did it so thoroughly that she stumbled and almost fell. When she stumbled, the flowers in her hair slipped down to one side. I wanted to rearrange them; she said that it would be better if we had a mirror, and we resigned ourselves to her wearing them in disarray and walked on. In the opposite direction came a pale, round woman, with almost no eyebrows and goggle-eyes. She stopped, arranged Valentina's flowers, and called her "my love." I watched her, not too pleased. Her hands seemed made of sugar candy.

"Why are you looking at me like that?" she said, smiling. "Jealous?"

We went on, and I was aware she had stopped and was watching us, murmuring endearments. I kept turning my eyes toward Valentina, who answered my happiness by looking in turn at me like someone who is waking from a dream and smiling. The little gold chain against the dark skin of her neck seemed as if it would be hot if I touched it.

"Do you like Enriqueta?" she asked.

"No."

"She's pretty, though. I wish I were like her."

"There's no one prettier than you."

"I wish I were, though. Especially now that I am your sweetheart."

I put my arm around her waist and felt her shoulder against my chest. She turned and looked at me with quick smiles. I should have liked us to evaporate into that afternoon light which was amber like the figures on my watch and Valentina's legs. Valentina talked about herself. She wanted to tell me what she liked to eat, and she added that when she had gone to bed her mother came to tuck her up tight and she pretended to be asleep so that her mother would kiss her, and her mother kissed her. Hearing this, I couldn't do anything but kiss her hair. And Valentina went on talking. What she liked best was, when she got home after running and jumping and sweating all afternoon, to take off her shoes and put her bare feet into an old pair of slippers she had. Remembering the pleasure of it, Valentina closed her eyes. "I must try it," I said to myself.

But heaven sent catastrophe upon us. Round a curve in the street came our old carriage, an unwieldy contraption from my grandparents' time, full of children. My father was on the box.

I wanted to get Valentina out of the way, but there was no side street near. Besides, my father had seen me. And when the carriage stopped beside us, Maruja put out her arm and, pointing her finger at me, shouted:

"He has on his new suit and his watch!"

My father said, "Where are you going?"

"I am taking Valentina home."

After a silence full of menace, my father gave his orders: "You go home. And when you know your lessons for tomorrow, if you want to go out, come and ask my permission."

I felt so humiliated that I did not know what to answer.

My father said to Valentina, "Get in, child."

Maruja's impatience and her broken exclamations showed that she had much to tell Valentina.

"I'm on my way home," Valentina said, remembering her duty as my sweetheart.

But things were to be as bad as possible.

"Get in. We'll drive you home."

There was nothing else to do. She got in. I watched the carriage turn around. In vain I hoped that an axle would break, that the horse, which was very old, would die suddenly. But the carriage was lost once more round the turn in the road, and I made my way home bathed in a cold sweat. I climbed the stairs like a ghost and shut myself in my room. I took off my hunting jacket with a feeling of utter ruin and flung myself on the bed. I did not cry, but I bit the counterpane until I tore holes in it. My breath struck the bedclothes and came back in my face like fire. I looked up. On the wall was an old painting of the child Jesus, who looked like Maruja. I knew that behind the picture there was a sort of niche in which were old papers, inscriptions on parchment, a portfolio of untanned leather, two antique pistols, and a dagger which had doubtless been made from a file because between the two cutting edges the steel was still roughened. The day I discovered these things was an unforgettable one. I kept my secret, and, though I was not sure that I could use them, the fact of having such arms gave me great strength. I took the dagger and put it in my belt. Then I got off the bed. I didn't know what to do or where to go. I imagined Valentina listening to Maruja's confidences. "Maruja will tell her that I have been whipped, that I got twenty strokes, and she will imagine me naked, receiving the strokes and crying ignobly."

I went into the storeroom. In a corner there were eight or ten mattresses folded double and leaning against the wall. I, who had been caressing the handle of the dagger in my belt, threw myself on the mattresses and began to thrust at them furiously. To feel the blade of the dagger go in, to push it deeper and deeper, to strike again, gave me a pure feeling of revenge. I kept this up for several minutes. The wool bulged through the wounds, and a few flocks came out entangled in the guards of the dagger. My teeth were clenched; my fingers hurt from pressing so hard on the hilt. I thought of nothing.

But at last I thought of my father and I had to begin over again with even greater fury. Not a single mattress was left without seven or eight serious wounds. I put the dagger back in my belt and looked around, panting for breath. There in a corner was Aunt Ignacia, with a bag of camphor, beside a pile of blankets. She was staring at me, motionless.

"God in heaven!" she said. "He takes after his great-grandfather on his mother's side who staked his wife at cards!"

I climbed head first out of the window on to the roof and scrambled down to the chimney on all fours. There was a soft sky with little pink fluted clouds. I went back in again and returned to my room. On my way through the storeroom I saw Aunt Ignacia examining the rents in the mattresses, and I said:

"No accusations, now, mind!"

"Holy Virgin, he's after me with a knife! Me, who have changed his diapers a thousand times!"

I hadn't threatened her with a knife at all, but she must have seen the dagger in my belt and connected it with the threat in my voice. It seemed very strange to me. I went into my room and reviewed my arsenal. My air rifle, my pocket flashlight, two tops, a box of colored pencils. Bah, all that interested me there was the rifle and the flashlight. And I thought of Valentina and Maruja. Probably that fool Maruja, who never listened to anything and who when one of the others talked too much began to whimper and said, "Be quiet, I'm going to talk now"—probably the little fool was talking more than ever, for Valentina was not much of a talker out of deference to her sisters-in-law. I began to think up an adequate revenge, but each one that I considered had a reverse side which would put her in a good light. If I killed Maruja she would have a funeral like one I had seen. A white coffin covered with little crystal prisms, with eight wide ribbons hanging from it. Gentlemen in black clothes bowing one after the other. And all the bells in town tolling. No. That was too much. Besides, she might go to heaven. After long hesitation I decided to shut her up in the carriage-house with a goose. A ferocious goose that she was more afraid of than anything in the world. She would scream like a crane. Looking through my arsenal again, I found four small firecrackers and put them in my pocket. Then I went down to the poultry yard. On my way I passed another locked room which my father pompously

called the library; it was littered with magazines and unopened newspapers still in their wrappings and a set of bound volumes of *The Family
Museum*. *The Family Museum* was a large-sized, mid-nineteenth-century
magazine full of engravings. There were also a few dozen books. We
were not allowed to go there, but I had my skeleton key hidden in the
niche behind the painting.

In the poultry yard the savage goose came at me with head down and
wings half open. He did this to anyone he saw, but when he got close
enough to recognize who it was he made up his mind one way or the
other and either attacked or slunk shamefacedly away. When he recognized me he raised his head, shut his wings, and went off, dissembling.
I saw that he was in form, and went on to the pigeonhouse. In the morning, when the sun rose, the pigeons made a sound like a hurricane with
their cooing. I took a handful of corn from a sack in the carriage-house,
and when they saw me they perched on my shoulders, on my head, on
my hands, and when the corn was finished and I went to get more the
whole flock followed me. There I stayed all the rest of the afternoon until
the carriage came back. Then I went to my room again, but, looking into
the dining room, I saw Maruja warming her feet at the fire. "It's no use,"
I said to myself. "If I ask her she won't answer and if I threaten her she'll
scream for Mother." In an agony of uncertainty I went out on the roof
and threw my firecrackers into the chimney one by one. But I made a
mistake; it was the kitchen chimney into which I was throwing them—I
realized it when I heard the explosions from below and the uproar
among the servants. To this day they have not been able to account for
it, though Aunt Ignacia, when the cook talked of the devil, shook her
head and said: "Yes, yes. A devil who's the image of his mother's
grandfather!"

My father was striding up and down with the wrapped and folded
newspaper in his hand, complaining, "In this house no one ever reads anything." But he ended by going up to the library, leaving the newspaper
in a pile with all the others, and looking into a zinc chest to see if his
pipe tobacco, which he used to mix with rum or brandy, was dry. I had
been there before him and had taken a volume of Bécquer's poems to my
room. I read in it here and there but could not find anything suitable
for Valentina. Besides, I was too upset to apply myself to anything. What
had Maruja told Valentina? I put down the book and, taking advantage
of my father's remaining in the library, went to find my sister. As soon
as she saw me she began screaming, "Mamma!"

"Be quiet! I'm not hurting you. What did you tell Valentina?"
I knew that my other sisters would not have told her anything. Maruja raised her head.
"The truth—I told her the truth. That you're a big stuck-up!"
I moved toward her, threatening and furious.
"And what else?"
"Mamma!"
Mother appeared, and once again I went to my room. For some reason I felt much calmer. Perhaps Maruja had told her everything, but talking to the little idiot had had a quieting effect on me. In my room I began to look at Bécquer's poems again. Now every poem seemed fit for Valentina.

> Again the dusky swallows will return
> To hang their nests beneath my balcony.

Or that other:

> For a kiss—I know not what
> For a kiss I'd give.

And I thought: "My sweetheart loves me more than Bécquer's sweetheart loved him, because Valentina lets me kiss her and even said she would kiss me if I told her to." I started to copy a short poem which spoke of "the sound of kisses and the beating of wings," and of which the last line said, "It is love, passing by." And after that another, which ended: "To-day I saw her, to-day I saw her and she looked at me—to-day I believe in God." But when I had copied them to the end, I threw them into my desk, took out my notebook of Latin declensions, and wrote on it in large letters:

THE UNIVERSIAD

From my tutor's allusions to Greek and Latin literature I knew that there were poems of this kind with similar titles, in which someone's praises were sung. I wanted to begin and write the whole history of the world to show that everything had been created to the end that Valentina and I should love each other. But no ideas came, and, feeling cross, I began a nursery rhyme:

> The little pretty sparrow
> Sat in the lemon-tree.
> With her beak she pecked the flowers,
> With her beak she pecked the leaves.

I closed the book and began to walk up and down, trying to find verses for "The Universiad." Suddenly the door opened and my father entered.

"So this is how you study!"

He walked over to my pile of books. The first thing he saw was the notebook on which I had written "The Universiad." Next, my copies of Bécquer's poems. As I had hidden the book, perhaps he thought that the poems were mine, and he looked at me as though I had sprouted horns.

"Oh!" he said. "It seems we're not to be spared even this!"

He went away with the poems and the notebook, sighing; this time he did not slam the door. A little later my elder sister sneaked in, and I eagerly asked her what had happened about Valentina. My elder sister admired me because I lived on the top floor and didn't feel afraid. She imagined me studying there at night and could not understand my courage. She was studying history, too, and she always did it in the dining room; but even so, if there was no one else in that part of the house and her history book suddenly told of the death of some king, she shut her book with a bang and went running through the house until she found someone.

"What's up?" they asked her.

"Nothing," she said, a little ashamed. "Only Charles the Fifth died."

Even though she was growing up she did not lose these fears. Now she stood before me, and I pressed her with questions. She was surprised at my anxiety and assured me that Maruja had not spoken two words to Valentina; she had put all her energy into monopolizing my father in order to make it clear beyond doubt that the gentleman driving the carriage and talking fondly to her was *her* father, not Valentina's. Father, into the bargain, had patted Valentina's cheek, which had decided Maruja not to speak a word to her through the whole drive.

I showed my gratitude for this news by deciding to begin studying at once. My father had gone away, taking the poems, in the depths of despair. "Oh!" he sighed. "A poet! What trials God sends!" When my mother convinced him that they were only copies he said that he felt much relieved and came upstairs to my room again. It was already dark. My sister Concha was no longer there, and I had gone out on the roof with my flashlight. I sat down against the chimney, opened a small textbook of astronomical geography, and began reading and looking at the sky. "The Three Marys, the Great Bear, Capricornus, the Little Bear. The Pole Star. And some of the planets. Not all of them. The ones that aren't there must be on the side of the earth where it is day." This part of geography was elective, not compulsory. When I learned that, I took a great liking to it. It was the only thing in my studies that interested me.

My father did not find me in my room. He searched the house for me in vain. Finally I was discovered on the roof. "For astronomy, it's good to be able to look at the sky," I said.

"But that part of the course is not compulsory, according to what your tutor says."

I could not tell him that that was why I was so much interested in it. My father went away and I heard him saying:

"Something has got to be decided on."

The following day I knew my lessons well. In view of that, my tutor took me into the next room and handed me some pieces of rough stone which showed the impressed outlines of fishbones.

"These are fossils," he said.

That showed that he had made an excursion the afternoon before. He went on explaining them to me, but, realizing that I was not old enough to be curious about such things, he stopped and said:

"I should like to begin teaching you natural history."

While he talked he watched me covertly, trying to make out if my punishment the day before had made much of an impression. Mosén Joaquín was my friend and never babied me—that is to say, he treated me as a peer. He took his role with a seriousness which I have never seen equalled. When I found out from certain indications that it was a point of pride with Mosén Joaquín for me to get good marks on my examinations, I understood that he had a need for me and I adopted an almost protective attitude toward him. This was the secret reason why, from then on, I knew my lessons more or less thoroughly, and never went to class without at least having read them over.

‡2‡

When my relations with my father improved, the whole family seemed to feel greatly relieved. Mother, my brothers and sisters, Aunt Ignacia. My brothers and sisters chattered incessantly at meals, but if I began to speak they kept still. The only person who seemed to be offended by my new situation was Maruja, who could not bear to have my father speak to me with a smile.

Valentina came often. I could not go to her house as frequently, be-cause, though her mother liked me, her father had a great antipathy for me. He knew that I had said something against him at home and that everyone had laughed. I could not forgive Don Arturo for being Valen-tina's father. He had a clerk in his office who always wore black, an intelli-gent-looking man, silent and courteous, rather over-precise in his dress and his speech, but who—poor fellow—was lame and used a crutch. The clerk respected my father greatly; he liked me and began to treat me as a grownup. I caused great mortification to Don Arturo, who had published a book entitled *Love, an Essay Toward a Psychological Analysis.* It was his doctor's thesis, and he had sent two copies of it to my father, one of them inscribed: "To Don J. G., this book of stale ideas, with greetings from the author." My father said it was a very good book, but when my mother asked him if he had read it he answered vaguely and only reiter-ated that it was a very good book. One day I was in the further yard where Aunt Ignacia sometimes amused herself with the rabbits and goats; I was trying in vain to understand some of Don Arturo's ideas, opening the book here and there. In a moment of inattention the goats tore it to pieces and ate it. Fortunately, it was not the inscribed copy. Some days later when my father said at dinner that it was a remarkably good book I agreed with him and my mother looked at me, wondering. Maruja was all ready to be delighted at what appeared to be a forthcoming reprimand, when I said, perfectly seriously, "At least for goats." I explained what had happened, and my father hesitated between laughter and indigna-tion. I told Valentina about it, she told her mother, and the story reached Don Arturo. They tried to make a joke of it, but Don Arturo did not forgive me.

I continued to be in love with Valentina. I returned to copying Bécquer's poems and gave them to her one by one. There were no love poets in her house, but sometimes on the backs of calendar leaves she would find sayings of famous men; or short poems by well-known or anonymous poets, often very erotic:

> *Between your arms, soft chains,*
> *Love sings his lethal hymn.*

Whenever Valentina found the word "love" she carefully copied the poem and put it in the pocket of her dress to give to me. One day the poem was by a modern poet; it said, more or less: "When I met you I loved you and felt a thorn in my heart. The pain from the thorn would neither let me live nor kill me. One day I pulled out the thorn. But now, alas! I feel my heart no longer. Would that I could feel it again, even though pierced by a thorn!" Naturally, I was much moved, and I returned to Bécquer's book. So the weeks went by.

My father had forbidden me to go on to the roof; but seeing that I did not study except when I was sitting by the chimney, he decided to give me permission to do so or at least to pretend that he didn't notice. So now I went out there with a pair of field glasses which I took from the library and with which I could see the roof of Valentina's house. When I told Valentina about it, she decided to go out on to her roof at the same time as I. From then on I saw her from my perch, and a few days later she told me that she had found her father's field glasses and could see me with them. So I decided to make a signal code by which I could talk to her on the days when, for some reason, we could not be together. On a piece of cardboard I sketched every possible pose of arms and legs until I had got an alphabet. There were a few additional poses which were intended to represent whole sentences. Both arms raised with hands open and wiggling fingers meant, "I dreamed of you." Arms crossed and legs apart meant, "Pilar is a fool." I knew that this pose would be frequently repeated. One arm akimbo and the other raised straight up meant, "I shall come to your house." I made an exact copy of it for myself and added one pose which she was not to use and which meant, "for God's sake." I thought it indispensable to my masculine role.

Our first dialogue brought me to class an hour and a half late. Mosén Joaquín warned me that this must not happen again. When the sun rose the next morning Valentina and I were on our roofs. She gave me sensational news: her cousin had arrived. I answered with the sign for "for God's sake," and became very eloquent, while the cats pricked up their ears, watching me without knowing whether to run, and the pigeons sailed round in small circles with the sun making rainbows on their wings. I had to see Valentina's cousin at once to find out what he was like and how long he was to stay. He was the same age as I was and lived in a nearby town.

My lessons were catastrophic and I arrived late again, though not as late as the day before. The months were passing; spring was drawing near, and with it the examinations. Perhaps Aunt Ignacia had seen my dances on the roof; she had said nothing to me, but I saw horror reflected in her eyes and in the evasive way she answered when I spoke to her.

My tutor realized that something extraordinary was happening to me, and he said that he wished neither to tell lies nor to do me harm. So he refrained from putting any mark in my notebook. I left it on the dining table as usual, and my father mistakenly concluded that my standing was the same as that which Mosén Joaquín had benevolently given me the day before. Feeling grateful to him, I studied a little and then ran off to see Valentina's cousin. To make an impression on him, I put one of the pistols into my belt. Valentina was waiting for me outside her house. She called her cousin; I saw a boy in knickerbockers and a knitted jersey. He wore very thick glasses and was a little taller than I. In the shadow his white skin looked blue. His hair was neatly brushed. We stood looking at each other from a distance without saying a word. Valentina pointed to him and said:

"This is my cousin."

We continued to look at each other in silence; finally he pointed at me with his chin and blurted out:

"He wants to fight."

Valentina assured him that I did not. The boy kept on looking at me resentfully. I asked him what his name was.

"Julián Azcona."

"Related to the Deputy?"

Valentina answered for him, saying yes. His father was a liberal Deputy whom my father criticized unmercifully. Using words that I had heard at home, I said to him:

"You are the son of a nefarious politician."

"I?" he said, not knowing what to think.

I started toward him. Moving backward, he repeated:

"He wants to fight."

"Admit that you are the son of a nefarious politician."

He took another step backward and made the admission. He did not really know what "nefarious" meant. Valentina pacified him:

"He came so that we could all three play together."

At one side of the house there was a little hill. Before we set out for it Valentina's cousin said that he was going to get his gun, and returned with a target rifle which was the dream of my childhood. Not letting me touch it, he said:

"This rifle loads with real gunpowder and shoots real bullets. Yours is just an air rifle—Valentina told me so."

I told him that the one she had described to him was not mine but belonged to one of my younger brothers, and with well-simulated indifference I pulled the pistol out of my belt. Valentina's cousin hid his surprise.

"If I load this with powder I can kill a horse," I said.

The boy looked at Valentina, who affirmed with great gravity, "Or an elephant."

"And I can knock down a house if it isn't a big one."

Valentina continued to support me:

"Like ours."

Looking hard at his rifle, I added:

"And I can make an army retreat. Or at least," I conceded, "I can hold it back until reinforcements arrive."

The boy shook his head, clicking his tongue.

"No. I don't believe that."

"Why not? I stand on a narrow bridge where they can only come over one by one. *You* tell me what would happen then."

The boy looked at Valentina, who nodded her head gravely.

"And the bridge—where is it? Because there isn't always a bridge."

We were walking along but we stopped. Valentina's cousin was the first to speak. Pointing to Valentina with some satisfaction, he said:

"She's my cousin."

Hardly letting him finish, I answered:

"And my sweetheart. A sweetheart is more than a cousin."

Once again the boy looked at her, and once again she said yes. Then he smiled beatifically and said, "How silly!"

"What's silly?"

"To be sweethearts."

"And what business is it of yours?"

Valentina's cousin started moving backward again, saying, "I knew he wanted to fight."

Valentina took my hand. Nevertheless, his rifle gave him a certain prestige.

"What does it shoot?" I asked him.

"Cartridges."

I burst out laughing and added:

"He says cartridges."

"All right, bullets," he said, confused.

I laughed again, exaggerating the joke, and repeated, "He says bullets!" Then, turning to him again, and coming so close that my breath fogged his glasses, I added:

"What I meant was, what caliber is it?"

He blushed.

"Perhaps he doesn't even know what caliber means," I said to Valentina. However, we started off together again. The boy seemed as confused and as incapable of any reaction as I had supposed. When we had walked a long way he started to talk about the rifle once more. It was obvious that he was clinging to his weapon as his last shred of dignity.

"Whether you like it or not, this rifle shoots with powder and bullets, and if it hits an elephant in the heart it will kill him too."

As Valentina had never seen me with a rifle of such powers, I could not bear that.

"That rifle isn't even good enough to play dolls with."

"What do you mean, not good enough? This is the kind of a rifle they shoot in championships with and win them. And if you fire it at a man it goes right into his body and he dies."

Once again I burst out laughing, and Valentina seconded me, though it could be seen that she did not quite understand what I was laughing about.

"Is it loaded?" I asked him.

"Yes."

"Let me see your bullets."

He took one out of his pocket and showed it to me in his hand.

"That isn't a bullet," I said. "That's called 'target shot'."

"They shot a dog with this rifle," he argued, "a mad dog. And he was a big dog too."

"I don't believe it. It wouldn't kill a mosquito."

I put my hand on his rifle, but he clutched it, ready to resist furiously.

"Don't cry," I said, "I'm not going to take it away from you. I only want you to see what I think of your rifle."

I put my left thumb across the end of the barrel.

"Go ahead, shoot."

The boy's eyes grew wide, and he looked from Valentina to me, uncomprehending.

"I won't shoot, because if I did I'd blow your thumb off."

I put my right hand quietly on the lock and pressed the trigger. The report rang out; I felt my hand being violently pushed back, and held it out open to the boy. There was not the least sign of a wound. Valentina stood with her clenched hand to her mouth, trying to bite her first finger. The boy looked at my hand, uncomprehending. Unexpectedly the skin of the fleshy part of my thumb broke open in a jagged star and began to bleed, heavy drops sliding down and falling to the ground one by one. I rubbed my thumb against my first finger and smiled.

"You see? A mosquito bite! Am I dead, Valentina? Did my hand blow off, Valentina?"

I measured the owner of the rifle with a glance; he was terrified and wanted to go back to the house.

"I didn't do it—you saw I didn't!" he said to Valentina.

The shot must have lodged against the bone of my thumb, because there was no hole by which it had come out. I began to feel a dull pain, which was not localized in the wound but went all through my hand. But Valentina's small dark face, hesitating between laughter and tears, made me forget it completely.

As we went toward the house I thought, "Now that this has happened, I don't care if Valentina learns about the whipping." I kept my thumb bent toward the palm of my hand and my fingers closed over it to protect it. Now and again I felt a drop of blood run down my fingers, becoming more perceptible as it grew colder. Valentina's cousin had not opened his mouth again. When we arrived at the house he said that he had something to attend to and went off, but not before I had warned him that if he told anyone what had happened I would accuse him of having wounded me with his rifle and get him locked up in prison. He swore to keep the secret, and, after admitting once again that he was the son of a nefarious politician, he disappeared through the carriage-house door.

"Do cousins kiss each other?" I asked.

"Only when they arrive and when they go away."

The idea that he was to spend two days in Valentina's house troubled me. Valentina recalled the scene we had played and made fun of him merrily. But she did not know whether she should laugh or cry. Suddenly she asked me, "Does your hand hurt?"

I showed it to her, smeared with blood from wrist to finger tips. Valentina was horrified, but seeing me smile she smiled too. She said nervously:

"You'll come into the house now, won't you, and we'll wash it?"

I said no, so offended that she did not dare to insist. With my wounded hand I grasped my pistol by the barrel, put it into the other hand, cocked it, and aimed at Valentina's house.

"If this were loaded I'd blow up your house right now."

Valentina felt that she was in the presence of a real danger, but I quieted her. She pretended to be brave.

"What I'm afraid of is the noise. Give me time to stop up my ears and I won't care."

When we reached my house we went to the bathroom. Aunt Ignacia saw to it that a boy and a girl never went into the bathroom together, but this time she said nothing. Valentina found some cotton and began to wash my hand. I said that we had a bottle of eau de cologne and that would be better. Valentina did not hesitate over applying the cotton to the wound itself, and I felt a sudden burning pain. I bit my lip, but my forehead was covered with sweat and the end of my thumb burned like a torch. Valentina finished washing my hand.

"Does it hurt much?"

"Yes," I said, gritting my teeth. "But it doesn't matter because it is for you."

Valentina did not understand, and I was not sure that I knew what I meant any better than she did, but in a confused way I felt that it was all for her sake. Valentina had no doubt that what I said was so, but she listened to me and looked at me as if she had entered a world she did not know.

"I've finished."

I stood up (I had been sitting on the edge of the bath) and warned her, "Don't tell anyone." Valentina understood that the consequences of mischief, even when they were bloody, had to be kept secret to avoid trouble. She did not know what to do. She put her crossed hands on her shoulders, stood first on one foot and then on the other, and kept looking into my eyes as if she wanted to say a great many things and did not know where to begin.

"Are you suffering for me?" she said at last.

And, remembering a religious phrase, I told her that suffering makes us worthy of bliss and many other things. Valentina listened in ecstasy. Neither of us mentioned her cousin again. The pain of my wound, I felt the shot against the bone now that it was growing colder, lifted us to another plane. I took out my handkerchief, very dirty and bedraggled. She looked for hers, which was cleaner, and wound it round my thumb. I held it steady myself in my half-opened hand. She asked me if it was better.

"Yes, much," I said gravely, and added, "Besides, I can still use my right hand and that's the important one." I held it up for her to see that it was not hurt. I took out my pistol with it, put it in my left hand, and explained how if the enemy came from the right I could aim this way, or another way if he came from the left, and demonstrated that the wound in my other hand had not put me out of commission at all. Then I gave her two kisses, and we went out.

No one noticed my hand, which I kept in a natural position with the thumb discreetly hidden. Valentina did not leave me for an instant; her idea was to fetch anything that I wanted, to let her little hands supply the lack of my useless one. Maruja watched us in great surprise, realizing that there was something new between us. My elder sister Concha came, as she always did, to offer me protection:

"Papa is in a very bad humor. He has asked several times where you were. You had better go up and start studying."

"In a bad humor, is he?" and, shrugging my shoulders, I said, "Bah!"

My sister shook her head sorrowfully and left us. In another storeroom on the first floor, the house was full of storerooms, they were starting to play theatre with puppets and our little cardboard stage. We went there, but Valentina and I preferred another kind of theatre in which we were actors and audience. We made up improvised plays; and that day the protagonist was an armchair, but the armchair was I. I sat on a stool with my knees bent at a right angle and my arms stretched out, and they put a sheet over me and covered me all over with it. My head and shoulders were the back of the chair, my extended arms were the armrests, and my thighs and knees the seat. So I remained, in perfect silence. The others hunted a criminal who had committed numerous crimes. When the criminal thought he was safest he came and sat down quietly in the chair, and I began closing my arms slowly but implacably until I caught him around the waist. The criminal had fallen into the trap, and all his cries were in vain. When he realized that his attempts to escape were useless, the questioning began. The next was to be Valentina. It pleased me that Valentina would come to sit on my knees and that I should embrace her.

It took a long time to find her because she had had the clever idea of hiding under the sheet, right beside me. She had come there only to ask me if I was in pain and to look at my bandage. I kept her by telling her that no one would find her there, and she crouched down on my knees. She had to give a little squeak, to guide her pursuers, each time they asked her where she was. At last she was caught, and we all solemnly agreed that no one could hide there again because then the victim would learn the secret of the chair and if he knew what would happen he wouldn't sit down in it. It was a long and earnest discussion. But the maid who usually came for Valentina appeared at the door. We all wanted to begin over again, but the maid was in a hurry. She was a large, coarse woman, with hair on her upper lip and a calm expression.

"I can't wait, because it is late already," she said.

Then she added, "And tomorrow is Sunday."

"What has that to do with it?"

"I have to get up early to go and see my betrothed."

She went every Sunday to see her "betrothed"—as she called her fiancé, who lived in another town ten miles away—and she had to rise early. Each Saturday she told it all over to anyone who would listen.

"Joaquina," I asked her, "what is your 'betrothed's' name?"

"It's a bad name—they call him The Lizard," she said seriously.

I went as far as the street with Valentina. Joaquina, the maid, looked at me with an ineffable expression and said, "So polite! He's a perfect little gentleman." The lamp was burning on the wall of the court, throwing two cones of shadow on the pavement. Our dog was asleep at the foot of the stairs. He raised his head with a rattle of his chain and began to growl because at night he was much fiercer, but when he recognized me he stopped growling and wagged his tail. I went to him:

"León, give me your paw."

He did not give it to me. I sat down on his ribs and León did not give me his paw, intent on some new smell on my body. Probably the blood on my hand. He sniffed and sniffed, worried and alert, with one ear half-cocked. At last he reached my hand and licked it. He realized that I was wounded.

He went on licking the back of my hand with his long tongue. Valentina found the courage to touch the end of his tail from a distance.

"He is very brave," she said to the maid, referring to me.

"It's because the dog knows him, because he's its master," said Joaquina.

When we parted at the door I whispered in Valentina's ear that if she ate nine olives before she went to bed and drank a glass of water she would dream of me. I would do it too, and dream of her.

That night I did not have to study, but the next day, having dreamed of Valentina (I did not remember the dream, but it had left me the flavor of a festival, like my father's saint's day), I went out on the roof with my signal code in one hand and the field glasses in the other. For more than an hour I danced and watched Valentina's dances. Three times she put one hand to her waist and raised the other in the air. She was coming to see me. I told her that we were going to Mass at the convent, and that if she went there we should be together. We already knew the poses of our code by heart, and we made them quickly, in a graceful succession. The cats watched me, more astonished than ever, and not even my red cat dared to come near me.

My hand was much the same. I did not think of it. The flow of blood had stopped, and my thumb was rapidly becoming inflamed. Valentina's little handkerchief, which had gone round it three times before, now only went round it twice. It hurt less, but if I ran or did anything that required an effort I felt it throbbing painfully. The only thing that troubled me about it was keeping it hidden.

Valentina and her mother came to Mass at the convent, and Pilar and her father went later at the parish church. We talked to each other in church. Over her bunch of white and green flowers she wore a small black veil, which she pushed back from her ear to hear me better—I spoke in a whisper—and perhaps also to show me her ear which was always nicely washed.

But—alas!—things had changed. Her cousin's parents were to spend the day at her house and take the boy away in the evening, the maid was not there to come and get her at my house, and her mother would not let her go out. To make up for this, Valentina told me the dream that she had had with the olives and the glass of water: My hand was well again and I went to her house and killed her cousin and her cousin's own father said afterwards, "It's a good thing he's dead because he was stupid as a tame duck." Her cousin did in some way resemble a duck, and I burst out laughing. At that instant, Mosén Joaquín, who was saying Mass, turned round to say, "Dominus vobiscum," and looked at me meaningly. Valentina's mother, who was uneasy over our whispering, made us keep still. At the elevation of the Host the bells rang like crystal. Mosén Joaquín, grave and concentrated, elevated the sacred form. Valentina put on the devout and contrite expression which her mother had taught her, but she kept stealing glances at me, and I opened my book of devotions, looking for something. I soon found several lines containing the magic word "love." And I read loud enough for Valentina to hear:

"The heart that is bursting with love seeks a safe road, and in vain love shows it one road after another, and the heart goes on blindly, burning with disillusion and impatience, until it meets with Thee."

Valentina searched her little white prayer book with gilded clasps, and found:

"Lord God of Hosts, behold me a slave at Thy feet, speaking with Thy voice and awaiting a look from Thine eyes."

That sounded very good. Valentina nudged me and explained with satisfaction, "The place to read is in the part in italics where it says 'Words of the Enamoured Soul seeking God'."

Her mother began saying "sh-h-h" again. We opened our missals once more, and Valentina pointed out the place, spelling out the title "in italics": "Words of the Enamoured Soul seeking God." It was easier for her than for me, because the soul is feminine and so what it said was appropriate. I decided to change the gender in my invocations, but as I was reading her a beautiful sentence I came unexpectedly on the word "immolation." And I did not know what to do with it. It was impossible for me to pronounce it straight through without hesitating. Besides, I had no idea what it meant. But Valentina had taken her turn:

"My perverted flesh goes to the deceitful world of pleasure, but my soul seeks and finds Thee, O Lord."

"The effluvium," I read with difficulty, "of Thine insubstan . . . insubstantial divine love heals my wounds."

My book was full of strange words, but looking further I found another section, also in italics, entitled "Words of God to the Enamoured Soul." I showed it to Valentina, much pleased, and said, without any modesty:

"I am God and you are the Enamoured Soul."

"Yes. I," she repeated slowly, "am the Enamoured Soul."

But she started reading her book with a solemn intonation:

"Like the flowers in the fields and the wind in the woods, like the singing of the stream and the breath of spring, my enamoured soul feels Thee by my side, O Lord."

"Flee the world and its deceits, put out of mind the impurities of the flesh, and raise thyself to Me if thou wilt have eternal life."

"As he who is thirsty goes to the spring, as he who is sad seeks after consolation, so do I seek after Thee, my Love."

"Come unto Me and slumber in My lap."

That seemed to me very appropriate, because Valentina liked to be kissed when she went to sleep. Then Valentina read a long paragraph:

"My whole being trembles before Thy greatness, yet it knows that to come to Thee there is the way of love and to Thee it comes, seeking peace, rest, ambr . . . ambrosia, O Lord, in Whom all beauty waits to receive me, O Lord of love, of wisdom, and of dominations."

Instead of reading myself, I leaned toward Valentina:

"Read that again."

She sweetly obeyed. That ending, "O Lord of love, of wisdom, and of dominations," left me confused. At that moment the organ sounded from behind the high screen of the cloisters.

". . . of love, of wisdom, and of dominations."

I had let my book fall (my wounded hand was numb), and with an entire lack of gallantry I let Valentina pick it up for me. When she gave it to me I kissed her hand. Valentina closed her book, smiled, and stood up for the end of the Mass. I too. She said to me, "I'll learn that part by heart so that I can say it to you when I am alone at home."

I continued to feel a strange greatness, which dissolved with the voices of the organ into the dimness of the church. I could have flown and routed armies, even without a narrow bridge. Without knowing what I was thinking or feeling I looked at a statue of Saint Sebastian in a niche in the wall, almost naked and stuck full of arrows. Mosén Joaquín turned to us with a rustle of his starched alb: *"Ite, missa est."* Valentina crossed herself. She had a rosary of little yellow beads wound round her wrist. She was dressed in white, and her dark face, the color of brick, seemed luminous. I looked at her. She told me that when her cousin and her aunt and uncle had gone, in the evening, I could go out on the roof and talk to her. I added, "Even if it is very late, you mustn't fail to go on the roof. If it's dark, I'll bring my flashlight and put it by my feet so you can see me."

"But can you see with field glasses at night?"

"Yes, just the same as in the daytime."

She was smiling all the time we talked, but I was very serious. "Lord of love, of wisdom, and of dominations." I would have abandoned everything—parents, brothers, and sisters, studies, the safety of home—to walk the roads until the end of the world, or the end of my life, hand in hand with Valentina, listening to her speak those words. That, for me, was everything.

I gave her the handkerchief from my thumb.

"Take it. I don't need it now because it's stopped bleeding."

"And who will take care of it for you today?"

She warned me that I ought to put on a new dressing of cotton and eau de cologne. And she wanted to be at my side to blow on it for me.

We went out of the church. In the vestibule I kissed Valentina twice on the cheek. Her mother—of whom I was very fond—gave me a kiss. I found that my elder sister was right when she said that Doña Julia put too much powder on her nose, and just as I was starting off the sacristan came up to me and said:

"Mosén Joaquín wants you to go to him in the sacristy."

I re-entered the church. In the sacristy, which was very small and placed behind the altar, there was a turntable fixed in the wall. It turned on its axis, and through it the nuns sent their chaplain the wine for the Mass, the hosts to be consecrated, and the little starched cloths which were used to cover the chalice. Through the turntable likewise a nasal voice would occasionally be heard, saying, "Hail Mary immaculate!"

Mosén Joaquín would lean toward it and speak in his strong, rustic voice:

"What it it?"

The answer to the nasal voice was supposed to be "Conceived without sin," but Mosén Joaquín did not seem to rate the nuns' ceremoniousness very highly. They would say something on the other side in a sorrowful whine, as if one of them had died, and the priest would answer a little brutally. I found it very diverting.

"I sent for you," he said to me, "to tell you that we will not have lessons tomorrow."

What could be happening? Perhaps a visit from some relative, or a great religious festival in the convent. Mosén Joaquín looked at me wonderingly, as though he had noticed something he had never seen before.

"Did you hear me?"

"Yes, but what is happening?"

"There is to be an eclipse, and we are going to observe it. Have you a pair of dark glasses at home?"

"No."

"A field glass?"

I said yes and that I would bring it. It was an eclipse of the sun. After that, Mosén Joaquín paused and looked at me again, wonderingly.

"How old are you?"

"Ten and a half."

He continued to look at me. I asked him what "immolation" meant, and he told me, smiling. Then he asked me to come up on to his terrace. I had breakfasted, but he gave me some fruit and sweets. On his table there was always a mechanical lighter and an ashtray full of cigarette ends. Today the ashtray was clean.

"What do you want to be in life?" he asked me suddenly.

"Oh, I . . . nothing."

"What do you mean, nothing? That is not possible. You have to be something."

He seemed to be waiting for an answer.

"Nothing," I repeated. "What I am."

Mosén Joaquín opened his eyes in surprise.

"What you are?"

"Yes."

Mosén Joaquín walked silently up and down the carpet, revealing a slight limp.

"And what are you?"

He realized that it would be difficult for me to answer.

"Don't you want to answer me?"

"Well, I'm—who I am."

"Good, I agree. But exactly what is your 'who I am'?"

In a rush of untrammelled sincerity, I said:

"Since you insist, I will tell you. I am the lord of love, of wisdom, and of dominations."

I saw that he wanted to laugh and that he restrained himself as if he realized that he was about to do something offensive. In order to keep from laughing, he put on an appearance of severity:

"And since when have you known that you are all that?"

"Since this morning."

Mosén Joaquín said: "I have no doubt that you are what you say you are, but other people find it difficult to accept such convictions, and I think you had better keep it to yourself, don't you?"

I would not give in.

"You are right about that. But I don't need to have anyone else accept them."

"Why?"

"There is a person to whom I am these things, and that is all I need."

"There is such a person? Who? A girl?"

"Yes."

"Valentina, the notary's daughter?"

"Yes."

"I do not doubt it, my son. But every man must make himself worthy of his own thoughts of himself. I mean he must work, he must develop the gifts which God has given him."

I was drunk with myself; it was this that the priest had seen when I entered the sacristy.

We arranged that I should bring my binoculars the next morning, and, with the prospect of two days without lessons before me, I walked home. I went through Nun's Alley, passed the bishop's cousin on her balcony with a flower in her hair as usual, and went through the back door and into the poultry yard—not without having heard Clara make a pitying allusion to my bare knees.

The family had gone to Mass at the parish church. They concurred with that other world in which Don Arturo and Pilar lived, even in the choice of a church. I kept my wounded hand out of sight. Nobody had noticed it. The secret of it, which I shared with Valentina, enchanted me. Being my sweetheart, she had to believe what I told her, and I had been too confident when I belittled her cousin's rifle to leave her any room to be afraid.

I went up to the roof several times, but she did not appear. I resigned myself, and sat down against the chimney and played with the red cat. I went in and got my book of astronomical geography to find out what an eclipse really was, but I did not understand it very well. All I learned was that there were total eclipses and partial eclipses. Mosén Joaquín had not told me which kind tomorrow's was to be, and I returned to his house to ask him; I wanted to dazzle the family. He told me that it would be partial and would hardly be visible except as a slight decrease in the sun's brightness. It would be caused by the moon passing in front of the sun's disc.

"But you, who are the lord of wisdom—don't you know all about it?"

I heard him laugh, half-aghast and half-benevolent.

During dinner I announced that there was to be an eclipse. At first no one heard me. My mother said:

"Put your other hand on the table."

I did so, hiding my thumb; but a little later, without realizing it, I had it in my lap again. I repeated what I had said about the eclipse, and my father immediately became attentive:

"What? An eclipse?"

I elaborated. It would not be total, the sun would lose a little of its light and the moon would pass in front of the sun's disc.

My sister Maruja said, with her mouth full:

"Nonsense. There isn't any moon in the daytime."

"Yes there is, but we don't see it," said Concha.

My father favored this explanation, and I put my tongue out at Maruja, who protested:

"Mamma!"

My mother told me again to eat with both hands, and I put my left hand beside my plate but I did not use it because I could not hold a fork with it. When the meat was served, since I could not cut it I said that I was not hungry. My mother insisted angrily and I thought I was lost, but my father intervened:

"Don't force him to eat if he doesn't want to."

I felt grateful to him, and when he asked me more questions about the eclipse I brought out everything I knew, mentioning in passing the planets which were nearer to the sun than the earth and those which were farther from it. When I spoke of the rings of Saturn, Maruja said:

"Nonsense."

She was disgusted because I had become the center of attention.

My mother kept her eyes on me.

"Put your hand on the table. And don't make me say it again."

I did so, artfully. No one would have supposed that I had a lead bullet in my thumb. Although it was considerably inflamed, I could still bend it inward.

My father asked for the paper, perhaps intending to read about the eclipse, and my mother said that she remembered a total eclipse which occurred when she was my age. It became dark as night at midday, and the chickens and pigeons went to roost, and the cook was as stupid as they were because she asked whether she should cook dinner or supper. Maruja burst out laughing. My father left the newspaper beside his napkin without having opened it or taken off the wrapper.

There it still lay in the evening at supper time. During supper I talked about the eclipse again.

"How is it that you know so much about it?" asked Concha.

"I know everything."

"You say you know everything?" my father asked.

"Yes," I said simply. "Everything."

I was in a bad humor because I had not been able to communicate with Valentina from the roof all afternoon. However, I felt sure of the evening, and I had my field glasses and my flashlight laid out ready on the bed upstairs. No one could make me explain in concrete terms what I had in mind when I said "everything."

"And how do you happen to know everything?" my father asked banteringly.

"Because I do."

"You remind me of Escanilla, our old coachman. Every year when the special preachers come for Lent he goes to church and listens to them with his mouth wide open, and afterwards he shrugs his shoulders and says, 'Bah, that's just what I was going to say myself.' He has done that for seventy years. He knows everything, too."

I was offended and said nothing. I hid my hand, which was really hurting me. As we did not eat meat at night I did not have to use my knife or hold my fork in my left hand. My father insisted:

"How do you happen to know everything?"

I stood up, throwing my napkin down on the table and pushing my chair back:

"None of your business."

A chill passed over the table. I walked slowly away and disappeared in the direction of my room. My father muttered:

"That is no way for a boy his age to behave."

My mother looked at him sorrowfully.

‡3‡

I wanted to be alone because I was in a hurry to be on the roof. I collected my instruments and climbed out on all fours. I looked through the field glasses in vain; I could see nothing. Things far away had disappeared and Valentina's house was sunk in shadow. I became confused, focusing on lighted windows behind which vague shapes were visible. The sky was clear, and there was no moon. Perhaps the moon would rise later. But Valentina could not stay there all night; they would make her go to bed. I thought that perhaps she was watching for me and turned on my flashlight. It gave a bright light; it was a large flashlight, and though it was called a "pocket" one, no pocket would hold it. Propped between two tiles, it threw its beam on me. And sure that Valentina was watching me with her glasses, I spent more than an hour opening my arms, letting them fall, raising one leg, squatting down, and as I made all my motions quite fast it was like a dance. I repeated the *"Words of God to the Enamoured Soul"* for Valentina:

"Come hither and sleep in my lap."

And then I added:

"Come to me, the lord of love and dominations."

I did not dare to say anything about "wisdom."

And my father had come upstairs to watch me. He saw it all and went away without speaking.

But the next day he came to my room as soon as it was light. He was obviously worried. He sighed, he gave in to me over everything. He kept calling me "son." Later I learned that my father was thinking of a relative who had died in a lunatic asylum; he had long feared that one of us might "take after him."

"Get dressed quickly," he said, "we're going out."

I obeyed, feeling curious. The only thought in my mind was the eclipse, which was to be at eleven o'clock. My father did not believe that there was to be an eclipse—he supposed that was part of my mania.

"What were you doing last night on the roof?" he asked me, as if it were not of much importance. "Was it something connected with the eclipse?"

I saw that he had offered me a good explanation, and said yes. I did not think that he referred to my dancing but simply to the fact of my being on the roof. My father sighed and went to the dining room with me, where we breakfasted; then we left.

We went straight to the doctor's house. The doctor was an old man, kind-hearted and a little eccentric.

He had just risen; he came to us with his newspaper open in his hands and said cheerfully:

"There is to be an eclipse today, Don José."

My father appeared to be much surprised. He asked the doctor to examine me. He made a sign to the doctor's wife, who took me into the next room, while the two of them remained together talking. My father wanted the doctor to tell him frankly whether my case was serious. The doctor listened without half-hearing what he said. When my father, who was unwilling to use such words as "madness" or "idiocy" even to himself, spoke of "serious upsets," the doctor lost patience and said, "Well, let me take a look at him." Having me there in person, he did not care what my father might have to say about me. And the good doctor repeated:

"An eclipse. With a piece of smoked glass, we shall be able to see it."

Then, indicating the newspaper, he said that it was curious that "science could predict them thousands of years ahead," and that it gave him great hopes for the future of humanity. My father obstinately called his attention to "my condition," but the doctor interrupted him:

"I'll go and take a look at him now." He hated family diagnoses. He rose, telling my father that it would be better if he waited outside.

When I saw the doctor come in I thought: "I've been found out. My father has found out my hand is hurt and does not want to reproach me." I felt grateful to him for his delicacy. As the doctor came in he said to his wife:

"Undress him."

She was younger than he and very agreeable. She began to take off my clothes. It made me feel somewhat ashamed, but each time I was about to protest the doctor said implacably: "Undress him." He looked to see if there was a fire in the fireplace. By now I was naked from the waist up and the doctor began his examination. He kept making gestures of surprise; he seemed to be disappointed. Then he asked me, as if he were irritated:

"Where is the pain?"

"Here." I held out my hand.

The doctor asked what had happened and began to gesticulate and shout when he heard that I had a bullet in my hand. He went out of the room and spoke to my father.

"Why didn't you bring him sooner, Don José? What could you have been thinking of? And I haven't even an X-ray machine!"

My father listened, perplexed.

"An X-ray machine?"

"Yes. We can't have everything in a town like this. And an X-ray would make it much easier. But in any case we must do something at once. If he had come a day later I should have had to amputate."

My father could not understand a word of what he was saying.

"Allow me—" he said.

But the doctor did not "allow" him. His patients' relatives annoyed him.

"The boy seems brave, but without an anaesthetic it will hurt him. And I don't want to give him a general anaesthetic. If I had an ampule of cocaine, that would do nicely."

I saw that everything was becoming terribly complicated.

"Can I go to see the eclipse?" I asked timidly.

The doctor said to himself, "The boy is my kind," and, after a moment's hesitation, asked:

"Will you be brave?" and without waiting for an answer added: "Let's get started."

He began taking scalpels, bistouries, and cotton out of a glazed cabinet.

His wife made me sit down in a chair and stood behind me, holding my head against her chest. The doctor said:

"Are you going to cry much?"

I answered him by smiling ironically, which seemed to satisfy him. But he went to another cabinet and took out a large clean handkerchief which he handed me:

"If it hurts you, bite on that. It doesn't matter if you tear it."

And the operation began. The doctor cut and scraped; I felt the cold steel inside my thumb. I moaned softly once or twice, like a "grownup." It never occurred to me to cry. I suppose that my father, hearing me from the other room, did not know what to make of it.

The operation ended with the doctor extracting the bullet and sewing up my thumb. He and his wife bandaged my hand in gauze and cotton and put it in a sling, and the doctor led me into the other room, carrying the bullet in a pair of tweezers.

"A hero," he said, "a real hero."

My father took the bullet in his hand without knowing what to think and looked at my arm with its bandages and the sling. The doctor asked me:

"How did it happen?"

"An accident," I answered, shrugging my shoulders.

My father looked from my thick white layers of cotton to the doctor and demanded an explanation, if any explanation were possible.

The doctor turned to my father:

"Nothing easier. You brought the boy here with a gunshot wound, and I have extracted the projectile."

My father stared at me, openmouthed:

"We have all of us gone mad."

Then, suddenly calm again, he turned to me and added:

"Explain this to me, son."

"Let him alone," the doctor said. "Let him alone now, and I'll come and see him tomorrow."

"Can he get back home on foot?" my father asked.

"Yes, but first I'll give him a little glass of something I have here."

The doctor's wife, who reminded me of Valentina's mother although there was no powder on her nose, came in with a vial of some liquid which she was stirring with a glass rod.

The doctor waved her away:

"None of that. We don't give boys like you orange-flower water, we give them a good glass of wine."

Turning to my father, he added:

"It is the fine wine Mosén Joaquín says Mass with. I send the nuns purges, and they send me their wine."

My father did not know whether to laugh with the doctor, to condole with me, or to scold us both. The doctor's wife came back with a glass. The wine was a dirty white and smelled delicious.

"Bring another for Don José—he needs it more than the boy does."

My father declined, took me by the hand, and we went out.

On the way I could see that my father was impatient to learn what had happened, but he refrained from asking questions. When we reached home he retired to the library and told me to go and lie down for a while. "We'll talk later." My mother was in another part of the house and did not see us come in. I was thinking of Valentina and of going out on the roof, but I found the window in the storeroom nailed up. As if that were not enough, it was also made fast by two wooden crosspieces, so that I could not even dream of getting it open. Particularly with one hand in a sling.

I came downstairs, furious, and went to my tutor's house with the field glasses hung round my neck. I had to give a long explanation on the subject of my arm. The eclipse was not at all spectacular. Mosén Joaquín had smoked a number of pieces of glass to look through, but by smoking the big lenses of my field glasses we were able to see everything much nearer and more clearly. Mosén Joaquín tried holding different pieces of smoked glass in front of my eyes; then he said I should use the field glasses. So we passed the morning. It was a bore.

I went home thinking of Valentina. Arriving by way of Nun's Alley, I found her walking arm in arm with one of my sisters in the open space in front of the carriage-house. When they saw me they both burst out laughing. I could not believe that my arm in its sling was so funny; but that was not the reason; it turned out that the end of my nose was black with soot from the pieces of smoked glass my tutor had held in front of my eyes. Part of my forehead, too. When I found out I tried to wipe it off, but they told me I was only making it worse, and we decided that they would wash my face for me. It all turned into a joke, and I came out of it with a clean face but with a slight feeling of resentment toward Mosén Joaquín. To make a fool of me after he had heard me say that I was the "lord of wisdom, love, and dominations!" I began teasing my sister, although it was not Maruja but Luisa, who usually behaved well toward me. She finally said:

"What you would like is for me to go away and leave you alone with Valentina, because she's your sweetheart."

She left us to ourselves. Valentina asked me if the doctor had hurt me, and I told her that he was going to cut off my arm but that he had no anaesthetic so he had left it for another time.

"Is he really going to cut off your arm?" she asked, wide-eyed.

"Yes, but it doesn't matter, because it will grow again."

And I told her the story of the eight brothers who were born with wings. An old woman like Aunt Ignacia wove shirts for them out of cobwebs. When she had finished a shirt and one of the boys put it on his wings fell off and his arms grew. But their old Aunt Ignacia died without finishing the last shirt. It had only one sleeve. And one of the brothers grew up with one arm and one wing. The fact that their wings fell off and their arms grew for such a simple reason ought to keep Valentina from being afraid. If my arm was cut off another one would take its place.

Valentina had no doubt of it, and I kissed her several times. The pigeons came, but not as close as they usually did because Valentina was there. She went a little distance away and I showed her all my tricks. The pigeons lighted on my shoulder and then, balancing themselves with their wings, climbed my arm to my hand, which I was holding up full of corn. When I got tired of it, I joined Valentina and told her that I did not like them because they only came for something to eat.

Valentina looked in her pocket and took out a piece of paper on which she had written the words which the Soul speaks to the Bridegroom. I read it aloud, kept it as a tribute which was my due, and, remembering the information Mosén Joaquín had given me in the sacristy, said:

"Now I must perform an immolation for you."

"What's that?"

"The homage that the ancients paid to what they adored."

"And you adore me?"

"Yes."

"And you don't tell me to kiss you? If you don't tell me to kiss you, I can't."

It was true that when I kissed her she never returned my kiss. Now I said to her:

"Kiss me."

Valentina put her two hands on my shoulders and kissed me on either cheek.

"Say that you liked it."

"Yes," I said. "But now I must perform an immolation for you."

I went back where the pigeons were and held up my hand, full of corn. Three or four came immediately. I caught one by the feet. It was pure white; it beat its wings desperately.

"Go to the kitchen and get a knife."

She was afraid to, because she had been given a thrashing at home for taking a knife. Oh, a thrashing—I thought—and she isn't ashamed to say so!

I handed her the pigeon. Valentina wanted to be brave, but she was afraid it would peck her. I showed her how she should hold it for a minute while I went into the house. When the pigeon flapped its wings hard she shut her eyes and gritted her teeth but she did not let it go.

I went to my room and returned with the dagger. My tutor had told me that there were many different kinds of immolations, but that the most usual procedure was to sacrifice a pigeon. There I stood with my dagger.

"What are you going to do now?"

"Don't be afraid—I shan't do anything to you."

"What am I to do?"

"Lie down and shut your eyes."

Valentina obeyed. I quickly but carefully swept the space around her with a bundle of olive twigs. The traces of the twigs made a sort of halo on the ground. Valentina continued to hold the pigeon's feet fast, her two hands brought together at the level of her waist. The bird had ceased to flap its wings. When I thought everything was in order, it occurred to me that I might have done my sweeping before Valentina lay down.

Then I took the dove in my good hand, held it against the ground by standing on its wings, and thrust my dagger into its body. Its breast was the whitest part of it, and the blood was so red that it seemed to shed light. I picked it up in my good hand and sprinkled the ground all around Valentina. Then I let some of the blood drop on her breast, on her arms and legs, and even on her hair. The pigeon was no longer alive and looked like an old rag.

"And now what will you do with the pigeon?"

We sat down and plucked its feathers so that we could give it to the dog. We took it to him, and he received it with great satisfaction. Later, the presence of the remains of the pigeon between our dog's paws gave rise to lengthy family discussions. No one could believe that a mastiff chained to a stairway could catch a pigeon, pluck its feathers, and eat it.

We ran through the yards, the stables, the upper galleries, and Valentina's dress and arms and legs dried but the stains remained. They were dark brown. A maid came for her and she went home. I went to my room. I was sweating; my feet were burning in my boots. I took off my boots, then my socks, and put on a pair of old slippers. The pleasure of it made me close my eyes, and I thought of Valentina. We had agreed that when she did it she would think of me too.

Valentina arrived home covered with bloodstains, and caused a sensation. Her mother searched her in vain for non-existent wounds. Pilar looked at her scornfully. Valentina kept our secret. No one could have made her confess.

I had shut myself in my room. My mother had been calling me for some time. I did not answer, sure that when they saw I did not come they would leave me in peace; instead, I opened my notebook of Latin declensions and went on with the "Universiad." That is, I began over again, for I crossed out the nursery song, which had no connection with my idea, and, feeling tremendously inspired, wrote:

> *In the beginning everything was dark.*
> *The birds, the fish, the trees.*
> *Men there were not yet.*
> *But had there been, they too must have been black,*
> *Because there was not light for anyone.*
> *And still there was no day and it was always night*
> *And the animals, the fishes, and the plants,*
> *The birds and the men,*
> *The men who were not yet,*
> *To know themselves must wait,*
> *Wait, wait, forever wait,*

The coming of a storm, of lightning-flashes.
God did not want to put light in the world,
And lingered for a million million centuries
Before he made it, for he did not want
Anyone to see his work,
Because he was ashamed to have it seen
Until there were palaces, until there were fountains
And nightingales, and until the birth
Of our two mothers, Valentina's and mine.

I went on, writing with great facility, trying to remember what I could of the account of the creation in Genesis so as to keep in accord with at least the order in which things were made.

But my mother continued to call me, and I went downstairs. She stroked my bandaged hand and asked me if it hurt, rearranged my sling, and, seeing bloodstains on my cuffs, was horrified.

"It's not my blood," I said, to pacify her.

"Whose is it then?"

"It's from the immolation."

My mother pressed me so with questions, entreaties, and bribes that I had to make a great effort to keep the secret of my wound. I did not tell her because I knew she would go tell Father. At last she admitted defeat and begged me not to go on the roof and to study hard so as not to anger my father.

"But isn't it possible to live without studying?" I asked.

"It is possible but it is not right. Everyone must work."

"Aunt Ignacia's husband never studied."

"But he is a laborer. I don't think you would like that."

"Why not? If Valentina would like to live the way Aunt Ignacia does, it wouldn't matter to me."

My mother looked at me in horror:

"Don't let your father hear you say that," she said.

The following days things grew worse. Valentina had been punished for the bloodstains. She did not come to see me. I could not go out on the roof because, apart from the window's being nailed up, my bandaged hand made certain movements impossible. And the doctor did not take off the dressing until the fifth day. During those days I did not see Valentina, and I could only learn from stray bits of information that she was still in disgrace, and that she spent her days sitting at the piano, crying because she could not visit me, and practicing scales. My thumb was almost well, and I was wearing only a glove with the four fingers cut off to hold down the light strips of gauze which were all the dressing it now needed. As long as I wore the sling I met with a degree of tolerance. Mosén Joaquín explained my lessons to me and did not ask me to recite. But the day came when my hand was well again and the window was still nailed up and Valentina was away and my father was in a rage because he could not make me confess what had caused my wound. I would not study. My father, on one of his excursions to my room, found the "Universiad" and tore it up. He threw the pieces into the fireplace. I began over again the same day:

> In the beginning everything was dark,
> The trees, the birds, the fish . . .

I persuaded Concha to deliver to Valentina a large sheet of paper on which I had drawn a brightly colored flower. Innumerable petals fell from it, each one a different color, and in the center of each petal was a sentence from the *Words of God to the Enamoured Soul*. My sister assured me that she had given it to Valentina and that the poor child was condemned to practice the piano seven hours a day, and was not allowed to leave the house. Concha knew a good many grown-up secrets, and she told me that my father was in a bad mood because the bank was asking him for some sort of guarantees to cover the operations of another landowner for whom he had given an endorsement. My father had perpetual dealings with banks. Almost every day he received a letter from one bank or another, and it seems that he owed money amounting to something more than the value of our properties. Until now, however, he had never been placed in a difficult situation. The banks themselves seemed to want to make things easy for him, and my father sometimes boasted that richer men than he could not get loans from the banks without his signature. It was on such an occasion that the present misfortune had befallen him, according to what Concha said.

Mosén Joaquín tried once more to be patient with me. But a day came when he could no longer contain himself. When he handed me my notebook I saw the well-known scribble, this time with a figure 30 beside it. Thirty strokes. Very well. All these days I had been trying to reach a decision. I was almost glad, because now I should be forced to take some step which would change my existence. Fortunately, my father was not at home when I came in and was not expected back until evening. On account of the banking trouble he had gone to the country, to a friend's estate. I kept my oilcloth-covered notebook to myself and talked more than ever at dinner. I looked around the table and said:

"It is all over. Things are going to be different. I cannot breathe this air any longer." The family asphyxiated me, or so I thought.

And at nightfall I stuck my pistols in my belt, put my air rifle over my shoulder, and, with the "Universiad" in my trousers pocket, went quietly out the front door and walked down the street.

I left the town, got into open country, and, forsaking the road where I might perhaps meet someone I knew, set out across the fields toward the distant blue mountains. I had left a letter saying that they were not to think of me again, that I was going to Zaragoza to live my own life. I knew, from having heard people say so, that Zaragoza lay beyond the blue mountains. I thought that I could get there before midnight, but the distance was over fifty miles.

I was not worried about the separation from Valentina. I felt sure that as soon as I told her where I was she would hurry to my side. On I went, and everything looked pleasant and familiar—the green trees, the dry bushes, the roots of the oaks, the red rocks. A poem shaped itself in my imagination, modeled on a popular song:

> All in my father's garden
> There grows a little vine.
> Tell no one, no one, no one!
> Let it be yours and mine.
>   'Twas you, 'twas you
> I saw beneath the yew!
> I knew, I knew
> How fair and firm you grew.
> For you, for you
> Turtledove and turtle true. . . .

I dedicated it to Valentina.

I thought it must be very late. However, I should have gone on if I had not come to the river, a river so swift that it could not be forded. I looked in vain for a bridge. It would have been better—I thought—to stay on the road that leads to the bridge; but I could not find that either.

And I was hungry and sleepy. Nothing would make me return home. Neither did I want to go near the town, because they must be searching for me.

In my uncertainty I saw, quite far behind me, a house with smoke coming out of the chimney. It was Valentina's house, but not the side of it that I was accustomed to see from mine. I tried to think what to do, but before I had made up my mind I found myself walking toward the house. Although my desire to go to Valentina's house had awakened only at the last minute, the truth was that when I first thought of running away it was what I had subconsciously intended. I reached the garden gate, entered it, and had the good fortune to encounter Doña Julia coming out of the house behind the maid who used to come for Valentina. Night fell at six o'clock, and although I had been wandering in the dark for two hours it could not be much later than eight. I told Doña Julia that nothing in the world would make me go back to my home and that I wanted to stay here with Valentina forever. Doña Julia took me into the house, remembering that she had been surprised one day not long before to hear Maruja, who was playing with her dolls at home and chattering to them, say quite reasonably: "If Pepe and Valentina love each other, why don't they get engaged and marry?" I looked everywhere for Valentina but did not see her. Her mother told me that she had gone to spend the day with her cousins in the next town, and that Julián (the cousin I had met) was spending the day here in exchange. Valentina would be arriving any minute—her uncle was driving her over in his carriage and would take the boy back with him.

At that moment the boy appeared in the hall.

"I've already met him," I said. "Come on in, don't be afraid. Who are you?"

Valentina's mother looked at us in surprise:

"You know who he is—Señor Azcona's son."

"Excuse me," I interrupted. "Let him answer."

And with great emphasis I asked him again:

"*Whose* son are you?"

"Me?"

"Yes, you."

He looked at my hand, not understanding how I could still have all five fingers and no bandages.

"I am the son," he blurted out, "of a nefarious politician."

Doña Julia retired to the kitchen to laugh. A little later she returned: "My son," she said, "the whole town is out looking for you. I have sent word home that you are here."

"I won't go home."

"No," she said. "No one will make you."

Soon after, Valentina and the "nefarious politician" arrived. I pretended to be busy with something until he and his son had gone. Pilar had come too. She looked at me from the height of her twelve years, and the notary walked up and down, occasionally coming to a stand in front of me:

"This business of running away from home is for bums. But if you will study I will let you live here."

At home, they were so happy to know where I was that they did nothing about making me come back. We dined in state, with the notary at the head of the table. Before we had finished, the maid announced that, in case she should forget it, she had brought my books from home and had just left them on the table outside. After dinner Don Arturo went to his club. Across the table Valentina pretended to be doing needlework. Her mother watched us tenderly. She had told her husband that he ought not to stay out late because he would need to have a clear head for work the following day. He was preparing for an examination for a better position. His wife had rosy ideas of the future, expecting that the new position would make him rich. (And so, as I learned, it later came to pass.)

I looked at Valentina without speaking. The white collar of her dress, her jet-black hair, which was tousled over her forehead and temples and which on holidays she twisted into ringlets behind her ears. Every one of her glances bestowed an unexpected value on all those charms which it seemed no one was as well aware of as I was. I had written several new stanzas of the "Universiad," and I wanted to take advantage of our silence and privacy to read them to her. Pilar kept entering and leaving the room; her exaggerated walk and the way she called the maid or spoke to her mother denoted an insolent disrespect. I read the beginning of my "Universiad." Valentina did not understand a word of it, but she felt herself caught up in the fire of my enthusiam, sensing it with the excitement of some small wild creature. When I had finished she asked me about my troubles with my family. Her mother began to listen attentively. Perhaps she wanted to find out which had had the greater influence on my decision, my hatred of my father or my love for Valentina.

Pilar felt offended by the indifference of three people to whom she seemed to mean nothing. But Valentina was perfectly happy; I perceived it in the fragrance of her hair and in the serene friendliness of her looks. I suddenly said to her mother:

"Doña Julia, I want to go to bed."

"So early?"

"Yes, because I want to talk to Valentina. We are going to sleep together, aren't we?"

Doña Julia did not know what to answer.

"My dear children," she said smiling.

Valentina clutched her arm:

"Please, Mamma, please!"

I looked at my sweetheart and thought of the times I had slept in the same bed with my brothers or with boys I knew. It had always been uninteresting and uncomfortable, but the possibility of having Valentina beside me in bed made me feel an emotion close to tears. Doña Julia did not answer and, perhaps to ease the situation, asked Pilar to sit down at the piano. Pilar did not want to play "for us." However, she would mind it less if Valentina played too. As she could not say so, she announced that she really didn't know anything but the two sonatas for four hands. Everything about Pilar was false and affected. Valentina rose and took her place at the piano. Doña Julia seemed pleased, but I was annoyed at having to listen to Pilar at the same time as Valentina. The piano sounded cold and crystalline. Valentina had the bass part; they went wrong twice, and both times Pilar tried to put the blame on her sister. I intervened. I turned to Doña Julia, because I did not want to start a discussion with Pilar, and said that Pilar had bigger hands and because she had studied longer she knew the sonata perfectly and played it too fast. Pilar answered me angrily. Although she used other words, she tried to tell me that I was a blockhead and ought to go back back to my books. Her mother remonstrated:

"Pili!"

I seized the opportunity to say in a low voice:

"Pili! That's the name of the ugliest cat we have!"

Valentina burst out laughing, and Pilar said that she would not play any more. The evening seemed to be becoming complicated, and Doña Julia said it was bedtime. I still believed that Valentina and I would sleep together. My disappointment when I was undeceived made me wary in matters of love, which appeared not to give one the freedom of a better world but merely to be a continuation of the troubles engendered by family, studies, and the general course of life. Doña Julia found a reasonable excuse:

"If you sleep in the same bed you will talk all night and not get any rest at all."

Pilar disappeared into the kitchen again:

"Sleep in the same bed! I never heard of such a thing in all my life!"

‡ 4 ‡

But the next morning Valentina brought me my breakfast in bed, just as she brought her father his. She explained that she had already had breakfast and that she was very fond of coffee with milk in it. She took more sugar than her sister and not in a cup but in an earthenware bowl, an ordinary pot with a lip round the inside, against which she squeezed out as many as six little rolls one after the other with her spoon before she ate them, so that there was always some coffee left for her to drink at the end. Pilar laughed at her for this habit of hers. Valentina repeated that when she woke up she felt famished, and as she said it there was a mysterious light in her eyes. I listened, and her words reached me together with the cooing of pigeons. They had as many pigeons about as we had at home. And watching her, no longer hearing what she was saying, though I knew she was still telling me about her breakfast, I found in her the grace of painted, wooden angels, and a reason for my mad adventures, from which I always saw myself emerging victorious or dead. Valentina's every gesture and every word, even when I did not catch their meaning, aroused a concrete emotion in me, evoked something that I had already lived or something for which I hoped. Valentina continued talking, and I continued to follow my separate thoughts. I considered them terribly philosophical. Everything is violent, contrary, and noisy. Arguments with my younger sisters, the clatter of dishes in the kitchen, the gabble of geese and hens and pigeons in the yard. My father's angry face, my mother's sighs. I lived surrounded, enveloped, by all that. And now, by the simple fact of being with Valentina, here was my life changed into a sort of smiling calm. No one could prevent it.

Valentina left me, and I dressed and went out. Her house, like mine, was uninhabitable in the morning. At least, it was only habitable for women—no matter where we went, we "men" were made to feel "in the way." Furniture all in the wrong places, feather dusters and cleaning cloths. We could think ourselves lucky if we did not find pails of soapy water running over the floor. Doña Julia told me that I would have to continue my studies, and there was nothing for me to do but to go to Mosén Joaquín's. I intended to go, but I never reached there. I thought it pleasanter to climb the hill and go hunting for male crickets: they would soon begin to chirp, because spring was already on the way. I was very clever at catching them, and when I had no other means at hand of forcing them to come out, I urinated into their burrows, which I could easily distinguish, and they immediately appeared, although never by the entrance into which I had urinated but by another which served as a "side door." I could tell the males from the females because they were smaller and their wings were harder. From talking so much about "male crickets," we boys who hunted them had got into the habit of calling them simply "males."

I returned to the house long before dinner time, with more than a dozen crickets nestled against my chest under my shirt. When I arrived I showed them to Valentina, and we agreed to go and find more that afternoon. Part of the large garden which surrounded her house was devoted to vegetables; the lettuces already displayed their leaves on the ground with a humid fragrance. Since crickets prefer lettuce to any other food, we let them loose there; and, as it was still long before dinner time, Valentina called to her mother and asked if we might go to the hill to catch "males." Her mother said yes; and, considering that it would not be proper for me to urinate into their burrows in front of Valentina, I took a small watering-can full of water. We returned in time for dinner with two dozen more, for which we had searched not only the hill but the turf of a nearby grove as well. We let them loose in the lettuce patch, where they must have caused great damage, and sat down to dinner. Valentina's father was in a cheerful frame of mind and felt inclined to make a little fun of me. He mentioned goats that ate books, and for the first time in my life I found myself facing a play of irony in public. But to pacify him I told him that the goats had liked a Latin book of mine much better—they had eaten forty pages of it. Don Arturo laughed at that, and his laughter made a noise like the clatter of wooden rattles in Holy Week.

At home we ate more ascetically. I mean so far as manners are concerned. No one ever saw my father or my mother show any indications of gluttony, of sinful delight in food. We children were brought up in the same way. It was always: "Keep your mouth closed, don't make a noise, where is your other hand, don't look at someone else's plate, sit up straight." Not infrequently one of us would be punished by being forced to eat with a book under his arm to remind him not to raise his elbow high enough to hit his neighbor at table in the ear. Whether for better or worse, dinner at home was an orderly affair. Don Arturo's dinner was punctuated by ill-concealed belches, his moustache dripped soup or wine, he heaved a sigh after drinking, talked with his mouth full, and kept both his hands busy among the side dishes without ever abandoning the main course. He looked drunk, and not from wine, but from the pure pleasure of eating.

"I ran away from home once, too," he said.

Doña Julia asked him to tell the story, and he told it, never stopping chewing except when he interrupted himself to take a drink from his glass. He dwelt on his fear of his father, and it was clear that it had been his only motive. He added that when he had gone home he had received a whipping which had taken the skin off his shoulders. When he said "shoulders" he winked, and they all thought it very funny. I was the only one who did not laugh, and I said that I was not afraid of my father and that no one would whip me if the day ever came when I should be so unfortunate as to have to go home. Don Arturo went to the club again, and I told Doña Julia that I never studied at home until "the lights were turned on." She accepted my schedule, and Valentina and I went into the garden. We looked at our crickets. Most of them had chosen the zones they wanted to explore and were hard at work chewing up the tenderest lettuce leaves. They probably thought they were in paradise. When we saw that they had no need of us and that they could not escape because the garden walls were high, we left them to themselves and I went to get my air rifle. I came back with a bag of ammunition (heavy bird shot) hanging from my belt and with a folded sheet of newspaper in my pocket. The paper was a part of my hunting equipment too; before I charged my rifle I had to wrap the shot in a scrap of paper so that it would fit tightly against the inside of the bore. In this way, the projectile was expelled with force, the paper dropped off it, and it flew straight to the mark. Or at least I believed so.

With my rifle charged, we went up on the *solana*, a long, open gallery where there were two folding chairs, several others of straw, a table split by exposure to the weather, and in a corner some packing boxes and pieces of sacking.

"Have you never seen me hunt sparrows?"

I looked around, and once again my eyes were arrested by the pigeons' feeding stand, nailed high up on the wall. It was like a fanciful wooden commode, very wide and with several perches around a receptacle which held wheat and corn. The sparrows patronized it as much as the pigeons.

We dragged three of the packing boxes to a strategic point and covered them with sacking, leaving room enough between them for us to sit on the floor side by side. This was to be our ambush. Valentina became excited, watching me coming and going to put the finishing touches to it and talking all the time in a careful whisper. When everything was prepared we crawled inside on our hands and knees.

"The sparrows that are here now have seen us," I said, "and none of them will come close. We'll have to wait until they go away and some new ones come."

So I put the loaded air rifle at my side and we began to talk in low voices. When Valentina replied, her breath felt hot on my cheek and her hair touched my face.

We heard her mother calling us, but we did not answer. We decided to keep still until she tired of calling, and she went into the house again, saying:

"Where can those children have gone?"

I said:

"Tell me about your mother. Who does she like best?"

"I don't know. But Mamma is very bad."

"Why?"

"Because she doesn't want us to grow up."

"She doesn't?"

"No, she doesn't. She is always saying that the bigger we get the more trouble we give her and that she wishes we had always stayed two years old."

I thought this extraordinarily perverse. I looked out through a crack between the sacking and the packing box.

"Have the sparrows begun to come yet?"

"A few."

I could see two males with their black cravats on their breasts. One of them was on the top of a brick pilaster that projected from the wall, the other on the railing of the *solana*. They both looked all around them and then exchanged distrustful glances.

"Keep quiet."

"Why?"

"You'll see. There are two males there."

"Are you going to shoot crickets too?"

"No. Two male sparrows."

"That's what I thought. Because when crickets are so easy to catch, there's no use shooting them."

"No. These two have come to see whether we've gone."

The pigeons came and went with the rustle of silk in their wings. The sparrow on the pilaster gave a hop and flew a little nearer to the grain. Valentina looked out too.

"There he is."

"No. Wait. When he doesn't see anyone he'll call the others, and then a lot will come."

"How will he call them?"

"Like this: 'chow, chow'."

Valentina laughed and softly repeated, "Chow, chow." And a flock of six or seven females flew up and went straight to the food dish. The sparrow on the railing began calling furiously too, as though he were disappointed that the others had stolen a march on him. Many more sparrows flew up, and the eating place was covered with them. Now and again a pigeon grew angry and advanced on one of the sparrows threateningly. But the sparrow would only retreat a little way and flutter around for a moment, then settle again in a different place. I got my rifle ready.

"There are so many of them," I said, "that I don't know where to aim."

But I was a good huntsman who chose his game. I slowly aimed at the male of the flock which was nearest to us. I fired. Valentina drew a deep breath of relief.

"What a fool I am!"

"Why?" I asked, looking at the empty feeding place and searching the ground in vain for my quarry.

"Because I felt afraid."

"You can talk out loud now. Don't you see that they've all gone?"

The pigeons had gone too, but no farther than the gallery. The sparrows, on the other hand, had not stopped until they had reached the nearest roofs. I was standing up outside our hiding place.

"Where did you hit him?"

Valentina never doubted for a moment that I had made a bull's-eye, and she came out to look for the sparrow.

"I hit him," I lied, "but it was in the foot and he was able to fly away."

Valentina told me that I should aim at their wings and then they couldn't fly. But they were a long time coming back. And I didn't intend to aim at their wings but at their heads.

Feeling under a cloud of failure, we hid ourselves once more and I drew Valentina to my side.

"That flock," I said, referring to the sparrows who had escaped, "are frightened to death; they won't come back to-day. But there's still a chance that some others will."

"Do they eat only wheat?"

"Who?"

"Sparrows."

"No. They eat mosquitoes, too."

"And what do mosquitoes eat?" Valentina was becoming curious. But she clapped her hand to her forehead: "What a fool I am. Of course I know! They eat people."

"They do?"

"Yes. One bit me yesterday."

We talked softly. It enchanted me to whisper to Valentina because it made me feel that we had done something we should be punished for or were just on the verge of doing it. I loaded my gun again and we waited. I did not bother to look through the crack because I knew it was too soon for the sparrows to return. Valentina, who had seen the pigeons angry with sparrows and threatening them, asked:

"Can a pigeon eat a sparrow?"

"No. Pigeons only eat wheat."

"And corn."

"Yes. And bread crumbs too."

"And they don't eat pigeons that are smaller than they are?"

"No. But if they peck them hard they can kill them."

"Then that's why the sparrows are afraid."

We waited for a while in silence. The pigeons came back, but not the sparrows. And Valentina said:

"For a sparrow, a pigeon is like a giant is for us."

"Yes."

"And have you ever seen any giants?"

"Yes, once."

"And giants don't eat men, either?"

"No, but they can kill them. I don't think they ever eat them nowadays."

This seemed to set Valentina's fears at rest. But she did not stop asking questions:

"How many giants did you see?"

"Two. A man-giant and a woman-giant."

"Did they talk?"

"Yes, but I didn't understand them."

"What language did they speak?"

"Giant language."

"Don't you understand it?"

"No. But they don't always talk. They don't talk to us because they know we can't understand them. They just make a sound like 'Uuuuuh'."

Valentina was frightened and came closer to me.

"And what is giant language called?"

"Gigantish."

We remained silent.

"You know everything." Valentina said.

I took a look around. Valentina looked too.

"There's the same sparrow on the railing."

"That's very strange."

I looked again.

"It's not the same one," I said. "It looks like him, but it's not the same one."

"How can you see that?"

"I can't see it, but it's not the same one because the ones that we frightened won't come back until they've been to sleep and forgotten it in their sleep and it will be another day."

"Oh."

The sparrow on the railing was another male, with his black decoration on his grey throat. Not far from him, on the same railing, there was a female, smaller, trimmer, and earth-colored. The male seemed to be scolding her for her imprudent boldness, but she only answered:

"Chow, chow."

They began to approach. But they did not leave the railing. Valentina's mother called again from the garden. We did not answer. Valentina laughed slyly.

"Those children—where can they have gone?"

She went back into the house.

"Do you know something?" said Valentina contentedly. "I'd like to stay just like this always. Hiding here, and have them call us, and we not answer."

I signed to her to be still and began getting my rifle ready again, little by little, being careful not to make the slightest sound. My precautions excited Valentina. She sighed and said:

"Oh, what a fool I am!"

"This time I'm not going to aim at a male because they are too clever and when they hear the report they give a little skip to one side and change their position while the shot is on the way. The females are stupider. You'll see how after I fire they sit still and look around for a second and then give a chirp and fly off."

I aimed slowly, very slowly. I made up my mind to fire; then I had to wait once more because the sparrow had moved. I aimed all over again, held my breath, and was ready. Valentina put her hand to her throat and sighed: "Oh, what a fool!" At last I fired. They all flew off again; my quarry did not fall to the ground; not a feather fluttered in the air; there was no sign that I had hit anything. I was furious. It was not that I had ever killed a sparrow with my rifle, but I had never before had such a perfect opportunity. Valentina looked at me in surprise.

"This rifle doesn't work very well," I said.

Valentina never doubted.

"It's harder," she said, to console me, "to hit one in the beak or the foot than in the body."

I did not say that I had not aimed there. I carefully closed the gaps in our hiding place. I did not go out as I had the time before. It was obvious that not one had been touched, not one.

They took much longer to return. I amused Valentina by telling her more about giants. She listened with perfect faith. She had seen giants every year in the Corpus Christi procession, seven or eight of them at least, as high as her house, marching in pairs, man-giant and woman-giant; they stopped and danced right in front of her house, opening their arms lightly when they whirled around, and then dancing rigidly in one spot with their arms outstretched. So Valentina believed that all giants were like those, harmless or stupid. But I told her terrible things which made her really afraid, only to revive her again with my prowess and courage.

The sparrows did not come, and I continued to talk in a low voice.

"The giant Caralampio will come to my house one day and carry off Maruja if I tell him to."

"And Luisa too?"

"No."

Valentina was silent for a little while, and then she said:

"Luisa is very clever for her age, isn't she? I'd like to have her for a sister."

A few sparrows appeared, and for the third time I raised my rifle—not without some uneasiness. When I fired I gritted my teeth fiercely, but it was with the same lack of success. Unwilling to admit another failure, and in order to show what a good hunter I was, I announced that I was going to kill some pigeons too, besides the sparrows.

"That is much harder," Valentina said.

"One pigeon is as good as forty sparrows."

I found the largest shot I could, wrapped it in chewed-up paper, pumped the rifle until it was fully charged, and hardly had to wait at all —perhaps the pigeons had decided that we were harmless.

"Those are the ones papa likes best," said Valentina, pointing to one with an iridescent breast and red feet.

"Let's begin, then."

I fired, and the pigeon gave a jump, tried to fly, and fell with one wing spread out and its beak wide open. I went out for it and found that it had a broken wing; its beak opened and shut slowly in time with its heart beats. I brought it back to the ambush and threw it down as a trophy, closed the sacking again, and got my rifle ready once more. I was radiant, and Valentina stammered excitedly:

"Now another. Bang! And another. Bang! And another."

"What shall we do with them?" I wondered, seeing that we now had six.

"We'll take them to the kitchen."

The day was one which foretold the coming of spring. The sun had been shining directly into the garden, and the air was almost warm. One of the crickets began to chirp; two or three others timidly followed its example. Valentina and I came down the stairs of the *solana* loaded with dead pigeons and started toward the kitchen. Doña Julia saw us enter the house; her first question was, "Where did you get those?" From the impatient way in which she spoke I knew at once that we should find stormy weather ahead. We tried vainly to think of an excuse, and, just as Valentina was saying that we had found them in the street, Don Arturo came in through the garden gate. When he saw us he came straight to me:

"Those are the pouters I bought in Zaragoza for breeding. What happened?"

He picked up two of them by their bloodstained wings. No one answered. We looked at one another, and I felt a strange sensation, as if my ears were growing larger.

"I want to know what happened!"

The only answer came from the cricket in the garden, now clearly accompanied by two others. Don Arturo waved the incriminating evidence in the air and said:

"I made nests for them myself, and they had just begun to lay! Fifty pesetas they cost me! Ten a pair!"

No one answered. There were ten crickets chirping now instead of three. Don Arturo looked out the window angrily:

"What is going on out there?"

Doña Julia came over to me, pacifically:

"Tell me what happened. Just tell *me*, Pepe."

"We found them in the street."

Don Arturo took my rifle and removed the loading tube. I had fired it over thirty times, and it was hot.

"In the street, did you?"

His round head turned red. The blush began on the crown, which was bald, and spread down toward his nose. He shook his fist at me, which I thought was going too far, and, turning to the window again, exclaimed through the chirping of thirty or forty crickets:

"Do I hear that, or is something the matter with my ears?"

The well-fed crickets chirped with all their strength. Doña Julia put her head out the window too, not knowing what to think.

"Heavens!" she said. "The plague has broken loose!"

Valentina, seeing that her father and mother were not watching her for a moment, gave me her hand.

"You killed them yourself. Admit it."

Don Arturo waved the two pigeons before my face. I gathered up my courage and answered:

"They'll be very good with rice."

"Did you hear him, Julia? Did you hear what he said?"

Doña Julia left the window and addressed me:

"What did you say?"

Valentina, in an access of heroism, spoke:

"He said what is perfectly true. That they'll be very good with rice."

"Be quiet, stupid!" her father interrupted.

Doña Julia knelt down beside me and took one of my hands in hers:

"Come, come, Pepe! You are in our house, you are our guest . . . What did you say?"

Valentina broke in again, repeating what I had said.

Don Arturo directed himself to me. He spoke, and his spittle showered on his wife's face and mine.

"Say that again, if you dare!"

I did not answer. Then, as Don Arturo continued to provoke me and I began to feel that I was being made ridiculous before Valentina, I repeated what I had said, and added:

"And if you won't let me stay here, I have a house of my own that's bigger than yours and a father who isn't like you and hasn't—"

"What do you say I have?"

I realized that I was going too far and said nothing. But I looked so hard at his stomach—a truly monstrous stomach— that Doña Julia wanted to laugh.

"What were you going to say?" insisted Don Arturo.

"Nothing."

"Tell me, Pepito," coaxed Doña Julia.

"No, he won't tell. Criminal instincts go with lying and deceit. And do you know, you good-for-nothing, what every one of those pigeons would cost me if I had them cooked with rice?"

The crickets were no longer three, or even thirty, but a multitude, and their voices shattered the afternoon stillness, penetrated the house to its farthest corner, and forced Don Arturo to raise his voice:

"Three pesetas for every wing," and, rushing toward the garden—this time not to the window but to the door—he shouted like a madman:

"Who is responsible for this racket in my house? Or is there something the matter with my ears?"

Doña Julia, to calm him, assured him that there was nothing the matter with his ears because she could hear the noise too.

I went to the kitchen door and threw in my one remaining pigeon.

Valentina did likewise with hers; I took her hand and started into the garden.

"Where are you going?"

Don Arturo clutched at my sweetheart's dress and pulled so hard that she almost fell backwards on to the ground. Not feeling at all sure what the outcome would be, I said:

"He feels safe enough with her; with a defenseless little girl!"

Don Arturo danced round the room, waving his arms and calling to his wife to make him an infusion with a dash of cognac. I thought that he was coming after me to catch me, but I would not walk any faster. I went slowly away, and when I reached the doorway I saw that Don Arturo had gone out on the *solana* and was kicking my ambush to pieces.

"Do you need any more proof, Julia?"

Between the *solana* and the dining room there were more than sixty crickets chirping in unison. I set out for home, but the farther I got from the problem of the pigeons the nearer I was to the problem of my father. I shortened my strides, wanting to arrive as late as possible. I realized that it would have been best for me to wait until everyone had gone to bed, or at least until all the children had, because the things that troubled me most in my conflicts at home were Luisa's pity, Concha's worry, and, most of all, Maruja's perfidy. Realizing that if I stayed out until the "grownups'" supper time things would be even worse, I entered the house. I went to my mother. She was very glad to see me:

"So, my son, you have realized that this is your home?"

Bah! My mother was always saying obvious things. I turned my back on her and went to my room, but long before I had got there I realized that she was following me. I went to the storeroom to see if the window was still nailed up, but the thought that my mother would follow me there too, and see the damaged mattresses, made me turn back. I went into my room, and my mother entered and shut the door.

"Are you going to study?"

I suddenly showed a tremendous eagerness to study, then I shrugged my shoulders:

"I haven't any books."

They were still at Don Arturo's. It was dark, and my mother would not want to send a maid for them. I thought I was perfectly safe. But half an hour later all my books were brought to the house by Don Arturo's gardener. It was his revenge.

‡5‡

I locked myself in my room and thought, "One conflict at Don Arturo's and another here." I began to feel depressed, but a voice spoke inside me: "Am I not the lord of love, of wisdom, and dominations?" However, the same voice told me afterwards that it was not enough for me to believe it but that others must accept it too.

For the moment I decided to study.

To open a book was an act of heroism in itself. No one cared whether the subjects of which my books treated really interested me or not. In the first place, the authors of the books had shoveled their knowledge into them perhaps with no other intention than that of demonstrating that they could compose a really difficult text. Feeling rather inattentive, I took a long time learning my geography, the rivers of India, and my geometry, the first lesson in the second part, on solid geometry. Latin I didn't bother with.

My thoughts wandered away to my exploits of the afternoon; I wondered what would happen to Valentina, and revived my anger against Don Arturo. I studied at a small table, which was covered with a particolored cloth made from a piece of carpeting. The lamp was an old oil lamp remodeled for electricity. The cord ran through the aperture where the wick had been; the narrow, hollow base that had held the oil, and the wide porcelain shade, slightly tinged with blue, remained as they had been. The shade reflected the light on to the table in a wide nimbus. And where the nimbus ended, the darkness of the room, which so frightened Concha, began. But at the meeting place of these two mysteries, in the zone where light and shadow were parted, there was a yellowish halo in which the colors of the velvety table cover became brighter. Curious things were to be seen there: state coaches with footmen in gloves, garlands of flowers, dancing dwarfs, giants sleeping, or fallen, or possibly dead. Some of these things were so minute in proportions, so small and so distant, that, without realizing what I was doing, I took my field glasses and began examining them with their aid. Most of the illusions remained. Some vanished, but the glasses revealed in their stead an even smaller world. Between the thick knots of the warp and woof, which looked like hills and mountains, there was a whole flora. Grasses, shrubs, trees. The grass was sometimes blue or red, the trees mauve. I could make each shadow into a whole creature by imagining arms and legs for it, and bring it to life by endowing it with a purpose. When I grew tired of my game I sighed mournfully and returned to my books. I should have liked to be sitting there beside one of those red hills under a mauve tree, waiting for Valentina. And for her to arrive, freed from parents and tiresome pianos, those instruments of torture as black as coffins. I should find a river there where we could drink when we were thirsty, and honey from the hive, and apples.

And quite soon, I think, I saw myself there too. And Valentina's cousin came up, announcing:

"I am the son of a nefarious politician."

But I walked away with Valentina and, with our arms around each other's waists, we repeated the *Words of the Enamoured Soul.* I remember that, imagining myself with my prayer book open, I read the italic letters in the shadow of those little red trees as if I were actually reading from the book. I was the lord of love and dominations. The doctor had already said that I was a hero. But . . . lord of wisdom? I doubted that. I began storing new verses of my song for Valentina in my memory:

All by the shore of the fish-pond
Bend down, your face to see.
It will be you, it will not be you,
And a fish in every tree!

'Twas you, 'twas you
That made the reeds so bold.
I knew, I knew,
Because you shook with cold.

But I had to return to the rivers of India. They were not as large as I had thought. The largest river seemed to be the Ganges. It was the longest, if the figures in my text did not lie. I should have liked the Ebro to have been the longest, and I felt disillusioned and wounded in my patriotism. I finished my lessons—I never learned them thoroughly, but they were at least sketched in my mind and the next day I would go over them and make more sure—and then I had time left for the "Universiad." I had to begin it all over again. I went to the library for paper, first taking my skeleton key from behind the picture in my room. I slipped down-stairs like a thief and had put the key in the lock and was just beginning to open the door, when I saw that there was a light inside. I was afraid my father was there, so I took the key out and returned cautiously to my room. I had already reached the top of the stairs when I heard someone open the door and, after making sure that there was no one in the hall, close it again.

I sat down at my table and gave myself up to my landscapes once more. I could see little people on the cloth in the zone between the lamplight and the darkness. And in those miniature landscapes I now saw Valentina clearly. She was dressed in her Sunday dress, the same one she had worn to Mass at the convent. With my field glasses I could even see her yellow rosary wound around her wrist. Some of the figures in my landscapes jumped like fleas, but she remained still and looked at me. "To those beings, except for Valentina," I said, "I must be a kind of God." I opened one of my books at the blank pages at the end and began writing down all the things I could see: a rivulet, two trees, a tiny wagon loaded with grass and wildflowers. A bird. And another. All the birds were sitting still on the ground. One of them seemed to be a peacock with its tail folded, or perhaps a pheasant. And Valentina came walking among them—I could see her perfectly through the field glasses—and waving her bare arms she said: "Papa beat me. Now that it is Papa who beat me, you can kill him." And a smile came over her dark face, as it always did when she spoke. I promised her I would, and asked her what she thought of my latest exploits. She answered by saying only that "one pigeon is as good as forty sparrows," with which I felt perfectly satisfied. Meanwhile I was looking for her father through the miniature landscapes on my table, and I could not find him. I was aware of a delightful feeling of laziness. It had been only a short time since I had begun "to have supper with the grownups." Until then I had had supper with all my brothers and sisters—except Concha, who was twelve—at nightfall at seven o'clock. By eight I was already in bed. It must be half-past eight by now, and I had not eaten even yet because now I "had supper with the grownups." The younger children were in bed. I fell asleep, and woke with a start when someone came to look for me.

Luckily, my father was too preoccupied by his private worries to want to inquire into the facts:

"Oh—so you're back, are you?"

My studies began to go better. Since I could no longer go out on the roof and it was impossible for me to study in my room in the daytime, on sunny days I went out to the second yard, where the geese and the pigeons lived, and climbed the tiled roof of a shed to a point about halfway up the kitchen wall. I could not see Valentina's house from there, but with the cats and the sparrows I persuaded myself that the scene was much the same as the one from the other roof. The absence of a chimney, however, made it decidedly inconvenient. There I studied, thinking of Valentina. I had told my elder sister all that had happened, and she promised to find out for me what my beloved's fate had been.

On the other side of the wall opposite, which ran between the poultry yard and the stable of the next house, there was a narrow hanging terrace where clothes were dried. There was someone very interesting on this terrace. It was Carrasco. We were the same age and next-door neighbors, but we had never spoken to each other. Yet we could not see each other without instantly plunging into desperate combat. When Carrasco saw me in the street he bit his first finger, showed his teeth, wrinkled up his nose, and emitted a series of low snarls. I heard the snarls and thus knew where he was. And almost before I had seen him I flew at him like lightning. The neighbors sometimes separated us before we had come to blows, and sometimes, seeing that we were about to meet, one would hold me and another would hold him until we had passed by each other. I had forgotten him because we had not had a fight for five or six months. But when he saw that I had discovered him from my roof he began to bite his knuckles and snarl. The wall was thirty feet high. He couldn't come down and I couldn't go up. He threatened me with a slingshot; I replied with my empty pistol, which filled him with admiration; then, without exchanging a word, he put his slingshot away, I put my pistol away, and I went back to my geography.

The afternoon sun colored part of the opposite wall. The pigeons flocked to the roof on which I was sitting and surrounded me. As I did not offer them anything to eat, they did not perch on my body but they fluttered about and came to rest within reach of my hands. Then, seeing that I had nothing for them, they went away.

I was studying the mountains of Russia without interest. The only mountain that interested me was "Roland's Leap," which I could see from my room. So I looked at the opposite wall, where three lizards with heaving flanks were warming themselves in the sun. I had never seen anything prettier and more delicate than a lizard's head. The timorous eyes, the little nostrils the color of baked clay, the fine mouth which was always shut and ended in such a well-modeled snout, enchanted me. Carrasco's snarling aroused me from my abstraction. I looked up.

"Come on down!" I said, laughing. "Come on down! I'm waiting for you."

"I have your grave all dug for you."

It was probably the first time that we had spoken to each other in our lives.

"Come on down!" I insisted.

He seemed to be quite willing.

If there had been straw or hay below, as there sometimes was, he would have come.

"I have your grave all dug for you," he repeated.

I pulled out my pistol and aimed at him:

"Get out of here before I count ten."

I began counting aloud. When I reached "eight" he disappeared. I was sure that he had gone into the street to wait for me. In times past he had sometimes waited for me a whole morning. His dream was to triumph over me, but I knew his tricks and, except for the first time when he took me by surprise and succeeded in knocking me down and strad-dling me so that I couldn't get away (even then he could not claim a victory because I hit him in the nose and he went home dripping blood), our battles had ended either indecisively or in my favor. I knew of no concrete cause of his hatred for me, but later in life I learned that such hatreds are the most envenomed.

It was hot that afternoon, with the silent heat that falls on villages, when the pigeons seek the shade and time seems to halt and grow deep with a thousand small sounds. I was sweating and I left my lookout, considering my lessons learned. Just then I heard a voice calling my name from a window.

"Pepe!"

It was Concha, and there was no need to ask why she had called me. Valentina was in the house.

When Doña Julia came to our house in a hat and gloves my mother received her in the drawing-room. If she came "just passing by" without her gloves and hat, they stayed where they were and Doña Julia helped my mother to put away linens or take them out—the two ritual labors of the home. If my mother went to Doña Julia's house in a hat and gloves she was likewise received in the drawing-room. When one of them, on leaving, announced that "this visit didn't count," it meant that the other was not obliged to return it. These things were the manifestation of a perfectly serious formality. It entailed no other obligations. As for my father and Don Arturo, they saw each other at the club.

This time Doña Julia had come wearing gloves and a hat. Valentina was "paying a call" too, and etiquette required three details: white socks with white garters, black patent-leather shoes with white buckles, and the green and white flowers in her hair. The drawing-room was a large, old-fashioned room surrounded by phantasmal armchairs swathed in white covers. There were family portraits on the walls, among them one which I prized highly, although my father often joked about it. It was my childish pride: the portrait of "our uncle, the Colonel." The other portraits were uninteresting. My parents in their wedding clothes, we children dressed for our first communion. There were also three or four darkened oil paintings, of which my father used to say, "The frames are very good."

What interested Valentina and me was a glazed cabinet containing marble figurines, fans of painted silk and feathers, wedding presents, and two Manila shawls full of birds-of-paradise and strange flowers embroidered in soft yellows and greens on a white background. I told Valentina that I would give her all the things in the cabinet when we married.

"What about your sisters?"

We looked at these things while our mothers exchanged compliments, and little by little stole toward the door. Doña Julia saw what was happening and threw out brief warnings which consisted only of her daughter's name:

"Valentina!"

Valentina, as though she had been caught committing a crime, approached the center of the drawing-room, and soon after we began edging away again. At our third attempt her mother called her to her side, took her hand, and made her sit down on the carpet. I came slowly over and sat down too. Before I entered the drawing-room I had to scrub my knees thoroughly, it was the most arduous part of my toilet, and put on my green velveteen suit.

Doña Julia, extremely polite and proper, told my mother that her garden had undergone a veritable invasion of crickets and that on these warm nights they began chirping at twilight and did not stop till morning. No one could sleep. But it was obvious that they wanted to talk about me, and my mother asked me from time to time:

"Pepe, haven't you anything to do? Shouldn't you be studying?"

I said that I had finished my lessons already and asked Valentina to come out with me. Her mother refused for her. So I sat down beside her again, intending to keep them from talking.

"I wish," Valentina said, "that it were Sunday again."

We exchanged the sheets of paper which we had hidden to give each other. Valentina's mother, who was watching our every movement, put her hand out and took her daughter's sheet.

"What is this?" said my mother smiling.

It was nothing less than three lines from a sonnet by Baudelaire. Valentina had found it in a review to which her father, who was fond of literature, subscribed:

> *Permit my heart, intoxicate with spring,*
> *To plunge into your eyes as in a dream*
> *And sleep beneath the shadow of your lashes.*

It was the most beautiful thing Valentina had sent me. For my part, I was continuing with Bécquer. Her mother took it too and read it to herself:

> *When they had told me, in my very heart*
> *I felt the strength of steel and felt its chill.*
> *And then I knew wherefore it is men weep,*
> *And then I knew wherefore it is men kill.*

There was more of the poem, and I had altered it so that what "they told me" was not that she had been unfaithful but that her father had beaten her. Doña Julia was amused and amazed. We were both ordered to leave the room, and we went away feeling very pleased. And then our mothers began to talk about us.

I took Valentina to my room, closed the shutters, turned on the light, shook the tablecloth to rearrange the lights and colors, and began to show her where I had seen her, how she had raised her arms and said her father had beaten her, and so on. I invited her to look through my field glasses; and so we spent a long time. Then I showed her my arsenal, and my "ammunition dump," an old tin powder box of my father's into which I put small quantities of gunpowder which I stole from his new ones.

"In less than a month," I said "I'll have enough powder to blow up your house."

Valentina looked at me doubtfully:

"No. They're disgusted enough already about the crickets. I tell you," she insisted, "that they really are awfully disgusted."

"All right," I said. "But I may have to do it."

We went to the first yard and then to the second. Aunt Ignacia was there, giving the ducks and geese and pigeons and goats their supper.

The next thing I saw—after Aunt Ignacia—was Carrasco on the top of the wall. He bit his knuckle and snarled. When I began to point my pistol at him he said in a terribly grown-up voice:

"Colaso's son is here and wants to talk to you."

As if there were not enough, he added, in a stupid sing-song tone:

> "I don't want to fight any more, I don't,
> And if you are willing—why, let's be friends.
> I don't want to fight any more, I don't,
> And if you are willing—why, let's be friends."

When he thought he had chanted it often enough, he said, in his speaking voice, that Colaso was outside the door of my house, waiting to talk to me about something very interesting. I asked Valentina if she would like to come with me and find out what he wanted. With my arm around her shoulder and skipping every three steps we made our way to the court. We did not have to go through the house. There was a passageway which ran beside the oil and wine presses. León started growling again when he saw us, but soon stopped.

I found Colaso where Carrasco had said he would be. He was the leader of the other gang, though of all my enemies he was the only one who said that I was worth something and that it would be better to persuade me to join his gang than to attack me. The difficulty was that if I joined his gang, bringing with me my entire arsenal, I could demand to be made leader, and this the present leaders would not tolerate. I turned to Valentina:

"Wait here a minute and watch everything that happens."

I went out of the door and walked up to Colaso, looking as unfriendly as possible:

"Here I am."

"People who are always fighting don't amount to much," he said, sententiously.

"I'm not always fighting."

"I don't mean you."

The matter which had brought him to see me was a really serious one. His gang went to the bank of the river every day to challenge the boys of the adjoining town. They carried hemp slings and a good supply of stones of the proper size. The boys across the river were not less well-equipped. And the struggle began. The last few days the battle ended in favor of my townsmen, but when the enemy had suffered more than three casualties (boys who had been hit in the head and ran home dripping blood) their fathers came out with rifles, embarked in boats, and rowed out to a good shooting distance. Colaso's slingers attacked them and probably made a few hits, but when the fathers reached the middle of the river they aimed their rifles, which they had loaded with kitchen salt, and gave us a scorching. Every boy's calves were scarred by the grains of salt which "got under the skin and burned terribly." While our wounded danced up and down, smarting, the boys from the enemy town laughed and made fun of them. And this had been repeated for three successive days and was not to be borne. They wanted my advice, but the best thing would be if I would join them. There was to be no battle that evening.

"Why not?" I asked.

"Because if you don't come with your reinforcements, it's useless."

"What kind of reinforcements?"

"Why, reinforcements enough so that we of this town won't go down as cowards."

"My gang?"

"That would be the best thing. Your gang, and you with your arms."

They all knew that I had daggers and pistols. I accepted, and made an appointment with them for the next day.

Colaso went off. National unity had been sealed. Anyone who had been told that Carrasco was going to fight at my side would have thought that he was the victim of a very harsh joke. I returned to Valentina and said:

"My enemies have come. Colaso and Carrasco and all of them. It is clear that they have come because they need me."

"What for?"

"For a battle that we are going to fight tomorrow."

Valentina felt uncertain, as usual:

"Mightn't you be killed?"

"Me?"

"It's because I saw Colaso doing like this, as if he were aiming a rifle."

"But they only shoot salt."

I intended to load my two pistols with gunpowder and good wolf-ball.

"I'll go too," she said.

"Who ever heard of women going to war?"

"They go to look after the wounded."

Valentina looking after my wounds seemed to me a beautiful idea, but I did not give her permission. Besides, after what had taken place at her house she would find it very hard to slip away.

We went up to the dining room, where our two mothers and Concha were having chocolate. My new plans made me absent-minded, and Concha and my mother noticed it at once. My mother asked, wonderingly:

"Where have you two been?"

And added, with her usual lack of tact:

"Always in corners, always hiding in corners."

Valentina threw her arms around her mother's neck and explained to her that she had to marry me. Her mother was offended:

"Very well. And you don't want to marry me any more?"

This was a new problem. Valentina solved it very cleverly:

"No. Because I have to marry a man. You and Papa. Pepe and I. And everyone else."

"But why?"

"Because that is how life is."

I affected a masculine contempt for this female chattering. I was annoyed when Valentina embraced her mother, because her embraces belonged to me.

"You'll have a very untactful husband."

Valentina turned to me:

"She says you will be very un-tact-ful."

It was a new word to her and she had to pronounce it carefully. Valentina's mother explained:

"It is very untactful when you try to win your father-in-law's admiration by killing his pigeons."

I looked at Valentina. Had she betrayed me? Had she confessed everything? I looked at her in a way which admitted of no doubt, and she answered me by putting out her tongue, winking charmingly, and shaking her head in a decided "no." She and I, face to face, were stronger than our elders. And besides, I was thinking of the next day's adventure with such pride that I could regard everything else with benevolence. "I?"

"Yes, you, Pepe. Now you'll be angry with me because I have just told your mother all about it."

"Doña Julia, I don't understand. And you needn't worry, because I shan't be angry with you."

In truth I could never regard Valentina's mother or my own as real enemies even in the worst situations.

I wanted to take Valentina on to the gallery, but her mother would not let her go:

"No. She is going to stay with me now. When you are married you can have her with you all the time."

Concha served chocolate and brought in some pastries. I kissed Valentina good-bye and was leaving the room when her mother asked me if I hated her too much to kiss her too. I returned and kissed her hand. I did not like to kiss her face because there was always powder on it.

I went and prepared my equipment.

My father had gone to the country again, to the estate of the landlord who was involved in the same difficulties as he. For the moment I had a clear field. I went to the library, where he kept his shooting material. I soon found three canteen-shaped tin boxes full of powder. And other boxes full of cartridges made of some transparent material through which the charge was visible. And still another with lead ball for wolves and wild boar. I took powder and bullets and went to my room. There I found that the ball fitted my pistol barrel loosely. There was room to spare. I decided to do as I did when I loaded my air rifle, that is, to make the projectile fit the barrel by means of chewed paper. And seeing that I had all the things I needed, I hid them behind the picture and began to walk up and down. I opened the window and looked out, calculating the distance between it and the roof; then, sure that I could not cross it but unwilling to resign myself, I went into the storeroom and found to my surprise that the window there was open. It seems that my mother had had it unnailed in order to ventilate the part of the storeroom intended for jars of jam and preserves. With my field glasses slung across my shoulder, I went out on to the roof and settled down against the chimney. The sun was beginning to set; I could hear a cricket far away. I remembered the ones we had left in Don Arturo's garden. I began to look around. There was not a cat in sight, but the birds were returning to their shelters to sleep, chattering as they always did. A number of sparrows approached the holes which the supporting beams left here and there in the wall and were noisily expelled by other birds, who came out furiously to defend their homes. Twilight fell in an impressive calm. Everything was sweet and yellow like honey. Behind the nuns' tower the sky filled with clouds. Valentina was going home, and I imagined her walking modestly along beside her mother but thinking of me. Then there happened what always happens to me when I have a pleasurable feeling of myself. Distances vanished, the past too dissolved in a confused cloud, and nothing but the present remained. Yet out of this delicious moment strong roots reached down into the depths of my being, and something rose from it too, like branches and strange, iron flowers. I felt stronger and at the same time dehumanized, like a stone or a beam. Watching the sunset, I saw the opposite of what I had seen in my tablecloth under the lamplight. In that sunset, which surrounded me like an immense glass bell, I saw the same fantasies, but monstrously enlarged. The same light that poured down on my roof, on the chimney, and on the wall where the birds were chattering, entered my eyes like a torrent. Beyond the nuns' tower the clouds were the same white as the washing hung out to dry. Other clouds formed amber-colored figures. Staring out, I began to see my dead grandmother's head with its white cap, in the bed where she always lay ill. I remembered too how the poor creature used to say:

"O Lord, let this cup pass from me!"

Then I saw Valentina too. Not her face nor even her legs, but the whole of my Valentina was made of the substance of those lights and of that crystal of the sky into which I felt myself falling.

I had my field glasses, and I focused, just as I had on my tablecloth, on the distant clouds. The impression did not increase, but the glasses isolated the sunset and excluded the sights immediately around me. I should have liked to escape into those regions where all words die, where all desires are enriched in silence, and I came to believe that perhaps I could arrive there through the black tube of my field glasses. When I heard the convent bell, which rang just then for prayers, I dropped the field glasses into my lap and spoke with closed eyes:

"O God, I too am the lord of love and dominations, and one day," I said modestly, "I shall be the lord of wisdom. But Thou who canst do all things, make Valentina's father die and mine too, and make our families very poor, and let Valentina and me walk the roads forever. Amen."

After that I found I had one firecracker left, and I threw it down the chimney, this time quite sure that it was the dining room chimney. I waited and listened and, hearing nothing, went downstairs to see what had happened. The fire was out, and Maruja was studying her catechism two steps from the place where my firecracker had fallen. Alas! I picked it up and, opening my mouth and pulling the corners of it back almost to my ears with my fingers, I stepped quietly up to my sister. She flung down her book and ran to the door:

"Mamma!"

"Mamma, Mamma! Always Mamma!"

I started to slip up to my room again, but suddenly remembered that there was something I still had to find out and went to the poultry yard. And indeed I had no sooner arrived than I heard Carrasco's voice from the top of the dividing wall:

"Three o'clock to-morrow at the little ford."

The nearness of the battle made me more reasonable. I will not deny that in the midst of my grandiose plans I suddenly remembered the rifles that our enemies' fathers loaded with nothing but salt, it is true, but the salt crystals were sometimes as big as bird shot, and they penetrated the calves. But I would never succumb as Carrasco and Colaso had succumbed. All we boys knew that a wound from salt caused such an itching that dancing up and down, at least for the first minute or two, was unavoidable. It was useless to scratch—indeed, it made matters worse. The best thing was to dance, and, in any case, it appeared that the dancing was unavoidable. This was the real calamity of the last few days; this was why the boys all felt so ashamed. I looked through my wardrobe for a pair of heavy socks which were long and turned over at the top, but which, if I wore them in battle with the tops pulled up, would protect my legs completely. Would they be a sufficient defense? I had an inspiration, ran down to the kitchen, and returned with a handful of salt, with which I loaded the tube of my rifle. I hung the socks on the foot of my bed and fired. Salt penetrated between the threads of the weave.

"All right, but I fired from too near. From a distance the salt can hardly have that much force."

But in any case, my plan was not to let them fire. To surprise them before they reached the middle of the river. I had to think it all over very slowly, as real soldiers think.

I clicked my tongue, shook my head, and, hearing supper announced, slid downstairs on the banister. Before I dismounted I called down the stairway to León. I heard his tail wag against the ground.

I was so impatient for the glories that awaited me that I could not sit still at supper and that night I hardly slept at all.

‡6‡

I woke very early. The battle was in the afternoon. It was a sunny day. I slipped off to the scene dressed in the oldest trousers I could find and a knitted jersey worn through at the elbows. In my belt underneath the jersey, which came down over it, I carried two pistols loaded with powder, shot, and tight-fitting wads of paper. In one of my trousers pockets, a fuse of the kind peasants use to light their cigars; in the other, an innocent box of wax matches which I found in the kitchen. To all appearances I was the most inoffensive being in the world, and I smiled ironically when people passed me and said paternally:

"God keep you, Pepe."

When I reached the ford they were all ranged in battle array, awaiting me. Three or four boys were sharpening their teeth with a file that belonged to the apothecary's son. It was one of our customs to do this before a regular battle so that we could bite more fiercely; and today, in view of the possibility that the enemy would come ashore or we succeed in crossing the river and engaging him hand to hand, the file was passed from one to another and I could hear it rasping against the boys' incisors.

Colaso came forward as the delegate of the allied gang. The troops were such veteran warriors that some of the boys who had been wounded on the previous days had succeeded in escaping from their homes and had reappeared at the post of duty. They faced not only the risks of battle but later unpleasant consequences behind the lines. Across the river two boats bobbed up and down; they were moored to the rocky shore, and their oars were aboard. Carrasco invited me to review the troops. I silently admitted that they knew more than I did, for I had not supposed that troops had to be reviewed before a battle. But a whistle sounded across the river, and out of the streets at the edge of the enemy town, which was visible about three hundred yards from the river, poured a howling multitude of small boys. It was impossible to make out what they were shouting, but they were certainly repeating the extremely dirty and offensive refrain which they had dedicated to my townsmen. Naturally, our boys wanted to shout too and pay them back in the same sort of coin, but I stationed myself ten yards ahead of the front line, turned my back on the enemy and cried:

"Silence!"

Carrasco, Colaso, the apothecary's son, and the son of the woman who kept the tobacco shop stepped forward and informed me that they were the leaders.

"If you are leaders," I said, "where are your arms?"

"Do you mean you don't want us for leaders?"

The enemy was yelling louder than before, and the first stones struck.

"Get your slings ready!"

"All ready!" came voices from here and there.

As the stones were falling like hail, I said angrily:

"Break the troop up into guerrilla parties. Can't you see that we're too close together?"

Before the other leaders had repeated the order the troop had carried it out.

"Fire at will!"

The gang which was usually against me was composed of more veteran fighters than my own followers. Carrasco bit the first finger of his left hand and grunted, while he whirled his sling with his right hand and raised his left foot to put the strength of his whole body behind his missile.

"This looks like a real war," I heard several boys say in satisfied tones.

We were better slingers; it could be seen from the way our stones skimmed across the river without rising. If a stone thus slung struck an enemy in the head he fell down unconscious. We had made the experiment many times, and it was our countersign and our military advantage. The enemy, you might say, fired, looping the shots.

The apothecary's son was hit in the ankle and fell to the ground cursing like a real soldier. He called out to me:

"Get out your pistols now."

But I could not sacrifice victory to please the apothecary's son. Our enemies had stopped shouting on the principle that you cannot both ring the bells and march in the procession, and they were now giving all their energies to the combat, Carrasco, still biting his finger, had already knocked down two of them and was raging up and down like a devil, waving his empty sling in the air and yelling:

"There are two that confession can't help any more!"

The others imitated him and made skimming shots. Carrasco called out instructions to a boy who was putting too big a stone in his sling. He said that small stones were better because they flew faster and the victim could not see them coming. That was his method, and he demonstrated it, whirling his loaded sling in the air, biting his finger, and raising his left foot.

The leather of the sling cracked:

"A rebound is worse than a direct hit. It will knock anything down. I'd rather be hit by ten straight shots than by one rebound."

We attacked with fury. One of the two enemy wounded got up with his head smeared with blood, the other lay motionless on the ground. They were less intelligent than we, and they gathered into groups which were easy to hit.

Colaso came up, uneasy:

"We've wounded two of them already; it won't be long before they bring on their rifles."

"Let's make it twenty before the rifles get here."

The battle continued, and at the end of two hours the famous reserve of rifles had not appeared. The enemy casualties had not reached twenty, but they were not far from it. On our side the wounded were the apothecary's son, who limped but was still firing; Carrasco, who had received a glancing blow on the head; and a small boy, the son of the barber, who had been hit in the right forearm and who, when I asked him why he had stopped firing, held out his arm to me, fractured—it swung in either direction like a broken reed. Gritting his teeth with pain, he said:

"Take my sling if you want it because I don't know what's happened to my arm. It bends both ways. Take it," he insisted, "it has a sweet tooth."

He meant to say that it was gluttonous, that is, that stones it threw always hit someone in the head. The others continued to fire without incident. I had my back to the enemy when my troops warned me:

"Here it comes, here it comes!"

I thought that they referred to a stone which was coming my way, but the gestures of some of my followers who were preparing for flight told me that the moment had arrived. I turned to face the river; there were the two boats full of peasants and bristling with rifles. They seemed to be looking at us in astonishment and exclaiming:

"There are more of them every day!"

The peasants were surprised to see how calm we were. I took out my two pistols. I was sorry at once, because I needed two hands to fire, and I put one pistol back in my belt. I lighted the fuse with a wax match, and with a pistol in one hand and the fuse in the other I waited.

"Fire on the boats!"

The stones from our slings skimmed over the water. We heard them clatter against the wooden sides of the boats. Two or three stones found their mark, and we clearly heard groans and the voices of adults. The first boat fired two rifles at us. The report was so loud that I felt myself weaken. Some of our boys started running, but I commanded:

"Keep your places! Everybody down on the ground, and protect your heads with your arms."

Most of them obeyed. I had pulled up my socks, so that the tops covered even my knees. The apothecary's son, who was unlucky that day, was hit by a few grains of salt and danced the inevitable dance, which was even more grotesque than usual because of his injured ankle.

With all the power my lungs could muster, which was not much, I shouted:

"Fall back. Everyone, fall back! Or you'll all be killed!"

Another burst from the rifles answered me. Promptly disregarding the itching of my legs, I applied the fuse to my pistol. I fumbled for a moment without being able to ignite the powder, and then I do not know what happened, but the pistol flew out of my hands with a report much louder than the rifles had made. The boats stopped. The silence after I had fired was so great that I could hear Carrasco scratching his head.

"Watch out, they're firing bullets!" someone in the boats said.

Our side rose, reanimated, and sent off a hail of stones.

"Watch out, they're firing ball—I heard it go by," we heard someone say in the first boat, which, instead of coming on, began to turn to one side, perhaps preparing to retreat.

I was amazed that there were no dead and no wrecked boats. But I still had another pistol. The second time, I fired with my eyes shut. The report was even louder, and the men in the boats, who were already falling back before our hail of stones, turned round and rowed as fast as they could for the farther shore. Amidst their shouts we heard the words "mayor" and "police." It appeared that some of them had heard my ball whizz by their ears. The boys of the enemy town, when they heard my shots, took to disgraceful flight. Left masters of the field, we cheered loudly and decided to withdraw in proper formation. Long before we had entered the town, an incomprehensible terror had seized that handful of heroes. Some feared their mothers' slippers, others the room where rats were, the majority that they would be deprived of supper. We parted, thoroughly satisfied with our exploit and resolved to maintain the sacred union of the two gangs; "each for all and all for each," we affirmed, and reminded each other that the principal part of our alliance was keeping our secret from those ignoble and stupid beings, our elders. Colaso embraced me and said that they would make me their general. The apothecary's son, thinking that colonel was a higher rank, added:

"And colonel after the next battle."

Carrasco bit his finger and said:

"I'm colonel and Pepe's admiral, because it was a naval battle."

I did not dare to confess that I had lost my pistols. They had vanished, the devil knows where, when I fired.

"Was it a naval battle or not?" he insisted.

"Mixed. Land and naval, both."

We parted, repeating our cautions in regard to secrecy. A precaution which turned out to be most useful, because the people of the other town protested to the authorities, and when the investigation began six of our boys were held—just as if they had been of age—and gave evidence for several days before a children's court which was constituted for the purpose in the municipality. I had to go too, but not as a presumptive delinquent like the others. At home I pretended to be surprised by the summons to testify and affected indifference, although really I felt that we had gone too far and that we might all end up in a reformatory. My father, still preoccupied by his difficulties with the bank, did not pay much attention, although he had given me to understand incidentally that if I were guilty he would do justice with his own hand—nothing short of cutting off the arm with which I had offended!

My testimony before the investigating commission consisted of denying everything that might point to me and defending my comrades. I said that, according to what I had heard, my friends had gone to the river to play and several inhabitants of the town on the other side had attacked them with rifles. The tribunal heard us attentively. It was composed of three peasants, one of whom was a member of the town council. I had heard my parents laugh about him, which gave me a certain amount of sang-froid.

"With rifles?"

"Yes, and in that case what could my friends do but defend themselves? So they defended themselves with slings until they were obliged to run away."

"We all have scars on our legs," said one.

The apothecary's son, whose wounds were still open, was examined, and when the tribunal was thoroughly occupied we said that of course they had fired only salt.

"Even so . . . ," said the councilman, shaking his head.

I was afraid they had learned of my shots, but they had not. The peasants from the other side of the river were checked by the consideration that it was undignified to enter into a boys' quarrel. The story of the salt, which no one had mentioned before (to such lengths did we carry our policy of not talking before adults), changed the course of the affair entirely. My comrades were set free, it being considered that they had been sufficiently punished by their three-day confinement in the grain-loft of the town hall; I went home; and the peasants from the neighboring town were condemned by their mayor to a fine of two pesetas for firing—even though it was with salt—at human beings, and one of them who did not have a hunting license had his rifle taken away and had to pay a fine of five pesetas. Our triumph was complete, but, after three days of real panic I had become wary. (I had not been afraid of punishment, or even of prison, which would have been an adventurous consequence, and worthy of me; what I feared was the scandal at home and, above all, Don Arturo's satisfaction.)

Meanwhile, my situation among the boys was a really privileged one, and I felt it at every step. Carrasco appeared on top of the wall and saluted me, asking for orders and instructions. In the street, if I asked a boy for anything he had with him—a top, or a mat made of playing cards, or whatever it might be—he gave it to me at once. Even among the boys of the more distant quarters, with whom we never played, I had a certain authority. The news had gone round, and when I passed I often heard: "That's Pepe, Pepe from the Plaza." And they left their games to look at me. I considered that I had deserved all this—a naval victory in a place where there was no sea was something that did not happen every day—and sometimes I would go up to them, patriarchal and magnanimous. I remember that one day a small boy from one of the more distant quarters had a bird in his hand. Since they were looking at me as if I were a superior being, I had to behave in accordance with their expectations. I had to do what a superior being would do.

"Give me that bird."

The boy gave it to me, but it was obvious that he was sorry to part with it. I looked the bird over knowingly:

"You haven't clipped its wings?"

"No."

The bird was not hurt. Its heart beat strongly against my fingers. I raised my hand and opened it. The bird gave a surprised chirp and launched itself into the air with all its strength. Its joy and surprise were so great that they caused a repercussion in its stomach and, as it flew, we saw a speck of white matter fall through the air. The bird came to rest on the edge of a roof and turned and looked at us. It gave another happy chirp and flew away. The boy watched it, not far from tears. I took five centimes from my pocket and gave them to him:

"Don't go thinking I took it away from you," I said. "I don't take things from people. I bought it from you with my own money."

To a small boy five centimes were a fortune. The youngster considered himself generously reimbursed and, still not quite believing in his good fortune, walked off, for fear I might change my mind. I told the boys who remained that they must not catch birds, because birds loved freedom more than anything.

"I kill them sometimes, but that's different. It's all right to kill them, but not to catch them alive and make slaves of them."

I thought these ideas were worthy of my prestige, but possibly I was sincere. I was not sincere in the price I paid for the bird, because giving five centimes for a bird—I, who could catch any number of them—seemed to me a piece of extravagance.

I continued to reap the fruits of my popularity, and it gave me such pleasure, such calm, and such self-confidence that I felt that now I really was the lord of dominations. Lord of love I had been for some time. I only needed to become the lord of wisdom. And I settled down to study, with the idea that I must raise myself to the stature which was mine.

I had not seen Valentina for a week. The poor child must be stitting at the piano with her scales and arpeggios. At home Maruja and Luisa had begun taking piano lessons too, and all day long you could hear their slow struggles from the direction of the gallery. Luisa did not like

it, but Maruja boasted of it and talked about "studying a lot," saying that
I never studied anything, as if we were equals.

When Valentina was allowed to come, we met with all our accumu-
lated desire to be together. She had learned what had happened at the
river, because her father had talked of me scornfully, accusing me of
terrible crimes, and she had asked the boys and they had told her.
Valentina did not admire me any the more for it. I had raised her to a
delirious plane long before; beyond it, it was impossible for her to go.

"I'll soon be leaving for Zaragoza," I told her.

"What for?"

I answered as I had sometimes heard my elders answer:

"On business."

Valentina added:

"For the examinations?"

"Yes, that too."

"Will you send me a post card?"

"Yes. One every day."

"Who are you going with?"

"With Mosén Joaquín, because he has business there too, and we
happen to be going the same day."

Mosén Joaquín was satisfied with me. He had tried to obtain a recital
of the latest events from me, but, seeing that I maintained my reserve,
he did not insist. We were "both studying," because Mosén Joaquín had
had the intelligent idea of telling me that he had "forgotten a good many
things," and that "the sciences, too, had advanced since he had studied
them," and, in conclusion, that he ought to study every day at the same
time as I did. It was a miraculous revelation. And now I found great
pleasure in doing just what he was doing. He at his table in his study
beside the flowery terrace, I on the roof, leaning against the chimney.
Sometimes I even permitted myself to say to him in class:

"Mosén Joaquín, you are mistaken. You have that wrong." And we
would turn to the textbook and see that I was right. I think now that he
must have done it on purpose.

Our friendship increased. One day he saw me walking through the
Plaza of Santa Clara with Valentina. There was a merry-go-round in
another square not far away, in the opposite direction from the convent,
and I had invited her. When Mosén Joaquín, who was on the balcony
of his terrace, saw us, he gave us a friendly smile and waved his hand.

I spent my money prodigally on the merry-go-round. We did not like the horses, and the pigs even less. After we had taken two rides on the horses we decided to sit in the back of a charming landau, close together. It happened that the music was the tune to which I had composed my poem, and I sang it. The second time, Valentina knew it:

Come and play and sing,
All in the ring
Of cinnamon-bread.

'Twas you, 'twas you
That made the reeds so bold.
I knew, I knew,
Because you shook with cold.
For me, for me,
Valentina and Valenti.

And I ended, with the last notes of the tune:

Dindle and dandle!
Here comes the notary,
Bringing his candle!

The last lines pleased Valentina very much.

Mosén Joaquín saw us returning, and waved to us again. The next day he said:

"I should like to be the one to marry you on the day you finish your studies, eh?"

I promised him that no one but he should marry us.

"That is, if you're still alive," I added seriously.

He laughed heartily.

"You think it will be so very long before you have finished your studies?"

He laughed again, and that day we went out on the terrace and had lessons there, walking slowly up and down in the sunlight. I saw that Mosén Joaquín had become fond of me. He made jokes and interspersed his teaching with stories.

But his enthusiasm led him to speak of me to the Jesuits—members of a permanent mission which had been in the town for some years studying the possibility of founding a college. At the time they had only a chapel and an old sprawling house, along whose verandas they sometimes strolled in the middle of the afternoon. Their chapel was generally known as "the Society." "I'm going to the Society," "I've come from the Society." My father had a great respect for the Jesuits, but he had never cultivated their friendship. He considered them too worldly. He preferred the Augustinians, the Carmelites, the Benedictines.

One day after class there appeared at Mosén Joaquín's house a Jesuit with a huge belly held in by his black sash. He and Mosén Joaquín talked of things that did not interest me, and when lessons were over the Jesuit invited me to walk with him. I accepted, and we set out.

The monk assumed a beatific and protective attitude, which was the worst he could possibly have taken with me. As if that were not enough, he took my right hand and held it between both his against his belly. And so we walked slowly along, he talking to me all the while with a cloying and maternal condescension. I was half-crazy at the idea that my brothers-in-arms might see me in such a situation. I kept looking around but, fortunately, saw no one. The monk, beating time with his slow steps, was saying:

"We have football games and a library of adventure stories, but we have something even better, something you would never dream of."

"What is it?" I asked curiously.

"A moving magic lantern. What is called a cinematograph."

It interested me, but if I had to pay for it by exhibiting myself with him in the street, my hand in his, walking slowly in time with his immense belly and listening to him talk the way Aunt Ignacia talked to my little sisters when they first began walking, I renounced even the cinematograph. The man wanted to destroy my work of years in an instant. I pulled my hand away and ran until I had reached home. The next day I had to explain to Mosén Joaquín, and I told him what had taken place. My tutor looked at me strangely—I don't know whether with sympathy or with sarcasm—and said:

"Obviously that is no way for a bandit chief to walk down the street, is it?"

"I am not a bandit chief," I said seriously.

I saw in his look his fear that the course of our relations would change and I would stop studying again.

"Then what are you?" he asked, without a trace of sarcasm.

"I told you that one day."

"Ah, yes," he said, and was silent, remembering with an effort.

The following weeks were entirely calm. I studied, because I felt that I was really on the road to becoming the lord of wisdom, since there were days when I knew more than Mosén Joaquín, whom my father held to be a man of high culture. And the love between Valentina and myself was beginning to enter the pleasant and peaceful plane of habit. My father had found a solution to the difficulty with the bank, according to what my sister Concha told me, by making an even larger venture. I did not understand the nature of it. My sister spoke of my father's emerging victorious, and so it must have been. My father was satisfied and bought a small cabriolet. He retired our old horse, whose activities thereafter were restricted to eating grain and walking about, and bought a young one. My mother protested against the expense, but she ended by catching my father's enthusiasm. He was so pleased that although he found my fifth "Universiad"—this time with more than ten pages written on both sides—he did not tear it up.

The pleasure of taking off boots and putting on slippers after running around was greater every day, because now the sun was strong. For the same reason, Valentina and I indulged in our enjoyment much more frequently. My father began to have faith in me, and, though he knew that I studied on the roof and sometimes danced there both by moonlight and by sunlight, he did not take it too badly and gave up trying to understand it. But I remained isolated. "When I have passed my examinations," I said to myself, "I'll put the question of marriage to Don Arturo seriously." I knew already that if you were out of money you asked the bank for it, and if they didn't give it to you right away you had to go and spend a week in the country, at the farm of a relative of ours. When you came back from your excursion, the bank gave you money.

My sister Maruja never liked to ride in the "stylet," as we called the old carriage, the name being a diminutive of "sty," which is the place where pigs live—because it was soiled by pigeons and hens. For my part, I liked to ride in it with the old horse because I was allowed to drive. I no longer took Maruja seriously because my conduct in respect to my studies had given me a pre-eminent role, and I was for ever teasing her about the "stylet." She found out things about my past—fragments of fact, misunderstood information—and went to my mother with them, hoping that they would be brought up against me all over again. She told a story of my having made a blunderbuss and having killed seven people with it by the river.

My comrades did not look kindly on my abandoning them and began conspiring, but just when the atmosphere had become unbreathable I set out for Zaragoza with Mosén Joaquín. We went to the station, which was some distance away, in the new cabriolet. Maruja flew into a rage because she had never been in the new carriage. It was obvious that Mosén Joaquín was going with me, but he was going "to keep me company." She wanted to come to the station, but was not allowed to, and stood in the porte-cochère muttering:

"If he fails, he'll be apprenticed to a shoemaker."

The train took three hours to reach the city, and we went to the Hotel Fornos on the Arco de Cinegio. We were taken there from the station with other travelers in an immense horse-drawn omnibus whose wheels made a tremendous racket on the pavement and whose windows buzzed in a thousand corners. All through the journey Mosén Joaquín had treated me as a friend. Not once did he mention studies or textbooks or examinations. Seeing the landscape through the window turning slowly round us like a disc, he had said: "See that? It shows that the earth is round." That was his only scholarly remark.

When we arrived, Mosén Joaquín went to see some acquaintances—professors in religious colleges—who, it appeared, were friends of my examiners. I went out into the Arco de Cinegio and reconnoitered in all directions until I had established landmarks. I had fifteen half-peseta silver pieces (seven and a half pesetas in all) which my mother had given me. I found a shop and bought five post cards with views of the city, making sure that they all showed "tram lines." I also bought stamps, and then continued my inspection of the quarter. In one direction I went as far as the Calle de Don Jaime, in another to the Plaza de la Independencia, in yet another, in which I had to go quite a distance through narrow alleys and then through a covered arcade full of brilliant shops, to the Plaza de Sas. In the center of the Plaza de Sas there was a kiosk which sold newspapers, flowers and birds. I went to it and was much surprised to see behind a lattice dozens of huge frogs in buckets. I asked the price of them. They were ten centimes apiece, and I bought five. One for Valentina, one for Concha, one for Mosén Joaquín if he wanted it, and two for myself. I took them back to the hotel, dropped them in the bath, and sat down to write my first post card to Valentina.

"It is different here. All the streets are paved like the rooms and the sidewalks at home. Also there is nothing but love everywhere. In the vestibule of my hotel there are a lot of newspapers fastened to sticks, like flags, and you sometimes see in big letters: 'The Love of My Life,' 'Love of All Loves,' 'Wounded for Love.' It appears that all this happens in the theatres. A big hug from your unforgettable Pepe. P.S. I have just seen a tramcar in front of the hotel with a sign saying 'Madrid.' I shall go to Madrid and write you again from there. Farewell." I wrote the address, put on a stamp, and dropped it into the hotel letterbox.

Mosén Joaquín returned feeling satisfied. It appeared that everything was going well. I would be examined the following day. We did not talk about books or studies. It seemed that the whole tangle of classes and declensions and theorems had been left behind in some remote sphere. After dinner Mosén Joaquín went out again, leaving me, with some other boys in the court, in the care of the hotel manager and making me promise not to go beyond the districts that I had explored in the morning. But I had to go to Madrid, among other reasons because I had told Valentina that I would. I went to the Plaza de la Independencia and boarded a tram marked "Madrid." The conductor gave me a ticket, and we traveled through avenues and streets and squares and finally through empty lots for half an hour. When we stopped, the passengers all began to get out. Everyone except myself was carrying a satchel. I looked out the window and saw the metal roof of a railway station, a number of slate-tiled buildings, and two or three chimneys. The conductor said:

"Here we are."

"Does the car go back?" I asked.

The conductor said yes and got out to turn the trolley around. Then he turned over the seats. I looked about and said to myself, "This is Madrid." I had to buy another ticket, and at the end of the journey I found myself opposite the Arco de Cinegio and felt that I had been through an adventure which, if it was not perilous, was decidedly "manly." And I sat down to write another card to Valentina:

"I have just come back from Madrid. The boys there don't seem like boys any more than the ones in Zaragoza. They wanted me to play in the hotel but I preferred to go to Madrid. On the way, there was a wooden fence with large letters on it saying, 'The Triumph of Love.' When I got back I saw that they had changed the printed cards in the revolving door and that instead of the one that said 'Wounded for Love' they had put another that says 'The Last Battle.' I send you many embraces from your unforgettable Pepe. P.S. I take the examinations tomorrow. It was to be another day but I got them to put it forward for me so that I can be back sooner. Farewell."

During the night an incident occurred of a sort that frequently marked my comings and goings. The frogs started croaking, and in the concavity of the bath their voices were like thunder. Although I was asleep and did not waken, the servants unlocked my door and shook me until I told them where the frogs were. I could hear people protesting in the corridors and the adjoining rooms. They wanted to take the frogs away from me, but I protested and said that they were mine and I would not allow myself to be robbed of them. I put them on the balcony in the bottom of a flower pot, but they continued to be annoying. The protests began again, and I declared that they would croak no more. I put them back in the bathroom but this time I left the light burning. Frogs never croak when it is light.

The examinations were like a family gathering, everyone pleasant and smiling. I began with Latin, and Mosén Joaquín could not laugh at the professor because the latter was ill and his assistant, who was a priest, took his place. Mosén Joaquín believed that only priests had the right to know Latin. My examination was brilliant. The professor assured us with great seriousness that many of the questions were really more suitable for "the higher faculties."

In the geography and geometry examinations I did less brilliantly, but the professors seemed to want to show me that they liked me, and they exchanged smiles with Mosén Joaquín, who was present, seated near the examiners. When the examinations were over we stayed, walking up and down the cloister waiting for my marks. It was already noon, and we were very hungry, when a beadle appeared with a packet of certificates. On my three examinations I had got two "outstandings" and one "excellent." Mosén Joaquín was radiant.

I wrote Valentina another post card:

"I was only the lord of dominations and love before. I tell you this in confidence. But now I am the lord of wisdom too. I was awarded two unanimous 'outstandings' and one 'excellent.' This afternoon we are going to a play at the Fuenclara, a big theatre where they give edifying plays, according to Mosén Joaquín. The play is called *Saint Catharine of Siena*, and it is a pity because to-morrow they are giving another one called *Divine Human Love*, which seems appropriate for us. You are the first person I want to know the triumph of your unforgettable Pepe. P.S.

Don't show this to anyone except your mother so that she can be the one to spread the good news. Farewell."

In the afternoon we went to the theatre. I thought that "edifying" had a different meaning and expected something special like battles in the colonies with plenty of dead, but it was nothing but well-dressed people facing each other and arguing interminably. Afterwards I inquired and learned that "edifying" plays were those in which virtue finally triumphed.

The next morning we rose early to catch the train and reach home by dinner time. I was received in triumph. Valentina had had only my first post card; the others did not arrive until the following day. But Mosén Joaquín had sent my father a telegram. Everyone knew except Valentina.

For the examinations in September, I still had three subjects left that we hardly took seriously: grammar, calligraphy, and physical education. Grammar was the only one that I had to study a little, but no one reminded me of it, and we were already making preparations for our summer holiday and I did not even have a copy of the textbook. My friends were dazzled, but they continued to conspire against me, and I received news of several intrigues in which I was obliged to intervene if I wanted to maintain my authority. Carrasco was one of those who rose against me. The basis of the rebellions was the fact that my two empty pistols had been found near the ford. Losing them, I lost my power.

About June 10 everything was ready for us to leave for the castle of Sancho Garcés Abarca for the summer. To part from Valentina seemed intolerable when Doña Julia told me that they were to spend two weeks in August at San Sebastian. San Sebastian was the fashionable resort, the favorite beach. I told Valentina again that the boys in the city were like onions—it seemed that their heads had been kept under ground and they came up white, with shining skins. They always walked hand in hand with grownups and their hair was so well brushed that a fight seemed an impossibility.

I begged Doña Julia—fruitlessly—to allow Valentina to come with us. When her mother almost yielded, her father intervened clamorously:

"What a place, what a place for her to go!"

My mother said that the castle was extremely comfortable and really in the mountains, almost among the peaks of Navarre. It would be healthy, especially for children. Doña Julia looked at me and said:

"The seashore would be good for Pepe—sea air is soothing."

My father conferred upon me the honor of arranging our journey. We had to use both carriages and carry two mattresses and a quantity of bed linen in the old one. One of the mattresses was for my mother's bed, the other for Concha's. They were the only two proper beds we took, although I liked the others better because they were called "campaign beds," which is to say "camp cots." They were small single beds composed of a steel frame inside which was stretched a piece of canvas edged with leather. Through the leather, which was perforated with metallic eyeholes, a waxed cord was looped to the steel frame, making it possible to keep the canvas taut and springy. We children were to sleep in these single beds, which pleased me.

In the first expedition all of us except my sister Concha, my mother, and Aunt Ignacia set out with my father. My father went ahead on horseback with a corporal of rural guards whose sector was precisely the territory surrounding the castle. Our old coachman drove the cabriolet, and I followed in the old carriage—the sty—in which, among saucepans, mattresses, and blankets, Maruja had been unwillingly installed. Only the maids rode in the sty, and Luisa, who sat beside me on the box. The old horse seemed perfectly contented now that he had the young ones for company. My father had bought a third horse, a saddle horse, and he liked to show off riding it. The old horse had three bells hanging from his breast strap, and the cool early morning put us all, except Maruja, in a fine humor. We should be installed in the castle before noon; in the afternoon my mother, Concha, and Aunt Ignacia would follow on a second trip. The old horse was to remain at home when he returned; two journeys in one day would have been too much for him.

As soon as we got into the open country I began to sing. The castle of Sancho Garcés stood on the topmost height of a conical mountain. My father sometimes indulged a weakness for saying that our family had originated there. Sancho Garcés had been King of Navarre, which at that time included half of present-day Aragón. The main portion of the castle—the old fortifications—was in ruins. A wall completely surrounded the highest part of the mountain and extended like a steep series of stairs down the declivity which connected the high peak of Sancho Garcés with a chain of mountains which continued into Navarre. The wall had lost more than half its height, and the great hewn stones had in the course of time rolled down the mountain. What was left of the wall did not, however, seem like a ruin. Within the wall there was an enormous level space which had been the parade ground. The portion which faced the north was closed off by structures of great solidity; walls whose doors and windows sometimes showed a thickness of six feet. On one side of the parade ground the chapel displayed its Romanesque lines; opposite it at the other end of the immense space there was a group of one-story stone buildings which surrounded the yards and stables; with their Romanesque doorways, they bore witness to the multiplicity of offices which were needed in a castle where six or eight generations sometimes lived without leaving it and neither grandparents nor grandchildren knew any horizon but precipitous rocks and eagles' nests. The castle overlooked a space of fifty miles in every direction except the north, in which the series of abrupt peaks was continued. One did not need to know much about war to realize that not a bird could pass that chain of mountains without permission from the occupants of the castle; but for fifty miles to the southward too, nothing could move without their being aware of it.

The rest of the family arrived before dark. From the castle we could see our town in the distance, with the nuns' tower, which was as high as the tower of the parish church. Through my field glasses the tower was so clear that it seemed surprising not to hear the bell. The only inhabitants of the castle were the old sextons who looked after the chapel and the corporal of rural guards who, with his wife and children and two or three other families, lived in a part which had much the appearance of a deserted village.

In this barbarous and romantic combination, it was impossible to tell where man's work ended and nature's began. There, on a block of stone which projected beside my window, was a pair of birds of prey; they gave their hoarse cry when they saw me and were off in high, easy flight. On top of the ruined keep behind the chapel, some storks were perched among the yellow mustard and the vines. They were migrating storks, resting a moment on their journey to other lands. At night we sometimes heard the howling of a vixen.

‡7‡

The day after our arrival my father rose very early and set off with his gun. About eight o'clock I heard shots, and dressed and went out to investigate. More shots gave me the direction, and at last, with the aid of my field glasses, I discovered my father on the side of a hill at the foot of the mountain. Then I saw him raise his gun to his shoulder again and fire. Through my field glasses my father's shots produced a charming effect. A jet of white smoke issued from the barrel in perfect silence, and it was only long afterwards, when he had the gun under his arm again or was reloading it, that I heard the report.

After waking several times to listen to the wind, which seemed to want to tear down the castle, I had slept well and was thoroughly recovered from the emotions of our journey; the morning was cool and bright and the wind seemed to have fallen. I walked around the chapel until I came to the ruined keep, immense and square. In the midst of untamed nature there were spots carefully paved with blocks more than a yard square. A great sundial on the octagonal corner tower of the chapel, bore a sentence in Latin: "All wound, the last kills." Next, I explored the wall which ran round the parade ground. I calculated that the parade ground would hold over forty thousand men drawn up in formation. There was a place where the ground ceased to be level and a ramp began which led down to where the wall was closed by a rudely carved gateway. The top of the gateway was on a level with the parade ground because the ramp made a steep descent. The wall was continued beyond the gateway along the road, which descended the mountain in violent zigzags, but it was soon lost among the rocks.

The corporal greeted me from a distance; he was dressed like any other peasant, except that he wore a wide diagonal belt of braided leather with a copper disc in the middle of it inscribed: "Forestry Section, District of Ejea de los Caballeros." He told me that he was going to fetch water from the "spring of the wild goat." The water from it contained a great deal of iron.

"Is that what makes it good?" I asked.

"There's nothing to equal it."

The corporal went to mount his mule. I followed him, but when we started out I heard someone call me from a window. Aunt Ignacia, who was very sorry for us all because we had come to live in such a place when we owned a "decent" house, threw down a sweater to me:

"Carry it over your arm and put it on when you begin to perspire."

I folded it, tucked it under my belt, and started off with the corporal, looking covertly, with an envy which I cannot describe, at the copper-mounted Remington carbine slung from his saddle.

I asked him if he had ever shot anyone.

He said that he never had, and that he earnestly hoped that the occasion would not arise.

As I went along I collected grasshoppers, which I put under my shirt. Some of them escaped through the most unlikely apertures, but I found I had four or five left, which were enough to put in Maruja's bed. They did not bite or do any harm, but they would give her a good fright.

There was a small stone vault over the spring, built to prevent the wind from blowing dust into it. On the right side of the vault there was a bas-relief of a religious subject. Beside it the words "*Sancta Maria*" were engraved on the stone in Romanesque letters.

"It was made in the old days," said the guard, "to protect the spring from the corrupt winds that sometimes blew from France."

"Eh?" I said, not understanding.

"Yes, and it still happens now. When you drink from a spring hereabouts you must be careful not to open your mouth too wide, because the demons who travel on the winds lie in wait beside springs to enter your body when you drink. And if you yawn while you're on the mountain, even if you are not near a spring, make the sign of the cross on your mouth at least three times, because if you don't they can enter your body."

He added that on some nights they came in legions—hundreds and hundreds of them—and groaned as they passed over the roofs, and that the wind sometimes "smashed the heads of some of them" against the corner of his house.

"Yes. I heard them last night," I said, and it was true.

When we had loaded the mule with four jars of water from the spring, which was about halfway down the mountain, we started back. Before we had reached the gateway in the wall we saw my father coming up too. He was carrying a number of partridges and rabbits and had tucked a large white handkerchief under his canvas hat to protect his neck and ears; it danced in the breeze.

"Getting sunburned, Don José?"

The corporal congratulated my father on his success as a hunter, but reminded him that he need not go to so much trouble—with a little skill and patience he could shoot partridges from the window of his bedroom. My father asked him numerous questions concerning the habits of partridges and presented him with a rabbit.

I went up to my room to write to Valentina. I still had two of the post cards I had bought in Zaragoza, and I wrote on them both. I put stamps on them, though later I was told that they were not necessary. I mentioned on the post cards that I was "no longer in Zaragoza and that if I wrote to her *from there* it was because I had had more than enough." My father read them and asked me what I had had more than enough of —post cards or Zaragoza? I answered, both. I went on to say in my post cards that the castle could hold a thousand warriors, and that if she came with her mother one day I should be able to see them through my field glasses as soon as they left their house. "There is no love here—nor theatres, nor books of poems—but I have found a very ancient spring where Sancho Garcés' warriors used to drink. There is iron in the water, and they say that makes it very good, but I don't believe it because I've never seen anyone sucking a nail. There is writing on the wall which says:

> 'Santa Maria
> A star shines in the sky,
> Guiding sailors through the sea.' "

The last two lines were of my own composition. And I added: "I am a wanderer, traveling the roads alone and blind, but I see the star in the sky and it is you and you guide me." And I ended, as always, "Your unforgettable Pepe."

When there was anything lyrical in my post cards my father read them and showed them to my mother, in alarm. My mother soothed him, and once she said to me:

"You are fond of poetry, my son. You take after me in that."

I looked out the window. All the windows opened on to emptiness and faced some wild scene beyond. In the distance I could see a peak like ours on which there was another castle of Sancho Garcés Abarca, the ruins of which continued down the slope. It was larger than ours; sometimes clouds hung round it, with a turret visible above them. It was now uninhabitable. There was not even a road leading to it.

In the afternoon my father, who seemed impatient to explore everything, go everywhere, and hunt anything, asked me to go out with him again. We forced our way into unlikely places through shrubs and tall weeds, or slipped dangerously on big rocks. In the end we had to climb to the top of Sancho Abarca by goat-paths because we were far from the road. We arrived at nightfall, exhausted. We had been exploring the possibilities of hunting the larger kinds of game. It had not been dark an hour before everyone succumbed to drowsiness, and we were in bed by nine o'clock. Once again the wind howled and made the walls of my room tremble; in the comfort and warmth of my bed I felt that I was being hurled through space in an enormous projectile. Finally I fell into a heavy sleep.

The next morning the corporal had brought letters, and my father had to put on civilized clothes—except for his riding boots—and go to town. He said that he would return by evening. I was left alone—I mean, I was the only man left—and I decided to explore the other castle.

It took more than two hours to reach it. There were lizards warming themselves in the sun among the ruins; when they saw me they raised their heads, uncertain whether to run or not. It was all far more ruinous than it appeared to be from a distance. I found a rusty key, ornamented with a complicated design, and kept it as a trophy. Just then I heard a sheep bell. I started toward it and found that I had to leave the castle, go round it, and descend the last ramparts. Down there I found a very old shepherd wrapped in sheepskins and wearing sandals [abarcas] that were doubtless of the same pattern as those worn by Sancho Garcés' men. Around him, scattered among the ruins, were several hundred ewes.

"Good morning!"

"Your father," he said, without any preface, "is fond of hunting. There are mountain goats around here."

He pointed with his staff to a nearby wood. He added: "If you go through there on your way home you'll see one jump." Apparently the shepherd knew my father or had encountered him on his wanderings. Or perhaps the shepherd knew everything.

"Did you come to see the castle?"

"Yes."

"What are you looking for?"

"Nothing."

"But you have something in your hand."

I showed him the key. He looked at it for a time in great surprise, as if he did not know what to say. Finally he spoke:

"The lord of this castle lost one battle. Only one."

I knew it already from having heard my father tell it. He lost one battle because once, when he was encamped with his host in a nearby

valley, the enemy came and when his military councillors told him that
he must move his camp so that he could give battle successfully, he saw
that the swallows had nested among the tent poles:

"How can we break camp?"

Above the edges of the nests appeared the ugly, hungry beaks of the
young swallows. "How can we break camp?" And they did not break
camp. And they went to meet the enemy in another place, and lost the
battle, though half the host was able to return to the camp and wait
until the young swallows could fly. Then they broke camp and returned
to the castle, which the enemy was besieging, and they broke the siege
and entered the castle. That was the story my father had told me. The
shepherd said:

"On that hill over there, there is a small castle, and another over
there. And another there. Look! And the lord of this castle had many
bastard sons and only one legitimate son whose name was Garcés. And
the bastards were given such names as De Dios, Esmeralda, De la Peña,
Del Castillo. This district is full of those names. One day the Moors
came up through the valley, and it looked as if the battle next morning
would be an ugly one. And the lord went to visit the small castles, which
had been built in the ravines to give warning, one after the other. And
when he came to that one, he called out, without dismounting from his
horse: 'Ave Maria. Who dwell within there, and what is their toil?'"

"'Here within,' answered one of his many bastard sons who were
awaiting the enemy, 'dwell six score sons of whores all ready to lay down
their lives for you, our father and lord.'"

And looking dreamily at the ruins, the shepherd added:

"That is why that little castle is called by a bad name now, 'the stronghold of the sons of whores.'"

Then the shepherd gave me a leather purse which he had tanned and
made himself, and I hung it at my side from my belt. I tried to think of
something to give him, but I had nothing of any value. The shepherd
smiled and, seeing that I was ready to leave, repeated:

"If you want to see mountain goats jump, go carefully through that
little wood."

I went down the mountain on the side opposite the castle, entered the
wood, whose trees were so closely interlaced above that no light at all
came through, and continued walking, guided by a distant brightness.
I arrived in time to see a stag and three fawns disappearing among the
trees. In the center of the wood there was a pool of rain water in a bed

of rock. The fawns went there to drink. I told my father about it when I reached home and thus escaped a reprimand for having been lost in the mountains all day. Luisa stared at me in real alarm. She looked strange in that rocky place. She seemed like a doll which the sun or the wind or any stone would hurt and destroy if she wandered six feet from my mother's skirts. When she looked at the savage majesty of the rocks, the mountains, and the clouds, her face wore the expression of one who has received a personal affront.

Maruja, on the other hand, wanted to be thought brave, and even went out beyond the gateway, all by herself. She always said that she was going to "catch males," but they made her come back. My hate for her had disappeared. From the height of my triumphs in matters military, naval, amorous, and academic, I could not look upon her as an enemy. To keep up the old custom, I tried to tease her, but in small, unimportant ways; the shine on her nose—which was not shiny like a nose, but shiny like metal—the same shine that appeared on her forehead and the point of her chin was the most frequent subject of my jokes. There was a certain tenderness at the bottom of them, and this my mother understood when Maruja ran to accuse me of "having insulted her." But only a few days after we came to the castle something happened which I cannot recollect even now without terror. We were on the second story of the principal part of the castle. There was a wooden balustrade that ran from one side of a large room to another above the stone staircase which led down to the story below. Maruja was sitting playing on the floor by the balustrade, and I was preparing a sort of framework out of sticks and string for the blind I was thinking of making. My little sister was angry with me and kept insulting me. Her way of being insulting was to repeat over and over again, mechanically and passionlessly, the whole possible repertory of childish insults. I finally became annoyed, started toward her, and, when I was halfway, saw her disappear between the balusters and fall into space. I heard a soft thud followed by absolute silence. She is dead, I thought. She is dead. I did not dare to look down the stairs for fear I should see positive proof. I heard my mother, Aunt Ignacia, and one of the maids arrive, lamenting. Then I went down. My sister had fallen on the stairs. No blood could be seen, but she looked as if she were dead. We picked her up, and the news was spread through the house. I believed that I was guilty of the crime; but fortunately there was no crime. My sister recovered consciousness a little later, and arnica dressings were applied to her head. The first thing she said when she opened her eyes was that I had picked her up, lifted her over the balustrade, and let her drop. I heard her, and could not even wish that she had been killed, because she was so frail and defenseless that it was impossible to wish it. Yet it was the only thing that could save me. My father was alone in denying her accusations. When I heard him say that Maruja was lying, I began to feel that perhaps we could become friends. Maruja, seeing that she had failed, began to weep bitterly and said that she hurt all over. It was not true. Nothing hurt her and she had suffered no injuries. A bump on the head, like others we had received without losing consciousness or accusing anybody. It is true, none the less, that I have never understood why she was not killed.

Two days later we went after the deer. My father and I had gone to bed at six o'clock the evening before, with the sun still above the horizon. By two o'clock in the morning we were already up, and the water was splashing in the washbowl where my father bathed every morning amidst stormy sounds of water. We set out. We went straight down in total darkness after crossing the beds of two streams grown over with brambles and strewn with great grey rocks. Before dawn we had circled the other castle, and as we entered the wood the sky began to lighten in tints of cinnabar red. A few seconds later the whole firmament was a dome the color of bull's blood. My father hurried me along:

"Come on, quick! If we don't get posted before dawn the deer will scent us."

On the farther side of a little open pool in a clearing in the woods we rapidly built a blind, taking advantage of the natural disposition of the rocks and tree trunks. It was not exactly beside the pool but about twenty yards beyond it in the opposite direction from the wind.

My father, looking out through a loop hole, asked softly:

"Where did you see them run off?"

I pointed to the place. "That is where they will always run to," he said, "because when an animal is surprised and in danger it never runs to a place it does not know."

The deer had not appeared, but they would come because there had been no moon and it is only on moonlight nights that they go to drink before dawn. Our ears kept deceiving us with the illusion of leaves rustling among the trees. The wind brought us the faintest sounds.

But nothing came. The tension of the first minutes had disappeared when we heard a faint hissing. It seemed as if there was another hunter present who was warning us to be still. And into the open place in the woods came two large snakes, chasing each other so agilely that our eyes could not follow them. At last they stopped and began to lift themselves into the air on their tails. And they started dancing. I am not joking. They started dancing, and they danced for more than half an hour. Sometimes they stretched themselves upward to their full length, and they measured more than six feet. My father had never seen anything like it. I did not know whether to laugh or to start running. The kingdom to which I laid claim was not the kingdom of snakes.

When the snakes seemed to be growing quiet, we heard the noise of trampled leaves. The snakes fled as fast as they had come. My father got his gun ready, and what appeared was not a deer at all but a bear. A big old bear, who looked in our direction, suspiciously.

"A bear!"

"Quiet!"

My father was as frightened as I was. He fired both barrels together, and the bear, who did not seem to have been touched, raised his head and looked in our direction. At the same moment the shepherd whom I had encountered in the ruins of the castle walked up to the bear and scratched him under the chin. The shepherd cupped both hands around his mouth and, turning in our direction—we were still in our hiding place, unable to comprehend what was going on—shouted:

"Why, what harm did Mateo do you?"

My father looked at me and finally said:

"Son, pinch my arm."

I pinched it. The shepherd said:

"The mountain goats don't come here. You have to go farther up."

And he walked quietly away with the bear. Farther on, toward the ruins of the castle, we could hear the bells of his flock.

My father and I came out of hiding and returned to our castle. We did not mention our failure. My father appeared to be deeply preoccupied, and only exclaimed now and again:

"It's just like what happened to Uncle Monico."

I realized the drama of the situation and did not dare ask what that was. But he repeated it once more, and I felt obliged to.

"Was it about a bear too?"

"No, a wolf. But I am not going to tell you about it because you are too young to understand it."

I did not insist. We reached the castle at noon. My father went into the chapel, intending, apparently, to turn to God in his perplexity. I too. The chapel was wrapped in a delicious humid darkness. My father lighted the lamp before the altar and knelt down. The alabaster image went back to the time when Sancho Garcés had lived in the castle, and was even much older. It was covered to the neck by a conical mantle embroidered with silver and gold. The image was rather large for this sort of statue in Spain, and while my father prayed I noticed that some moving thing was peering over its shoulder. I fixed my attention on it. It was a lizard. Later I saw tobacco-colored squirrels in the holes of the chapel vault as well. My father continued praying, and I kept quiet. The lizard remained perched on the shoulder of the image and seemed to be looking curiously at us and the lamplight. It sniffed at the ear of the image, descended to its embroidered mantle, on which it looked like an additional ornament, and slowly returned to its post on its shoulder.

Later on I told my mother about it. Aunt Ignacia, who was present, said quickly:

"That was not a lizard."

"What was it then?"

"The devil. In places like this even the Virgin has the devil round her neck."

My mother smiled. She was less religious than my father, contrary to what is usually the case in families.

Before dinner I walked round the parade ground with a heavy iron-tipped walking stick.

I had written Valentina another letter and sent her new variations on the song. Melancholy ones, now:

> *Come along and play,*
> *Play till time for bed,*
> *Playing in the ring*
> *Of cinnamon-bread.*

> *All in my father's garden*
> *Tall grows the tree*
> *Full of empty nests*
> *For you and for me.*

For me, for me,
Valentina and Valenti.
When I kissed you
And started away
I knew that you
Would cry all day.

Dindle and dandle!
Here comes the notary
Bringing his candle!

Valentina would learn to sing them to the music. I wrote the last stanza in the hope that she would sing it at home.

The next day I was wandering around the parade ground, and, for lack of something better to do, I began poking with my stick at a large flagstone whose outline was lost under earth and grass. I noticed that my blows produced a hollow sound, and I went to tell the corporal. He found an iron bar, which the peasants call a *barrón* and which they use as a throwing stick or javelin, but after violent efforts we were able to move the stone only a little. My father became interested and brought another lever, and between the two of them they succeeded in raising the stone. Beneath it was an opening, regularly circular and more than a yard in diameter. My father and the corporal looked at each other in astonishment, and the corporal said that these mountains were full of caves and that in one of them the cup which Christ had used on the Mount of Olives was hidden. But this opening must be a well. There might be water in it and there might not. They threw in pieces of burning paper to light the shaft. There was no indication that it had ever held water. The walls were of hewn stone, smooth and well fitted. The corporal offered to go down and explore. I too offered to go, but they both agreed that I might not. They fetched a rope, a lantern, and a pickaxe. The corporal let himself down by the rope with the lantern on his belt and the pickaxe over his shoulder.

The corporal shouted up from below to say that everything was clean and in order and that there was a blocked-up door there which he was going to break open. My father went down too, and soon afterwards I heard the monotonous sound of the pick separating stones and mortar. I protested so much that they finally let me join them. I descended rapidly. As soon as a part of the wall gave way they put the lantern through the hole and looked in curiously. It was the beginning of a gallery which ran straight on for over a hundred yards. They enlarged the opening, and we all three entered. I wanted to go ahead so that I could tell Valentina I had been first, but my father kept calling to me and forced me to stay in the rear. My father was not aware that it frightened me to stay behind, and I ended by taking a place between the corporal, who went first, and my father.

I looked about anxiously. I believed that the world was made from the inside out. Beneath the place where we now stood there were other subterranean passages containing fragments of yet earlier lives. What I saw interested me greatly on account of my "Universiad," in which I should have to describe it. My father, who was not particularly strong in history, put his hand on the wall and exclaimed:

"A great people, the Romans!"

He immediately added that, though Rome had invaded us, the principal Roman emperors thereafter were Spaniards, like Trajan. And he told us wonderful things about Trajan.

The gallery that opened off to one side had a clean, flagstoned pavement. In order not to lose his way, my father took a piece of paper and began to make a map, starting at the point where we had entered. It appeared that the gallery ran on for hundreds of yards. To the left there were some fairly large square chambers. In the first one we saw a clay jar. It was full of blackened coins which, under a tightly adherent layer of dust, could be seen to be silver. We left them undisturbed, with the intention of returning for them later. They were of the ninth century, to my father's great disappointment, who wished they had been Roman. In another chamber which opened off the gallery a little farther on there was nothing but a rope hanging from the roof and under it, on the ground, a heap of human remains and bits of rotting cloth. This discovery was enough to check the curiosity of all three explorers, but we went on.

The gallery ended in a round chamber in the middle of which was a large square block of stone. We struck it with our sticks to see if it was hollow or not, but it was a solid block. From this chamber four more galleries ran in four directions.

"Here," my father said, "the persecuted Christians said Mass."

The guard insisted that the chalice of Christ's passion was hidden in these caves.

We continued our investigations, but as it was a task that would take nearer to a week than a day, we decided to return. When we were out in daylight again, we met the rural priest who came on Sundays to say Mass for us. He had already said two, one in the village and another in a saint's chapel, and as he had swallowed two good mouthfuls of wine fasting, he was a little dizzy. He was in a great hurry to say his last Mass and have breakfast, and we all went to the chapel. The sexton was present in his new clothes and assisted him. He did not speak his sentences in Latin but uttered their phonetic equivalent in Spanish. For example, when he was supposed to say, "*Et cum spiritu tuo*," he said, "*Según se mire es tuyo*." The long prayer of the "*Oremus*" was something which produced an uncontrollable laugh in my father. When the priest elevated the Host, the sexton heard the corporal's dog scratching himself and, forsaking his bell, chased the animal out of the chapel:

"God damn it, this is no place for a dog to get rid of his fleas," he said.

After Mass the sexton spoke to my father:

"Haven't you forgotten something, Don José?"

"What?"

My father had once jokingly told him that he knew as much about the Mass as a priest, and that he would buy him a chasuble for feast days and he could say Mass as an auxiliary deacon. On this account, the sexton there and then began to chant the Epistle of Saint Paul after his fashion. The priest and my father restrained their laughter. Later my father said, nodding his head:

"God is better pleased with his absurdities than with the prayers of many bishops."

The priest breakfasted heartily—the state of slight intoxication he had manifested when he arrived disappeared as he ate—and then took his departure. My father accompanied him as far as the foot of the mountain.

We did not return to our subterranean explorations that day. During the night I woke frequently because the wind was making a louder noise than usual, and I connected its wailing with the mysteries of the crypts we had discovered. My father had told of our discoveries at the supper table before we went up to bed. Since he had spoken, I did not feel obliged to keep still and chattered on unrestrainedly. Afterwards I went to my room and wrote to Valentina: "With the discovery of the vaults," I said, "I shall soon be able to finish the 'Universiad'."

The next day the corporal appeared with a long ladder, much more practical than our ropes for getting up and down. We descended—my father, the corporal, and I. We reconnoitered the territory we had already explored. From time to time we were made uneasy by a distant sound of footsteps, and we stopped until we discovered that they were only the echo of our own. My father tried to account for our confusion by saying that there might well be fox dens thereabouts, but the corporal said that foxes preferred holes which were not deep and into which the sun shone.

He knew a great deal about foxes and had promised my sisters three pelts for collars and cuffs.

"Will you have to go far to find them?"

"No, sir. They come right to the door of my house. When I go over the mountains I fasten a little piece of pork rind to my boot and drag it all the way along. Then I set my trap at the door of my house, and the next day before I get up I hear the fox downstairs in the trap."

We continued our explorations. In a vault whose roof sloped down to meet the floor we found another jar containing coins and parchments. The value of the coins was decidedly questionable, but we all felt as if we had discovered a treasure. My father gathered up the parchments to take home and announced that all these things belonged to the Provincial Museum of History and that no one must touch them. In a corner we found more calcined human remains. We returned to the circular chamber, from which a wide gallery descended at a steep slope. On either hand there was a long file of niches into which no one dared to flash the lantern because they were obviously tombs. The air was not damp, but it was cold. My father and the corporal were in their shirt sleeves, I in an undershirt. I was so cold that my teeth almost chattered, but I kept from showing it so that my father would let me go on. At the end of the descending gallery we found another large circular chamber with galleries running off in different directions. We decided to take the first, which turned to the right. Unlike the gallery we had been following, this one ran upward until it ended at a place where the roof met the floor at a very acute angle. My father told the corporal to dig into the obstruction. After half an hour's work, daylight appeared. The corporal said that the exit had been stopped up in the course of time by the natural accumulation of soil. We walked out, and found ourselves among the servants' quarters of the castle, in a small court surrounded by irregular buildings. Here must have lived the smiths, the wool dressers, the master crossbowmen, the armorers, the weavers.

Later when we were talking to my mother she asked me if we had closed the entrances to the subterranean passages again, and we were obliged to tell her that we had, in order to keep her from feeling afraid. My father, full of self-importance, retired to his room and tried to decipher the parchments, but was quite unable to make out a word.

We had invited Mosén Joaquín to visit us, and one morning he arrived and came limping up to the top of the castle. There he wiped the sweat from his face, sat down on a block of stone before he had greeted anyone, and said to my father:

"This is the kind of air that agrees with me."

Aunt Ignacia brought luncheon to us where we were sitting: two partridges in pickle—prepared with oil and vinegar—and two bottles of wine. The corporal had come to kiss Mosén Joaquín's hand and looked at the tray, twirling his moustache. My father invited him to eat. Like Mosén Joaquín, he could tell where wine came from by its bouquet:

"This wine is at least eight years old and comes from the vineyard of Almoravides—right?"

My father answered that it was not eight years old but ten. It had been bottled the year I was born. As to the vineyard, he was right.

"This isn't wine, it's mother's milk," the corporal said.

Comparing wine to mother's milk seemed to me rather a strange kind of joke. My father laughed, feeling flattered. Mosén Joaquín wanted to go to the chapel. The three of us went together. I continued thinking about wine and mother's milk. Why did mother's milk have to be the best thing in the world. I would not have taken milk from a wet nurse, or even my mother's, although at that time I imagined that I had. Babies who sucked mother's milk aroused pity in me, because they had no teeth. Mosén Joaquín knelt for a moment with bowed head when he passed in front of the image, then, as he rose, continued to my father:

"You are right, Don José. That wine came from Almoravides."

They entered the sacristy and a little later returned. I was saying that I called the image "Our Lady of the Lizard" because there was always a lizard on its shoulder. Mosén Joaquín knelt again, bowed his head, and murmured for a few seconds. My father simply crossed himself, and I repented of having said what I did, although it was the first church I had seen where you could talk out loud just as you did in the street.

We went down into the vaults. I do not understand why Mosén Joaquín hoped to find fossils there. As we did not find any, he wanted to leave at once; he was completely uninterested by the other things.

In the afternoon as I saw that no one was paying any attention to me, I went to the ruins of the other castle hoping to find the shepherd. Since

I had seen him caressing the bear I had been devoured by curiosity. I still wore the leather purse and the old key of the castle, one on the right, the other on the left. The shepherd was there, under an arch as usual, with his body in the sun and his bearded face in the shade. He received me kindly and at once reminded me that I had the key of the castle and that I must keep it carefully.

"Yes," I said. "But where is the bear?"

"What bear?"

"The one you brought to the wood the day we shot at him from our blind."

"What blind? What wood?"

I explained and he listened attentively, but denied that he owned a bear or had ever brought one to the wood.

"However, it is possible that you saw me, because there are lamias hereabouts. And lamias make people see things that aren't so."

He explained what they were. Female wood spirits, with webbed feet like geese or cloven hoofs like goats.

"Have you seen one?" I asked.

"Yes, more than one."

"Are they very ugly?"

"No, they are the prettiest women I have ever seen. They have a little dimple here."

He pointed to his bearded chin. He added that they were not to be trusted and that the first thing to do was to look at their feet. They were accustomed to wear very long skirts to hide them, but, that being the case, it was sufficient to lead them on to a place where the ground was damp, and look at the footprints they left.

"But what I saw was a man, not a woman."

"With a bear?"

"Yes."

"Then it was the veterinary's nephew—he has a bear."

Not for anything would he himself have one, because every lamia has one of her own to ride on and there are as many lamias as there are bears, and if anyone has a tame bear then there is a lamia who has to go on foot and she will persecute him and when a son is born in his house she will put a bone from a cemetery in his swaddling clothes.

We remained silent. The shepherd went and lifted up a stone which was hot from a fire he had built on it and took out a piece of meat from among the smoking embers. From his bag he took bread, salt, and oil, seasoned the meat heavily, and began to eat. He said that he had hunted a rabbit, and that he never lacked fresh game.

"Have you a gun?" I asked him.

The shepherd laughed and said that when the rabbits saw a hunter with a new gun, leggings, cartridge belt, and a woolen muffler round his neck (I thought of Don Arturo), they danced for joy. "But when they see this"—he held up his shepherd's staff—"they call for confession." He offered me something to eat, and I accepted. When we had finished, he said:

"Come along if you like and I'll show you the wine cellar."

We went about twenty paces and he got down on his hands and knees, pushed aside some shrubbery, and disappeared between two rocks. I did likewise, feeling the agony that I have always experienced when I think of myself in a too confined space, but beyond the rocks the passageway became an enormous cavern which instantly reminded me of the galleries under our castle.

"Come this way."

I followed him and saw him stand up by the wall, put his hands into a vaulted niche which had the sepulchral look of those I had seen before, and pull out the neck of a wineskin through a crack in the tomb. It had a stopper which unscrewed. He took a small leather wine bag from his belt, removed its stopper too, and let a stream of wine pour from the skin to the bag; I could smell its fragrance. He stoppered the wineskin again, and we made our way back in silence. When we emerged the shepherd burst out laughing and said:

"There's where I keep my wine. The bishop himself doesn't drink any cooler."

"But isn't that a tomb?"

The shepherd looked at me for a time in silence:

"Are you afraid of the dead?"

I shook my head, but the shepherd wanted to convince me:

"I've been keeping wine there for thirty years. My father and my grandfather kept wine there before me. It hasn't yet happened that the dead man—whoever he is—that lives there has drunk a single drop of it."

I remained silent. After he had drunk a long draft he offered it to me and I drank a little. The wine was almost ice-cold, and the shepherd took it away from me before I had finished, saying:

"Be careful, because it's strong wine and if you drink much of it you'll have to stay here and sleep it off or I'll have to carry you to the castle on my back. Neither of which would be proper."

The afternoon was wearing on, and the sky began to grow pale. The shepherd considered the sun and the distance that separated me from the castle:

"You must start now, and if it gets dark before you arrive don't be afraid, for when anyone has had a drink of this wine the lamias can't do him any harm."

I looked at him, enchanted with it all, and asked him if it was to exorcise the lamias that he kept the wine in the tomb.

"Yes, young one, but you mustn't tell anybody because it is a custom that I inherited from my father and he from his grandfather and he from his great-grandfather and he from his great-great-grandfather and so on back to the time when God walked the roads."

To show him that I was grateful for his revelation, I made him another. I told him that I had discovered the underground passages of our castle and that I had gone exploring more than a league under the earth gathering coins and old documents, and that one of the passageways connected with the castle in whose ruins we now were.

"All by yourself? I don't believe it."

"Why not?"

"You say you had to dig into the ground and break through walls. When did you do it?"

"Yesterday."

"Let me see your hands," and, taking them and turning them palms up, "where are the marks of the pickaxe?"

I felt so completely disarmed that I could almost have lain down and cried.

"If we are to be friends," he added, "no more lies! And now be off with you, because it is going to get dark."

I wanted to prove to him that there was some truth in what I had said. At least the passageway connected with the castle. The shepherd understood how dramatic it would be for me to be able to convince him and he accepted part of what I said.

"Not this passageway, though. It may be another, but not this one."

"Why not?"

"Because this one leads to hell. My grandfather wanted to go in once, and a devil appeared before him who knew the whole history of my family. He stood there telling him about his father and his grandfather and what their names were and what they thought about things, and from that day on my grandfather had a void in his guts that stayed with him until he died. So now, none of us ever go in any farther than the fourth tomb because—and don't forget this, young one—anything that is bad is good too if you take only a little of it. So, if you go far in you will find yourself with a void, and if you go still farther you will fall right into hell. But if you stay near the entrance like I do and keep wine in the tomb you get strong and the lamias can't do anything to you."

And, feeling the wine bag, he shook his head and added:

"It's too cold, it goes down without your knowing it, and where it goes it gives such joy that there's nothing to do but go on drinking it. And now you see for yourself, it has gone to your head."

He was right, but until he said so I had not realized it. It could not be said that I was drunk, though I did not know for sure what intoxication was. Well, I wasn't falling down, or even staggering, I talked normally, and I could come and go without having the road wriggle in front of me, and besides, if the shepherd had drunk much more than I had and wasn't drunk, why should I be?

"All drunkards tell the same story."

"What story?"

"That they aren't drunk. But don't worry, young one—I'll take you home."

Refusing any help from the shepherd, I thanked him for his kind intentions and set off. I ran most of the way back. When night fell I realized that if I ran I felt afraid, and I went along slowly, peering at the shadows on either hand, although I knew that the lamias would not harm me even if they appeared. I sang Valentina's song:

> *Dindle and dandle!*
> *Here comes the notary*
> *Bringing his candle!*

‡ 8 ‡

When I reached home, everyone was uneasy, although they were becoming accustomed to worrying about me and having it come out all right in the end. There were new guests at the castle: the doctor and his wife. They welcomed me as an old friend. My father did not like to be alone for long and had invited them to spend Saturday, Sunday, and Monday. The doctor was enchanted, and his wife tried to approve of everything, saying "How lovely!" in a tone of great conviction, as if she were at a bazaar. Like Aunt Ignacia and Luisa, she found nature, except in photographs, unconvincing.

When they understood that I did not intend to give any explanations —a thing which I had always considered humiliating—we went in to supper. Of the children, only Concha and I were present—the others were already asleep.

It was holiday fare, which is to say that supper lasted three long hours. My father had brought up wines to which Mosén Joaquín and the doctor did honor. The doctor's wife, who thought that the wines were harmless, immediately became flushed, although she drank very little.

After supper Mosén Joaquín, who had promised to read us his translation of the parchments we had found in the vault, produced several sheets of paper. At first the doctor fidgeted in his chair, expecting to be bored, but little by little he became interested, put first one elbow on the table and then the other, leaned toward Mosén Joaquín, and made gestures of approval. The silence grew deeper and deeper. Concha and I listened with intense interest. The parchment ran, in a style which suggested the original Latin:

"Preface made by me to the ordinances of this castle built according to recorded history by Sancho Garcés Abarca which is to be read once a month on the fast day of our Holy Mother and at the hour of vespers, before the captains and lettered men, by the Master of the Order of Santiago below signing and which preface all shall bear in mind, according to their obligation, to conform their souls to it in time of peace or war as may be agreeable to the blessed service of God. Amen.

"Of three classes of men is made the fortune and the glory of this land, and in general of all lands not inhabited by savage and barbarous peoples.

"First, those whose good will in dealing with their neighbors, whose hearts which love God and mankind, whose sense of right, and whose inclination to help others have blotted from their souls all passions and evil desires and whose lives have no substance save the reflection of their virtues. This class of men are saints.

"The next are those who, by long study and experience and much fighting in their youth against Moors and bad Christians, and because God was pleased to distinguish them with this privilege, have been able to penetrate further than ordinary eyes into the inwardness of things and, feeling whiteness descend on their hair, for the honor of their sons and the arms they had won and with fiery love were able to set down in good rhetoric sacred hymns and profane songs and famous chronicles which the men of tomorrow can read for their edification. The first of these men—of our time, I mean—is that King Alfonso X, of Castile and León, named the Wise. And this class of men, which we shall call the second of those who make the nation in our land or in any other, is the class of poets.

"Finally, the third sort of men necessary to establish our greatness is the class of those who seek out adventurous deeds and the enemy's steel, to write with their blood, for so it can be said that many have done, the devices of their shields. These are heroes.

"The three sorts of men, then, most necessary to establish greatness are saints, poets, and heroes. A land can be very rich without these virtues but it will not achieve greatness. And God our Lord has not been chary in giving us in this land these three classes of men, for we have them at our side every day and we see them in their virtue, wisdom, and heroism, edifying us with their deeds. There are some who have more than one of these qualities, but it is enough for each of us to have one only, because if we possess it utterly, as God desires that men should possess things, then there can be no true poet without a touch of heroism and no true saint without a touch of the poet, nor, finally, any of the three without some of the virtues of the others.

"The first condition of the saint is to neglect everyday values for those whose home and splendor is found only in eternity. And this is also the condition of the hero. And of the poet. The first condition of the poet is truth and beauty, for which he will give his life if necessary, and this is the condition of the hero. The first condition of the hero is not to turn his face from danger but to advance on it with greater courage. The greater the danger, the greater the glory of conquering or dying. In these qualities are also included beauty, truth, and the holiness of love for just causes. It cannot be said, then, that each quality exists separately from the others and is in and by itself sufficient for greatness, because if this were so some qualities could be opposed to others, which is impossible.

"And I say to you that in this castle of Sancho Garcés the hero is to be accounted first, and then, in the same place, the saint and the poet. And that on your heroism depends the careful stimulation and growth of the

other virtues, for, however much some may tell you that they are qualities of peace, I tell you that they are also qualities of war, for war is as
it were the highest and bravest part of life, and in war these high qualities increase and are heightened, just as at the moment of greatest
curvature of bow and crossbow all the qualities of wood and steel are
put under tension and increased. And so I tell you, O my captains and
knights, that the ordinances which continue in this castle must be im-
pregnated with these sentiments and bring it to pass that our privileges
won by long centuries of struggle must be regarded as such without pride,
and that submission must be received without causing humiliation, and
that our law must be like the law of saints and poets and heroes, stable
and pleasing for the greater good of all men and for the greater good of
our country and the service of God, and that all you who are high in
fortune and courage and nobility shall keep in remembrance those words
of Saint Paul where he says: 'One man esteemeth one day above another:
another esteemeth every day alike. Let every man be fully persuaded in
his own mind . . . For whether we live, we live unto the Lord; and
whether we die, we die unto the Lord: whether we live therefore, or
die, we are the Lord's.' So we must all be, for perhaps God leads us
along this path, toward the true glory of obtaining in this stronghold of
Sancho Garcés some man who, reaching the highest state of the three
virtues of heroism, holiness, and wisdom or poetry, will better the path
of mankind as was done by Saint Paul in Rome, the Cid in the camps
of the infidel, or Alfonso X in his Christian kingdoms.—Amen."

No one had interrupted Mosén Joaquín. My sister Concha was
yawning because at first she thought that the parchment would be like
Fabiola, which she was reading and which related the loves of the
Romans. My mother sent her to bed. There we remained—we men, and
my mother, and the doctor's wife, all equally enthralled by the reading.
I did not entirely understand it, but there were words like torches, and
the document as a whole was as warming as the shepherd's wine. My
father was the first to make a comment:

"What style!"

"You are right," said Mosén Joaquín. "The style in Latin can only be
compared to certain of Seneca's epistles. My translation gives but a faint
idea of it."

"There are no such men in these days," said the doctor's wife.

Her husband protested:

"Plenty of them—everywhere."

My father thought the same. He believed that the cultivation of the three virtues, rather than college educations, engineers, and economics, would restore Spain to greatness. The doctor did not believe that past greatness ever returns. He did not believe that anything that was really dead ought to return. If it had died, it was because its hour had come. "But," he added, "true greatness never dies. The source of it continues in other channels."

"In what channels?" my father asked.

The doctor gave an example. In this region, in these castles, the liberties of modern Europe were born. Here, and not in the French Revolution—which was only a small affair of bookish tradesmen. My father interrupted to declaim against the spirit which the diffusion of commerce—deceit, untruthfulness, lack of trust, the false honesty always based on repression—had brought in. The doctor listened carefully and said:

"Yes. But what are we to do?"

"You have just told us. The liberties of Europe were born in this country. While African barbarism was being held back, first here and later at sea—Lepanto—the parliaments of Aragón were laying down laws in which liberty was for the first time organized. Out of these parliaments were later born the idea of liberty in France, the old legislation of England. The relations of the nobility and the aristocracy with the people and the king. The statutes in which pure juridical entities were formed, independent of . . . ," he went on, but I was no longer listening.

Mosén Joaquín nodded his head as if he were in ecstasy:

"Oh, if we would dare to be what we all, more or less, are within ourselves!"

"What do you believe that we are?" asked the doctor.

"Heroes or saints or poets. Each of us is born with one of those seeds in his heart."

I said that I wanted to tell them something very important that had happened in one of the outer castles, but that first I must ask a question.

"What kind of question?" said my father, made wary by experience.

"What does 'bastard' mean?"

They explained as well as they could. I saw that there was some mystery about it into which I was not to inquire, and, not quite able to understand it, I began the story the shepherd had told me. When I came to the sentence: "Here within dwell six score sons of whores all ready to lay down their lives for you," they all burst out laughing except the ladies, whose reactions were very different. While my mother stared at me as if she had never seen me before, the doctor's wife blushed and said:

"Oh! . . ."

My father continued to laugh, but when everything was quiet again, he asked me, suddenly serious:

"Where did you hear that?"

"Someone told me."

"Who?"

I should have kept my secret, because it was not normal behavior for me to tell everything that happened to me, but in the document that Mosén Joaquín had just read it said that the poet was a man of truth and beauty. I took this perfectly literally; so I told my story. Afterwards I added:

"What were those men in the castle? Saints or poets or heroes?"

My father did not know what to answer:

"Poor unfortunates."

"But they must have fought well."

"Yes," said my father, "there are men without spirit who behave heroically or wisely or holily if those who guide them can inspire these things in them."

My mother was still looking at me uncomprehendingly:

"This boy . . ."

"In that case," I said, "bastards are men without spirit, are they? A pity!"

"Why?"

"Because I should like to be a bastard."

They decided to ignore me. Mosén Joaquín was the only one who looked me in the face, and now and again he rolled a little ball of bread across the tablecloth to me and I would send it back to him. However, I asked:

"Are six centuries much in the life of mankind?"

"No. They are nothing," said the doctor.

"Well then, we are just the same as the people who built this castle, are we?"

"More or less."

"And what are we, Papa? Are you a bastard?"

No one answered. They talked about something else. I considered myself half hero and half poet. I said so. The doctor and Mosén Joaquín looked at me sympathetically. My father took the map of our explorations from his pocket and spread it out. My mother asked again if the entrances to the vaults had been closed, and the doctor's wife seemed to be relieved too when we said yes. When the doctor heard about our discovery of the skeletons he remembered that he needed one for his study but that he had not dared to ask the gravedigger for one because his corpses were comparatively recent. "One of those from down below would suit me," he said. But he added that it must be "perfectly clean." I thought of the shepherd. I told the doctor that I knew someone who would clean it for him but that he would have to pay for it because the man was very poor.

"I'll give him fifteen pesetas, if he really cleans it properly."

My mother was horrified again:

"Where do you pick up such acquaintances?"

I did not answer. The doctor, remembering the operation, said:

"He is really a brave boy."

My father looked at the map. There was a gallery which protruded beyond the sketch and was prolonged to one side in an imaginary direction.

"And that gallery?" Mosén Joaquín asked.

"It has still to be explored. There are tombs on both sides."

I broke in:

"It goes to the other castle. And the tombs too. And in the last tomb there is cold wine and if you drink it the lamias won't hurt you."

"Bah! Wine in a tomb! What foolishness!"

They continued to pore over the map and wondered where the gallery, which had been prolonged in an imaginary line, really led. I wanted to speak, but my mother interrupted me:

"Are you going to tell us more nonsense? Be quiet."

My father seemed to forget the map for a moment:

"If we were to remember those virtues, those ancient virtues . . ."

"I said before, Don José, that great things that have died ought not to be prolonged."

"But you also said that true greatness never dies."

"No."

"Where is it today?"

The doctor tried to find examples. Finally he pointed his finger at me:

"Anywhere. Here, even. That boy is not contaminated yet. He would give his life to have a share in defending this country with the six score bastards in the castle."

I could have hugged the doctor.

"Papa—" I said. "Let me explore that gallery. All by myself."

"Are you mad?"

"No. Let me do it alone."

"When?"

"At once."

"At night?"

"It is always night down there."

"My son, you are afraid of the vaults. So much afraid that the vaults have become a hallucination with you. And you think that to explore an unknown underground passage is the most heroic thing in the world."

Mosén Joaquín rose and retired to a sofa in the corner. He lighted a candle, took out his prayer book, and began to read vespers. When he rose, I had risen too, thinking that he wanted to speak to me privately, but when I saw him take out his book I returned to my chair, disappointed.

"Let me go to the vaults."

The doctor was to stay for three days. They agreed to explore the new gallery to the end the following afternoon. They were undoubtedly incited by my forwardness.

"I believe," I said, "that the lamias sleep in there with their bears. By day they come out and haunt the woods. But I am not afraid of lamias."

My father stood up, really angry at last, and ordered:

"To bed."

I rose quietly and turned to the doctor:

"Do you want the skeleton?"

"Certainly, but you . . ."

"Pay no attention to him," said my father.

And, soon after, he returned to the theme of past greatness. A man. If a man would appear who had all three qualities, like Philip II, like . . . The doctor stopped him:

"No, surely not he! I respect your opinion, but I don't believe that Philip II had one of those three qualities. Besides, the relations between nations, the relations between interests, the ease of communication, the whole of modern life make an anachronism of any armed national enterprise. Conquest, Empire: anachronisms. But the old greatness goes on."

"How?"

"We were once a strong people. A people of saints, heroes, and poets, as the document puts it. With power in our destiny to influence other peoples. We are still a strong people, Don José. We are not asleep. You will yet see one day how awake we are. But no people will again become great through arms."

"Perhaps."

"If yesterday Spanish Catholicism was able to conquer the world, to-day a new conception of humanity will arise among us too. That is to say, our empire can and should be spiritual. Today's heroism does not consist in giving your life in the advance of a regiment. It was long ago that Gracián gave a definition of the hero which has more of the saint and the poet in it than of the hero. In the fight against darkness, through knowledge."

" 'The Mansions' of Santa Teresa," said Mosén Joaquín from his corner.

"Yes. And men of science. Today, in reality, holiness, wisdom, and heroism are one and the same thing. And from that substance, without arms or conquest of territory, the new empires will be made."

The doctor's wife looked at him in ecstasy. She took advantage of a silence:

"Promise me," she begged him, "to give up your idea of having a skeleton."

My father suggested playing ombre. A game was immediately arranged. Two women and two men. Mosén Joaquín remained in his corner with his book. My mother spread a green cloth on the table and brought the cards.

I went to bed but fell asleep very late. I was trying to mature my plan for the following day. At first I actually thought seriously of going to the vaults, but afterwards, when I was alone, I began to realize that if the idea had occurred to me before an audience it had really sprung from a desire to show off, and now going seemed a more difficult matter. Even so, I planned to explore the gallery the next day. My father had said that they would start in the afternoon. I would go to see the shepherd, and approximately at the time they were entering the gallery at one end I would enter it at the other. We would meet halfway; I would convince them that I had been right in saying that it connected with the other castle, that I was enough of a hero to perform the feat like a real "bastard." The word seemed to me to denote undisciplined but all-conquering heroism.

‡9‡

I rose early, saw that the others were asleep, and went to the Romanesque fountain. There I wrote another letter to Valentina, in pencil. The corporal was going to town that day and would carry it.

"Here I am, and now it's no longer naval battles but subterranean ones with skeletons and hanged men. Everything has changed. Before you go to San Sebastián I want to tell you that there are lamias who ride on bears and have webbed feet like geese or cloven hoofs like goats. I know what you have to do so they won't do you any harm. Only I don't know whether their bears bite or not, but I'll find out soon because the shepherd will tell me.

"And I'll tell you what I am going to do this afternoon. But this, now, is something that grownups don't do because the shepherd himself doesn't dare to. I am going to explore the worst gallery all by myself, it is all black and long. It takes two hours to go through it and one castle connects with the other. That is the truth. Don't be surprised if you find out that now I am a bastard.

"Before I begin this adventure I write to you so that you will know where I am and that I am your unforgettable Pepe. P.S. Leave this letter on a table somewhere so that your father will see it."

Dinner was as ceremonious and complicated as supper had been and lasted terribly long. Unlike the previous evening, I said nothing. My father was surprised and asked the doctor whether my behavior did not follow the pattern of some neurosis, because I was bursting with things to say and without any apparent motive, I was dumb as a statue.

"He is not so dumb," said the doctor, "because what he's doing is hatching some devilment."

Taking advantage of my elders' remaining at table to talk, and sure that they would begin to explore the last gallery about five o'clock (not before, for digestion's sake, and also because it was already late in the afternoon), I set out for the other castle. Nothing worth relating happened on the way. I heard a fox bark, but they are harmless animals. Not a lamia nor a bear appeared.

The shepherd was lying motionless, as always, with his body in the sun and his head in the shade.

"Didn't anything happen to you yesterday?"

"You can see for yourself."

"I'm glad."

"Give me a little cold wine."

"Won't you get too fond of it, young man?"

"Me? Give me some." I drank a deep draft. "Against the lamias," I thought; and, remembering my doubts about the bears, I asked the shepherd whether bears would bite people who were immune to lamias.

"The bears only do what the lamias tell them to," the shepherd said.

Well, so much the better. Then I told him that I had kept him in mind and that if he wanted to earn fifteen pesetas he had only to get a whole skeleton and clean it and take it to the castle within two days, because after that the doctor would be gone. The shepherd shook his head:

"That's as much as I earn in three months. That and my bread and wine and oil. But I say no. Tell the doctor no."

"Why?"

"Because I say no. It's like the barber in my village who said to me one day, 'Bring me a mountain goat after he has shed. Bring me one, and I'll give you two pesetas.' 'What do you want one for?' I asked. 'To make me a good brush out of the hair that grows on his chin.' But a mountain goat has to have a beard on his chin, and so does a man. The only use for barbers is to put on leeches when someone is really dying."

"But this is different."

"Why?"

"Because it's for science."

"Ah—" He remained in meditation for a moment and then said: "No. The dead in their graves. May they sleep in peace. And the mountain goat in the woods."

"The dead would be glad to be able to help the living."

"They help already. They help quite enough. And tell anyone who doesn't believe it to come and ask me."

He began to say that the spring of medicinal water where people were cured of anemia passed through two old graveyards and received the water that filtered from another. "The dead wash themselves well, and those who don't want to die drink the water. And they get rosy and fat."

I dropped the subject, drank a little more wine, and asked if it was five o'clock yet. He looked at the shadow of a tree and said:

"It's already a handbreadth after five."

"Goodbye, then."

I dived into the dark shrubbery, went round the boulder, and entered the gallery. I turned on my flashlight. There were places in the wall which sparkled under the light. Perhaps fragments of quartz. At the start, under my first impulse, I went about a hundred yards without pausing. Then I noticed that the gallery was descending and I began to wonder whether the shepherd was right, whether it would lead me to hell, but it started running upward again and continued in a gentle slope. "Now it is heading for the castle," I said to myself. From time to time, feeling the wine in my veins, I cried impetuously into the shadows:

"Hah, I am a son of a whore too!"

I knew that the word "whore" was improper, but I did not really understand what it meant and it did not sound badly among men. Besides, I wanted at any price to be one of those six score who loved their father as little as I and defended him perhaps only to humiliate him. Because I began to see that, among other things, "to be a bastard" meant "to hate your father." I advanced with more courage and felt the beneficent influence of the wine in each beat of my pulse. I turned to look back and could no longer see the rocks at the entrance. Without realizing it, I had gone round a turn and the gallery stretched away in a gentle curve bordered by tombs and vaults. I went on, looking at nothing but the farther end of the space which my flashlight illuminated. It was all the same, and now I saw my tranquillity as a spectacle which gave me a superior idea of myself. Farther ahead I heard a noise of suppressed laughter and breathing: "It's the lamias." And I went resolutely forward, knowing that they could not harm me. There were no lamias; the sounds were produced by trickling water. The paving seemed to be covered with water. And I had to go through it, wetting my feet over my ankles. When I reached the other side where the footing was dry again I had the feeling that the flow might increase and that the water would prevent me from returning if any unforeseen encounter should make a retreat advisable. Thinking that I had gone far enough, I shouted so that my father, who surely was not far away, should hear me:

"Papa!"

The last echo sounded very far away. I thought that one of the echoes was my father's voice or the doctor's. I went on. Again I heard a distant sound of laughter. "Water," I thought, not too certain; but just as I came near enough to find out, my flashlight began to flicker. It was going out. I imagined that it would not last long enough for me to return and decided that the best thing was to go ahead as fast as possible, calling to Mosén Joaquín instead of to my father. I began to run, but stopped, because when I ran I felt afraid. I held myself to a fast walk.

"Mosén Joaquín!"

I had not considered that my flashlight batteries might fail, but the beam now penetrated only a yard ahead. Ten more steps and it would go out. I dropped it on the paving, producing a noise that reverberated in the profound blackness, and leaned against the wall. Keeping one hand on it, I resumed my advance. I felt that I still had courage, but it was an empty courage, beyond consciousness. I walked on, touching the wall. I knew that the galleries were not obstructed and that I should not encounter danger, but from time to time I heard my feet knock something aside with a light, dull sound.

"Bones."

I went on, but the wall ended. My hand groped in the air. "It makes a turn here," I thought, and felt the hair rise on my neck. I followed the curve of the wall and realized that I was entering another chamber. It was useless to hope to get my bearings myself. However, my will was strong, it acted beyond consciousness, as the will must do in madmen, and, as in them, with no concrete purpose. I stumbled over something and saw that it was a stone step. It was clean, very cold, and very damp. I sat down on it, put my head between my hands, shut my eyes, and cried:

"Valentina!"

A multitude of echoes returned upon me from the very vaults of the chamber in which I sat. I decided to remain there and wait. I closed my eyes and opened them again, but it was all the same. I felt neither my body, the stone step, nor my hands on my knees. Anything could happen, and I waited only for what really was to happen and to know whether it would be favorable or adverse. Fear? I was living in fear, I breathed fear, fear sustained me. In front of me the shadows, in which I could dimly distinguish outlines, began to move.

Above one shadow, higher than the head of an ordinary man, I could see a warrior's helmet, faintly illuminated. It was copper red, black, and white. I have never known whether I really spoke and was really answered, because the dialogue proceeded without words. I knew what the other felt, and he knew what I was feeling and said:

"Ah, what a struggle!"

"Why?"

"I am a bastard, too. Sancho Garcés was a criminal and sent me down here, and since then I have not been able to get out."

"Do you know the way?"

"Yes, but you must take my hand. If not, I will not go."

I stood up and gave him my hand. I could feel nothing, but the shadow said:

"Go first and lead me."

I obeyed, but came up against the wall.

"If I have to go first and don't know the way—how can I?"

"Go straight ahead now. I'll tell you the way."

As soon as I took his hand I began to hear the ring of iron everywhere, particularly one sustained sound as if someone were reshaping the point of his lance on an anvil with a hammer. So much noise prevented me from hearing the shadow, who was talking to himself, or to someone else:

"I didn't do it. O God, I didn't do it, and I have to pay for him.

The voice was barely audible. I dropped his hand and all was still. But I was in the gallery again and had reached the farther side of the chamber. Sure that the wall would not fail me now, I went on. "Where could that man have gone? And who was he?"

I heard footsteps behind me.

"Don't run away."

I gave a shriek. The words reminded me that I was surrounded by terrible things from which I must flee. "Don't run away."

It was the same shadow, the helmet still faintly luminous. The rest was invisible. I gave him my hand.

"Are you a hero?" I asked. "Or a saint, or a poet?"

"I am only a poor mortal. We are all poor mortals—here, and up above."

"I don't believe that is how a hero talks. But are you a saint?"

"Where are the saints? Golden crucifixes, golden chasubles, golden censers, golden mitres. Where are the saints?

"Forward. Go forward. I made saints. A few saints. I was not a hero or a saint. Perhaps a poet. But I made statues when I was too old to fight. I made the Virgin of Sancho Garcés. And people began to say that an angel had brought her image, and when everyone said that an angel had brought it I believed it too. But I had made it, and then the Virgin began to perform miracles, and people said: The Holy Virgin has given us victory. An angel brought it, and it cured my wounds. Everyone said that it came through the air in the hands of an angel, and I believed it too, but even though I believed it I was sent down here and one day I felt a blow between my shoulders. Probably they wanted to kill me, but they did not succeed. And here I am, and I cannot get out."

"Mightn't it be that they really killed you?"

He vanished again, but this time did not return. I called to him but he did not come. I decided to go on, but I stumbled again and this time fell. I did not have the heart to get up, but not through fear, because I was in the midst of fear, I lived on it, breathed it, it pulsed in my temples. Other shadows swayed before me. They wore something luminous too, but it was not a helmet. It was a cap and a feather.

I do not know whether I asked or was asked:

"Who are you?"

Now I could see that the speaker was not the shape with the feather, but another shorter figure before him. Little by little light fell on him from in front, and I was able to make out the black cowl of a monk dressed in white. His face I did not see. I never saw the faces of these apparitions. The monk was not as short as he had appeared at first, but bent. Old and bent. The monk spoke:

"Six hundred years have passed since I was sent down here because Sancho Garcés favored the Knights Templar. They put my head and my legs in the stocks, and after a while I heard footsteps behind me. I thought they had come to feed the hawks which were perched in a corner with their heads hooded in cloth, but I felt a blow from a mace on my head, and since then I have known nothing until now, when I see you before me. Who are you?"

I told him who I was.

"Are there templars still around?"

"No. Only Mosén Joaquín."

"I was fastened head and foot in the stocks without having been accused of anything."

"And they killed you, didn't they?"

The monk did not answer; his shadow slowly vanished. I sat on the ground, which was wet and cold, and I do not know how long I remained there.

Finally I went on and traversed a considerable distance without seeing or hearing anything. But I found myself in an obstructed gallery. I would have to climb a series of ledges and let myself drop on the other side, but I was afraid to drop in the darkness. I sat down and stared fixedly into the shadows. Fixedly, without winking, as I had done before. The first thing I heard was someone panting with effort.

"To the postern," he said. "Everyone to the postern!"

I saw a helmet with the visor down become luminous.

"Who are you?"

Suddenly there was silence. Then I heard a distant voice, which, however, came from beside me.

"Is there anyone here?" I asked.

"Yes, I."

"What are you doing here?"

"I am imprisoned. I am imprisoned and asleep. They could only have taken me asleep, my brother and my mother. I had spent twenty years fighting Sancho Garcés' men from the castle of Ejea. Wherever I fell on them, nothing remained but the memory of terror. But always in honorable Christian fashion. And to make peace with the lord of this castle, they decided to give me up. They waited until the sleeping potion had put me to sleep, and then they left me to Sancho Garcés' men, and they brought me here asleep."

He removed his helmet, and I saw his shoulder and his headless neck appear beneath it.

"Did they cut off your head while you were asleep?"

The shadow vanished.

"Good!" I said to myself. "They killed the saint, they killed the poet, they killed the hero. I am a bastard, a hero, and a poet. Will they kill me? Even if they kill me, I am not afraid."

I climbed the mound and went carefully down the opposite side. When I felt the pavement under my feet I let myself drop. And I went on through the gallery again in the darkness.

I no longer expected anyone. Neither my father nor Mosén Joaquín. I was ready to remain there forever. Again I heard the sound of laughter, but I identified it as running water without investigating it. All I remembered was that it was Sunday. That fact had some relation to Mosén Joaquín's presence in the castle, but I could not remember exactly who Mosén Joaquín was.

Another shadow took shape before me. It was a very fat monk, who laughed and repeated:

"He, he, he, he! Good goat cheese. Good blood of our Lord in a Moorish jar."

"Go away!" I cried.

"He, he, he! Wine in the Mass is the blood of our Lord. That is a poor honor for such rich wine. He, he, he, he!"

The fat monk lifted his frock and danced with his bare shanks.

"Let me pass, imbecile!"

"Who are you, lad? He, he, he!"

"And you?"

"I? The brother cellarer, the only person in the castle who died because God willed it—died a natural death, I mean, from indigestion. And you, lad? Who are you?"

"A hero. A bastard hero."

"Hero, saint, or poet . . . he, he, he! There are many here, and their heads fell one after the other, before they were ripe. I am the only one who died when his hour came." I pushed forward, but I passed easily through his shadow. I heard him laughing and dancing behind me. He did not molest me. From a long way off I could still hear him:

"He, he, he . . ."

He seemed to be laughing at me, but I felt so strong that nothing could make any impression on me. Something like a snake hung against the wall, but it was so long that it could not be a snake. I leaned over to touch it and realized that it was a rope. As I touched it, I felt a strange certainty:

"A gallows rope. If I cut it, the pieces will turn into snakes."

Far away at the end of the gallery I saw light. "What shadows will come now? More warriors, more saints, more poets? Perhaps executioners, coming for me." I approached and, when I least expected it, I heard familiar voices. Familiar voices together. My father, the doctor, Mosén Joaquín. And others. Perhaps others. I looked around, trying to find a way to escape. This was really horrible. The gallery was not intersected by any other.

I gave a scream.

Among the group of explorers was Don Arturo, who had come to spend Sunday at the castle, and Valentina. They had been traveling through the gallery for over half an hour, keeping up their spirits with talk on indifferent subjects. But when they heard my scream, they stopped dead. Don Arturo could not control himself, and ran. The doctor tried to master himself, shouting:

"That was a human voice!"

They made no move to advance. Valentina shrieked:

"Oh, God, it's what I thought. That is Pepe!"

She reached gropingly into the shadows and found an extinguished lantern. There was another that was still alight, but the corporal would not let it out of his hands.

Mosén Joaquín came up with a burning cigar lighter. Valentina lit the lantern. Mosén Joaquín tried to trap her, saying:

"Come here."

But she would not:

"That is Pepe! Oh, God, it's just what I thought."

She escaped him and came running toward me. Mosén Joaquín limped along behind Valentina.

I came to myself, but it took me a little time to get things clear. Valentina told me how they had left home, how she had arrived, how my father had thought of inviting her to come down into the vaults.

"Are they here?" I said. "All of them?"

"Yes, but let's go somewhere else."

I walked away, leading Valentina by the hand. She still had the lantern. Seeing the sureness with which I retraced my road, she was much pleased.

We heard voices behind us. The party was advancing, calling our names. We began to run. We soon came to the place where the trickling water covered the width of the gallery. Valentina said that she could cross, but I made her put her arms round my neck—with the lantern over my shoulder—and picked her up under the knees, holding her tightly against me. Her skin felt warm, or perhaps my hand was unusually cold.

And we reached the end of our journey without further accidents.

I had looked in vain for the shadows I had seen before. I began telling Valentina what had happened to me, but I could not remember it exactly, and all that I knew was that heroes, saints, and poets were all treacherously slain in the castle.

‡ 10 ‡

We emerged and found the shepherd beside a great cauldron of boiling water. He was keeping up a wood fire under it, and from time to time he took up his crook and slowly—respectfully, you might say—stirred round the body of an old woman. I prevented Valentina from seeing it. The shepherd looked at us uncomprehendingly but without too much surprise:

"Are you sure he will give me the fifteen pesetas?"

I said yes, and without warning him that others would be coming out of the gallery or answering his questions about Valentina (he kept looking at her feet) we went slowly off in the direction of the castle. The excursionists reached the entrance to the gallery and the corporal enlarged the opening with his pick until it was high enough for them to pass through without going down on their hands and knees. The shepherd, hearing someone digging his way out of the gallery, went round to the other side of the castle. And when they all emerged and discovered the abandoned cauldron in which a half-disintegrated human body was boiling, they retreated with very different feelings. Mosén Joaquín took out his prayer book, the doctor put on his spectacles with shaking hands. My father looked cautiously round, and after a long silence during which each felt that he was the victim of a bad dream, the notary stammered:

"We must draw up a deposition."

But first they must commend the poor human victim to God and put out the fire. The corporal pulled the burning logs apart and trampled them or threw earth on them.

But, seeing the fire being pulled apart, the shepherd came running:

"Hey, what are you doing?"

They all looked at him in silence. The shepherd pointed to the cauldron and said:

"She doesn't want to let go of her skin, damn her."

Night was falling, and Valentina and I walked on toward the castle with the lighted lantern. I was carrying it now, and the flame attracted dragonflies, moths, and other insects; they fluttered round it in crazy circles. I held the lantern away from my body, so that they could pass round it without hitting me, but a few moths lighted on my hand and my bare forearm, and I said that they tickled. Valentina wanted to feel them too, so I had to lend her the lantern. We did not put it out because it would soon be dark and we would need it then, and besides, we had no matches to light it with.

Far off behind the castle of Sancho Garcés the sun was setting in a splendor of greens and golds. Such a variety of light intoxicated me after the darkness of the vaults. We talked. It seemed as though we had always been walking toward a castle like this, talking and carrying a lighted lantern.

"Did you have to fight with the dead?" she asked.

"Yes. And they had me surrounded once, in the ring, in the ring of cinnamon-bread."

We were walking hand in hand. Valentina gave little cries of alarm when a moth clung too tightly to her bare arm, and ended by giving me back the lantern.

"Bugs frighten me," she explained, "all except crickets."

We were in so little of a hurry to reach the castle and be back among grownups that we sat down at the foot of a tree, setting the lantern beside us. Yes, Valentina was all made of amber now. And she, in turn, told me that I "seemed to have a light inside me." The lantern stood beside us, still alight. And Valentina cried, and I wanted to be brave, but I felt my throat tighten too and my eyes filled with tears. Shortly after, we fell asleep.

Someone shook us violently. My father, Don Arturo, Mosén Joaquín, the doctor—they were all there. The light of our lantern had guided them. And Mosén Joaquín kept saying:

"You'll catch cold, children."

"No, no, no!" cried Valentina, who was still asleep.

"Eh?" said the doctor.

I was not awake yet, either.

At last they woke us. The doctor treated us affably, but all the others seemed cross. I do not clearly remember what happened then, but I know that we arrived at the castle like criminals. My mother walked up and down, saying to the doctor's wife:

"He's not my son. He's a changeling."

Everyone was in consternation except Maruja, who finally went over to Valentina:

"I have only one thing to say: if you marry Pepe, I'll be sorry for you."

Valentina did not know what to answer, and blushed. Later she went away without my being able to say goodbye to her. I have not yet forgiven Don Arturo and my father for that.

I thought of the vaults, and felt I wanted to go back, but . . . why? If Valentina could not come to save me again, dead men and monks and lamias lost their interest for me. And Valentina—this idea obsessed me—was going to San Sebastián three days later, with her parents and her sister—her hateful sister.

My father ignored me. He was convinced that there was something wrong with me, despite all the doctor's assurances. The vaults remained closed, and my father said that he would notify the Provincial Museum so that they could take charge of the contents.

Sometimes my father looked at me as if I were a monster and said: "I cannot understand what is happening to you."

One day before we returned home, my father called me to him and asked me to tell him what had happened in the vaults, and how I had entered them and why I had gone alone and without any light. This time I explained everything, including the monk, the warrior, and the poet who was also a sculptor. Naturally, my father stared at me more perplexed than ever. But if he could accept nothing of what I had said, he had to accept the cauldron with the human body boiling in it. Starting from there, the rest became credible.

We returned to town, but Valentina was away.

Little by little I became aware again of the realities that surrounded me. I realized at once that I had lost my leadership over the boys of the allied gang, and that my own gang was being terrorized by Carrasco. Carrasco appeared on the wall and, biting his finger, grunted disrespectfully:

"I have your grave dug."

I wondered once if it might be true. My destiny as a hero and a poet was to die, but it was not any Carrasco who would kill me, but executioners with arms of steel in the dark cellars of the castle, while fat brother cellarers danced.

After her vacation in San Sebastián, Valentina had gone to Bilbao to stay with her aunts for a couple of months. Her aunts were to come to our town for Christmas, and would bring Valentina back with them. I saw a maneuver against me in this arrangement. I tried in various ways to find out Valentina's address, and one day when I saw her mother in my house—on a formal visit, in the drawing room—I went to her and asked her. She gave it to me and stroked my hair. Ah, she understood us! She was the only person who understood us.

I sent Valentina forty pages of the "Universiad" and a letter in which I praised her mother's good qualities and thoroughly vilified her father. To mail it, I had to steal almost all the stamps in the library.

I remember that the following day some other boys and I performed an experiment that we repeated from time to time. We caught a live bat and undertook to burn its nose, expecting to hear it utter oaths and dirty words. Although the poor beast only shrieked and whimpered, we all believed that we had heard them. When I told someone about it he remembered similar experiments in which he had heard the bat cry out filth and blasphemies. Neither he nor I was lying. We were certain that we had heard them.

That same day when I left the house I found Carrasco waiting for me on the corner. He snarled more than ever, but I passed without looking at him and he did not dare to attack me. However, he muttered:

"You're brave with the castle ghosts, but not with me!"

The day was one of the coldest we had had that autumn. When night fell the wind that arose announced the first snowfall in the mountains. And I walked home disgusted and dissatisfied.

‡ 11 ‡

Then an incident occurred. The following day Clara came for her pension, but she did not come alone. With her arrived, timidly, a widow fifty years of age. When Clara's voice was heard downstairs we children came to watch until my mother sent us away. This time Clara's voice was loud, but it was not raised against us but against her neighbor:

"North wind! North cold! North Christ!" she was screaming.

Her neighbor asserted that she did not want to cause any trouble and that the whole commotion had arisen quite against her will. She would not even have come.

My mother asked them in, which seemed to please Clara greatly. The widow knotted her kerchief under her chin. My mother asked her:

"Aren't you Señora Rita?"

"Widow of Agustín the younger, at your service."

"Widow, widow! Six months you were married," Clara grumbled. "That's a marriage for you! Six months!"

"And three years acquainted before it," the widow added, knotting her kerchief again.

They had brought a serious case which they wanted my father to judge, but my father was not at home. In his absence they confided in my mother. The widow had been married at twenty; she was now fifty. Six months after the wedding her husband had died of pneumonia. The widow shut herself up in her house and made her living by sewing. She did not go out, she gave no occasion for scandal. Her balcony door was always closed. She lived next door to Clara in a house whose roof was somewhat higher than hers. And for almost thirty years, whenever she believed a north wind was blowing, the widow would take her husband's clothes out of the closet and hang them on the terrace on her roof to air. Each time she filled her terrace with the clothes of her deceased husband they cast a shadow on the terrace of her neighbor which the latter maintained was prejudicial to her own freshly washed underclothes. Clara said that her clothes must dry in the sun to bleach. At first she had complained only of being deprived of sunlight. Now she insisted that this shadow of the deceased brought bad luck into her life of single blessedness. The outer habiliments of the deceased and Clara's underclothes had produced a conflict which, in the course of years, came to a head: Clara had climbed on to her neighbor's terrace, had thrown the clothes of the deceased into the court, and had scratched his widow. Clara complained very bitterly that the widow said that there was a "north wind" every three or four days and cast an "evil shadow" on her petticoats. The argument grew heated. My mother tried to pacify them, but she could not. And since my father was not at home—he knew the law and would have settled the matter—the conflict waxed. "North wind, north wind," Clara insisted. "Six months you were married, and all that north wind!" It looked as though my mother would be overwhelmed by the storm, when Aunt Ignacia arrived.

"Well, well," she said. "I never saw the equal of this. So much noise over a pair of empty trousers!"

"I haven't said anything," the widow excused herself.

"Eh?" said Clara doubtfully, feeling that she was no match for Aunt Ignacia.

"Run along with you now! And you," she said to the widow, who was sobbing, "don't spend your life sniffing the air to see if the wind is from the north or not. There's no husband in your husband's clothes—may he rest in peace!"

When Clara reached the door, to which Aunt Ignacia had pushed them, she seemed to want to begin again, but Aunt Ignacia would not let her:

"Be off with you, and don't come here with your stories, because I can say 'God' and 'Christ' too."

My mother disappeared into the hall, laughing.

This incident gave me something new to think about. The widow, enslaved all her life to one memory, and Aunt Ignacia's allusion to "empty trousers," gave me the idea that there was a tremendous mystery in a man. I was the lord of love, but the mystery was something else, and I did not connect it with Valentina. It was something else of which I was ignorant. I went to my mother. For the first time she saw me almost docile.

"Mamma," I said, when I had made sure that we were alone, "tell me the truth."

"What do you want, my son?"

My mother was delighted to see me so much the little boy that it pleased her to imagine me.

"Am I," I asked, "what they call a 'handsome man'?"

"In the first place, you are not a man but a boy."

"But will I be a handsome man?"

"I don't think so. No one could say that you are a handsome boy, either. No, you will not be handsome. But you will be one of those men who please all women."

She said it with such certainty and pressed my hands so sweetly—the latter was the more persuasive—that I felt convinced.

I started to my room. I had just given way to a tremendous weakness, but no one had witnessed it. And perhaps my mother would not tell anyone. Just in case, I returned to her side and begged her to keep our conversation secret. She wanted to embrace me, but I struggled away, saying:

"Enough!"

I went to the street. When I returned it was almost dark. At the corner, the gas flame of an early street lamp was flickering in the icy wind. And there under the street lamp was an old beggar with his stockingless feet in an enormous pair of boots. The old man had a scanty white beard. He leaned against the wall, weeping silently. I went over to him, impressed:

"What is the matter, good man?"

Then I saw that he was blind and was holding a piece of cord in his hand. His dog had been stolen, someone had cut the cord, and now he was perfectly helpless. He had just finished telling me, when I heard Carrasco snarling on the other side of the street. I had an inspiration which told me that he had done it, and I was right. But for the moment I preferred to pretend not to know.

"Where did you want to go?"

"To shelter in a cave I know beyond town, on the other side."

"Lean on my shoulder and come along. Don't worry. I'll lead you."

The beggar, still crying, put his hand on my shoulder. We set off, walking slowly. Carrasco jumped up and down on the opposite sidewalk like a demon, insulting me. I didn't want to listen to him.

People who saw us pass crossed themselves, unable to believe their eyes. I walked firmly and gravely along, listening to the poor old man's litany of thanks. He had stopped crying; now he sighed and said: "I wish —God willing—I could get Pinto back!" He was a dog who, the old man told me, knew the houses where alms were given, and the caves which afforded shelter from the wind.

In this manner we traversed the center of town and entered the outskirts. The old man walked very slowly, and it took us a long time. Once at our destination, I had to go back to one of the first houses to ask for matches to light a fire, because the poor old man was stiff with cold. When I related what had happened some peasant woman gave me raw potatoes and ends of bread, and one of them called me back after I had started away to give me a paper of salt.

I stayed in the cave for some time, showing the beggar where to step without burning his feet, where he could find the potatoes, which were roasting in the hot ashes, and so on . . . and once again the whole town was mobilized to search for me. It was very late before I had finished, and when I returned about midnight, crossing the Plaza of the Three Crosses —there, on the top step of the stone platform beside one of them (for there really were three) stood Carrasco. He had followed us all the way.

"I've buried the beggar's dog in your grave, and I'll bury you there too."

This was too much. I rushed at him. Luckily, only that morning I had roughened the soles of my boots with the kitchen grater, a necessary precaution against slipping on stones in case of a fight, and the moon shone down on the most ferocious combat between boys of which any record remains. We rolled over three times, four times, clinched, Carrasco digging the fingernails of one hand into my cheek and I holding his head back by the hair and hitting him on the nose, on the mouth. When he saw that he was lost, being unable to roll me over again, he used his free hand to tear my clothes. This was the last resource of cowards—to make sure, when they could not hurt us themselves, that we would be chastised later at home. But I was bleeding too, from my cheek and my neck.

People came running, and separated us. Two peasants took me by the hands and led me along. They were visibly delighted to have been the ones who had captured me.

My father received me, pacing up and down the court like a wild beast.

"This is the end," he repeated again and again.

When we arrived, he began to listen to the twenty-seven versions of each of my attendants. I must have presented a lamentable appearance, though none of my injuries were at all serious. My appearance, however, was nothing in comparison with Carrasco's, who limped, had one ear torn, and had to walk with his hands in the air to stop his nose bleeding.

When everyone had become calm, my father repeated:

"This is the end."

I finally understood. He had decided to send me to boarding school. My mother said that I would have to have more underclothes made, but my father insisted:

"Tomorrow morning!"

I told about the beggar, but said nothing of Carrasco. It was the matter of the beggar, however, which had made them angry. I went to wash and caught a glimpse of my face, which was really impressive. Mosén Joaquín, my teacher, had arrived; by the time the rumors had reached him they were sufficiently alarming. When he saw that the matter was unimportant and that the story as I told it was simple and edifying, he took my side and began to defend me. My father seemed to be listening, but when my champion ended, he said:

"He goes to boarding school tomorrow."

I did not leave on the following day. Various preparations had to be made for the journey, and in the afternoon I went to call on Mosén Joaquín. I asked him why heroes were killed.

"I'll answer you if you will tell me how the idea occurred to you."

I explained as well as I could what had happened to me in the castle, and Mosén Joaquín said:

"These things are too deep for you to understand. But you once asked me what the word 'immolation' meant. That is it. There is the answer. You are impressed by that parchment we read. The end not only of heroes but of poets and of saints is thus, almost always."

I asked for further explanations. So far, I had not understood a word.

"I will not tell you any more, my son. Remember that word 'immolation.' One day when you are older you will understand it yourself."

This only increased the mystery: "immolation." The word reminded me of nothing except Valentina receiving the blood of a wounded pigeon.

The preparations for my journey continued. We were not going to the Jesuits at Zaragoza, but farther away, to Reus, where my father said there was a "much more efficient" school. My father was unsympathetic to the Jesuits. He said that in spite of their reputation he had never met a really intelligent one in his life. The monks of the Holy Family offered them keen competition. Their professors, better prepared—he mentioned several well-known scholars—their more comfortable buildings, their more brilliant social position, in which, unlike the Jesuits, they aroused no jealousies. When everything was ready, I asked if they had heard any news of the beggar. No one knew anything about him. I said that I would not go to school until I knew that the beggar was being cared for, and two days later they told me that they had put him in an asylum.

It was cold. My father, having received a telegram from the director of the school, Father Llovet, whom he knew, said that we would set off at once. The farther we went, the milder my father became. When we reached the station he bought two second-class tickets.

The journey increased my father's mildness, although he was on the point of relapsing at several of my questions. Thinking of the last letter I had sent to Valentina, I asked him:

"Do saints marry?"

As there were other people in the compartment, my father mastered his nerves and answered me. Saints never married.

"Then is it a sin to marry?"

My father turned the knob of the radiator as far as it would go and asked the ladies' permission to open the windows. Then he answered me in more detail, saying that, as a saint, as a being in a state of beatitude, no one married, but that certain married people had been saints. "And now," he added, "all married people are martyrs." The sentence was received with smiles which opened the way to conversation. In the midst of which I was forgotten: so I spent my time looking out the window until we reached Reus.

We went to an hotel on a small square that had been lately watered; the asphalt reflected street lamps, cyclists, and varnished carriages, which passed silently on their rubber tires with no sound but the measured clopping of hoofs. In the center of the square, which was surrounded by stone buildings, there was an enormous equestrian statue of General Prim. I was enchanted with the square and the hotel, and would gladly have stayed there, but my father made a telephone call and announced with satisfaction:

"They are expecting you."

We took a carriage, and a little while later I was surrounded by monks in the reception room of the College of Saint Peter Apostle, an enormous building on the Avenida de la Estación, three sides of which gave on as many walks lined with carobs and strawberry trees. The fourth gave on a narrow street, on the opposite side of which was an electric power station with two tall chimneys. I observed all this while I was getting out of the carriage.

The monks showered me with attentions. My father conferred with the Father Prior privately, and told me that he himself would see to buying the regulation table service for me and having it engraved. They told him the number to have marked on it. My father, much pleased to know that he was going to be rid of me, made the acquaintance of all the monks . . . Behind me I heard, "Professor of Higher Algebra," "Professor of Latin Grammar," "Professor of Language and Literature." Then long compliments were exchanged. The Father Prior, seeing me looking toward a court from which shouts and cries were proceeding, said:

"Look out there, if you like. There are bicycles and skates and a football."

When, after my father had left, I went into the court, three boys about two years younger than I looked at me in great admiration and said:

"He didn't cry!"

I was well received, though I noticed that the boys came up to me and wanted to stay with me out of curiosity. There were Romanesque arches everywhere, like those in the castle, only they were made not of stone but of concrete, and where they ended the red brick wall began, to be pierced above by another arcade. The whole building, therefore, was red and grey. I was keenly observed, but I observed my surroundings no less keenly.

Supper was good, but we had to pray first and say grace afterward. In the immense dining room there was a little pulpit of carved wood, from which one of the pupils read aloud while we ate. "I like it," said my neighbor, "when it's my turn to read, because then I eat by myself afterward and they give me jam and preserves and anything I want."

The monastery was immense. The stairways were like those in the castle. The echo of footfalls was lost in the enormous arcades. My father was out of sight, and I was free and alone in wide, sonorous spaces. When I went to my room—we all went together in two files—we said our prayers standing in line in the gallery, and then each retired to his cell. Mine had a very large window on the side of the building that faced the center of the city. The blinds were closed, and when I opened them, because there was no light in the room except what came in from the hall, I retreated in amazement. In the darkness the city seemed to be raising hundreds of arms of light into the sky. Gilded reflectors fantastically illuminated the weather vanes and crosses of the highest buildings, and all the spires of the city's towers and domes were strung with thousands of yellow electric lights, which climbed up the sky to culminate in crosses on which there were letters reading: IN HOC SIGNO VINCES.

I went to the lavatory. Boys were running down the corridor hitting each other and trying to escape the vigilance of a solitary monk who was standing guard where three corridors met.

I asked why the city was illuminated.

"Haven't you heard?"

Others came to tell me. They were very nice to me that first day. The entire city was decked out to celebrate the sixteenth centenary of Constantine the Great.

I returned to my cell and lay down, leaving the blinds open.

I remembered my adventures in the castle. I was a hero, and heroes were killed. I was a poet, and poets were killed. Saints too were sacrificed. Perhaps Constantine the Great had been killed in a dark vault.

Would I be killed? I stroked the sheet, whose surface was cool and smooth, and I said, feeling a great firmness in my heart: "If I am killed, what of it? Now I understand immolation. I shall write and tell Mosén Joaquín." But it was a lie. I understood nothing.

That came much later.

‡ ‡ ‡

II

Violent Griffin

translated from the Spanish

by FLORENCE HALL SENDER

‡ 1 ‡

THE TOWERS of the city were still illuminated at night. Strings of electric lights outlined the towers, windows and eaves. From the darkness of my cell the city was a phantasmagoria. The sign IN HOC SIGNO VINCES and the labarum of Constantine seemed to float in the sky. That day I had learned the name of an emperor: Constantine the Great, and a rather ugly adjective that everyone was repeating: *constantinean*.

My silverware—knife, fork, spoon and napkin ring—engraved with the initials "J. G." and the number "101," arrived the next day. The boys who ate at my table said that mine was a lucky number and would bring me success in my examinations. They talked and laughed—it was Thursday, when talking was permitted in the dining hall—as if they were drunk. They were all gay and excited over the *constantinean* centennial festivities.

The first day was filled with novel experiences—faces, names, Catalonian accents, looks of indifferent curiosity—in which I was somewhat lost because of trying to see everything all at once.

I received two letters. One from my sister Concha and another—and very long one—from Valentina. Valentina always used the same phrase to express her sweetheart's devotion: *"Mi cielo"*—"My heaven." She called me her *"cielo."* And apropos of our separation, her mother had taught her a very wise proverb in verse, which she copied:

> *Absence is a wind*
> *snuffing little fires*
> *and fanning big ones.*

I felt happy thinking about Doña Julia, Valentina's mother, concerning herself with our troubles in this way. I answered Valentina that very day, although letter-writing was only permitted on Sundays. Since I had just arrived at the school they granted me this privilege, supposing that I had urgent things to tell my family about getting settled.

My father had left Reus the day before and I was still immersed in all that magic which was mine, and which seemed to have been motivated by my arrival in the city. Since coming to Reus I had been realizing that life had spaces and planes heretofore unsuspected by me. In the immense building where everything was so well organized and so clean, through whose windows great castles of light were visible by night, something extraordinary and new had to be waiting for me, beyond any doubt.

In my village I had somewhat skeptically accepted Catholicism as an appropriate religion for old ladies and aging devils, but in Reus it began to take on a certain real grandeur. Most impressive, however, was that nocturnal squandering of light, and the allusion to a Roman emperor and noble things that had happened fifteen centuries ago when, as a friar told me, the cross, the sword and the law were one. Although I did not believe this too fervently, I was dazzled by the festival lights.

The friars I had met at first impressed me as cold and verbose. Beside Mosén Joaquín, the chaplain of the Santa Clara convent, and my old teacher, the monks of Reus looked like well-combed functionaries demanding admiration in the name of what I did not know. Generous Father Miró, natural and somewhat simple. Solid Brother Pedro, gruff and veracious as an old peasant. From the very first, Brother Pedro struck me as the best.

At school the students wore blue and white blouses with belts and large, square sailor collars. This looked like a rather absurd bourgeois refinement to me. The black-robed friars, with cassocks and girdles like those the Jesuits wear, seemed solemn men. Despite the apparently free movements of the students, discipline was ever-present. The first days were rainy and dark. The nights with their festival lights appeared brighter.

"Are you Castilian?" a boy asked.

They called everybody Castilian who was not Catalonian. Then turning to his friends, the boy added:

"This fellow talks the way they do in the theatre, because he's Castilian."

We were in a patio surrounded by stone cloisters. It was misting. The asphalt pavement turned black and glistening in the rain. The boys told me that I would have to kowtow to the little cock-of-the-walk in the first and second terms. They pointed out the hero who was leaning against a pillar and staring at me from afar without blinking. He was older than I. He was in the third term, and although very thin he was obviously strong and athletic. His name was Prat and his father was the mayor of Gerona. He affected a grave and virile voice which occasionally cracked in his throat, sounding sharp and high-pitched.

I took shelter from the rain under the porticos with several companions. The others continued skating on the wet asphalt which reflected the cloister columns like a mirror. Of my first three friends two were brothers whose family lived in Amposta. Their names were Pere and Pau (Peter and Paul), which everybody always found amusing. They were blond and inseparable. The third—Roig—came from Castelbell. Roig went over to Prat to tell him all about me. Prat listened with an impatient and annoyed expression. "Why?" I wondered and said to myself: "This looks bad. We will have to fight." We would have to fight, unquestionably. Prat had the advantage, as far as size was concerned. I pretended otherwise, however, busily weighing the pros and cons.

In one of the rather wide lateral cloisters, the boys were still playing soccer as if possessed, screaming, kicking and jumping. Behind one of the goals, indicated by the space between the last cloister column and the stone wall, was a row of fifteen or twenty latrines. The doors were not always closed, and when the ball struck one that was ajar it slammed shut with a terrific clatter. Pere, Pau and I were talking some distance away, beside a pillar. The evening was still gray. There was a rare kind of intimacy in the air as if the low, cloudy sky were the ceiling of a room where a sick girl might be convalescing. Prat lost no time in joining us.

"Where are you from?" he asked.

"Aragón. And you?"

"That's none of your business."

This was a bad beginning indeed. Prat turned to Pere and Pau:

"Did he do anything to you?" he asked.

"No, I should say not. We're friends and feel like we've known each other always. His name is Pepe and he has a sweetheart in his home town. A real sweetheart who writes him letters."

Prat eyed me impertinently:

"I have two. Only one is really my cousin. But if you're looking for a fight," he said solemnly, "you've got something in store for you that's going to be really good."

I realized that if I took this insolence the first day, I was lost. In this patio, risky as well as propitious things did not mean the same as in the village, but were like events at the court of a king that could be related in refined ballades.

The situation was becoming serious. Prat looked at me without saying a word and spat on his forefinger. According to Pere, wetting the adversary's ear was the sign of servitude. And Prat touched my ear. At that very instant, and just as I was gathering my strength to respond properly, the soccer ball flew through the air like a projectile, struck Prat full in the cheek, knocked his head against the post, and the hero from Gerona fell unconscious at my feet. Pere and Pau ran to the infirmary for Father Salvá, and I did not know what to do, feeling both innocent and guilty. On the ground, under the dark clouds, Prat looked really lamentable. His legs stuck out into the patio where the rain fell on them furiously. The students crowded around. The boy who had kicked the ball so opportunely was Planibell, who had a face like the archangel St. Michael and could doubtless perform miracles. Prat regained consciousness, picked himself up, and prudently I walked away. From a distance I heard him ask:

"What did the Castilian do to me?"

He rubbed his cheek thinking that he had been given a terrific slap. And he had, not by me, but by chance. Nonchalantly I took a bicycle out of the storeroom to practice riding. Two or three boys helped me out as a gesture of courtesy toward the newcomer, or because they thought I could be a rival of Prat's. His eyes followed me:

"What did the Castilian do to me?" he repeated.

‡2‡

In class the boys sat according to their student rank, and in Latin there were two rival bands reviving the ancient passions of the Punic Wars: Carthaginians and Romans. The first day I was given the fourth place in the Roman section.

All the boys had nicknames and they called me *"el Castellá"*—"the Castilian." My neighbor was called *"Caresse"*—"Missing"—because in

French class, where he heard the friar occasionally ask for nonexistent tenses of irregular verbs, and the students answer *"carece,"* he found it very convenient to answer every question with that handy little phrase, dragging out the "s" sound of the "c" in the Catalonian way.

The classes were somber and sad. Dull as they were they did not actually become torture, although my lack of interest coupled with the too-present authority of the teacher aroused in me a trying impatience.

Spanish was the language of the classroom and mine was somewhat better than that spoken by the others, which gave me small privileges.

A red-haired boy was called "Bubu" because in French class he pronounced *"vous"* as "bu," and the indignant monk had exclaimed:

"What is that 'bu, bu' business, anyway?"

Then the pupil, opening wide his eyes, replied:

"Fus afez . . ."

When Prat and I realized that we had no choice but to kill each other or form an alliance, we became good friends. Sometimes I felt inferior to Prat, who was older and made a distinguished and naturally arrogant impression. He was a city boy. I came from the village. The difference was enormous, but I carefully concealed my feeling of inferiority.

Some days I assisted at Mass in the chapel, and did so mechanically, distracting myself with many little devices such as counting the human bones embroidered on the altar cloth, and the skulls, hearts, flames or tears of gold on the chasuble.

Two weeks after I entered the school the friars started preparing a festival program. The main feature would be the performance of Calderón's *Life Is a Dream.* The school had a theatre that would seat almost a thousand persons, with an independent street entrance and broad stoop used only on special occasions.

The feminine roles of *Life Is a Dream* were omitted. This was no great loss, since the women had nothing to do with the philosophical scheme of the play. After comparing my Castilian pronunciation with that of the Catalonian students, the friars gave me the protagonist's role: Prince Segismundo. This was a distinction that made me half-dizzy for days.

It took me a month to memorize the part. From the rehearsals of single scenes I had no idea of the complete play, which I had not read. The friars did not think it indispensable for us to know the entire work in order to do it well. I only knew that I had to appear melancholy and dreamy in the cave, irate in the palace, vacillating again in the cave, violent in battle, and compassionate at the end, after the victory. Today I do not understand how I could have found it so exciting, ignorant as I was of what was going on in the drama and of the motivations for my long verse tirades.

During the first complete rehearsal, however, I learned what it was all about. The geometry teacher, when I began to declaim, "Alas! Ah, wretched me! Ah, wretched me!" made a sound of clanking chains, and from that moment forward the adventurous and romantic background of the play began to appeal to me. I was more than pleased with my rôle.

Afterward I remarked to Father Ferrer:

"Do you know why Segismundo wins the battle? Because he believes that everything happening to him is a dream, and he has no fear of being killed."

No one could get this idea out of my head: "Everything turns out all right for him because he believes that he is dreaming and doesn't take what he's doing seriously, and isn't afraid of anybody or anything." On the other hand when, for a moment, the prince did take his real position as heir to the throne seriously, he tried to kill Clotaldo, threw a nobleman out the window, insulted his father, and became involved in useless scrapes. Things went badly and again he found himself in prison chains. I saw an important mystery in all this, but Father Ferrer only half-listened to me and exclaimed:

"Bah, stuff and nonsense. Just do as I say."

Factory strikes provoked occasional street disorders in the city. Since Reus was an industrial town, such events often had bloody consequences. The school was an enormous building, completely isolated and surrounded by gardens. Across a not very broad avenue at the back was an electric power plant with two very tall chimneys of red brick.

Even though the friars were fearful during times of violent strikes, I never took such dangers seriously. The people in the street, the common people, to me seemed incapable of harm. At night, from my cell window I saw the smokestacks against the background of the centennial illumination and thought—I don't know why—of the friendliness of the men who worked there. If they besieged the convent some day and set fire to it, they would rescue me just as the conspirators rescued Segismundo. They would perhaps behead the Clotaldos in cassocks, chasing them through the cloisters, and this would be sad but inevitable, as on the stage. I had heard that the monks used to connect the iron fences of the park and the lower window gratings with high-tension cables, in time of danger and disorder. If this was true, I ought to find out where the switches were and at the critical moment cut off the current, at the risk of my own life. The workers would then come in without danger and behead all the monks except Brother Pedro and the Father Superior. Brother Pedro was my friend. The Father Superior was a placid, fat priest for whom I felt respect.

As for the first- and second-term students, if this came to pass, I would take a hand to see that they were spared, and even the terrible third-termer, Prat. And then the explanations would begin. How had they been able to besiege the convent if the fences and gratings were connected to high-tension cables? And I would declaim, like Segismundo, except for changing the word "vassals" to "workmen":

> For the loyalty you exhibit,
> thanks, my workmen. See in me
> one who will this land deliver
> from a stranger's alien yoke.
> Sound to arms: you soon shall witness
> what my valor can effect.

I had asked the geometry teacher several questions about the meaning of various episodes in the life of Prince Segismundo and the friar, without paying the slightest attention to my ideas, replied:

"Wait until the last scene and you will see. All this is only a symbol."

The friar was very busy fixing up wigs on the spindle-like posts of chairbacks. And I was thinking about the workers again. What they needed was a good chief, like the conspirators in *Life Is a Dream*. Maybe I was too young to be their leader, but my youth could be an advantage. I was just as young on the stage, and still the enemies of the Polish king acclaimed me. The friar said:

"In the first act you will wear an ugly old wig. In the second the first servant wears that wig and you will wear this one."

He held up a very beautiful wig that fell in golden ringlets to the shoulders. Prat came up with a shaggy rag in his hands.

"This scabby old wig can't be for me," he remarked.

Brother Pedro looked at the lining and saw written in purple ink: *First Servant.*

"Yes, my son," he told him. "This wig is yours. It says so here. And in Father Ferrer's handwriting."

Prat argued:

"I am a servant of the King and that is just the same as the Duke de las Torres, who is secretary to the King of Spain."

"Just look at the vain one. But I am deaf in the left ear," said Brother Pedro, "and besides, if you think that you should play the leading rôle because you have a better figure than Pepe, I must tell you that your Spanish sounds like the cackling of a hen."

This must have been a terrible blow to Prat's pride but it was the sweetest of music to my ears.

During those rehearsal days, with my nerves still tense with the excitement of outside life and the night lights of the city, I felt as if I were floating in a pleasant confusion and went about repeating the stanzas of Calderón de la Barca. On Sunday I would write Valentina, telling her all about everything, and reminding her of a number of things she should do, like taking care of the crickets in the garden and sending me a recent picture of herself. I had heard my older sister use that expression about *recent* photographs.

Sometimes Prat was friendly, sometimes resentful towards me.

Besides his Catalonian accent, Prat could not say two words without his voice cracking, and he was such a bad actor that he always missed his cue for the single sentence he had to speak when Segismundo woke up. His sentence was:

May they sing again?

I, Segismundo, replied:

No, no;
I do not care to hear them sing.

In the middle of a very animated dialogue in verse, precision was important, but Prat always came in too soon or too late. Father Ferrer corrected him and the boy became so nervous that when he was waiting for his cue he would arch his back like a cat ready to spring. Again his timing was bad and anticipating rebuke he said, "If I have to wear that wig I don't want to play the part, either."

He was the most insignificant actor and the one who caused the most trouble. But Father Ferrer was too busy with me:

"Repeat the second part of the tirade in the cave with more emphasis."
Thinking of the general beheading of monks, beginning with Father
Ferrer, I stared at him and recited:

> *If Rome could see me on this day*
> *amid the triumphs of its early sway,*
> *oh, with what strange delight*
> *it would have been so singular a sight*
> *its mighty armies led*
> *by one who was a savage wild beast bred,*
> *whose courage soars so high,*
> *that even an easy conquest seems the sky!*

Father Ferrer appeared satisfied:
"You do get on well with the monologues and asides," he said, as if I
were a great actor.

In those days I had Father Ferrer mastered and subjugated, to the
amazement of my companions. The monk, who had a rat's mobility and
sharpness, and who was in all places at all times, flattered his actors and
especially me, on whom his success as dramatic coach depended.

Occasionally Father Lucas, pale and evasive, crossed the stage like a
shadow. The boys said that he had been burned in a raid on a convent
during Barcelona's tragic week. He had an ascetic and gloomy
expression. Looking at him, I recited:

> *What is life? 'Tis but a madness.*
> *What is life? A thing that seems,*
> *a mirage that falsely gleams,*
> *phantom joy, delusive rest.*
> *Since a life is dream at best,*
> *and even dreams themselves are dreams.*

Father Lucas looked out of the corner of his eye—without turning his
head—and went his way, silent and distrustful.

I did not study. What for? Although I realized that the stage had no
connection with real life, I took my prince's rôle as a victory. And
during recreation hours—off stage—I had everything that I could desire:
skates, bicycles, games of all kinds. It was merely a question of going
to the storage room and choosing.

But let us return to the stage. For the battle, which promised to be memorable, Father Ferrer had a supply of firecrackers of different sizes: for muskets, artillery, pistols. I wrote Valentina describing what those weapons would be like if we really had them, and their calibers. (About the calibers, I went into great and pedantic detail.)

A lay brother was busily painting in his shop. Father Ferrer asked me to go remind him that the door to the cave should have a grating that could be opened and closed. In the workshop I made exciting discoveries. The lay brother's cassock was hanging on a clothesrack and he was wearing ordinary corduroy trousers such as peasants wear. His shirt-sleeves were rolled up above his elbows. His hands, calloused from handling chisels and brushes, and his face, which was sad and dramatic when he was silent and radiant when he talked, made a lasting impression on me.

"Are you a father, too?" I asked.

"No, I am only a brother."

"Why don't you come to the study hall or to church with us?"

"Oh, little friend. I'm worthless when it comes to such things."

I gave him Father Ferrer's message and the lay brother listened attentively and then went to a corner of the shop where there were some crossed sticks of wood nailed together. His movements were unhurried, but sure.

"This is the grating," he said. "It's unfinished, and still has to be painted."

I decided that the lay brother was not giving the matter the attention it deserved. Looking at those sticks of wood I told him that the grating should be stronger, because it belonged on an old prison. The lay brother smiled:

"Never mind, little brother. From the auditorium it will look like iron. Besides, see here."

He turned it on its hinge and it screeched realistically. Then the lay brother spread out a dirty sheet of paper covering most of the shop floor.

"This," he said, "is the mountain with the fortress on top."

I saw nothing except some rough brush strokes and the outline of a stone wall twisted by the wrinkled paper. How could that possibly be a mountain?

"Here," said the lay brother, still smiling, "is a little window closed with transparent paper. We will put a little candle behind it. From a distance it will look as if people are living in the castle at night."

I did not see how those painted papers could create the illusion of a mountain. The scenographer, however, seemed sure of himself. He asked:

"Isn't there a storm? In great plays there is always a storm."

I declared, very sorry indeed, that there was no storm.

"But, on the other hand, there is war," I added.

The lay brother raised his head and clicked his tongue twice against the roof of his mouth. He did not like war. He took me to the back of the shop, and with both hands grasped the top of a large sheet of zinc, lifted it up and shook it again. The thunder it made was better than the real thing.

"A pity," he said. "I also have twilights and dawns, and lightning and hail. But if there is no storm . . ."

I talked about muskets and cannons, but the lay brother did not care to listen. Again he moved about the shop as if nothing in the world were worth the effort.

Beside the wall, on a carpenter's bench, was a long glass coffin. Inside, the head of a reclining Christ with closed eyes, yellowish cheeks, and pained mouth was visible. The rest of the body did not exist. In its place were some rough wooden sticks ending in two wax-colored, wounded feet. Scandalized, I protested:

"What an outrage! Who would ever have expected a thing like this? This is deceit."

"No, little brother. It is not deceit, but figuration. With a coverlet embroidered in gold and silver we hide these rough sticks during Holy Week, so that only the head on the pillow and the naked feet are visible for worship. The devout file by and kiss them.

Then seeing me skeptical, he added:

"But I must not leave it uncovered, because boys of little imagination like you may come."

"That imagination business," I was thinking, "must mean believing in images."

The lay brother covered the sticks with a white cloth, leaving only the sculptured parts visible. Where the knees and chest should be, the sticks of wood gave the proper relief. Then the lay brother went respectfully to the foot of the urn where the feet were showing, and kissed them. As he did this I was immediately aware of the Christ's reality.

"Little gentleman," said the lay brother, "haven't you already forgotten about the rough sticks of wood? Tell the truth."

"Yes."

"But you know that they are there, underneath?"

"Of course."

"And nevertheless you have forgotten. I myself made the image with these hands, but when I kiss the foot I am convinced that I am kissing the foot of the Son of God. What do you think of that?"

"How silly!" is what I thought. But behind that silliness I sensed a mystery I could not explain.

A plump, nude child with outstretched arms and legs lay on a carpenter's bench. I went over toward it. It was strange to see it there, on its back. The lay brother came up:

"When I was carving it the Virgin Mary said to me: 'Make the little rump rounder, the little heel softer.' And so gradually I finished it. And there it is now."

The infant was a graceful doll. Later I would see it on the altar surrounded by luminous acorns, silver garlands, enveloped in clouds of incense and canticles. The lay brother looked at it, contented.

"You will worship him. You will sing songs to him in the choir. And that's the way it should be. You are thinking that it is only a piece of wood. But who would dare to say that wood itself is not a miracle. Isn't God in the wood? Why don't you try to make a piece of wood?"

Now the lay brother pretended to be angry, to tease me. I remembered the song about the peasant who, having watched the carving of an image of the crucified Jesus, looked at it suspiciously and said:

> *Holy Christ of the Miracle,*
> *I knew you as a cherry-tree;*
> *the miracles that you'll perform*
> *you can put them here behind me.*

And I touched the seat of my pants. The lay brother laughed—a kindly laugh—and asked:

"What play are you putting on? Did you tell me the name of it?"

"*Life Is a Dream.*"

"Yes, that's right, little gentleman. Life is a dream of God."

Again he laughed and added, "Look how the light comes through the windows making shadows on the reclining Christ. In a moment those shadows will be gone and others will take their place. Everything is a dream. A dream of God."

I glanced between the legs of the baby Jesus and saw nothing.

The lay brother became very solemn:

"What part do you have in the play, little brother?"

"Prince Segismundo, the protagonist."

"Ah, a prince. Now you are a prince. Later you will be a sinner, then a saint, still later an unbeliever, according to the light God sheds on things. Life is like that. And do you already know your part?"

I began to recite:

> The king dreams he is a king,
> and in this delusive way
> lives and rules with sovereign sway:
> all the cheers that round him ring,
> born of air, on air take wing.
> And in ashes (mournful fate!)
> death dissolves his pride and state:
> who would wish a crown to take
> seeing that he must awake
> in the dream beyond death's gate?

The lay brother applauded. His hands were small and chubby. I did not regard that lay brother as a friar, since he was not wearing his habit, nor even as a man—he was too gentle and meek—but as a graceful and inoffensive animal. When he laughed he looked like a puppy. When he was sorrowful he had the sad profile of a bird. Of a crow, perhaps— how strange.

"With actors like you, Father Ferrer can really shine," he said.

He showed me other pieces of scenery. The backdrop—for the battle —was still to be painted. A field. Rocks at one side. A low, distant horizon. He showed me a sketch of it.

"Smoke," I said. "There has to be a lot of smoke, because of the firing cannon."

"Ah, no, little brother, highness. I won't contribute to the illusion of war. What I can do," he added, after a moment's reflection, "is put in some distant clouds that the audience can take as it pleases."

We looked at the sketch. It wasn't bad, I thought, even though not a soul could be seen. Other important things were also lacking.

"There must be some carnivorous birds in the air," I told him. "The ones that are going to eat up the dead."

The lay brother hesitated:

"Impossible. If I put carnivorous birds in the air they will always be in the same place and the illusion will be false."

"In my home town I have seen sparrow hawks flying and yet remaining still in the air, not moving either up or down. And they were real sparrow hawks with their beaks and claws, too."

"Ah, yes. They were hunting. All right. I will add some. How many?"

"Eight."

With a pencil the lay religious added a few lines to the sketch.

"No, better ten," I corrected myself.

The friar added two more. I also wanted him to put in a piece of broken artillery with dead bodies at the foot of it.

"No, I told you no once before. Do you, brother, think that the people in the audience will feel compassion if I put that in? What they will feel is the desire to go out and kill their fellow creatures."

"Who cares about that?"

"What do you mean by who cares? Are you mad, little brother?"

He looked at me with astonishment, adding:

"No. Ask me for anything you like, anything but that."

He picked up a can of varnish and went toward the infant Jesus to put on the finishing touches.

"Leave that," I said to him. "Father Ferrer told me that you must leave all that to finish the scenery. Don't you see that this is more urgent?"

"All right, all right," he answered laughing. "It will be ready in a minute. *Life Is a Dream* seems important to me, too. Life is a dream of God."

Suddenly he became very serious:

"Don't tell Father Ferrer that I said anything. For since I am not ordained it can sound like pedantry."

"What can sound like pedantry?"

"Talking about the dream of God."

Recalling words heard a thousand times in church, I asked:

"But don't the birds in the trees sing the glories of God?"

"You are very sharp, highness, little brother," and he roared with laughter, "but you don't know anything about such things. I can only do like the birds. Sing the glories of God. That's what I do," and he pointed to boards, canvases, carvings, "but I must not hold opinions because, as I told you, I am not ordained in theology. And I would never be able to get myself ordained either, supposing I had the ambition. I don't have the gray matter, little brother. I've always been a dunce."

The lay brother spread the last piece of scenery out on the floor and prepared the brushes. I walked about the shop.

"Why are you always laughing?" I asked. "You act like you're drunk."

Again the friar laughed at my words:

"Yes, I am drunk. But not on wine. On the breeze, the little light, the distant sound, what others say. Everything intoxicates me in some way. Now it is you who come and talk to me. When you leave I will be so sad I'll look like I have the toothache."

The lay brother made a clown's face as he said this.

"And why will you be so sad?" I asked.

The lay brother kept on laughing:

"Don't you want your supper, highness? Aren't you going to supper tonight?"

He walked to the door with me and saw me off. In the refectory I told my friends that I had been in the shop and that the lay brother was not a human being.

"Well, what is he then?" asked Pau, who believed everything I told him.

"Something like a puppy. He frisks about and barks and wags his tail."

The others also seemed impressed by my remarks. We spoke in a whisper because this was not a *de parla* day—when talking was permitted —in the refectory.

‡3‡

No sooner had I told them about the lay brother than some of the boys wanted to peep into the shop. They really believed in the barking, frisky friar. Some boys went so far as to say they had seen him on all fours, sniffing the wall repeatedly, and finally lifting up a leg. These

versions quickly made the rounds and one day Father Ferrer sent for me
to ask if I had said this about the lay brother. He seemed to be in a
friendly mood and I confessed. Father Ferrer looked very severe: "You
are going to give him an explanation." And he took me to the shop. He
left me there, warning the lay brother that I had something to tell him.
As soon as Father Ferrer disappeared the lay brother returned to his
naturally gay mood:

"What do you have to tell me, little brother?"

"Nothing. But I like to come see you."

"That's what I imagined. That was an invention of Father Ferrer's,
a father of great learning who will be Prior some day."

And he started telling sensational things about dogs he had known,
and which were more loyal and better than persons. The man was so
contented that he yelped once in a while as he talked about dogs. It was
all so simple and funny that it never occurred to me to apologize. He
asked me to recite something else from *Life Is a Dream* and I did not
have to be coaxed:

> *Heaven, here lying all forlorn,*
> *I desire from thee to know,*
> *since thou dost treat me so,*
> *why have I provoked thy scorn*
> *by the crime of being born?—*
> *Though for being born I feel*
> *Heaven with me must harshly deal,*
> *since man's greatest crime on earth*
> *is the fatal act of birth—*
> *sin supreme without appeal.*
> *This alone I ponder o'er,*
> *my strange mystery to pierce through;*
> *leaving wholly out of view*
> *germs my hapless birthday bore,*
> *how have I offended more,*
> *that the more you punish me?*
> *Must not other creatures be*
> *born? If born, what privilege*
> *can they over me allege*
> *of which I should not be free?*

The lay religious listened, disappointed.

"I'm sorry, but I don't like some of those things. That invoking and defying of Heaven is not right. It's blasphemy."

After a moment's silence the lay brother added:

"And being born is not a crime. The man was desperate. That is likely to happen to important men like princes and millionaires."

He led me to one end of the shop where he had religious statues. I was talking to him in a slightly arrogant manner, in the tone of my rhetorical rôle on the stage. I said that they had given me the part of Prince Segismundo because they needed a valiant and fearless man. The word *man* made the friar turn his head, surprised:

"Are you really fearless?"

"Yes. I've never been afraid."

"Never?"

"Never. What for?"

He showed me his statues, angels, demons. In one corner stood a dragonish, wooden monster, which at first glance somewhat resembled a turtle. Unseen by me the lay brother touched a spring and the monster stretched its neck and roared like a lion. I jumped back in spite of myself.

"Pardon me, highness, little brother," said the friar. "I thought you would not be frightened. This is La Tarasca that takes part in the Corpus Christi procession. It only scares tiny tots who are still crawling about on all fours, but it has frightened the valiant prince. Of course it caught him by surprise, but even so . . . Little brother, one must not boast because even the most valiant are at bottom insignificant. Very insignificant. Worm food."

I felt humiliated. My heart was still pounding and I had nothing to say. Finally I looked at La Tarasca scornfully:

"That certainly is a fraud. What does La Tarasca have to do with religion?"

"Ah, ah, little brother. You are really brave, but you are indeed a little donkey. Everything in our Holy Mother Church exists for some reason. La Tarasca is the memory of something that happened in the first century of our era. I will tell you about it briefly."

And sitting down, he continued, "When Jesus died on the cross his disciples scattered over the world preaching the holy gospel. To each country went an apostle in accordance with the tastes and idiosyncrasy of the particular country. To Spain came the apostle *Santiago*—St. James.

St. Jacob, that is, because I don't know if you are aware of it or not, but the name comes from the Latin way of pronouncing *Sant Jacob, Santiacob, Santiago*. Well then, here came the apostle who was in time to become the patron saint of Spain and of the Spanish knights who fought for the faith. But to tell you the honest truth," he added, lowering his voice, "I don't believe that it is necessary to fight with arms, not even for the faith. Don't repeat this outside the shop because I have not received holy orders and can therefore be mistaken. One of Jesus's dis-ciples went to each country, according to the customs of the land. And to France—who would you say it was? Martha, the friend of Mary Magdalene. Haven't you ever heard of Martha? She is in the gospels. Well, Martha went to France in one of those little boats you have seen sketched in your history book. Almost all the little boats sailing the Mediterranean then were Phoenician or Greek, with lots of oars on each side. So Martha went on one of these and disembarked in Marseilles. When she stood on land she said . . ."

"Did she know how to speak French?" I asked.

"No. And don't interrupt with silly questions, little brother. One can be brave and still be an ignoramus. At that time French was not yet spoken, but Latin. Martha naturally spoke Latin. Well, when she dis-embarked she saw a meadow full of flowers, and those at the river's edge were red and had a shape that Martha had never seen before. She asked the sailors: 'Why are these flowers blood-colored and dragon-shaped?' 'Because they are watered by a red stream coming down from Provence,' they said. 'And what's happening up in Provence that makes the water so red?' 'There is a city up yonder where the children are slain at birth, and some of them before they are born.' 'Who kills them?' 'Tarascio.' 'And who is Tarascio?' 'A dragon half turtle, half alligator, half man . . .'"

"Hey, hey," I said. "He couldn't have three halves, brother."

"Why not? A monster can have three halves, and five or more. That's precisely what makes him a monster. Tarascio, furthermore, let out great roars, talked like a man, and killed children. Martha said: 'Take me to that city.' And the sailors improvised a litter with the oars and put Martha on a bed of roses. They walked upstream until they came to the place in Provence today called Tarascon. There Martha alighted and entered the city singing the glories of the Lord. The townspeople told her the dragon had all the countryside terrorized. 'Where is Tarascio?' Martha asked. Everyone trembled for her, little brother, seeing what a weak little woman she was. And no one wanted to tell her where Tarascio was, so as not to be responsible for what might happen. She finally learned that he lived in a cave across the river. Martha crossed the bridge. In one hand she carried a bunch of the red flowers picked in Marseilles, and in the other a piece of the cross on which Jesus had died."

"How big?"

"Just a chip. About the size of my hand. Don't be a dunce, little brother. Don't imagine that she carried a club. The miracle was wrought by the divine nature of Jesus, not by brute force. How could a weak woman be more powerful than Tarascio? Well, at once Tarascio came out of his cave amazed at the daring of that strange woman. He was spewing fire out of his nostrils and making the mountains tremble like an earthquake. In spite of everything Martha went up to him unafraid and asked: 'Who are you, dragon?' 'I am the master of Tarascon. And you, who are you?' 'One more among women.' 'A friend of sin?' 'No, a friend of the crucified Jesus.' And so they went on talking. And Martha mastered and subdued him."

"How? She must have carried a sword. She had to have something."

"Legend says that Martha immobilized the dragon by saying some words in Latin. And while the monster was harmless the people of the town, armed with pitchforks and clubs, killed him. That was Tarascio. That's why we call this strange animal La Tarasca. And we take it out in the processions so that the people will not forget. In France, it seems, Tarascio comes back to life now and then and kills the children."

"You said that he killed children before they were born sometimes. That's impossible."

The lay brother, who had returned to his work, stood still for a moment with his brush poised in mid-air. He just looked at me, nonplussed. Then he nodded:

"You may be right, my boy. Times have changed."

Mechanically led along by the theme I started declaiming again:

> . . . *since man's greatest crime on earth*
> *is the fatal act of birth.*

"I may be wrong," the lay brother repeated, "but to me those lines sound like an insult to the Lord, to the life the Lord has created."

"But why?"

"Because they say that being born is a crime. A crime?"

He looked around and added:

"It's better to be like a puppy than to say things in verse or prose in such an arrogant way. Birth is a miracle, little brother. The greatest miracle of love."

Father Ferrer arrived just then and glanced inquiringly at the lay brother. He hastened to say that I had been very kind and generous, giving the father to understand that I had apologized. The lay brother spoke without looking the priest in the face. He always looked down at the ground when speaking to older people. He walked to the door with us and as he returned to his work started humming a little song in Catalonian: *"El bon Jesuset—s'en putxa a la vinya . . ."*—"The good little Jesus—climbed up to the vineyard . . ."

I was ashamed of not having apologized, but the lay brother with his cordial attitude and teasing was to blame, since he did not permit me to be humble. That friar who seemed simple as a little animal was suddenly revealing obscurities and labyrinths in his character. And he had a strange gaze, as if his eyes did not belong to him but to someone else.

I tried to find out what Latin words St. Martha had spoken to Tarascio. They would surely be an effective conjuration in time of danger. But the lay brother did not know them.

‡ 4 ‡

The first complete rehearsal of *Life Is a Dream* took place the following day. I had received a letter from Valentina with sensational news: she had washed her hair and the church tower had been struck by lightning. As always she copied verses from the almanacs, choosing those containing the word "love." They were quite inappropriate at times:

> *By smoke one knows*
> *where there is fire.*
> *Where there is love*
> *jealousy also goes.*

I paced the stage repeating my lines. The lay brother was also busy hammering here and there, and Father Ferrer was shouting louder than necessary to tell where each piece of canvas should hang.

With the stage finally set and the actors in costume, we had the dress rehearsal. The lay brother, in the auditorium, seemed pleased. It was a novelty for everyone to see the little friar who never left his workshop. With the instinct boys have for recognizing the most insignificant member of any group, they realized that the poor lay brother, who was neither priest, professor nor study hall proctor, could be the natural butt of jokes. Prat barked twice and when Father Ferrer went to admonish him he found the boy wearing the wig with the curls. The friar took it off and, holding it in his right hand, lovingly stroked it with his left. Prat seemed resigned. He remarked, however, that his uncle and aunt would be attending the performance, along with his cousin Ines, of whom he spoke as if she were his sweetheart. His favorite sweetheart, of course, for he had two.

Ervigio, a frail and delicate-looking boy, sometimes surprised us with his bantering spirit. And whenever he saw Prat he started chanting:

> Ines, Ines, Inesita, Ines,
> Ines, Ines, how pretty is she.

If Prat was near enough he aimed a kick in Ervigio's direction, but Ervigio dodged. Prat was still eyeing the First Servant's wig dubiously. To go on stage wearing that old rag made him very unhappy. He said that Ines had the most beautiful hair in the whole city of Gerona. The contrast made the wig more wretched still. I was pacing back and forth on the stage saying that I was a man among wild beasts and a wild beast among men, and giving terrible vibrations to my intonation. Pau, the blond boy from Amposta, called out from the auditorium:

"Father Ferrer, how good he is."

"Who?"

"Pepe."

The friar nodded, pleased. But Pau had not finished and in a tone of naïve admiration he added:

"He looks like the Virgin Mary."

The priest turned his head nervously:

"Who uttered that nonsense?"

I was wearing the gala wig at the moment. The impertinent remark helped me to play my rôle better. I looked about treacherously and moved my head with every word, shaking my body with aggressive rage. I spun around while staring at the father from head to foot and clenching my fists. I also gazed suspiciously at the wig that had suggested such an absurd comment to Pau. I would willingly have given it to Prat except for the thought that with it my enemy would appear more important in the eyes of Ines.

I felt uneasy on the stage when the lights were turned off. The extremely high-vaulted ceiling full of ropes and ladders like a sailing vessel, with immense wings moving up and down, did not make a very reassuring impression on me. Besides, those great masses moving in depths "way up high" made me dizzy.

The next evening the school took on the air of a great festive occasion. The grand stairway had been opened. Potted palms stood on the landings and in the corners. Families were arriving and going out onto the terraces overlooking the playground, where there were also much larger palms in jardinieres resembling rough tree trunks. Dressed in their Sunday best the pupils were strolling about. I wound my sandal laces around my legs up to the knees where the animal skins of my costume began. Before the performance they took flashlight pictures of us and the explosions frightened the little boys.

The excitement of the preparations was such that I had no time to think about myself and so the stage did not intimidate me.

At six o'clock the curtain slowly rose. The first act went off without a hitch and the house burst into enthusiastic applause. Prat, who did not go on stage in the first act, also took his bow, and when the curtain fell he started looking for his cousin through the peep-holes.

When the curtain rose again there was a serious setback. When it was time for me to go on stage I looked for my wig (I did not put it on until the last moment because it was too hot) and could not find it. I ran from one wing to the other until I spied it on Prat, who was crouching between two boxes. I tried to wrest it from him, he fought to keep it, fists started flying and we rolled over and over on the floor. Only Father Ferrer's intervention kept us from knocking down the scenery.

As was to be feared, Prat missed his cue and I had to ad-lib as during rehearsals. But Prat, refusing to be silenced, added a few extra lines, to impress his cousin. It was always something to do with the musicians:

He told them once to go away.

Or, with a haughty air:

Why would he have them sing?

I looked at Father Ferrer in the wings, and he was irate. (Prat at least maintained the rhythm of the verse, that is true.)

The boys in the auditorium were commenting on the fight—someone had taken them news of it—and arguing over the outcome. In spite of this and one or two other incidents, the performance went well. When the time came for me to throw the nobleman off the balcony I did it with such enthusiasm that the poor devil took fright and clutched me around the neck, absolutely refusing to let go. Then toward the end of the play I had to fire a shot at someone, the Duke of Moscovia, I believe. For this I had stuck in my belt an eighteenth-century pistol, empty except for a small percussion cap replacing the formerly used fuse. This was enough to give the illusion of real shooting. I fired. The percussion cap, which had always gone off during rehearsals, failed to explode and the Duke stood still, challengingly. Again I cocked the pistol and took aim, while Father Ferrer ran to the nearest wing and put a small lighted firecracker on the floor behind the Duke of Moscovia. I aimed, waiting for the explosion and repeating the lines. When the firecracker exploded it so caught the Duke by surprise that instead of falling he turned around to see what was going on and discovered the angry friar ordering him to drop dead. And so the perplexed Duke finally died. Only the spectators in the front rows seemed to be aware of the incident.

At the end of the performance there were eight or ten curtain calls and then Prat got rid of his wig and went to be with his cousin, who was pretty and dainty.

I also took off my wig and walked among the guests who were being served refreshments. They congratulated me and I relished my glory like a true actor. Father Ferrer, however, paid no attention to me and I felt cheated. I went up to him and asked what he thought of the performance, but he did not answer. He was walking around with some ladies, very polite and worldly. That friar was the most important teacher I had, and his opinion of my dramatic rôle would have repercussions— I thought—in my success or failure as a student. For the moment I gave up trying to discover his opinion.

With my head ringing with the echoes of success I was making my way around somewhat distractedly when vanity tripped me up.

Two very gracious ladies came up to me. Looking at my Van Dyke collar with its edges embroidered in imitation silver, one of them said: "How wonderful!"

Thinking that they were praising my histrionic talents, I remarked:

"But it would have been much better if Prat had not made so many mistakes."

At the same time—but too late—I realized that the ladies were merely talking about my costume and, to make matters worse, that they were relatives of Prat's. I blushed, and on the other side of the auditorium saw the "King's Secretary" with his young cousin. Very pretty she was, too, although not as graceful and natural as Valentina. Ines was a doll who looked as if she were made of gilded silver, with music hidden somewhere, in her chest or stomach or thighs. Ervigio, the jester, winked and repeated:

"Ines, Ines, Inesita, Ines . . ."

Then Ervigio and Roig approached a lady who was leading a very stylishly dressed and made-up girl by the hand. The girl was wearing an ornate cap and Ervigio said, patting her on the head:

"What a beautiful little *gorrina*—bonnet!"

Turning to the girl's mother, he added:

"Never in all my life did I see a *gorrina* like this."

Gorrina could be the diminutive of *gorra*—cap, bonnet—but it was also the feminine of *gorrino*—pig. The mother, however, never could have imagined that Ervigio was punning.

I was beginning to feel rather lost among the guests when Brother Pedro came up with a lady who was wearing those folding spectacles we called "impertinents." She opened and closed them constantly with a little click. They praised my acting, but having learned my lesson, I waited to be sure before thanking them. I looked around for the lay brother, in vain. He was never around when something pleasant or important was going on. He shunned people, I believe, as some animals avoid the light.

I was not accustomed to such brilliant festivals either. I felt nervous if people were not paying attention to me, and if they spoke to me I appeared rather distracted and superior. Brother Pedro brought me a glass of lemonade.

"It's very good for the throat," he said, as if I had tonsillitis.

In spite of his solemn serenity Brother Pedro was always joking. His peasant jokes were not very funny, however. The days we wrote home—Sunday afternoons—I asked him for two or three extra envelopes and he would look at me waggishly and say:

"Extra envelopes? I have nothing extra."

The friar took for granted that one of the letters was for my family, but he wanted to know about the others. Valentina's name, which he had seen on previous letters, was for him full of mystery.

I naturally wrote Valentina about the festival, reminding her that in *Life Is a Dream* I fought my father. And I had vanquished him, which should be no surprise to her, just as it did not surprise the audience. I repeated my ideas about dreams and reality. Believing that life is a dream was enough to make difficulties in life vanish. And I quoted: "What is life? An illusion . . ." In reality nothing was important. "Only you and I," I wrote. What was her father? A *frenzy*, a *madness*. And also a kind of animal dreaming that he is a notary. As for mine, why talk about him? Dreams. On the stage Planibell was my father, with a long white beard and a crown of gilded cardboard. Everything was a dream but us, Valentina and me.

That night as I looked out from my cell over the still illuminated city, I considered myself a part of all these wonders. The festival lights, which had been disappearing from the municipal buildings, were still burning on churches and monasteries. A few days later most of them were gone. They were never extinguished in my memory.

On Sundays we were allowed to read whatever we liked for two hours. I took out small volumes of sailing adventures, by Salgari, I believe, from the bookcases in the study hall.

During the next few days Brother Pedro frequently talked about my ability as an actor. From Father Ferrer I was never able to get a single opinion. It was as if he had forgotten the festival and Calderón de la Barca as well as my talents. I realized that the moment of glory was over. It was sad to return to the normality of hours, days, and weeks all alike.

Again I found an excuse to go see the lay brother in his studio. Since every hour of the day was occupied with some planned activity and the shop was off the beaten track, I had to slip away and later, if questioned, fib.

The lay brother was giving the last touches of varnish to the infant Jesus as I entered. I asked if he had seen the play and he said he had.

"You were very good, little brother, although a trifle too pompous for my taste," he commented. "This does not mean, however, that I did not applaud you."

This sounded like faint praise to me. The lay brother continued:

"I was in the auditorium because I wanted to see the effect of the scenery with the lights and actors. And once there I stayed until the end."

"The scenery wasn't bad," I said, "even though there wasn't any smoke in the battle."

The lay brother left the infant Jesus to dry and went to a corner where he uncovered a pink marble head. It was the head of a middle-aged man, grave and noble. But the nose was broken. The lay brother wanted to tell me something: "Do you like it? What a shame. I struck it too sharp a blow with the chisel and crack!—the nose fell off. Don't you think it's a shame, little brother?"

On the floor, at the foot of the tripod, was a small piece of marble. The lay brother looked at the noseless head with melancholy.

"What saint is that?" I asked.

"None. It is not a saint. Not everybody can be a saint. It is a head that I tried to make at odd moments for my own pleasure and only to show my . . . skill as an artist. As I chiseled I was doing something very similar to what you were wishing to do on the stage. Well, little brother, don't misunderstand. Yours was much more important. But I too wanted to say to the people: 'Eh, don't you see how smart I am?' This head was not bad, but beautiful or ugly it served no purpose. I only wanted to prove to myself that I have talent. Everyone wants to be better than everybody else, no? Foolishness. We are all unique and don't realize it. No one realizes that he is unique in life. Because, well, let's see: is there anybody else in the world like you? No. Your face is different and your way of looking also. All right, then, why do we want to be still more different? When I was carving the child Jesus and making the image of the Virgin or St. Joseph, and even La Tarasca, do you know what was happening to me? Well, inside my head I was hearing something like a chorus of happy simple people singing. They were not singing like professionals in a theatre, but like reapers or vintagers in September. I found this block of marble not long ago, little brother, half-buried in the garden. Since Roman times, maybe. And in that block I saw a face. St. Joseph? The Virgin? No, my lad. A dead yet living face, as we sometimes see in museums. Haven't you noticed how those faces in museums are dead and alive at the same time? Well, yes indeed, I set to work. What for? Only for me. And while I was working no one was singing here inside. I was a little mad, just as you were on the stage. My hands worked, not with love, however, but with a kind of secret pride. And then, unawares, I struck that blow with the chisel and broke the nose. One of God's lessons."

"What lesson?"

He looked around as if to make sure no one was within hearing:

"Yes, highness. A lesson. There came a moment when I thought: I am a great artist. And in that very instant the nerves in my arm became so stupidly happy they let themselves go. Crack! The nose broken. Everything lost. Now, what can I do? It's my fault. One is perhaps no more than a poor animal, but one wants to be a man. And more than a man. Madness, little brother."

"Now," I said, "that statue is worth more."

"Why?"

"Because it's ancient."

The lay brother burst out laughing:

"You have a ready answer for everything, but it's no use. I saw you in the theatre. You broke the Prince's nose, too. That is, you broke your own. On the stage you wanted to kill Clotaldo and your father and be more than a man. When I was making that head I had the feeling that I was a great artist forgotten by the entire world. How sordid! I felt it and this was worse than if I thought and believed it. That head seemed more beautiful to me than the infant Jesus, and the devil was talking to me and saying: 'You made the Child; they will put Him on the altar and the people will worship Him. If you make this head, they will put it in a museum some day and the people, when they see it, will adore you. You and not the infant Jesus."

The lay brother laughed:

"The old Nick is very smart. Smarter than you and I together."

Aware that he was talking too much he stopped. But it was not long before he came back to the subject:

"You also broke the Prince's nose. But don't worry. The audience did not notice. Yes, I saw it, because I know you. And because I don't like those arrogant lines invoking and defying Heaven. Nonsense. Well, then, you broke his nose. Is your Prince more ancient with his broken nose? Possibly, but that doesn't settle anything."

Unconsciously I touched my face and felt my nose. The lay brother was talking again and working with his brush.

"When someone comes to the shop and looks at me and I look at him like this, face to face, directly, I am tempted to say everything that pops into my head. Good? Bad? I don't know, but I can't help it. You're not annoyed by what I'm saying now?"

"No. Why should I? Besides, what you're saying isn't so. You don't say a word to Father Ferrer when he comes here. You don't look him in the eye, either."

"You are right. I don't say anything to him. What can I say to him? Father Ferrer is a scholar. I listen and obey."

"And when you're alone, what do you do? Pray?"

"Yes, I pray."

"In Latin?"

"No, I'm no student. I know nothing. Don't look at me like that. I am a real ignoramus, yes, I am."

I walked over to a kind of tomb.

"And here, what's this?"

"Nothing. It's nothing," he said, "but that's the way things are. When you come I talk too much. Do you know why? Well, because I put myself in your place unintentionally, as if I were you. You come, brother, and I see you. And by your manner of looking and keeping still I guess what you are thinking, feeling and wanting. When I have someone else before me I am not myself. I am only that person. I can't help it. Don't look at me like that for I am telling the honest truth.

"Inside here I have a soul. All right, my soul. Everyone has his own soul. But everyone's is different and mine, if I may say so, is liquid. When someone is near me it evaporates and then, presto, the vapor takes shape in the air like a phantom, with the form of the desires and feelings of the other. And there I am, without a soul. Yes, soulless. In the good sense, I mean. You mustn't laugh too hard at my foolishness. And when I talk I say everything the other person is thinking, feeling and wanting. And I answer what he would like to ask. But with you it is different, because you are a child and I have the impression that you are I myself when I was small. Do you know what happens then? Well, I would like to improve myself. That is, you. All right, forgive me, little brother; in reality, myself. Well, you understand. And as soon as you came I saw your intention. Yes. You know that your hand slipped a little because you were drunk. With the lights, people, applause. I, too, am slightly drunk with solitude and sunlight, shadows and sound and color. You were also, with yourself. And you were saying: '*Heaven, here lying all forlorn, —I desire from thee to know, —since thou dost treat me so . . .*' What did you want to know? Your hand slipped and . . . crack! bad luck. Now you think that with your broken nose Father Ferrer does not esteem you so highly and you come here for me to mend it for you. How? By telling you that you were a sublime artist on the stage.

"You were thinking with great justice and truth: the lay brother is the last monkey in the school and has not the slightest importance. I agree. On the other hand, you are a student whose father gives money to the community. And the lay brother who is as happy as a puppy is going to tell you that you were sublime on the stage because of your pretty face. All right, but this time you are mistaken. I have a liquid soul, and with a child like you I want to do exactly the same thing as with the wood and clay and stone. Haven't you noticed how water changes the shape of stones and makes them round and smooth and polished? Haven't you noticed how many pebbles there are, all alike, on the river banks? The water has been polishing them. Well then, what I am saying is that you want to be more than other people and I must warn you that this desire is foolish and commonplace. It is necessary to be like the rest. Yes, little brother. One must be simple, good and useful. Others have their merit. A great deal of merit. All men, the poor dears, have a great deal of merit. They live. That doesn't sound like very much to you? To live?

"I am quite worthless, do you understand? When I was young I saw my soul escaping through my eyes and going toward the people around me, and I thought and felt precisely as they did. Something different every time. Some became angry and said: hypocrite. Others thought: he is a fool. They were right in their way. I did not know how to live. They knew, but I did not. It was like a game where somebody who does not know how to play vexes the others by spoiling their sport for them. I did not know how to play. Then I said: the best thing would be for me to go away and let them play by themselves. And here I am.

"This community is made up of very deserving priests. Don't think that it is easy to teach so many students and run this enormous house with all its services, from the stewards who live in the basements to the father astronomer up there in the observatory. The fathers are wise and good. But within a few days after arriving here I was feeling just as bad as before. Or worse. Good for nothing. Will you believe me when I tell you that I don't even know how to assist at Mass? I was ashamed of my uselessness and went off into the corners to mope. Instead of looking at the holy and wise fathers of the community I looked at things: wood, stone. Before coming here I had been a cabinetmaker and door painter and was something of an amateur artist. So I began to mend windows and tables and make cupboards . . . well, easy cupboards, for kitchens and pantries. I also repaired the worn shoes of the brothers because I understand a little about half-soling, having worked with a cobbler as a boy. But the only thing that is of interest to us now is that I was looking at things. Wood, stone, clay. Gradually I came to see that these things also had their purpose and desire, and my poor liquid soul of a hypocrite and fool evaporated and went to them and took the shape of their desires.

"It is no joke, little brother. Don't laugh. So for ten years whenever I see a piece of wood I begin to feel that it wants to be something else: an *ecce homo* or cherubim. Or a dove, or the Holy Family's little donkey. And when my soul has escaped and I am a soulless boob without substance, I start humming through my nose like a poor animal and pick up my tools. Gradually what was inside starts coming out. And when it has fully emerged and I have varnished it, it is not my intelligence I see in the form and color, far from it. What intelligence could I have? I, who came here where they keep me out of charity, since I do not know how to earn my bread. When I see the love of my poor hands in the sculpture, then I pray. And it gives me a rather simple contentment. Now you see, little brother. By this I mean that one can be like a dog without a master and at the same time love people and have a little of the joy that God has scattered throughout the world. But you will not have it, highness, if you insist on being more important than other people. Because you too" —the friar laughed—"you also have a liquid soul. A little soul that escapes through your eyes. The bad thing is that you repress it out of conceit and then you do as on the stage and say: '*Because man's greatest crime is birth.*' Haughtiness, little brother."

Because I insisted on considering the lay brother inferior to the rest of the community, his opinions struck me as second-rate. I almost never saw him wearing his cassock and when by chance he did have it on the skirt was usually tucked up and knotted around his waist. When he occasionally appeared like this in the corridors he caused something of a sensation, for we boys had never seen a monk in trousers.

Thinking that I was being prudent, I asked:

"I don't care about the opinions of the others, brother, but if you can divine them, couldn't you tell me what Father Ferrer thinks of me as a dramatic artist?"

"Ah, little brother. You are very clever."

"You won't tell because you don't know."

"Oh yes, I do. Father Ferrer thinks that you did very well and that

the families of the students applauded you, saying: 'See how clever the
boys of this school are.' That's true. It's a pity your parents could not
have seen you. Are you sorry too?"

"Me? No."

"Ah, little brother. Do you also believe that you are better than your
parents?"

When the lay brother was silent his expression was quite dramatic,
as I mentioned before. He went over to the infant Jesus to see if the
varnish was dry. Then he said, with great conviction:

"We must love people as they are, little brother, and that is not easy.
For you it is almost impossible."

Glancing at the saints scattered about I asked:

"Haven't you ever made a demon? A real demon, I mean, of stone or
wood?"

"No, we don't need demons."

"Well, I saw one in the chapel, beside the Bible."

"Ah yes. But I didn't make it. That's factory-made."

"And why don't you make a devil?"

The lay brother led me by the hand to the shop door and, lowering
his voice and pushing me outside, said:

"I could, but I prefer to work on other things. Do you know why?
Because the devil is only intelligence. I don't like intelligence by itself.
Not at all. I am rather afraid of it, little brother."

I pondered this on my way to the refectory, without understanding it:
"How can he be afraid of a wooden devil?"

In the cloister leading to the dining hall the boys were standing, as
usual, in two long rows. I got in line in front of Pere and Pau, beside
Planibell. When he took his place at table and saw that the soup was
already served—we had a vegetable soup every night for supper—he put
his nose close to the dish and, if it smelled of cabbage, made a gesture of
repugnance, saying:

"I can't eat this."

This Planibell was a delicate boy, with a porcelain-like face, blond
eyebrows and a fragile chin, but he talked like a truck-driver. He was
the only one who deliberately cultivated an impudent and obscene style.
He gathered his table companions around him in a corner of the patio
and used the vilest words when talking to us. We answered him in kind.
We called these meetings our class in civic education. Planibell, who
had spent one year in a boarding school in France, added to his Castilian

and Catalonian repertory dirty French words which sounded quite innocent to us because of our unfamiliarity with them. Caresse joined the
group once in a while and we made him learn them. This boy, a little
simpleton, admired Planibell who told him:

"When Father Miró asks you for examples of the parts of speech in
class, you must say: substantive: *merde*. Adjective: *salaud*. Emphatic
pejorative: *espèce de con*."

The boy learned them and waited for his opportunity to shine.

Sometimes we had an auditor like Roig in these "classes." He was the
most colorless boy, and the one most lacking in personality, in the whole
school. He always laughed and agreed with everybody.

Ervigio kept on making fun of the little cousin Ines whose voice and
manner of walking he imitated. The girl had really made quite an impression on him but he did not want to admit it. He found the idea of
her being Prat's cousin intolerable. He went to Caresse and told him
that if Prat wanted to marry his cousin Ines, he would have to walk to
Rome, carrying a pilgrim's staff and cloak-cape, to ask permission of the
Pope. Caresse believed it. And he was of the opinion that this was not
worthwhile, since there are other women in the world one can marry,
without having to walk to Rome.

"Oh, no, you're wrong there," said Ervigio very seriously, "for you
haven't seen Ines. If you saw her you would really know something
good."

With all his simple-mindedness, Caresse had his dangerous side. He
was growing so fast that his sleeves came only to the middle of his forearm, revealing his bare, red hands covered with knots and tendons. He
had handed out two or three memorable cuffings. The boy seemed to
have more and heavier bones than anybody else.

Prat sometimes attended the class in civic education and after listening
to the French obscenities he would look at us haughtily, say two or
three forbidden Spanish words that sounded much more violent and
rotund, and disdainfully walk away. He felt a certain natural antipathy
toward Planibell, but they were halfway relatives of some kind or other
and refused to fight, out of clan solidarity. During summer vacations, it
seems, they had really beaten each other up.

In front of the friars we feigned a passive submissiveness. We knew
they sent secret reports to our families and that, regardless of the facts,
our parents would listen to them rather than us. Furthermore, being

priests, they spoke in the name of God. All resistance or conspiratory effort would be futile.

There were no flatterers or informers, however, among the boys. I never knew of a single case of disloyalty in all the time that I was there.

‡5‡

There were all sorts of friars in the community and our opinions of them must have been rather just, as is usually the case with children. On the whole, we were more inclined to believe in a brother than in a father. As they rose in importance we found them more and more suspect, although, oddly enough, we respected and loved the one at the top of the pyramid, the Father Superior. Because he taught no classes, maybe, and was therefore rarely seen.

Father Miró, educated in France where the church enjoys no official privileges, was gentle, understanding and reasonable. He was not, apparently, arbitrary or capricious by temperament, as were other teachers. And he looked at us with large and lingering eyes.

The day Caresse recited the phrases learned in civic education class, Father Miró blushed with indignation and sent him out to the corridor to await disciplinary measures. Then he pardoned him. Caresse did not squeal on us or our exercises in Franco-Spanish scatology. But he looked at us ever after with a skeptical eye as he thought about the dangers of trust and the disappointments and deceits of friendship. His long, bony hands dangled from his sleeves, threatening but useless, since the six of us at table made common cause with Planibell.

Ervigio came to tell me the well-known jokes about Prat and Ines. Some days he made fun of her and called her prim and dull. I said to him:

"Now let's get this straight! Did you or didn't you call her an angel?"

Ervigio said that if she and Prat got married he would send them a urinal as a wedding present, with Ines's name engraved on one side and the bridegroom's on the other. I warned him not to let Prat hear about this or he would pay dearly for the joke, but Ervigio defied danger with the words of Don Juan Tenorio:

Doña Ines of my soul . . .

Among the sixth-year boys there were two or three big husky fellows who were beginning to shave. They smoked in secret. The cigarettes were very expensive, however, since buying them not only involved feigning the need to go to the dentist, but bribing the servant who accompanied them. In the end, each package cost the price of ten. The blue blouse looked like a ridiculous disguise on such big students. One of them, named Planchat, with a deep voice and treacherous look, used half-words terribly charged with meaning when talking about the friars, and especially Father Ferrer. But if at that moment the friar appeared, Planchat behaved with gentle and submissive courtesy. After Father Ferrer had gone by Planchat would return to his poisonous looks and mutterings. He had the eyes of the bad man in a melodrama capable of killing for hire. This made a great impression on me and he may have been aware of it.

On this particular day Planchat was sitting on the cloister balustrade —on the second floor—staring at the toe of his shoes. He rarely raised his eyes, as if his upper eyelids were made of lead.

"The day everyone says what he really believes," he grumbled, "we'll see where Father Ferrer ends up. Because I know all his tricks by heart."

I looked over my shoulder at the patio where the friar was coaching football. This Planchat, whom I regarded as an example of what a boy can be like when he grows up, was repeating Planibell's words, not to show off, but spontaneously and seriously. Knowing that he was stronger than the monk, I did not understand why he did not give Father Ferrer a good licking some fine day. Planchat was again looking at the patio out of the corner of his eye:

"The day I get out of this place they'll see who I am. Because the Ferrer I like doesn't wear any cassock. The one I like is Francisco Ferrer."

"And where is he?" I asked.

"Where is he? Under the sod. They shot him in the moat of Montjuich Prison."

Then he lowered his voice to tell me that he was an anarchist, at the same time grinding his teeth.

"Who's an anarchist? Ferrer or you?"

"Both of us, man. Both of us, good God Almighty. Can't you hear?"

Every morning after that when I saw him at Mass in the chapel I always thought: "Some day he'll bring a bomb and put it behind the altar." If Father Ferrer happened to be saying Mass I would consider it well used, even if a little piece of shrapnel got me.

I told Planchat I had a sweetheart.

"A sweetheart to marry?"

"Sure, of course."

"Bah, that marrying stuff's a bore. Moronic."

"How come?"

"Moronic. I believe in free love."

He explained what this was and even though I was not sure I understood, the certainty of his contempt for matrimony seemed admirable to me. I did not understand the word "moronic" either, but I did not want to show my ignorance by asking what it meant.

We hated, as I say, Father Ferrer. We were all fed up with his false, friendly words and cold, reticent looks. The looks of an affable asp. This was when I learned that it is possible to hate someone who has dealt correctly with us.

I also learned that one can be silent, solemn, dramatic and even tragic, like Father Lucas, and yet provoke comic and hilarious reactions. Ervigio, always restless, whenever he saw taciturn Father Lucas pass by without noticing anyone (he never looked at us, not even when the cloister was full of students), would say to me as he wrinkled up his nose:

"Don't you smell something scorching?"

He would say it under his breath, but so the priest could hear. Father Lucas' presence aroused stronger reactions in Planchat than in Ervigio. "Priests are morons," Planchat said. But if, as he said this, a teacher approached, Planchat stood up like a soldier in front of a colonel, answering in short, very polite affirmations, "Yes . . . Yes, sir, of course. As you wish, Father." I could not understand these servile contradictions in Planchat's character. Later it occurred to me that he talked in this way to impress me and that at heart Planchat was as shy as a lamb.

I received a letter from Valentina. She had washed her hair again, but lightning had not struck the tower. For want of other news she told me that her sister Pilar was furious because I was an actor and had said that if Valentina married a second-rate actor she would dishonor her family forever. Otherwise everyone was well (ADG—Thanks be to God) and she copied some other verses for me that spoke of love; this time from San Juan de la Cruz, no less. I sent her the printed program of our entertainment, a picture in which I was dressed as Prince Segismundo, and Gutierre de Cetina's *Madrigal* that begins:

Light eyes, serene . . .

I had some misgivings, however, remembering Valentina's black eyes.

In the patio Planchat told me that on Sundays he did not read the lives of the saints, but Voltaire and Rousseau. I asked Brother Pedro for these authors and he was pensive for a moment before remarking:

"Those gentlemen bring me a whiff of sulphur."

Their books were not in the study hall bookcases. I told Planchat, who gave me to understand that I had not heard him correctly. He read them at home during vacations. He added that these authors were real men without prejudices, and that they were also enemies of matrimony. In their books they told the painful truth.

Father Ferrer heard about my wishing to read Voltaire and sent for me:

"How can you be interested in books written by the enemies of God?"

Shortly after this the history teacher, who was not a priest but a lay instructor who came in from outside to give us lessons—and never dared scold us—asked me in class:

"Have you ever heard me speak of Voltaire and Rousseau?"

He looked at me and his expression was as gentle as that of romantic lovers in the poet Bécquer's time.

"No, no, I haven't. Why?"

"I mean, have you ever heard those names mentioned in this class?"

"No."

"Then when the Father Superior asks you, will you kindly tell him so, Sr. Garcés."

"What do you want me to tell him?"

"The truth. The simple truth."

The next day the study hall desks were searched. There were rumors that made the older boys uneasy, since they often kept humorous and amorous magazines like *Papitu*, with pictures of large nude women in them, hidden there.

On Ervigio they only found some girls' addresses. Nothing important. He had a card index in a shoe box labeled "*Women*," containing over fifty filing cards with the addresses of girl friends and acquaintances. He had jotted down details like these on the cards: "Personality, sincere. Bust, swell. Legs, shapely. Age, 16." The monks took this away from him, which plunged him into mute despair. After this his jokes were more caustic than ever, especially those aimed at Prat and Ines.

Providence seemed to be helping him along with his raillery. During those days melancholy made Ervigio hang around me more than ever and I finally came to take him seriously. I showed him a letter from Valentina, hiding the signature with my hand. The line I showed him contained one of the most common expressions of love: *"Mi cielo,"* "My heaven," "Darling." But Valentina had forgotten to dot the *"i,"* and the following *"e"* looked almost the same as the *"i."* So Ervigio read a word with a ludicrous and rather indecent meaning. I turned pale with rage. Aware of this Ervigio jumped out of my reach, repeating:

"You are her *cielo,* her *cielo* . . ."

Except he did not say *cielo* but the other word. I decided then and there never again to show a love letter to anybody.

When two days later during "vigils"—that's what we called the three daily hours of study in the large hall proctored by Brother Pedro—I went up to ask for a dictionary, Brother Pedro looked at me with a smile:

"What word are you looking for?"

"Several," I replied.

He started off with his peasant jokes, heavy and humorless:

"Several words are no more than two and mean that: *several words.* One word and another are several. Now you don't need the dictionary."

I insisted that I needed to look up terms like *perplexity, homicide,* and *immemorial.* I knew that the dictionaries were a delicate subject. Only the sixth-term boys—who shaved—were permitted to have them at their desks. Brother Pedro did not believe me.

"Don't you know what *perplexity* is?" he asked.

"No."

"You perplex me."

These conversations in an undertone while I looked at the yellow snuff staining the front of his cassock made me impatient, but he did it on purpose:

"You don't know what *homicide* is either?"

"I'm not sure."

"Naturally, Planibell doesn't give you those words in the class in civic education, does he?"

Nothing ever escaped Brother Pedro, but he never informed on us. This was the secret of his authority over us.

He winked at me. I wanted to look up the names of Voltaire and Rousseau to find out the reasons for their enmity toward marriage. The friar told me that I should write down the words and that he would take the trouble to look them up for me.

The next day Father Ferrer led me into the presence of the Superior, whom we almost never saw. To reach his imposing office we passed through the classroom corridors with their signs: Lecture Hall 7, Lecture Hall 12, Auditorium, etc., and entered a dark cloister with a vaulted stone ceiling. On the right I saw the natural history classroom, which was not called lecture hall but laboratory. The door was ajar and in a corner I could see, hanging by its skull, a human skeleton that frightened the small boys. They did not call it a skeleton but "death." On the other hand the sixth-term boys, who were studying natural history, called the skeleton "Phillip."

The corridor was intercepted by a wooden grating, in the center of which was a small door of elaborately wrought iron bars. Above this door was a sign: Inner Cloister. Only members of the masculine sex could enter here.

The office of the Father Superior was large and dark and had a wooden platform, like the classrooms. There the Superior with his large impassive face was waiting for us. If Father Ferrer was as thin and agile as a snake—as Planchat said—the Superior had a sickly obesity about him. Nevertheless his three hundred pounds did not make him grotesque. The Superior seemed to draw from them a natural and unostentatious solemnity. Every gesture and word seemed to express cordial sincerity. In his utterly candid gaze a spark of authority sometimes gleamed, giving the great mass of his person a strong and hierarchical aura.

I remember the Father Superior's obesity very well because I had never seen a similar case, then or since. Above his cassock collar he had two double chins. His shoulders were broad and rounded and his chest bulged out spectacularly. Yet at the waist his fat disappeared, forming an enormous hump behind. In spite of all this which was probably caused—so I think now—by some functional disturbance the result of chastity, the Superior's figure was not grotesque. His speaking voice was amiable and confidential.

Being so fat he walked as little as possible. He occasionally came to the study hall to preside over "vigils," and in the silence of the room we knew when he entered, without turning our heads, by the uneven sound of his steps and his slightly asthmatic breathing.

He asked a question in Catalonian and Father Ferrer shook his head, then looked at me, smiled with his eyes—false, then with his lips—deceitful, and in a voice that sounded cracked to me remarked:

"You played the part of Segismundo very well."

The Superior leaned over the table to look at me:

"Is it true that you're from Aragón?" he asked.

Father Ferrer hastened to answer the question:

"He's a *maño*. A little *maño*."

"That's not so," I said. "*Maños* come from Lower Aragón. From Zaragoza and Teruel. I'm from Huesca."

"I don't agree with you about that, Pepe," the Father Superior answered. "All you Aragonese are *Maños*. Those of Lower as well as Upper Aragón. You should not mind. Don't you know what the word *maño* comes from? From the Latin *magno*."

That was something else. From *magnos* (great) came *magnificent*. So it was not ridiculous to be a *maño*. I looked at the Superior gratefully and said:

"The people of Upper Aragón are bigger than those of the low country, that's true. And I come from the province of Huesca where they killed Sertorius. *Urb Victrix Osca*, the Romans said."

The Father Superior seemed to be enjoying himself as he listened to me.

"All right, Pepe. Everywhere the mountain people are bigger than the lowlanders. But the greatness of the Aragonese is moral and has nothing to do with size. That makes it better and more worthwhile. Although not everything, of course, is virtue with the Aragonese. They are famous for their stubbornness. Isn't it true that you are a little . . . hardheaded?"

"Because we are right, Father Superior," I replied.

While the Superior was looking at me with real and sympathetic understanding, Father Ferrer kept up his uncomfortable giggling:

"Yes, we know. To Zaragoza or the puddle."

No one can be witty without some kindness and innocence. Father Ferrer was utterly devoid of both these virtues. He thought of himself as rather superior and this was the first trait we boys detected in his character.

"That story about Zaragoza or the puddle," I said with emphasis, "is what they tell about the *baturros*—Aragonese rustics. We people of Huesca are not *baturros*, certainly not."

The Father Superior's outstretched hand lay quietly on the table. "That's something else. The *baturro* does not come from the banks of the Ebro. *Baturro* is depreciatory. The term is *bato*, which means simpleton, boob. From the Greek *battos*, stammerer. Don Pepe is right in not wanting to be either *baturro* or *bato*, for he is neither. He certainly did not stammer in *Life Is a Dream*; quite the contrary. Don't you agree, Father Ferrer?"

Although I sensed something facetious in the Superior's words, he was incapable of being annoying.

"I don't know why people tell that story about Zaragoza or the puddle," I insisted. "It is nonsense. Like when they say *catalan fotut*, about the Catalonians."

At that time I did not know the meaning of those words.

"My son," said the Superior gravely, "that expression is in bad taste. But the phrase about Zaragoza or the puddle should not bother you. It is just a joke. They always tell such jokes on the peasants. And sometimes they are true, and sometimes not. The Galicians are stingy, they say, the Castilians haughty, the Valencians false."

And then the Superior on his platform started explaining the origin of the phrase "to Zaragoza or the puddle," which everybody has used some time or other when speaking of the Aragonese.

"It comes from a very old tale," he said. "A peasant was walking along the highway, and at quite a clip, when a stranger said to him:

" 'You seem to be in a hurry, my good man. Where are you going?'

" 'To Zaragoza. Tomorrow morning at seven I will enter the city by the stone gate.'

" 'God willing,' replied the stranger who was an angel.

" 'God willing or not, tomorrow at seven I will be in Zaragoza.'

" 'Look,' said the angel in a friendly tone, 'it's unreasonable to talk like that, for God could punish you.'

" 'Whether he punishes me or not, tomorrow morning at seven I will be in the San Pablo Inn.'

"Then the angel touched the peasant's foot with a little reed cane he was carrying and changed him into a frog. This about the frog is not capricious. The Aragonese peasants went many places then as now wearing knee breeches, and sometimes their legs do suggest those of that little animal."

The Father Superior continued: "The poor *baturro*, for he was a *baturro*, spent seventy-two years in a puddle near the highway, croaking

during the summer nights and enduring the winter cold as best he could.
When the time was up he recovered his human form, returned to the
highway, and started walking toward Zaragoza, just as if nothing had
ever happened. Shortly the same stranger reappeared:

"'Where are you going, my good man?'

"'To Zaragoza. Tomorrow morning at seven o'clock I will cross the
river by the stone bridge.'

"'God willing, brother.'

"'God willing or not willing.'

"Again the angel touched him with the small reed and the poor man
was again changed into a frog, spending another seventy-two years in the
puddle. He finally returned to the highway and started walking with
the same haste when the stranger reappeared:

"'Where are you going, brother?'

"The peasant took a good look at him, recognized him and replied,
somewhat disgruntled: 'To Zaragoza . . . or the puddle.'"

I could not understand why this was so funny. Father Ferrer, with
his rodent's smile or that of a man too smart for his own good, said:

"Come on, you are Aragonese. Not a *maño* or *baturro*, but a good
Aragonese. Why don't you sing a little *jota* for the Father Superior?"

"I have no objection," I said without looking at him, "provided you
dance it."

The Superior had to make an effort to keep from laughing. Father
Ferrer said:

"Anyone can see that you're ashamed of being Aragonese. No matter.
But at least tell the Father Superior where you got the names of those
wicked writers whose books you were asking for."

"Who? Voltaire and Rousseau?"

"Oh, you don't have to mention their names here."

Suddenly aware that these writers were more important than I had
thought, I felt an overwhelming desire to read them. Yet I was not really
interested in them but in their opinions on marriage.

"Who mentioned those names to you?" the Superior asked.

"The history teacher?" Father Ferrer insinuated perfidiously.

Naturally I did not want to accuse anybody. I said that I had heard
of them before coming to school.

"Not in your house," both priests commented at the same time.

"No. Nobody reads in my house. But I did want to read Voltaire,
anyway."

"What for? We have more experience, my son," said the Superior, "and we believe that such reading is not appropriate just now. When you are older, if your confessor authorizes it, that will be a different matter. They are two enemies of the church. Two reprobates."

I hesitated an instant, then decided that I could say what I was thinking:

"I can read everything and it won't do me any harm. I . . . well, I am different."

"Ah, different? May one ask how?"

"Yes. I have a liquid soul. But I don't mean to say that I'm the only one," I added, thinking of the lay brother in the shop.

"Ah," the astonished Superior repeated. "And how so?"

"Well . . . you will see. It's a little hard to explain."

I could not recall what the lay brother had said about the liquid soul, and even so I would not have wanted to explain in front of Father Ferrer with his dry expression. The Superior looked at me, intrigued. A distant bell rang and he dismissed us by saying that I should come back some time and explain what I meant by *liquid soul*.

"That's very easy," I said, suddenly remembering the lay brother's words. "It all consists in seeing a phantom of mist that comes out of one's eyes and divines the ideas of others."

"Come, come. A phantom of mist? I never heard of such a thing," said Father Ferrer.

Outside in the corridor Father Ferrer kept talking to me about Voltaire and Rousseau. Our shoes rang out rhythmically on the cold and shining tile mosaics. Every other step I had to skip to keep up with the friar.

"Don't you know? Rousseau was a criminal who died swallowed up by his own wretchedness. The death he deserved, the sinner. May God forgive him."

I understood that Father Ferrer did not want God to forgive Rousseau.

"And Voltaire?"

"Ah, Voltaire was a cynic full of vices and infirmities. When he was old a black dog appeared on his bed, walking back and forth from the head to the foot, from the foot to the head, until finally he curled up on Voltaire's face. The dirty, shaggy hair of that black dog asphyxiated Voltaire. Who do you think the dog was?"

The devil, I supposed. But I distrusted Father Ferrer. Surely the Superior would never have told me anything so hard to prove. Everything that Father Ferrer said became suspect to me precisely because he said it.

I learned less in the school than I had in the village with Mosén Joaquín. The only thing that really interested me in school was an occasional clandestine confidence of the boys in civic education, but above everything else the lay brother in the workshop. I never talked about the lay brother to anyone, and the students had forgotten him again after the jokes of the first few days.

During the recreation periods everyone revealed his natural self. Ervigio had a curious talent for mimicry and a rare cleverness at discovering people's grotesque sides. He still had Ines on his mind and made fun of Prat, behind his back. Even so, this mocking was risky.

In our books, as at the end of the religious leaflets and tracts, were the four initials A.M.D.G., meaning *Ad majorem Dei Gloriam*. Ervigio had found an impudent translation in Catalonian: *Al macho donauli garrofes* —"To the mule give carob beans." Many of the boys wrote those words beside the large ritual letters.

Ervigio was always the first to see even the slightest irregularity in others and he felt obliged to call attention to it in some way. (Just as he had seen it in Valentina's handwriting.)

He was constantly harassing Pau, who did not have much of a nose:

"Pug nose, don't you want a cake?"

Then he himself would answer:

"No, because it's moisoned."

He said "moisoned" instead of "poisoned," as if his nose were stopped up.

Father Ferrer sometimes walked with comical haste, his cassock flying, and talking to two or three boys at the same time, while interrupting himself to give orders here and there. He moved more than was seemly with priestly decorum. When Ervigio saw him like this he would say under his breath:

"Ay, what commotion! What a reverend commotion!"

Ervigio made many pert remarks about the fiesta performance of *Life Is a Dream* out of envy, since he had been given nothing but the obscure and anonymous post of prompter.

He also mocked his relatives, saying that his aunt gave him two pesetas when he arrived home with good marks and said:

"You are a good boy but too *precarious* for your age."

She meant *precocious*. But precarious was also quite fitting.

I wrote to Valentina complaining of our separation for the first time and saying that it would not be long until Christmas vacation. Then we would see each other and I would tell her a thousand things I had not written because they *were not to be trusted to the mails.* (I had taken this sentence from a novel.) In the inevitable postscript I added, "My grades for the second month are good, but the monks send them to my father. They are all excellent, I think, although I am not sure. You will see. *Vale.*"

That Sunday I read half of a novel of sea adventures. I was so fascinated that I could not wait until the next Sunday to find out how it ended, so that night, after the lights were out, I slipped out of my cell and barefooted went down to the lower floor. Our cells were all closed with the same key, from the outside. But we could open them from the inside, if we wanted to go to the lavatories. In this way they knew who had gone out, for we could not lock the door again.

I reached the study hall and took my book from the shelf. Passing by the natural history laboratory on my way back I could not help thinking about the skeleton. Since the door was closed I did not actually see it, but I had it in my imagination, which was worse. The sound of my bare feet echoed through the corridors. I could feel and hear other barefooted steps behind me. A skeleton, naturally, is not a living being, but in the darkness of the night one fancies it floating in the air and passing through a closed door, even a wall. Before reaching the door I was not afraid, but once past it, I could not keep from going faster and faster. There came the moment when I broke into a run. When the fear became unbearable I stopped and looked behind me again. I saw no one. Then I started walking again and in a moment the same thing happened all over again. Fortunately, when I reached the stairs to the third floor the echo of my steps had disappeared.

I did not go to my room since there I had no light. The lights were left on all night in the lavatories, however. Comfortably installed in one of the toilets I started reading, ashamed of my fear and recalling my bold deeds in similar circumstances during the preceding summer. I decided that community life, and especially in community with priests and older boys, was robbing me of strength and perhaps making a coward of me. In Salgari's novels I would recuperate my strength.

I had stopped on page 123—I remembered because of the order of the numbers—precisely when four starving men on board an unmasted ship had eaten the leather of a suitcase and were about to draw lots to see which of the four should be sacrificed to feed the others with his body. One of the sailors prepared several pieces of rope of different lengths, and the one drawing the longest would resign himself to death. Naturally the sailor who had awakened the greatest sympathy in the reader was the one chosen by fate. I was terribly distressed, sometimes identifying myself with the victim, and sometimes with the coldest and most insensitive of the other shipwrecked sailors, whose name was Jackson. "Very well," said the victim, "my only request is to be killed unexpectedly without my knowing anything about it."

The companions of so many heroic hardships passed through contradictory states of feeling. On the one hand, friendship. On the other, the instinct of self-preservation. I could not accept this as reasonable. Better to starve a thousand times than eat up a friend, but I granted that it could be possible among other peoples and under different skies. I devoured the pages.

It took a long time for the murder to come off and the lavatories with their white tile walls and bare floors were very cold. Finally the victim fell stabbed in the back, and the chapel clock struck two. I went to my room with a heavy heart and grieving soul. I had to give Father Ferrer's face to the poor dead seaman, in order to calm down. But on the whole that reading had restored my adventurous energies of the good old days in the village.

I had intended going down to the study hall to return the book, but the dead sailor and the skeleton on the other side of the laboratory door made me decide to wait until morning. Once the sailor was dead my curiosity lost its keen edge and could wait until the next Sunday afternoon.

I wrote a letter to Valentina bringing her up to date on the lay brother in the workshop and telling her the story of La Tarasca. After the signature I added in the postscript: "Now I must tell you that marriage is moronic and that we need not marry to be happy. *Vale.*"

A few days later it was my turn to read in the refectory while the others ate. The school regulations only permitted us to talk during Thursday and Sunday dinners. On these days, after taking our places in the dining hall, we waited silently for Father Ferrer's signal. When he clapped his hands there was an explosion of voices, exclamations, laughter, suddenly revealing the effort we had had to make to keep still. On other days we could only whisper, and hope to avoid being seen by the guardian friar. While we ate in silence one of the boys would mount a wooden platform beside the wall and read. The readings were not very stimulating: lives of the saints. The one who read ate alone, later, near the serving windows, and usually had special desserts and sweets. The day I read many boys seemed to be paying attention—which was not often the case—and I felt flattered. Their interest was not because of my Castilian manner of reading, however, but because of the extremely peculiar saint whose life it happened to be my turn to read.

It was a curious experience for me, also. San Benedicto José Labré was a truly engaging saint. As I was pointing out the peculiarities of the life of this man, Father Ferrer looked at me two or three times with surprise. It was the first time that he had heard the name of San Benedicto José Labré and in all probability he could not understand his case.

According to the text this saint had been a French citizen with no religious or civilian training, and without ecclesiastic office or benefice. A tramp. What the French call *clochard*. He walked the highways barefooted, with a sack on his back, and a stick. His friends were also vagabonds, beggars, who got along as best they could on the margin of civility and law. From time to time Benedicto called at a convent and asked to be admitted as a servant, saying that the highest ambition of his life was to become a friar. They gave him a piece of bread and brusquely sent him on his way. Sometimes, when they saw his rags, they gave him bread without deigning to speak to him. And sometimes they sent him packing, giving him only kindly words.

So he traveled through all the south of France and northern Italy. It was, if I remember correctly, toward the end of the eighteenth century, when the French were dancing the Carmagnole in the execution plazas and enacting their first democratic laws.

As I read I was thinking about the lay brother in his shop. He was not a vagabond, or ragged, but there was something about him of a marginal man. And if in my tone some sympathy for Benedicto José was evident, it was because of the lay brother in the workshop. Naturally my sympathy was not aroused by his virtues. What could I have known at that time about human virtue, and especially anyone's religious nature? I liked the lay brother because I could talk to him man to man, and the saintly vagabond because he was the exact opposite of Father Ferrer, who was always well brushed and combed and overnice.

Father Ferrer belonged to a community and our school was a convent. (The part where the monks lived was cloistered and there they led their monastic life.) Convents like ours and monks like Father Ferrer had humiliated and even insulted the holy man, according to the book. The poor vagabond Benedicto José had to sleep under bridges in the sad company of drunkards, thieves, even degenerates and murderers, in all probability. But during his last years all these people called him *saint*. And not because of his wisdom or the alms he gave. How could he give alms if he lived on charity? Nor because of sermons in the tapestried pulpits of cathedrals. These people must have seen other things in him, to call him saint. What? This mystery intrigued me.

After reading the first page of the biography I thought: "Just like the lay brother in his shop, Benedicto José had a liquid soul. The others saw his holiness because his soul came out his eyes, just like the lay brother's." But here I got into a muddle. Whose soul was liquid? The one who perceived the other or the one who let himself be perceived? Incapable of resolving this complicated problem I started thinking about the lay brother again. He could divine anguish or joy in others, but he also left the doors open so that we could enter into intimacy with him. I had a liquid soul too. I felt sure that the lay brother had told me this in earnest, and for nothing in the world would I allow them to have doubts about that quality which I considered a privilege. Although my liquid soul was not saintly but magical.

The reading ended with Benedicto José's arrival in Rome where he died as obscurely and wretchedly as he had lived.

Another detail made me link the saint to the lay brother in the shop. Just like the lay brother, Benedicto José was hard on himself, very gentle and kind to others. At least this is what the book said. Soon after his death came the vagabonds and thieves who involuntarily attracted the attention of the church. "The saint is dead," they repeated along the highways and in the nocturnal shelters of France and Italy. Long before the church did so, the vagabonds had canonized Benedicto José. I imagined him as dirty, ragged, with his sack on his back and a halo around his head. The dogs saw the halo and barked.

When the saint was in a jovial mood he joked, possibly like the old beggar who used to come to our house on Saturdays and cry out on the threshold in his thunderous voice:

"An alms, because if not . . ."

"If not, what?" some servant would ask.

"I'll go away," the beggar would timidly reply.

When I finished reading I was sure that I had succeeded in annoying Father Ferrer. In two passages of the text I had inserted an apparently innocuous phrase which, however, did establish a comparison: "like other ecclesiastics." Where the text read: "Benedicto José was neither cultured nor learned in academic sciences, nor careful in his dress and appearance . . ." I added: *"like other ecclesiastics."* And this addition went humming straight as an arrow at Father Ferrer. Without looking at him I could see his face like a pink spot in the air. And he had no halo.

The poor vagabond saint would never have dared come near our convent, I was thinking, with its entrance of Roman mosaic and two great doors, the second of which did not open until the bold caller had been identified. I found the idea of Father Ferrer's having to kneel before the ragged Benedicto José extraordinarily pleasant. But this saint was not in our chapel. He would never be in a chapel where the pulpit was inlaid with gold and silver, and where the frosted glass canopy etched with a dove, symbol of the holy spirit, shed torrents of inspiring light upon the orator preaching the sermon.

And yet Benedicto José was a saint and Father Ferrer only a sinner in a cassock. This struck me as just and wise.

The next day, Sunday, I wrote another and rather long letter to Valentina telling her about Ines, Prat's sweetheart. I said that even though she was pretty she was not fit to take off Valentina's shoes and stockings, and that she and Prat would be a good pair, since God breeds fools and they seek each other out. This expression was one of my favorites when I wanted to be satirical. In the postscript I wrote: "As I told you in my last, I am an avowed enemy of matrimony and a partisan of free love. I don't have time to explain today, but in the next letter I will tell you all about it. *Vale.*"

I had had another incident with Ervigio that day. Once in a while he asked me if I had received a letter from my sweetheart and I looked at him with murder in my eye, refusing to answer.

Pau was a year younger than Ervigio, who tyrannized him. Pau made some remark to him and Ervigio, looking over his shoulder, answered:

"I don't go around with you because the one who goes to bed with children gets soaking wet, et cetera."

To avoid the indecorous expression people usually say: *the one who goes to bed with children, et cetera.* But Ervigio put the *et cetera* where it did not belong and when it was superfluous. I told him so. Pau laughed and Ervigio boldly answered me back. I struck him. He hit me back. Then he sought refuge in the shadow of a friar. Ervigio had struck the last blow and I was resentful and apprehensive.

‡6‡

That night when I went to my cell I noticed that the last lights of the Constantine centenary had disappeared. The night no longer had those noble distances but now seemed stuck to my window, dark and commonplace, and the two power plant smokestacks looked taller and more vigilant.

Two days later I went to see the lay brother in his shop. He was very sad. Before making my presence known I had been watching him from the door. His cassock tucked up around his waist, the lay brother was mixing colors in a tin can near an alcohol lamp. The flame was barely visible in the daylight. He looked so melancholy that I hesitated to enter and wondered if I should go away. Finally, almost in a whisper, I said:

"Hey, brother . . ."

My voice must have echoed against the bare walls and cold corners. The brother was startled. Then he looked at me gravely:

"Does Father Ferrer know that you come to see me?"

"No. Why?"

He seemed confused.

"You should ask him for permission."

I saw that the nose had been glued on the pink marble head. The lay brother viewed his work with satisfaction, saying that he had not been able to resist the temptation to mend it. The statue had an expression the like of which I had never seen before. It occurred to me that it was the head of the vagabond saint. I talked about Benedicto José and related all the details that I could remember. I also told him how astonished I had been by this kind of saintliness.

"But what is it that astonishes you?"

"Well . . . a vagabond who does not work, who does nothing, who has never studied and who is, or looks like, an ignoramus. He shouldn't know much, I say, if he had never been to school."

The lay brother looked at the marble head:

"Don't you say that Benedicto José looks like this statue? And do you believe, little brother, that this is the head of a man who knows nothing?"

"No."

It might have been the head of a man who had never gone to school, but not of an ignoramus.

"Benedicto José had a liquid soul like ours and he could learn lots of things without studying," I said.

The lay brother asked me if I had said anything about a liquid soul to anybody and I fibbed and said no. "You know," he repeated, troubled, "that nothing intelligent can occur to me when talking about religion. I beg you, then, not to repeat anything I say outside the shop." I gave him my word and he asked:

"But why do you say this marble head has a liquid soul? This piece of stone has no soul, even though form is something like the soul of things, and in their own way all things have one, even those that seem most . . . crude."

I said that this sculptured face moved in the light like mine when I saw myself reflected in water. In still but rippling water.

"Your own face?"

"And sometimes others, when several of us boys peer into the Pardinas pond in my town. And one light comes and another goes."

"The Pardinas?"

"Yes, near the river. An old abandoned shrine is down there and it still has a bell. When the peasants come down the mountain to the village and pass through there, they say:

> *'Camporretuño*
> *without a single saint,*
> *they had one once upon a time*
> *but the devil made off with him.'*

"Camporretuño is the ancient name of all that district," I explained.

But there was the marble head, and I saw it as if it were at the bottom of a pool. The lay brother seemed interested and I continued: "That's why the face seems alive. Its ears are covered, but I'd say it's listening. The eyes are not looking at anything, yet they seem to be seeing. And furthermore, it is contented with life, yet could cry." After a pause the lay brother remarked:

"Yes, little brother, you are right about that. One could say that this man is contented with life even though he might be thinking frequently about death. At this moment I can imagine what the life of this individual was like, little brother. He is neither priest nor friar. He is a civilian. More than a civilian, a pagan. A patrician. He married very young, his wife died, he intended to marry again, but he was afraid that his new

wife would also die. Don't you see? He seems to be thinking that catastrophe lurks behind every joy. And now he is afraid of happiness. Don't
you think so? It's as if he wished to laugh and didn't dare. He's afraid.
But he is not a weak man, despite everything. He is some one, and that
is revealed in his forehead and eyebrows. Don't you agree?"

The lay brother seemed happy listening to himself.

"I glued the nose back on with a special kind of paste and now it is
tighter than before. Of course," he added sadly, "a statue should not have
breaks or repairs. It ought to be perfect."

He gazed at his work sorrowfully. He started mixing paint, muttering:
"I shouldn't be fixing up this head. If the nose broke it was for some
reason. I lacked unction and tempered nerves and, all things considered,
it should stay broken, my young friend. When things break it means they
should be broken."

Near the marble head was another one of wood, but turned toward the
wall. It was new, fresh, without a blemish. Underneath the chin was
a stick some six or eight inches long to be fastened between the shoulders
of some body that ought to be lying around somewhere. "This saint,"
I said, "doesn't look very serious."

The lay brother told me that he thought it looked like Father Ricart,
the priest in the observatory. To see whether the similarity really existed
or not he wanted to let several days go by without seeing the face. That's
why it was turned toward the wall.

"It's a saint you can't look at without laughing," I said. "Who is it?"

"St. Felipe Neri."

"Paint a beard on him and then he won't look like Father Ricart."

"But San Felipe didn't have a beard. If I put a beard on him he'll look
like St. Paul."

"Well, he doesn't look like a saint, that's a fact. He gives the impression
that he is making faces and feels like laughing and is trying to keep
from it."

"Didn't you know that San Felipe Neri was something of a jester? He
carried a tiny little monkey around with him tied with an enormous rope
like a ship's cable."

"What a saint!" I said skeptically. "How can saints be walking around
the world with monkeys?"

"But, man, have you forgotten Benedicto José Labré?"

"He didn't have any monkey."

"All right. But in any case happiness belongs in this world and God

wants us to laugh once in a while. But I see, little brother. You believe
that one must be solemn and important to be saved. Very well. I won't
deny it. But importance is given us by God, we are not obliged to give it
to ourselves. He gives it to us, little friend. To each the importance he
deserves. And the least He gives us is a thousand times greater than the
greatest that we can give ourselves. San Felipe Neri could play the clown,
if he liked. Why not? Others do when they want to and when they
do not."

Leaning toward me and lowering his voice, he added:

"Don't you know that true wisdom sometimes wears a clown's face?"

This was new to me. But I remembered that I had never been able to
laugh at a circus clown. The clowns impressed me as superior men who
did ridiculous things because they scorned us. I found the lay brother's
remark very complicated, however. Wisdom, a clown's face? I knew that
Father Ricart, the astronomer, was the most learned monk in the community and that he sometimes published important articles in *El Ebro*
magazine. And it was true that this father whom I had seen in the chapel
had a broad face with high brows, a small mouth and an astonished
expression.

"And you say that San Felipe Neri was a clown?"

"No, little brother, I would never say that," he answered, shaking his
head and noting that the paint mixture was just about right. "But he
could do clownish things without losing his virtuous and even saintly
character. Do you think that a man has to wear pontifical garb to be a
saint? Sobriety and solemnity are for God's ritual and service, but in
ordinary life a man is a man and often less. About this I can speak with
greater authority than others."

That day I helped him with his work, sandpapering two small boards.
We went on talking.

"Could San Felipe walk on his hands with his legs in the air?" I asked.

"I don't know, my little friend."

I clicked my tongue as a sign of regret and reproach. I liked to differ
with the lay brother. To provoke him again I told him about the image
of the Virgin in the chapel of the castle of Sancho Garcés Abarca, and
how Escanilla's wife brought a votive light once when they were changing the image's mantle. But when she saw only a small wooden pyramid
underneath the mantle she stared, wrinkled up her nose, and said:

"So that's all we have, is it? Well, I guess I'll just go right back home
with my little candle."

Then the lay brother recalled: "That's like the peasant who had seen the crucifix when it was still the branch of a cherry tree." We laughed and continued working. And the lay brother added, "Or like people who believe that miracles were only possible in antiquity. Do you believe in miracles, little brother?" I said that when God was walking the earth there could have been miracles, but that now it was not so likely. The lay brother exclaimed, "I knew that's what you were going to say." He stopped working and stood gazing at me with sadness.

"You believe that this period of time we are living in is the best in all the history of the world. Admit it, little brother. And that it is the only time when people really know what is going on. No? Why? Because you are alive. Not only this. But among all the other boys you also believe that what you think is best. All right. This happens to many. And it is because intelligence deceives them, deceives us. Maybe it can save us, but it can also ruin us, little brother. Come here and listen. Our time is not the best, but different, just like the past and future centuries. And everything was a miracle then, and everything is a miracle now. Isn't it a miracle that you don't believe in miracles? Isn't it a miracle that you are there on your two hooves?"—"Two feet," I corrected—"Well, two feet, and that you look at me and hear and understand me and still consider yourself above miracles? How can you stand there and think as you do? What have you done to be more than a piece of wood or stone? Ah, little brother. Smoke. We have nothing but smoke in our heads. Who are you, what have you done to deserve being able to talk and laugh and repeat the verses of Calderón de la Barca on the stage even though, to be quite frank, I do not like them? Come on, answer me."

I realized that the friar might be right, but things seemed simpler to me. "I am I," I told him. "I don't see any miracle in that."

"Ah, very well. You are you, little brother. But don't you ever wonder why you are you?"

"Well, each one is himself."

"Yes, but what has each one done to deserve being who he is?"

"God knows if we deserve to be or not."

"Ah, good. God knows. We agree on that, but you say it as the peasant would. You say it thinking: let God mind His own business. He must know what He is doing and why. That's what the cat would say, if it could speak. And meanwhile you eat good chops, play football, sleep like the blessed and enjoy life. You may even have a sweetheart, for all I know."

"Of course," I said.

"Very well, I don't blame you for that. But you say: God knows why. Well then, God has given you an intelligence so that you may try to find out also. And isn't that a miracle?"

"I don't deny it."

"Ay, little brother. I don't deny it. And you say it as if you were doing God a favor. Really, Pepe, at times you strike me as not being very intelligent."

Looking at me with a natural pity he dropped his brushes, came up to me and said, slowly:

"The other day you were reproaching me for not looking directly at people when I speak. You're right. I almost never look anyone in the eye. Because of the greatness of the miracle, my young friend. I look at you, it is true. Do you know why? You are not yet a man, and they are. And when Father Ferrer comes to the door and opens it and comes in, he, on two feet"—"On two *hooves*," I interrupted to say. The lay brother continued: "When he comes in looking so intelligent and says to me: 'Good morning, brother,' I am bowled over by the miracle for a moment. He comes, looks at me, speaks, saying that he wishes me a good morning. Furthermore, he sees that I am here, that I am the lay brother, that I am I. 'Good morning, lay brother,' he says to me, a lay friar. And he is a scholar. I am not. And he comes in and recognizes me. And I look at him and recognize him. Doesn't this seem like a series of miracles to you?"

"No indeed, not in the least."

Even though I was beginning to sense a mystery behind his words, I was still unconvinced. If he had used someone else as an example instead of Father Ferrer, it might have been more effective. The lay brother's face shone with inspired contentment as he talked. I looked at the marble head. The lay brother went on:

"Isn't it a miracle that my intelligence can move my hands, direct my eyes, and permit me to recognize, in a material object, a human being with his name and characteristics? Isn't it a miracle that my hands can make a human head out of a piece of wood?"

"No, because you learned how, and also because you have hammers and chisels."

"All right, little brother. Talking to you is like hammering on cold iron. It's a waste of time. No matter. Come along, bring me that saw. And don't be afraid of La Tarasca. It won't bite."

The saw was on top of the monster. I handed it to him.

The lay brother continued, showing great concern:

"You say that the marble head looks like Benedicto José? And that he has a liquid soul like you and me? How do you know? Because you have the impression you're seeing it under water?" The lay brother smiled, half-flattered and half-sad. "No. This head, even though it may have the same expression, cannot have a liquid soul. Because the first sign of the liquid soul is tears. How can it weep? You realize that's absurd."

"I don't cry either," I hastened to say.

In the intervals between the sound of sawing wood, the lay brother went on explaining:

"I'm not talking about the tears of grief or sadness. In that case everyone would have a liquid soul, for we all cry some time."

"Except me."

"All right, all right. So would you, little brother, if you had a great sorrow or someone in your family died."

"A sister of mine died a while back and I did no such thing."

"All right, but the soul is not liquid because of weeping when one is sad and grieving, but when one has no grief or pain at all. Only because of thinking that you are alive in the world and that God is concerned with you, just as if you were really important. Don't you understand? One weeps because of . . ."

"Joy? I saw one case in my family."

"No. With the amazement that comes from beginning to understand. All right, you are very young for that."

I asked him if he talked about these things with the friars.

"No, poor me. I only talk to you because you come to see me and ask questions. We started out talking about *Life Is a Dream* and since then we have gone on with La Tarasca and the images. I'd rather talk about the marble head than about your enemy Clotaldo."

I took the word out of his mouth:

> *Why, thou traitor vile and base,*
> *what need I to know the rest,*
> *since it is enough to know*
> *why I am my power to show,*
> *and the pride that fills my breast?*

The lay brother sighed:

"Look here, little brother. You would be an admirable person if you could just accept being one more and not special. You were born like everybody else. You will die like all the rest. Meanwhile you live like everyone. Do you hear? When you came to this very school your head was full of air. Would you dare confess it?"

"Why not? I thought that I was the lord of love, wisdom and dominations. I have been changing my ideas a bit recently."

I had entered the school two months ago, but it seemed like two years to me.

"The lord of dominations, too?" the lay brother asked. "Do you know what the dominations are?"

"Why, the battles won and empires gained."

"No, no. The dominations are an order of angels attending the Lord. The Lord has thrones, angelic powers, and dominations in the heavens. Attributes of power, but not like earthly ones. Very different. Without cannon or swords. Look, come here. Come over here, little brother."

He opened an enormous portfolio leaning against the wall and took out a sketch. It was unfinished and between broad pencil strokes were spots of color. "These are the dominations," he explained. I saw around two dozen angels, some with spread wings, others folded, some praying, almost all of them singing. They had faces of beautiful girls. Some had yellow and black wings, others blue and white. Sometimes one wing was open, and one folded, like the birds I caught in my hand when they tried to fly. One of the angels looked like Planibell, although surely it did not say *merde* in either French or Spanish. Another had a leg that was too thick.

"That angel's flat-footed and bowlegged," I said.

"All right, El Greco painted them like that. What do you think? These are the dominations."

If those were the dominations I had made a serious mistake. Lord of dominations? I also had my doubts about still being the lord of wisdom. Of love, perhaps. Suddenly the lay brother asked:

"What is your sweetheart's name?"

I did not answer. I finally said that I had firmly resolved not to mention her name at school, because neither the friars nor the other boys deserved to hear it. Ervigio made fun of everyone's sweetheart and had made up a song with the name of Prat's. No one would crack jokes with my sweetheart's name.

The lay brother looked at me surprised and said:

"Well, well. I see that you love your sweetheart."

About that time I received a letter from Valentina, with pictures. One of them had been cut down to eliminate someone I was not to see. I suspected her cousin. I wrote to Valentina inquiring about it. She answered by return mail saying that it was her sister Pilar, and that she had cut herself out of the picture because there were too many boys in my school, all busybodies and gossips. Pilar was right about that.

When I changed clothes one morning I discovered in the pocket of a new shirt a small silver coin. The money was not very important, since there was no opportunity to spend it at school. But occasionally we went out in two long lines to visit some interesting place like the mine pool, a picturesque spot. In the middle of a grove of carob trees there was a kind of cave with a tunnel at the back. We could not go inside as it was flooded with water and the gallery closed with an iron grill. It had been a magnesium mine and on the walls and roof were constellations of luminous little dots resembling stars. The water from the abandoned mine filled a large pool with green reflections and there was a low stone wall around the edge. We spent our money on the vendors who were usually at hand.

The coin in my shirt pocket was a revelation. My mother had put others in the clothing at the bottom of my trunk, figuring how long it would take me to spend what I had when leaving home. A minute later my cell was full of socks turned inside out, wrinkled shorts, undershirts strewn about. In many socks I found half a peseta. The yield of that search was considerable, in terms of my needs.

I put away the clothes again, happy with my treasure. My mother was mistaken if she thought that I was going to wait until I changed socks and underwear to find my money.

I talked to Planchat again and asked him to tell me about free love. With his ferocious air he said: "The thing's quite clear. What's the need of any blessing or red tape of the judges? Those are trifles and fools' traps." He had no intention of marrying. I listened to him with great curiosity.

I asked more questions. In our civic education class I had discovered the physiology of love, about which I had only had vague ideas before. I did not entirely believe the boys, although I took for granted that there was some truth in what they said. I did not find those half-notions as sensational as older people seem to think when they conceal them from children. For boys, sex is much less engaging than a mechanical bird or bicycle.

Free love seemed worthy of expert, heroic and unprejudiced persons like me. "I must explain it to Valentina," I thought.

‡ 7 ‡

At school it was easy to explore the basements, but one could only go up to the terraces on the top floor with some friar. Once in a while Brother Pedro would take a group of eight or ten boys up to see the observatory. Father Ricart demonstrated the big telescope and other apparatus. He also showed us the drawings he had made of stars and planets at different hours of the night and on different days.

When I went up almost the whole group from my table came along, and Prat besides. Since he had been in the observatory before, he put on airs and attempted to be our guide and lecture us. Among other things he whispered something absolutely absurd. Not even Caresse would have believed him. He said:

"You can look everywhere except at Venus because there women are taking sun baths. Real naked women. Anyone looking at Venus gets excommunicated."

Afraid that Brother Pedro might have heard him he raised his voice slightly, adding:

"I read it in an encyclopaedia of *astrology*."

He insisted that he had looked through the telescope at all the planets in the heavens except that one. He had also seen the moon, which was inhabited by men very different from earth men. Only their ears looked like ours. According to Prat the men in the moon were called selenites and were as slim as bar stools, despite the fact they had four feet. His details were so precise that you could not help believing in them to some extent. Skeptically, Planibell said to him: "Look here, Prat, you'll have to give me all of that in writing."

The observatory was circular and dark. Two small lamps with metal shades gave off a weak light on either side of the console above which the half-orange of the cupola turned imperceptibly. This had an open gash for the telescope to peer through. We spoke softly when we entered as if the place were a temple or someone had died. Pau opened his eyes wide and dared not make a sound.

Occasionally Prat anticipated Father Ricart in his explanations: the cupola moved by itself, from east to west, just like the telescope, obeying a clock mechanism synchronized with the celestial movement.

Pere asked a baby's question which shamed us. He wanted to know if he could see the gates of Heaven, because St. Peter was his patron saint. He supposed that he must be there with his wooden key.

Everybody laughed, but it was Father Ricart who laughed the hardest. This priest did have a face like the statue of the saint in the workshop. Smiling and not very . . . ascetic, shall we say. The lay brother was right. Father Ricart was smoking a Havana cigar, and having noticed something irreverent in us with respect to Pere's question he said, taking the cigar out of his mouth:

"My sons, the gates of Heaven are within our own souls."

Prat, more forward than usual, added:

"St. Peter! And why not St. Genevieve and the eleven thousand virgins?"

Without looking at Prat, the astronomer touched mysterious little wheels here and there, and said to him:

"Come, madcap, hush."

The eleven thousand virgins ought to be taking sun baths on Venus, I was thinking. Every so often something like a ratch or cogged wheel could be heard. The immense telescope turned with the cupola of the observatory and with the celestial vault itself.

Father Ricart was a little harsh with Prat in a friendly way. He had a finer sense of humor than Brother Pedro. He said that Prat was growing like a dinosaur. Sometimes he kept looking at him and added:

"You must be growing by stealth, at night. That way no one finds out about it."

Father Ricart's cheeks were red and he spoke as if he had too much air in his chest, in a cut-off and rather explosive way. Pau, suddenly feeling very bold around Prat, laughed over in the shadows at one side and repeated: "He called him a dinosaur." Prat heard and corrected him, offended: "That's not so. He said I'm growing like a dinosaur, which is different."

Prat had placed himself first in line to look through the telescope. He refused the help of the astronomer, saying that this was not his first experience and that he knew all about those machines. I tried to set my liquid soul in motion and looked at Father Ricart, thinking what a vast amount of knowledge was necessary to be really wise.

In the darkness, leaning against the wall, Brother Pedro was taking his snuff.

Seated on a rather high metal stool—I recalled the inhabitants of the moon—Prat put his face close to the complicated mechanism and, squinting one eye, started to look. The astronomer said:

"Now the telescope is pointing toward Mars because it is the moment of the opposition and I am making observations."

He showed us several drawings he had made on preceding nights, apparently all alike. "See how the planet is not round at all, but somewhat flattened, just like the earth, and that it has two caps of ice, one on each pole, like two white calottes."

Very seriously Pau remarked:

"You can't see the people in those drawings."

Prat, whose head had disappeared among the tubes, wheels and gears, declared:

"I see them now."

Father Ricart turned around, vexed:

"What people do you see, simpleton?"

Prat said:

"I don't see the people, but I do see their shining swords and bayonets."

The astronomer put his face close to Prat's:

"You're lying like a trooper. And besides, you can't see a thing because you're looking through a screw."

The lens was only an ordinary one such as field glasses have, and it was very hard to find. Prat had been confused among so many wheels and tubes, but did not want to admit it:

"Word of honor, Father Ricart."

"I'm telling you that you are looking through a screw, bedouin."

He made him get off the stool and had me sit down. Prat protested and the astronomer said:

"Don't you say a word to me, because we've known each other for a long time now."

Seated on the stool I put my right eye where the friar indicated. At first I only saw luminous, moving and fugitive spots. Soon, however, I saw a white disc, motionless in the center of the lens. It was slightly smaller than the moon seen with the naked eye. It was not quite white, but pinkish. Light green shadows were visible now and then. And some very fine lines came down from the North Pole toward the center. The North

and South poles were both very white. When I mentioned the lines
Father Ricart said:

"Those are the famous canals."

Then he added: "They are not real canals, as you know, but that's
what astronomers have taken to calling them."

I kept looking. Everybody else was still. In his corner Brother Pedro
sneezed. Planibell was in line behind me and touched my shoulder impatiently for me to let him have his turn. Pau asked:

"What else do you see?"

Before I could answer Father Ricart remarked:

"I hope you don't see soldiers too."

"I didn't say I saw soldiers," said Prat from the shadows. "Just the
light shining on their swords."

Brother Pedro interrupted to say:

"Last year you said you heard beating drums and marching troops."

Realizing that everyone was against him Prat explained that what he
had said last year was true and that the beating drums were sounds coming up from the street. Anybody could have been confused. Besides,
things might have been different on Mars last year.

"Maybe that day was the king's birthday," said Planibell, with irony.

"And there were celebrations," I added.

"Yes, civic celebrations," concluded Brother Pedro sagaciously.

What I saw did not interest me greatly. But I felt obliged to say:

"Some day people will go to Mars the way they now go to America."

"Nonsense," said Prat.

"Why not? Pepe is right."

Brother Pedro took my side, but since this monk usually helped the
weak against the strong, his help depressed me. I did not want to be weak.
I was younger, that was all. Planibell sat down before the telescope and
to keep him from going wrong, like Prat, the astronomer put his finger
beside the lens. I was more interested in the mysteries of the observatory
itself than in those of the heavens and I started looking around. On a
small table there was an open notebook full of algebraic formulas and
notes. I thought of the lay brother and wished I might be there with him.
Father Ricart was silent, chewing his cigar. On the small table beside
the notebook was a clay casserole full of cigarette butts. I concluded:
"Some nights the astronomer does not come down to the refectory for
supper because he doesn't want to leave the telescope and then they send

his supper up to him. That casserole must have contained a stew or a good roast and afterward the friar used it as an ash tray." Father Ricart smoked constantly, and as he talked and exhaled, the smoke formed curious ladders in the air.

Pere and Pau took their turns at the telescope, but dared not say a word after Prat's silly behavior. Ventós, a boy I barely knew, had gone up with us. He came from Villalonga, and looked like a little Moor or Hindu. He never laughed. Homesickness was responsible for his being so taciturn. He could not get used to living away from his parents, which I found quite incomprehensible.

Brother Pedro, holding a large blue-checked handkerchief in his hand, when invited by the astronomer to have a look, remarked:

"I see all that better with my eyes closed, Father Ricart."

The brother at times seemed to know a great deal about life; but in the way that peasants do, silent and sullen.

The observatory vault and telescope, which was like an enormous cannon, baffled me and seemed more mysterious than the whole of creation. The only thing needed to make the emotion complete was that little sound of a ratch heard from time to time in an indeterminable place.

Father Ricart did have a clown's face and looked as if he were going to pull suns and stars out of his sleeve to surprise not us, but an audience in some unknown place. Pere looked at him as if he were—while still being a clown—the St. Peter he was looking for among the constellations.

This mysterious spot seemed more suitable for praying than the chapel itself. I would like to have been there alone with Valentina. The astronomer was talking about light-years, millions of light-years. Trillions of light-years. In a low voice I asked the brother how far it was from where we were to Saturn. The astronomer, who heard me, answered my question by saying that the longest distance in the sky was nothing compared to the distances we have inside, between fear and hope, for instance. The fear of a death we do not know. The hope of an immortality we cannot imagine. He looked at me and asked:

"Don't you agree?"

I was grateful to him for talking to me seriously and I wanted to tell him that I was not afraid. Father Ricart's confidence intoxicated me even though I did not know exactly what he meant.

"I know what immortality is," I said. "It is like a statue."

Brother Pedro blew his nose, making a sound like the lowing of a cow. Prat again insisted that last year he had seen strange things on

Mars. When he saw that no one believed him he started biting his nails, suddenly indifferent to everything and eager to leave. Brother Pedro repeated:

"You must shut your eyes to see the heavens."

"I only close one," interrupted Prat, uncomprehending. "You should only close one eye."

"And put the other against a screw, eh?"

Prat crossed over to the other side of the rotunda when he realized that we did not take him seriously. Furtively he took two or three cigarettes from a pack on a small table, hiding them in his closed hand. Then, quite casually, he put his hand in his pocket. As always, Brother Pedro saw everything. He winked at me and started cracking jokes in Catalonian with the words Prat and *Rat-penat* (which means bat and also convict or punished rat).

We left with nothing unusual having happened. Prat asked the friar:

"Say, Brother, isn't it true that Mars is the god of war?"

"And Caco the god of thieves."

"Well, I read in books this size"—and he indicated the size of a missal as if this made the reference conclusive—"that Mars is the god of war and that's why they call the step of soldiers martial when they march off to war with music and drums."

Planibell said:

"No one goes to war with drums or music."

I remembered my father who, although he had never been a soldier, sometimes talked about war and told, as if he had seen them, of Aragonese soldiers attacking with bayonets while the regimental band played the *jota*.

The brothers Pere and Pau had become quite attached to me. Possibly because their study hall desks were next to mine and we were neighbors in the refectory, in addition to the fact that I was a "sophomore," they "freshmen." Or it might have been because they were both very blond —which in children suggests a delicate and refined personality—whereas I was very dark. In any case, something drew them to me with a reverential expression. I reacted with the natural inclination to protect them.

In Latin class the professor, an old but still robust and energetic priest, assigned us problems that obliged us to think for ourselves. Throughout the course we students remained divided into two bands: Carthaginians and Romans. I had gone over to the Carthaginians, preferring Hannibal to Scipio, and I was one of the best among them, thanks to the Latin lessons given me in my village by the chaplain of the convent of Santa Clara.

The teacher dictated a classic sentence to us, from whom I do not recall, asking us to make written comment upon it. The sentence was *Parva propria magna, magna aliena parva*. The teacher, whom we called *Chaveta*—Pivot—his favorite word for describing the most dissimilar things, was rubbing his hands together as he watched us jot down the Latin sentence. His use of the word *pivot* was picturesque: Sertorius had lost his pivot (become rattled) on different occasions in his life. Only a warrior who had lost his pivot would dream of being liberal and democratic, said the priest. Julius Caesar had also lost his reason, that is to say, his pivot.

Father Ferrer had been spared nicknames because he terrorized us with his smiles. Brother Pedro had been spared for the opposite reason: his friendly reticence.

Whenever I returned to the lay brother's workshop I could not escape the feeling that I was in the presence of someone who deserved to be pitied, for some reason or other. I mistook his simplicity for weakness. An important man had to be energetic, competent, commanding, as well as worthy of honors and triumphs in the Roman fashion, a bronze statue with a horse, equestrian, that is to say. Consequently the poor lay brother's authority over me—even though I was unaware of it and in spite of everything—was an unfathomable mystery.

That day the lay brother was working and humming through his nose. When he saw me his face lit up:

"Come, boy, and close the door," he said.

Then he added, with childish joy:

"Don't you know? I have a companion."

He pointed to a cat seated on the crosspiece of a crucifix that was lying on a carpenter's bench. The lay brother hastened to remark that since this image had not been blessed or consecrated, the cat's sitting on it implied no irreverence. The confusion of objects in the shop was such that if the lay brother had not called it to my attention, it would have taken me a long time to discover the cat.

"What do you think? We have mice. And mice when they find a piece of waxed wood chew on it, finally eating it. Not all, of course, just the surface, the part with its nice little sauce. So I had to fetch the cat. It's a beautiful animal, as you see, and a good friend, only he considers himself too smart. He thinks he knows more than seems right in a cat. But if that happens to us men, why should we be surprised?"

I stroked the animal, which pressed its cheek against my hand, purring. This sudden friendliness was always a pleasant surprise to me. The lay brother said:

"We know each other now and get along very well. The poor thing has work to do in this shop. But the mice are not his main interest. He spends his leisure hours glued to the windowpane watching the birds, and when he sees one close up he gets so excited his teeth chatter and cheeks tremble. The poor little thing can't help it."

I looked around for the marble head. I inquired about it and the lay brother said, rather surprised:

"Why does it interest you so much, little brother?"

"It's the most beautiful head I ever saw."

He looked at me slowly:

"You are a tempting devil. For some days I have been playing with the idea of smashing it and this morning I was resolved to do it when you arrived."

He pointed to a spot where several objects were covered with a cloth:
"There it is. Underneath there."

I was on my way when I heard him add in a supplicating tone:

"No, little brother. Don't uncover it. Leave it as it is. I understand that you want to see it and that you like it. So do I. Too well. It's just that I succeeded in giving it the contradictory expressions of a liquid soul, that's true. It has love in its eyes, indifference and pain in the line of the mouth. It has strength in its profile, plus goodness and refinement. It has, we might say, hope in the hollows of its eyes, and also desperation. Do you know something, little brother? What impresses me most in these statues is the silence. For it is a silence that appears to have been created by the artist himself, by me. Haven't you noticed how often the head of a stranger who does not speak is a head that says a thousand things all at the same time? Extraordinary things, too, important, sublime things. When he does finally speak he disappoints us because he only says one thing at a time. Yes, little brother. With his tone of voice and the insignificance of what he says he destroys the mystery. So long as he kept still our soul went out to him and attributed to him the grandeurs, confusions, yearnings and above all, the contradictions of our own life. He was good and he was bad. He was a saint and he was a criminal. He was alive and he was dead. But when he spoke the bird flew away."

"What bird?"

"The miraculous bird, little brother. But don't think that the miraculous is only to be found in the silence we were talking about. It goes much deeper than that. I am going to uncover the head and you will see."

After doing so he returned to my side and went on talking:

"That head has everything. Even the doubt of the pagans in ancient times. You, little brother, will ask: what doubt? A doubt that you will have when you're grown up, because you are intelligent. And that I have now. Look at that head. It could be Benedicto José, I don't deny it. It is above happiness and misfortune, pleasure and pain, love and hatred. Yet there is doubt in that head and the French saint you were telling me about never had any doubts, I feel sure. Otherwise he could not have lived as he did. Yes, I doubt sometimes. When I'm alone. But recently doubt has been giving way to a new feeling. Yes, little brother: the pleasure of having created a work like this with my own hands. Do you understand? Do I have the right to such happiness? I don't know. The only thing one must know is that there is pain in the world and that this pain can become prayer. Don't interrupt. Wait, brother. There are many ways of praying. What we are doing now, you listening and I speaking, and that head looking at us, is praying. Yes, little brother. When you make an effort to understand me, you are praying. But when I was making that head, I was not praying. When I make a head like this, do you know what I am thinking? Well, that I am very smart. And I am praying to myself, as if I were God. Go on, little brother, take this hammer and hit it on the forehead. In spite of my laughter, I mean it. Go ahead, smack it hard. You children like to smash things. Here is a good opportunity."

I picked up the large, heavy hammer and hesitated. The lay brother kept on smiling:

"Smash it."

"No."

"Why not?"

"It looks alive. I can't. How can I hit it on the forehead?"

I left the hammer on the carpenter's bench, near the dozing cat, which opened its eyes and perked up its ears. The lay brother said we were both cowards for not daring to break a marble head. And he looked at the cat.

"This little animal has a liquid soul, too, in its own way. A tiny liquid soul. See? Now it's looking at you and thinking: this boy is young. He is younger than the friar and comes to the workshop because he's fed up with studying. But I am going to attract the cat's attention and you will see what happens."

He coughed twice and when the animal turned its head the lay brother looked at it tenderly. With a rather silly tenderness. The cat, feeling caressed by the friar's look, purred contentedly. When the lay brother stopped looking at it the purring ceased and the cat's eyes half-closed. The lay brother coughed again and the cat woke up and purred again, friendly, as soon as their eyes met. Then it folded its little front paws and napped again.

"What's its name?"

"The poor little thing lived in the pantry and had a name it certainly did not deserve," the lay brother answered.

"What?"

"The brother steward called him Asmodeus."

"Who's Asmodeus?"

"A devil, little brother. A lame devil. I think it's unfair. The cat has a slight limp, it's true, because he caught his paw in a mousetrap and hurt it, but I don't think he'll always be lame because he's gradually getting better, and when he gets excited at the sight of birds he forgets about it and doesn't limp at all."

As I did not see the infant Jesus around I asked where the statue was. The lay brother said:

"On the altar. Do you know how many electric lights he'll have around him? Two hundred and sixty, all of them forming roses and lilies amidst a golden forest. For the Christmas festivities, which will begin in a few days. You won't be here because you'll be going home to eat turkey and marzipan. Everybody's leaving day after tomorrow."

"Everybody but me," I said. "Well, Pere and Pau are not going either, because their grandmother died yesterday."

"Oh, little brother. Did someone die in your family, too?"

"No, I'm not going because my family is moving to Zaragoza."

"Ah, I see. So you're going to live in the capital?"

I said yes. In one way I was pleased. But in another I was sorry because Valentina and I would be separated. Half of my family had already gone to Zaragoza and the others were still in the village. How many lamps had he said the infant Jesus would have?

"Two hundred and sixty. I must go now to finish setting everything up. But first I'll go down to the basement for some friction tape."

Between his hands he was pressing two boards that had just been glued together.

"I can go, if you like," I told him.

I liked the basement. It was like the hold of one of Salgari's ships.

"Wait. Take this note to the brother steward. Otherwise he won't give it to you."

He wrote two lines on a piece of paper. I left at a run. In the cellars other things in common use were stored besides provisions: tools of all kinds, boxes of chalk, notebooks, unpainted pine desks, and cloth for blouses, sheets, towels. Also, apparently, modeling clay.

But most of that great space was pantry. Tins of food, dozens of hams, tons of potatoes, hundreds of sacks of beans and chick-peas, boxes of dried fruit, chocolate, eggs, bacon. There was a dense and succulent odor about it. The ceilings were vaulted and the piled up boxes formed extensive passageways. In one of them, at the foot of a wall made of barrels and sacks, was a small wooden table and there was the steward, an old man with a decomposed and soft fattiness. He was wearing flannel trousers, a shirt with a Roman collar, and a canvas duster. There was no dust in the basements. On the contrary, it was very damp down there. The duster seemed to be stuck to his body the way damp shirts cling in summertime. The steward, dubbed "Don Genitive" by Ervigio, was every busy at his table, surrounded by pens and bottles of inks of different colors.

My first impression was that I had seen the steward before. I finally decided that he must be the same friar I had seen in the cellars of the castle of Sancho Garcés Abarca.

I supposed that he was keeping the pantry accounts in those notebooks. The steward stuck his pen behind his ear and raising his small hands laughed in a high key:

"I don't know who you are, little fox, but I know very well what you're after."

He got up, took two pieces of chocolate out of a metal box and gave them to me. In spite of his fat and his years—he must have been well over fifty—his movements were agile. Meanwhile I glanced at his notebooks and saw that he was copying Latin verbs in the most graceful Gothic script imaginable. The infinitives were written in the margin in red ink, the first person in green. The name of the verb along with the different tenses in large blue capitals. When he saw me so curious, he said:

"I am studying for the priesthood. Didn't you know? I've been studying for ten years. Next year I'll receive minor orders."

And again he laughed "hee-hee-hee." On the table were the leftovers
of his lunch and as he turned his face toward me I caught a slight whiff
of wine. Not brandy or any other vicious drink, naturally, but plain and
honest red wine. I remembered the refrain of a children's song about a
gluttonous little mouse that lived inside a cheese. That was the impression the steward made on me, as he looked at me with grandmotherly
complacency and said:

"You are a fine Latinist, I suppose. A fine and foxy little Latinist."

He looked bloated, as if he were stuffed with Latin verbs from head
to toe. I told him that we were doing some work in Latin for Father
Chaveta.

"And who is Father Chaveta?" he asked, suddenly grave. "Isn't that
the reverend father Don Fulgencio Honorato Cabrera?"

"Yes indeed, nobody else."

"I know that Ervigio gives them all nicknames. Look, I have them
jotted down here."

He showed me a long list of nicknames. Some of them I knew, while
others were new to me. They belonged to teachers of advanced courses
and others. There, for instance, was the very reverend Father Jenaro de
la *Calambrera*—Cramp-ton, the physics teacher. This nickname undoubtedly referred to the high tension currents of the window gratings. I
suppose the rumor was unfounded, but the boys liked to talk. They also
said that there were guns and munitions stored in long locked cases.
This I do believe.

Among the names on the steward's list familiar to me was "Chamus-
quina"—"Scorched." I did not have to be told that this belonged to Father
Lucas. The poor fellow had to put up with the boys' bad jokes because of
the fortuitous fact that he had been able to escape from a burning convent
that had been set on fire.

The brother steward seemed to forgive me for calling the Latin teacher
Father Chaveta and asked me what kind of Latin exercise we were doing.

"*Parva propria magna, magna aliena parva.*"

The steward folded his arms, tee-hee-ed again and said:

"Let's see, and what do you have to say about all this?"

My liquid soul suggested to me that this steward had a secret ambition
to be a Latin professor some day. But he had better hurry, because the
little hair left on his head was already silvery. Instead of answering I in

turn asked him what he was doing with that list of nicknames. He told me that he was studying our reasons for giving the teachers those names. No one had called him by any nickname, and they would not either. With that he offered me another piece of chocolate, and I realized that the poor fellow hoped to escape nicknaming through bribery. But too late. Ervigio had gotten ahead of him.

I handed him the note from the lay brother and he read it and gave me a roll of friction tape. I left, with the steward's "tee-hee" ringing in my ears. Back in the studio the lay brother looked sad:

"Now you see," he said to me. "You don't want to break that head. Tell me the truth. You're afraid. Why are you afraid? Since you mentioned it, I don't dare either. And there it is looking at us."

When I went back to the patio Father Ferrer tried to find out where I had been. I had lied before, but now it was impossible. I said nothing and thought: "Ah, he is spying on me." Suspecting that the lay brother could be blamed for my absences I kept still, preferring to be deprived of recess periods for two days.

I received a letter from Valentina. She was counting the days until Christmas—the poor little thing did not know that I would not be there— and told me that the sixty crickets we had put in the garden would die, which was a great pity. Her father kept repeating: "If only we get a good freeze that will put an end to all of them." But I read that letter with an omniscient grin. If freezes put an end to crickets, they would long since have disappeared from the earth. Those little animals knew how to burrow into the ground and wait for spring. When spring came Valentina's father would really see something.

In the P.S., Valentina said that if I was not in favor of matrimony, neither was she. She asked me to explain more about free love. And she copied a long paragraph on love, mystical love, from her prayer book.

I answered, telling her all about the observatory and the marble head and the lay brother in the workshop, saying that in spite of his wisdom— and he was wiser than Father Ferrer—he asked me for advice sometimes. Concerning free love, I said that it was the most appropriate for two people who were really in love, and promised her another letter soon with complete information on the subject. In a long P.S. I told her that my father would not let me go to the village for the holidays.

The students started packing their bags and two days later Pere, Pau and I were the only ones left at school. The building was all ours. We were lost in the refectory where we ate, talking a blue streak, with no one around to say anything to us, and no need to mount the platform and read. Afterward we went to the chapel, basement, study halls, everywhere except the cloister and observatory. No one bothered about us. The days seemed much longer in spite of my helping the lay brother in the chapel and accompanying Brother Pedro everywhere on his rounds.

Besides these voluntary activities I still had time to read. I exhausted the supply of Salgari's books and had to fall back on the lives of the saints. The missionaries sacrificed by the savage peoples impressed me, but the fact that they accepted martyrdom without making any effort to defend themselves robbed their acts of a great deal of human significance. How much more convincing was Magellan's death, fighting in hand-to-hand combat with the Indians on an island in the Pacific!

I moved about freely among the books, but the dictionaries were still locked up, and I looked through the glass at volumes R through V. Nevertheless I was happy during those days and I now think that this small prohibition made my freedom more pleasant. As for Valentina and not being with her, I found it uncomfortable but not tragic. For the time being her letters were enough.

Pere, Pau and I went out one morning with a *fámulo*—a lay servant who cleaned rooms, made beds and attended to other chores—and we took advantage of the outing to see the city. The *fámulo* was a rascal and used bad-sounding words and made fun of the priests. When he passed a pretty girl he would cock his uniform cap at a jaunty angle, pushing it back to one side, and say:

"What a girl!"

We walked through the heart of the city. Even though it no longer had the festival lighting of the Constantine centennial, the little city seemed to have such a fantastic beauty about it that I envied the people of Reus for being able to live there. To be a clerk, streetcar conductor, or waiter in a restaurant in that city would be wonderful indeed.

In the center of town the streets were as straight, the plazas as clean, the shops as magnificent as in Zaragoza itself. And I never tired of gazing at the General Prim monument in the Plaza de la Constitución, a life-size bronze horse and rider on a marble pedestal. This man had been assassinated, they said, and thereafter glory for me was a question of being shot and having a statue like that one in a plaza paved with small stones glistening in the rain.

The Christmas festivities were not so gay as at home, but they had their charm. Most outstanding was the chapel, shining like a golden ember. In the middle of the altar was the lay brother's image of the infant Jesus, lying on a bed of shining metal garlands and flowers covered with tiny lights. The child, his arms opened wide, looked as if he were inviting us to fondle him, and everything about him was so natural that if he had not had the halo back of his head we would have taken him for a living child.

One of those evenings I stayed in my room for a long while looking at the city in the rain. Ordinarily no student was ever in his room—the spot least familiar to him—except to sleep. Each cell had an iron bed with two pillows and a blue coverlet. Beside the window a clothes rack. On the other side an iron lavatory. Two chairs and a night table completed the furnishings on a floor of cold mosaic.

That evening I was in my room for a long time alone. And for the first time in my life I felt the anguish of absence. I felt lonely and far away. Naturally, I was thinking of Valentina. And that curtain of fine rain with shining threads amidst the gray, the blurred silhouettes of the buildings, the power plant smokestacks with their wet brick that turned from gray to a bright pink, were filling me with a sadness whose depths were lost in the remoteness of time, perhaps—I now think—before my birth. I would have liked to make my solitude more absolute and irremediable. I wanted to go where there would never be anyone but Valentina and me, and feel there the ultimate depths not only of delight but anguish, too.

At dusk I was afraid—I would never have admitted it, but I was—and returned to the chapel, now filling with the faithful. I sat with the community in the choir on the second floor behind screens through which we could see the audience but not be seen. The priests sang Christmas hymns to the Virgin to the accompaniment of the organ, and between songs they let Pere, Pau and me blow on clay whistles filled with water that produced marvellous imitations of birdsongs. The *fámulos* helped us in this task and Brother Pedro acted as conductor of the bird orchestra.

The organ music was also accompanied by tambourines, triangles (one was hanging on the corner of the organ), and castanets, and the lay brother was playing a flageolet called the *tenora*. With all this there was quite a din inside the church. The lights, the infant Jesus, the well-dressed worshippers, gave the chapel a gala atmosphere and an innocent gaiety:

> *In the portal of Bethlehem*
> *was born a red carnation*
> *which became a purple lily*
> *for the world's redemption.*

I sang with all my might and the brothers Pere and Pau were not to be outdone. The lay brother's face was radiant with inner joy, his eyes fixed on the altar with the infant in the center. I went over to him and asked:

"You made him and now you pray to him?"

He acted as if he were waking up:

"Hush, little brother. Didn't I explain that to you in the shop? All children who are born are like him. And don't they come from God just the same as this one? Who moved my hand when I was carving him? Who gave me the light of day to work by? Who made the wood? Ay, little brother, hush. Hush and pray."

The lay brother's eyes were moist. In them—so I thought—his liquid soul was visible. But now they were singing again, only this time in Catalonian. Pau nudged me with his elbow and said:

"I can sure sing this one. It's *La Pastoreta*—The Little Shepherdess."

For they sang not only religious but secular songs as well.

> *What will we give the little shepherdess,*
> *what will we give her to take her to the ball?*
> *I would give her a pretty little bonnet*
> *and in the little mountain take her for a stroll.*
> *For in the little mountain it never rains or snows*
> *and down in the valley the wind forever blows.*

Here they started all over again with the first line, while Pere and Pau went on with two or three more which, apparently, were not to be sung, because Father Ferrer hurried over with a finger on his lips. All the "don'ts"—small or large—always came from Father Ferrer, in the choir, classroom, or patio. As we were trying to decide what the order meant, the two brothers sang out, bawling like young calves:

> *In the shadow, in the shadow, in the little shady place*
> *flowers and violets and rosemary.*

Everybody was in the choir, even the steward, who had put on a cassock.

Afterward we went to the dining hall. We three students, as usual, ate in the immense empty room, but at dessert time Brother Pedro came to fetch us, leading us into the community refectory, a large room with a horseshoe-shaped table. All the priests and brothers were still in their places, having just eaten. On the walls there was only one picture of Jesus performing the miracle of the loaves and the fishes, and a crucifix above the head of the table. In the middle of the room, between the two sides of the horseshoe, was a wide empty place. There Pere, Pau and I sat down in front of the Father Superior, who was presiding over the table.

We three boys were in shirt sleeves, although I was wearing the vest of my green velveteen suit with silver watch-chain visible. Pere and Pau, being a year younger than I, seemed much more childish. We ate our dessert with the community. There were several kinds of marzipan, Jijona turron, roast almond caramel, Alicante turron, and fruit creams. We stuffed ourselves like the proverbial sheepshearer's son.

The lay brother was at one end of the table, attentive and silent.

Father Ferrer started joking and, looking at me, told how on a night like this the self-respecting Aragonese danced the *jota*. What a mania for the *jota* and dancing! I did not say anything, but Pere and Pau started shouting and saying that they would gladly do it. The bad thing was the absence of music. The lay brother went to the choir for his *tenora*. Meanwhile Father Ferrer said to me:

"Why don't you dance, too?"

I looked at him but still said nothing. I would have danced, had it not been a question of pleasing him. At that moment Pau felt so happy to be on such familiar terms with the friars that he was ready not only to dance, but dance on his head. He said to me in Catalonian:

"*Portes armilla i no balles?*—You're wearing a vest and not dancing?"

Everybody laughed. The lay brother's *tenora* could be heard as he came through the corridors playing. Brother Pedro had picked up a tambourine and the metal discs were jingling, the parchment thumping. Seeing that the two friars I considered my special friends were taking part in the celebration I changed my mind. When the lay brother entered the refectory, the music of the flageolet and tambourine so stirred up the atmosphere that dancing was natural and unforced. I started dancing with Pere and Pau. If I felt ill at ease for a moment I looked at Brother Pedro and, to encourage me perhaps, he leaped about striking the tambourine on his knees. The lay brother's cheeks were so exaggeratedly puffed out as he blew on his *tenora* that he looked as if he had two oranges in his mouth. We kept on dancing. But when the dance rhythm ended and the *tenora* marked the beginning of the song, I sang:

The sun rises in the valley,
in Monteargón the moon,
and in the castle of Apiés
the wheel of fate and fortune.

Pere, who had no desire to be left out, sang in Catalonian when it was
his turn:

For lunch they give me onions,
for dinner, onions and bread,
to keep from lighting a fire,
onions for supper I'm fed.

The monks guffawed. Again we danced. Father Ferrer was silent and
wore the grave look of someone disappointed about something. I was
thinking: "Ah, now I see. You wanted me to refuse to dance because
you had probably told the Father Superior that I am unsociable, as you
told me once." For me at that time, to be unsociable was to refuse to
dance. In some way it is true. Thinking that over I danced more lustily
still.

They applauded us enthusiastically. The Superior asked me to recite
something from *Life Is a Dream* and, still short of breath from the
dancing, I repeated:

And the rich man dreams of gold,
gilding cares it scarce conceals,
and the poor man dreams he feels
want and misery and cold.
Dreams he too who rank would hold,
dreams who bears toil's rough-ribbed hands,
dreams who wrong for wrong demands,
and in fine, throughout the earth,
all men dream, whate'er their birth,
and yet no one understands.

Again they applauded and I saw that among those applauding were
the lay brother and the famous scholar Father Ricart. Happily I recalled
that this priest had called Prat a dinosaur, a madcap and a bedouin.
The feastmaking soon ended. In the corridor I heard the brother

steward in charge of the basements, saying to Father Ferrer in a mournful tone:

"As I'm telling you, father, if I had followed the advice I give to others, I would now be at least a canon."

‡ 8 ‡

Boys always end big holidays with some illness. Pau had indigestion, Pere a cold. I, tonsillitis. Since they had no fever they could continue their normal everyday lives, the masters of the convent. With high fever I had to stay in bed. But I had paper and pen and wrote to Valentina, more or less as follows:

"I must tell you that I am well (ADG) and, as I told you in my two previous letters, the best love is what they call free love. This consists in our living together without any wedding at all, because matrimony is a moronic affair. Now you see what it is.

"I could not leave for my vacation. My father and yours have agreed that we must not see each other, but some day I'll get out of here, and then what?

"In our grandparents' time matrimony was taken for granted, but there weren't any electric lights then. Now it's different. Think about free love and tell me how you feel about it. With free love I will love you just the same as now, because more is impossible. You will see.

"About the lord of dominations, I must tell you that this was a joke. The dominations are choirs of angels, some green, some yellow, and still others a mixture, and God commands in all of them. Some are quite flat-footed and bowlegged, but that doesn't matter. I am stronger than other boys my age and size. This comes from my living in the country where it is not like it is here, because in the country the people live a more natural life and when they are old they die very healthy.

"Here I gave Prat a beating even though he is bigger, but that's because of something that happened my first day at school. I will tell you about it verbally.

Your unforgettable

Pepe.

"p.s.—I have seen Mars, the moon, the sun and the Milky Way with St. James seated on his throne.—*Vale*."

In a second postscript I added a song which I had "composed" for her:

A gold-finch cardelina
flew down from the high Pyrenees
to see an old sweetheart of mine
whose name is Valentina.

I spent the whole day in bed, quite bored. In the morning, about ten o'clock, Brother Pedro had come up to see me.

"Here I come with the holy oils," he said, jokingly.

He put a glass of orange juice and an aspirin tablet on the night table and left. The other boys were not allowed to come near me, for fear of contagion.

That day the sky was overcast and intermittently the rain hung out her sad curtains. At four o'clock in the afternoon the cell was dark and until eight, when Pere and Pau came up to bed and Brother Pedro brought me my supper, I was in darkness. For four hours the only light I saw was a small rectangle of yellowish light cast on the floor by the grilled peep-hole in my door.

In those four hours my fever rose and I saw and felt strange things that I still remember perfectly today. Through the windowpanes I could see distant clouds mingling with the smoke from the power plant chimneys. They were much taller than the school building, but from my bed I could see the top.

The sheets were cold. The high fever gave strange projections to my fear. I did not think of anything as I lay there half-asleep with the queer sensation that I was melting into the shadows of the room. When I woke up I thought of Valentina again. My reflections were pessimistic, but I liked them. The more pessimistic the better. I liked to think that I would never see her again. But if I did not see her—because my family was moving to Zaragoza—how would I be able to live without her? I regarded this as a hopeless piece of bad luck and would have preferred to become ill, worse, really ill. The low clouds and rain depressed me. I would have liked to die, if only to bother my family. What could I do to make my throat worse? A childish solution occurred to me: I would hold my breath. I held it as long as I could and only breathed again when I felt that I was suffocating. I felt sure that if I repeated this I would finally make my throat worse. But I did not notice anything strange and attributed it to the fact that I had not held my breath long enough. Then

something curious happened. When I thought that I was about to suffocate, I saw the shadows of the room turning rose-colored. This intrigued
me and I decided to hold it even longer. But when I noticed that the air
around me was deep red, I became frightened.

I repeated the experiment until my ears buzzed and the shadows
turned rose-colored, then black. After that, and at once, utterly red.
Frightened, I started breathing normally. And thinking of pleasant
things. The marble head, for instance. I had a strange idea. It occurred
to me that I myself, José Garcés, could be a saint like the tramp, Benedicto
José, without studying or learning anything. Or like the clown, San
Felipe Neri. Although I preferred the vagabond. Sometimes I felt as if
I already had a yellow halo around my head. But then I thought: this
is absurd. If I told the friars they would think I was crazy. Nevertheless
I could be a martyr, if not a saint. And martyrs had halos. In reality I
was a martyr or at least heroically unhappy, far from Valentina.
Maybe the halo came from that unhappiness, which was approaching
martyrdom. The halo of the martyrs of love.

The next day I was able to get up and resume my normal life. It was
still raining and everything seemed wet and far removed from the world.

In the chapel I thought I saw the yellow halo around my head. My
head of a martyr of paternal cruelty.

In the afternoon I went to the study hall and since I was alone and
no one was watching, I wandered among the bookshelves taking out
books and putting them back. Once again I looked to see if the dictionaries were accessible, but the shelves on that side had sliding glass doors
that were locked.

Some days before I had read a story about an ancient king whose
enemies wanted to poison him. They were unsuccessful because the
king always drank out of a cup made from the horn of a unicorn, in
which all poisons became harmless. I was intrigued by the unicorn and
went to Brother Pedro to ask him for the dictionary once more. After
great deliberation the brother took out volume U, looked up unicorn,
saying when he found it:

"Go ahead, read fast, because I have things to do and can't stay
around here all afternoon."

I read, fascinated by the engravings—I had never seen a horse with a
horn in its forehead. The dictionary said that it was a very fierce animal,
but gentle with virtuous women, and that only a virgin could approach

and master it. I returned the volume and while the friar was locking it up again, I asked:

"What is a virgin?"

The friar looked as if he regretted his indulgence. Finally he asked:

"Don't you know who the Virgin Mary is?"

"Yes."

"What do you know about her?"

"That she was a virgin before giving birth, when giving birth, and after giving birth. But . . . aren't there other virgins?"

The friar looked uncomfortable:

"Of course, many more. But the other virgins are . . . profane, if one may express it in this way."

He took out an enormous watch, looked at the time, and remarked that it was growing late. He left hurriedly and I heard him scurrying down the corridors. Outside, the rain continued falling.

I wanted to read, but the books on the lower shelves were almost all books of devotion, and I had already read the pleasure books. I stood on a chair and tried to reach the higher ones. The first volume had the word "love" on the back. And it was a thick book. It must contain a great amount of love. Although it was written in Latin, I decided that its teachings might therefore be more secret and difficult, so I took it. I assumed that I could understand a part of it all.

I realized immediately that the book was full of important things. The author was a priest, a Fray André So-and-so, chaplain of the King of France, and he had written it in the year 1170. Yesterday, as they say. It dealt with the courts of love in Provence and cited the names of persons living at the time, and even the opinions of a Pope, Innocent the Fifth of Avignon. It all seemed full of mystery and authority. Love. In those Gothic letters on the cover the word "love" looked really imposing. I was thinking of Valentina.

I took the book to my desk beside a large window opening onto the second floor cloister. Beyond the cloister it was still raining, sounding like a prayer in an ancient tongue. I took out paper and pencil, just in case a friar happened by. In this way dissimulation would be simpler.

I began with the index. My curiosity had been caught by a chapter with the following caption: "True love, can it exist between husband and wife?" The very question seemed scandalous to me. One by one I read many opinions of distinguished people: princesses, dukes, priests, all of whom said no. Matrimony made an obligation of love. The reasons, very long and philosophical, did not worry me, but the categorical affirmation made my esteem for Planchat suddenly rise. He had undoubtedly read this book.

I jotted down the Latin sentence where the affirmation was clearer, intending to send it to Valentina and other friends, translated. Still today I can recall it in Latin: *Dicimus enim et stabilito tenore firmamus amorem non posse inter duos jugales suas extendere vires.* (We affirm and sustain by the present declaration that love cannot extend its rights to two married people.) Then came the names of over fifty men and women quite evidently respectable in their time. Even priests and monks. It never occurred to me then that marriage in the twelfth century must have been quite different from marriage today. At that time the husband's rights extended to the life of the woman, and there were other and equally cruel conditions. If the husband could kill his wife, fidelity did not mean much. The wife was more conscious of fear than love.

The book awakened such greediness and inquisitiveness in me that I wanted to read it not page by page but all together and at once. Nevertheless there were parts I did not understand.

Naturally, I thought of Valentina, her parents and mine. That Latin sentence, ringing of law and edict, dogma and liturgy, seemed to me to be without appeal. Those very persons signing the tremendous declaration had written a code of love with over thirty parts. They all sounded sweet to my ears because they dealt with love. I remember some more or less accurately because I copied them and tried to learn them by heart, as some lawyers learn the legal codes:

"No one can be deprived of his right to love." (I thought of Don Arturo's arbitrariness.)

"Through the action of jealousy the aching of love is always increasing."

In those days I found particularly apt that expression about the "aching of love," because solitude and rain were making me feel for the first time that love could be the cause of sadness, and again and again I came to think of myself as a martyr with my halo and everything.

Still there were things in that code of love I could not understand. For example:

"The person who loves, grows pale in the presence of the beloved."

"The one in love is always fearful."

Then the code ended in a sad and contradictory way, saying that there was nothing against a man being loved by two women or a woman by two men. This was intolerable, and reminded me of Valentina's cousin, the son of the "nefarious politician."

The evening was painfully sad. The rain continued. It was not always rainy in Reus, but I don't remember the days of splendid sunshine so well. That evening it seemed as if the whole world were weeping because I had not gone home and could not be with Valentina. The first days of Christmas vacation were enjoyable because of the pleasing novelty of being alone in the school. Then I began to feel as if the universe were crashing on top of me. Neither Pere nor Pau nor I went to the storeroom to get bicycles or skates. We stayed inside all day long.

Now I turned pages and pages of the chaplain Fray André's book, bewildered by that last conclusion of the code of love. Nevertheless I could very well take what I needed about free love and leave the rest. The things that struck me as improper I took to be grownups' nonsense.

At dusk I heard a sound in the corridor leading to the study hall. It was one of those sounds that suggest the apparition of a phantom: slippers brushing the floor in a rhythmical way, and an asthmatic breathing. I supposed it was the Father Superior and having no time to put the book back on the shelf, I hid it in my desk and started writing a letter.

When the Superior saw me, he said:

"So it's you, Pepe. What are you doing here all alone?"

"Writing to my family."

The father came closer. He seemed to want to profit by the occasion to tell me something. He sat down at the next desk, beside me:

"Since you are here, I want to talk to you. They tell me that your marks are not good and you can imagine that it hurts me to have to send them to your family. I don't like to displease your father."

"You can send them. It doesn't matter," I answered, without the least concern.

"What do you mean, it doesn't matter? What are you saying? You must remember that your father loves you and is paying to have you educated to be a useful citizen."

"I don't believe my father is paying for anything except to get me out of the house. He doesn't want me there. Don't you see that right now he has obliged me to stay at school instead of going home on vacation like the rest?"

"Come, come. How can you think that?"

"Because it's true."

"What do you base this on?"

My own voice sounded impressive to me. I prepared to talk, sounding as authoritarian as possible. With the Superior I could not help being sincere. And desiring to convince him, I recalled the facts on which my most effective arguments were based. Once, for instance, when I was going down the street with my father an acquaintance passed us and remarked: "Don José, you don't have to tell me who the lad is because it stares one in the face. He's the very image of you." Later my father kept looking at me with a cold expression and said, "I don't know what's wrong. But I don't see the slightest resemblance between you and me." I commented to the Father Superior:

"He doesn't love me because I don't look like him."

"Come, come now. Don't be silly."

"Really, Father. He thinks that I am not his child."

The Superior looked at me astounded. His amazement made me feel ridiculous and I dug up more arguments:

"My mother doesn't think I am either. One day she said that I could not be a son of hers, and that someone must have exchanged me with somebody else when I was a baby in my cradle."

The Superior burst out laughing. Then he asked me to go to Pere and Pau when I finished the letter, because they were looking for me. He glanced my way as if he wished to go on talking, yet said nothing. In view of that I continued:

"In our country there are cases of babies exchanged in the cradle. I have heard such stories."

I realized that the Superior did not believe me. Outside the rain continued falling. Without saying another word the Father Superior got up, leisurely went toward the bookshelves, picked out a book and slowly left again.

Those places in the school where I had formerly been with the other boys, and which were now only for me, gave me a magical sensation of power.

I returned to my book on love.

The rain shut me off from the world. It could turn each cloister into a Moorish castle or phantom ship. The sound of the rain produced sadness, yet it was a pleasant sadness. I recalled afternoons spent at the Pardinas farm near my village when suddenly it started raining on what they called the "burned pond"—a broad pool—out of which the ducks came running, making a great racket. One afternoon I was there with Valentina, in a window, watching the rain. The rain was falling on the pool and Valentina said that little bubbles like glass were forming on the surface of the water and that when she was little she thought they were glass marbles. The ducks ran for shelter. In a truncated tower was a stork nest and when Valentina saw that the two big birds were getting wet she said, very solemnly, that she would like to take out an umbrella to cover the storks. I reassured her, saying that they had a feather cape better than all the raincoats and umbrellas in the world.

Valentina said many quaint things. She also told how the year before when she saw some boys on roller skates she thought that someone had put those things on their feet because they could not walk.

That evening in the school I also remembered an old beggar who passed by the Pardinas sometimes. Smiling, he would look at me and Valentina, and his smile made me somewhat uneasy, while Valentina smiled back at him with utter confidence. Then she said to me:

"Everybody seems so good to me when I'm with you."

I had evidently changed a great deal at school. I dared to admit to myself now and then that I was afraid. This, I believe, was because I was obliged to live with bigger and stronger boys around whom it would not pay to make a pretense of being brave.

This rain did not look like the rain I used to see at the Pardinas, at the castle of Sancho Abarca, and in the village. It hung a gray curtain behind the arches of the cloister and gracefully slid off the outside cornices and pillars. It was not cold. It was never cold in Reus.

Having finished my notes from the book on love, I replaced it on the shelf. Then I went down to the first floor, avoiding the places where I imagined Pau and Pere might be. I looked in the lay brother's shop. He was not there. I knew that a few days before he had gone to visit his family in a neighboring village. No one was in the workshop. No one but the cat, I mean, seated as always on the crosspiece of the wooden crucifix. The persistent curtain of rain could be seen through the wide windows. The cat opened its eyes and when it heard my steps looked at me. Then it closed them again.

I was vainly looking for the marble head when I heard a sound at the door. It was Pere and Pau, who had followed me, but they seemed intimidated by the place and hesitated. I went up to them:

"Outside. No one is allowed in here."

I was thinking about the secrets in the construction of the images, the wooden chests and false knees covered with gold-embroidered quilts, which should not be seen by small boys "without imagination"—those were the lay brother's words. I went out with them and locked the door, saying:

"This place is off bounds."

Just to make sure I went back to the door, and took out the key and stuck it in my belt. Pau looked at me admiringly. Pere, as if to compensate for my authority, showed me a letter from his father with a twenty-five peseta note inside. I thought of my father. "He doesn't send me money," I decided, "because I am not his son." This reflection gave me a strange feeling of importance in my own eyes.

From that day forward I determined to study less and be a worse student, convinced that I had a right to take revenge on my father for having left me at school during vacation. I stuck to it with the greatest zeal.

When it was dark the rain mattered less. The artificial light altered our feelings and we three boys went to the dining hall to play royal goose. This is a game that three or more can play, and it was Pere's favorite. Pau took small numbered balls out of a leather pouch. He referred to the number only by allusions and poetic similes that we already knew. For example, instead of fifteen he would say "the pretty girl." Instead of twenty-two, "the two baby ducks." For seventy-seven, the "Civil Guard." Instead of thirteen, "dirty face," and so on.

Although Pere and Pau were almost alike physically, their characters were very different. Pere was irritable and touchy, Pau patient and without nerves. I was on the point of asking them if they knew what a *virgin* was, but it seemed to me humiliating since they were smaller. I would wait and ask Planchat, because Brother Pedro's reaction warned me that it had something to do with sex and that I need not expect further enlightenment from any other friar.

Another letter came from Valentina. She said that she agreed with me about free love. But then I did not hear from her for many days and my sister Concha wrote that she had been ill, and was not allowed to go out. It seems that one day when there were guests at table and the talk was of marriage, her mother, Doña Julia, had remarked to Pilar that marriage was the most important goal in life. Whereupon Valentina had interrupted and scandalized them with her ideas. She began by saying that marriage was something moronic. Then she declared that she would never marry.

"And you who have a sweetheart say that?" her mother asked.

"Yes, mamma. But Pepe and I are not going to marry, because we believe in free love."

The father pounded the table so hard the salt shakers danced and, holding back his laughter, he ordered Valentina to leave the dining room. Not knowing whether to take offense or laugh, he muttered: "The little sniveler . . . I wonder where on earth she gets such ideas?" What amazed Don Arturo was the fact that his reprimands did not make the slightest impression on the girl.

‡9‡

Shortly afterward the students started returning, noisy and excited, as always.

I wrote to Valentina telling her that love was impossible between husband and wife and that later I would send her the declaration in Latin signed by the French scholars. Then I told her that I had a halo, that she had one also, since we were martyrs of our fathers and suffered for love, and that we both had liquid souls. I would explain all this to her when I wrote again Sunday afternoon.

The boys talked about their gifts received on the day of the Magi. Many still believed in Melchior, Gaspar and Balthasar. I myself had misgivings at times, and then as suddenly believed in their existence. This depended on who was talking. The innocent faith of the younger boys was contagious.

In study hall Brother Pedro sometimes looked at me and winked as he put snuff into his big porous nostrils. Presiding over the hall the brother looked like an ancient stone idol. Tired of immobility and silence I would occasionally go up to him and ask, wanting to know how much longer the torture of "vigils" would last:

"Do you know what time it is?"

The brother would take out his large nickel-plated watch, snap open the cover, put it back and say:

"Yes, I know."

It was another of his peasant jokes. Then I would ask him to tell me and, feigning surprise, he would say:

"Very gladly. It is ten after seven. But you only asked me if I knew the time."

The next day during recess I went to the shop. The lay brother had returned. He received me very happily and, still smiling, told me that his father was very ill and might die any day. I expressed surprise that he could talk so glibly about it and the friar arched his brows:

"Why not? What don't you understand?"

"It looks to me as if you were going to be glad of your father's death."

"Little brother, no, I wouldn't go so far as to say that . . . But the poor dear has suffered a great deal in his life and his reward is waiting for him. Of course I will not be glad when he dies. But neither does it strike me as catastrophe for him to change his eighty sad years for an eternity of beatitude. Doesn't that seem natural to you? Or, out of egotism, should I wish him to go on living among illnesses, shadows and bitter memories? No, little brother. That would be absurd. I love my father dearly, but I cannot love him more than God himself. It's not easy for people to understand, but you are different."

I was different? For me death was a terrible misfortune and only the death of Valentina's father or of mine could be accepted otherwise (especially my father's). I could not believe that the case of the lay brother's father was similar.

I brought the lay brother up to date on recent events. I had had a high fever and been in bed, and no one came up to see me. I also told him that since then I had a yellow halo around my head occasionally.

After a moment's reflection, he said:

"You'd better not come to the shop so frequently."

He believed that this illusion of the halo was the result of some of our conversations.

"It's better not to talk about such things," he added.

"Why?"

"Ordinary people don't understand them."

"But I do have a halo. Don't you think so?"

"Of course I do."

This really amazed me. Laughing I told him so. I knew that I did not have a halo, but I liked to imagine that I could, especially when I was unhappy.

"But you really do have one," the lay brother said.

"Can you see it?"

"Yes. I see it on everyone. All men have one."

"No. You forget about thieves, bandits, murderers, Moors, renegades
. . . "

"They too," added the lay brother, lowering his voice and glancing
around. "Only we don't see it. To see the criminal's halo one must know
more than you and I do, little brother."

Then, seeing me still confused, he added:

"Everybody has a halo, but please don't repeat these things outside
the shop. As I told you, little friend, everybody has a halo because there
is not a single man without his conscience and in it all men suffer and
purge their sins before death. The Providence that directs and watches
over everything knows full well that the wicked are just like everybody
else. When a criminal or a saint does something good or bad, with the
light or darkness of the good or evil they have done, Providence prepares
other events for them which no one can escape. And they suffer or
rejoice again, and so a chain is formed binding them to the rock of
destiny, just like us and everyone. Living has merit, little brother. A
great deal of merit. And all men deserve their halo, the good as well as
the bad, just because they are born."

The lay brother removed the canvas from the marble head. Behind it
the last afternoon sun was shining on an old broken cornucopia. The lay
friar contemplated his work:

"Now," he said, "this head does seem to be living on its own. It is
more alive than you or I, since we don't dare do anything to it."

I was thinking of what he had said about the halo. It seemed all right
to me, even though I could not accept the idea that someone like Father
Ferrer, and boys like Prat and Ervigio, would also have one. And older
men like my father, even less. The idea that my father could have a halo
troubled me.

"Now I see, little brother. You want the halo for yourself and your
friends, in any case. And that is not fair. One must be generous and
desire the good of others. Not only the halo, but everything. Do you
know what? If you were older, you would understand me. Every living
thing deserves respect and love. Some day you will be grown up. And
maybe you will go on being selfish and proud. And I will dare not speak
to you, brother. That's why I talk to you now. I will see you when you
are grown up and won't know what to say. For I will be so inferior to
you that I will feel ashamed to even look at you. Listen to me carefully,
now. We can have everything, but we will lose everything in life.
Everything, except what we have voluntarily given. Generosity and love

alone can save us, little brother. What is love? Above all, the desire not to be more than anybody else and to do what it is our duty to do in life. Don't you see? When you were speaking ill of Father Ferrer you were unhappy. Don't deny it, for I know better. Who knows to what extremes of unhappiness that hatred could carry you? On the other hand, if you tried to perform some act of humility around him and the boys who make you angry, you would see at once how much happier you would be. It's good business, to be good. I'm not asking you to do these things, understand, little brother. I'm just giving you examples. Such things are not done because another mentions them. Although when opportune it will be well for you to show them you do not hate them, and to forget any grudges you may hold. Are you listening, little donkey?"

"That's what the gospel says. Love your enemies. But honestly, brother, it's pure nonsense and you know it."

"Why?"

"Well, it's as plain as the nose on your face. Love people we don't like! Bah! Impossible!"

We went on talking about other things.

I mulled over this for several days and finally one Sunday morning, after confession and communion, I went to the patio ready to make friends with everybody. Maybe the lay brother was right. But Brother Pedro was there instead of Father Ferrer. Prat was trying to adjust some skates he had just put on and was sitting doubled up like a jackknife at the foot of a column. I went up to help him, screwed the metal clamps just right, then fastened the straps and he was ready. Prat bit his nails but did not object. I was almost in a kneeling position. When I finished, Prat skated away without a word of thanks. Then he came flying back, grabbed hold of a column, swung around it and said:

"Castellá, if you want me to give Ervigio a good beating, just say the word."

I wanted to tell him that I had done that myself several times already and needed no help, but held my tongue. I was waiting for Ervigio with quite different intentions. When that busybody saw me approaching he started reciting, grotesquely referring to what he had just seen and making theatrical gestures:

> *"In humble submission I bow,*
> *your clemency to implore."*

Ervigio could not possibly imagine that I had just saved him from a couple of Prat's punches. I looked at his head recalling what the lay brother had said about halos. With Ervigio he was mistaken. Some days Ervigio had a fried garlic head incapable of being related to anything as noble as a halo. But in spite of everything I told him:

"We are friends and you can say anything you like because I won't take offense."

I gave him a friendly slap on the back and left him completely baffled. As I moved off I heard him say to Pau:

"Prat has a new slave now: the Castilian."

But there was no resentment or sarcasm in his tone. Leaning back against the pillar, I watched the white clouds in the sky and felt grateful to myself. Then I remembered that somehow I had to find out what a virgin was. Maybe Planibell would know. Planibell had also seen me tying on Prat's skates. Acting as if he were losing his balance—he also was skating—he grabbed me and both of us rolled over on the ground. I skinned my knee, and it bled. The culprit tried to get away from that stern administrator of justice, Father Ferrer—one had to recognize this quality in him sometimes—who had suddenly appeared. He called him a savage and canceled his recess periods. I tried to help Planibell, insisting that it was all my fault. Bewildered, Planibell repeated:

"You see? He says so himself."

I went limping to the infirmary where they painted my knee with iodine. The priest still blamed Planibell, whom I timidly defended. I was so insistent, however, that Father Ferrer finally excused him. Then he looked at me with a distant expression, saying:

"What's the matter with you, Pepe? Don't you feel well?"

In the afternoon I wrote Valentina, sending her the Latin sentence on love. I also told her about the halo and that everybody had one except a few people like Pilar.

In study hall I loaned my colored pencils to Pau and helped Pere with a difficult problem in geometry.

I continued treating everyone like this and three days later I realized that I was beginning to have a saintly reputation. The brothers Pere and Pau were all but kneeling at my feet when I walked by. I went to the lay brother and told him what was happening. Everybody was talking about my saintliness. It was very difficult to be one of the common herd and pass unnoticed. The lay brother shook his head as if being a saint, or passing for one, were a misfortune. Then he said:

"You're right. You must avoid their talking about you, little brother."
Aware that the lay brother was right I decided then and there to be as
discreet as possible. I had noticed that after talking about my saintliness
the boys began to leave me alone when small details making me appear selfish and swaggering revealed that I was not so saintly. Their
disappointment in my saintliness evidently made me quite uninteresting.

I left the initiative for pranks up to Prat or Ervigio. Even jokes on
Caresse, who was usually my victim, just as Pau was Planibell's, and
Ventós Prat's. The strange thing was that we defended our victims from
the others, following the classical tradition by which the slave acquires
rights with his master.

One day in the gymnasium I asked Ervigio if he knew what a virgin
was. I told him about the unicorn and how only a virgin could approach
and master it. Ervigio said:

"All women named Mary are virgins. Don't you see that they are
baptized under the patronage of a virgin? María de la Concepción, María
de los Desamparados, María de las Angustias, and so on with them all.
Everybody knows that."

The boy, however, was busy with a secret plan, not concerning me
but Caresse. He went up to him looking very surprised, and asking:

"What's the matter with you? Aren't you in pain? You look as if your
head were swollen."

Caresse had taken off his uniform cap, and hung it on the hatrack.
Caresse looked at Ervigio and said:

"Get out of my presence, traitor."

He had recently taken to calling everybody traitor as a result of his
disillusionment with our friendship. The curious thing was that in spite
of everything he immediately fell into some new trap. He was busy
doing gymnastic exercises. Other companions, made wise by Ervigio,
went up to Caresse to say that his head appeared to be swollen. Meanwhile Ervigio had taken Caresse's cap and put inside, under the hatband,
several strips of paper so neatly that nothing wrong could be detected
from the outside.

When Caresse finished his exercises, went to put on his cap and
found that it would not go on, he turned pale. Ervigio ran up to console
him:

"With a week in bed and maybe a little operation on the ciriac glands
you'll be all right again."

"What are the ciriac glands?" Caresse asked.

We tried to pull his cap down on his head and when he saw that it really would not go on, Ervigio said:

"What a pity, at your age. It's the same case exactly as my aunt, only they took out her caryatid and then she got well."

Caresse went to Brother Pedro, who discovered the paper under the hat-band. The next day everyone was telling how Caresse had got the swell head in the gymnasium. The boy lost his patience and handed out two or three punches with his long, bony hands.

A few days later we made an excursion to the Riudecañas dam. We went by train, occupying several coaches, and well-provisioned with bags of peanuts, apples, oranges. Brother Pedro, despite the inconveniences of a trip of this kind, seemed to have a good time also.

We arrived in mid-morning.

The reservoir was like them all: an enormous stone dam built across a river bed. The dammed-up waters reflected a clear and tranquil blue sky.

We were shown the chambers containing the machinery for opening the locks, the turbine generators, and told about the resistance force of the dam, the expansion force of the water, and the energy liberated when the master lock was open. No one paid much attention. Ervigio was on the lookout for the peasants he called "*bucardos*"—wild goats—so as to have a good laugh at their expense. He spoke to them in a mixture of Catalonian and Castilian, saying incongruous things very seriously. They eyed him suspiciously.

We ate out in the open in an enjoyable rustic way.

At the bottom of the dam was an echoing wall and the boys went down there to shout. While Pere and I were arguing about how many villages in the valley would be flooded if the dam were destroyed, Pau came to tell us about the echo. Then Prat. I told Pau that there were echoes and echoes, and that they were not all alike. Ervigio nudged me with his elbow and said under his breath: "*Redeu*, this Pau swallows anything." Then he winked and whispered something in my ear. Pau asked:

"What kinds of echoes do you say there are?"

"There are some very shameless ones," I answered, thinking of what Ervigio had whispered.

Ervigio was in league with Prat to play a trick on Pau. I also was on more friendly terms with Prat since helping him to put on his skates.

Prat was hiding behind some rocks in front of the spot where the echo was formed.

We took Pau to the foot of the dam and first he called out the name of the reservoir:

"Riudecaaaaañas!"

The echo returned his voice, although slightly changed:

"Pelaaaanas!" (The word means "jackass.")

Unable to believe his ears Pau said: "It's wrong. Didn't you hear it make a mistake?"

Then he shouted the name of his town:

"Ampoooosta!"

And the echo replied:

"Idioooooota!"

Again Pau was amazed: "It doesn't say exactly the same thing that I do. It changes some letters." And he shouted again:

"This is Paaaau . . ."

"You are Paaaau . . ."

The boy turned around facing me:

"Now the echo's answering all right," he said.

We were all very serious. Pau shouted a woman's name, his sweetheart's, perhaps:

"Loooola!"

"Laaaay-low!"

"It's wrong again," Pau remarked, "and every time it makes a mistake it insults me."

He ran for Brother Pedro who came to see what was going on. Pau told him that the echo there was insulting people.

Again Pau shouted his name and Prat, who had no idea that the friar was listening, said two or three dirty words rhyming with "Pau." Brother Pedro was seized with a fit of spasmodic laughter that spread to all of us. Then the whole thing became boring and we left.

After our picnic lunch an airplane flew overhead in the direction of Tarragona. The friar told us that eight years before he had seen the first plane fly over Catalonia, and that it went from Reus to Tarragona in thirty-five minutes. The aviator was a Frenchman named Vedrines.

Brother Pedro did not believe that such inventions were necessary. Why such haste? I told him about an uncle of mine, a farmer, who had been advised to buy a car. The salesman argued: "Let us imagine that you start out with that car at nine o'clock in the morning. Well, at ten you're in Zaragoza." My uncle replied: "That wouldn't suit me. What would I do at ten o'clock in Zaragoza?"

I talked to no student about the lay brother in the shop because I considered his friendship a secret privilege. I think, however, that Brother Pedro knew of it. That friar knew everything related to us. I started speaking ill of Ervigio. The brother smiled, looked at me, took a pinch of snuff, and said nothing. I was never able to make him say anything bad about anybody.

A first-year boy hurt himself in the thigh when trying to break up a dead branch for firewood. The wound was small but deep, and three-cornered. While they were dressing it—it bled very little—I saw a layer of white fat that looked like pork flesh inside the wound and I wondered if maybe it could not be fried like bacon. I knew this was a stupid idea, but I could not help it.

We returned by train and at five o'clock were at school again.

I had misgivings regarding what Ervigio had told me about the virginity of the Marys, and asked Planibell. He was also confused and when I repeated Ervigio's opinion he said yes, that virgins were the women named Mary. I thought with discouragement of my little sister Mary. The idea of hunting the unicorn with her struck me as degrading.

Ervigio used to come up to my desk on Sunday afternoons when I was writing letters and look over my shoulder. I would cover the paper with my hand and turn around to look at him. Then he would go away dancing and repeating:

"Ines, Ines, Inesita, Ines . . ."

Ervigio used the name of Prat's cousin to refer to anybody's sweetheart, as well as love letters and everything related to these important questions in our private lives.

‡ 10 ‡

That evening I went to see the lay brother in his workshop. And something truly extraordinary happened. I opened the door, went in, but saw no one. Yet I felt certain the lay brother was there. Before long I discovered him flat on his back on the floor, at the foot of a St. Michael whose raised sword seemed to be threatening him. My first impression was that he was dead. From the crosspiece of the crucifix the cat looked at me and the friar, indifferent. I started backing my way out, but without taking my eyes off the lay brother who was still on the floor, motionless. "He must be dead," I said to myself, not knowing what to do, whether to run tell the other friars or keep the secret. As I reached the door I thought the lay brother moved. I went on out without making a sound and waited outside a moment. Then I peeked in and saw my friend at work, just as if nothing had happened. I went inside again. Two outside windows were wide open.

As soon as the friar saw me he was aware of my astonishment and asked:

"Little brother, you were in here before and saw me lying on the floor, didn't you?"

I said nothing. It seemed scandalous to me to have seen someone "dead" and then see him alive again. The lay brother realized this and repeated:

"You came, saw me lying on the floor, and ran away frightened. Isn't that right?"

I nodded. The friar continued:

"It's all over now. I opened the windows. I'm better now, although my head is heavy and my stomach upset. I may have to go to the lavatory to vomit. What did you think when you saw me lying here? That I was drunk? That I was dead?"

"No. I thought that you were in a trance like Santa Teresa."

The friar wanted to laugh but could not. He covered his mouth with his hands and turned paler still. Then he gave me a strained look and said:

"I lighted a little charcoal burner to do some tin soldering and the carbon monoxide fumes went up to my head. The same thing happened to me once before, brother. Now with the windows open there's nothing to worry about. As you see I'm pretty worthless. Weak. Two whiffs of gas and the man's flat on his back with his toes turned up. Were you scared?"

"No. Only when I found you dead at the feet of St. Michael, with his sword raised, you did look like the devil."

Then the friar laughed. And so did I. I did not believe what the lay brother had told me, however. He was lying, I thought, trying to cover up something, some grownups' secret, perhaps, like that of the virgins,

about which no one cared to give information. The friar sat down for a
moment and held his head in his hands.

"It's nothing," he said, "but I could have died, little brother. There
have been cases."

Encouraged by his words, I said:

"You were good and dead when I saw you."

"No, not dead. Just fainted."

"And what did you see when you were . . . in that fainting spell?
Did you see heaven? Or hell?"

"No, little brother. I saw nothing. Nothing at all."

I still did not believe him. I had the impression that I had discovered
something I should not talk about, and maybe that was why I wanted
so terribly to talk. The lay brother understood this and did not even ask
me to keep the secret, taking for granted that it would be useless. He
showed me the lighted burner and repeated: "That gives off carbon
monoxide. Understand? If you breathed this gas from near by you would
also faint, brother. That can happen to anybody."

I only half-believed what I was hearing. There was a mystery in it all
which I related to the halo at that moment. My eyes were searching for
the marble head. Another mystery. In one corner La Tarasca stood
staring with lowered head as if ready to attack. The cat on the crucifix
sometimes had a sea-green color in its eyes with a tiny perpendicular slit
of light. I wondered what the cat thought of so many figures and images?
Would it be as impressed as I was? The friar pushed me toward the door:

"Run along, son. I'm not feeling well. You might get sick, too. Run
along now and come back later, if you like, when the air is clean."

I left and, naturally, the first thing I did was to tell Planibell what had
happened, in strict secrecy. I had seen the lay brother looking as if he
were dead, I said. Planibell listened with a certain air of superiority and
explained that this was called trance and rapture, but that he did not
believe this was the case with him since such things cannot happen to a
lay brother. One must be an ordained priest.

I told Pere and Pau. They thought Planibell was lying since Santa
Teresa was not a priest and yet had frequently been in a state of rapture.
What happened to the lay brother was neither trance nor rapture, but
ecstasy. And they showed me an engraving in a prayer book of Saint
Ignatius in ecstasy. I kept on discussing this with the boys and within
a few days all the students were saying that the lay brother was a saint

and performing miracles. This time our gossip did not reach the ears of Father Ferrer or the other friars.

We played in our classes, especially French, although our teachers were not aware of this. I sat near the door where I had a little paper figure that we called the farmer's dog, all set to perform. It had four feet and a head and could just as well have been a cat or lion as a dog. I set it on the floor in front of the door. Pushed along by the draft blowing under the door the farmer's paper dog gaily raced over the mosaic floor. The teacher could not see it because he was behind a table on a low platform. When the dog ran it was hard to keep from laughing. Especially for the gullible Caresse who finally annoyed the teacher and was punished.

We had an extremely devout group of Catalonian boys among us. They were quiet, obedient, and two or three of them talked of entering the priesthood. They were greatly impressed by my account of the lay brother's ecstasy or trance, and listened with open mouths.

A few days later one of them whose name was Tarsicio told me that he was going to become a priest and would finish his training when he was nineteen years old. I said that they would surely not accept him unless he could produce an official document of "Catalaunum purity." The three other pious boys who were always hanging around Tarsicio came up to find out what Catalaunum purity was.

"It means being able to prove," I explained very seriously, "that your ancestors had nothing to do with the death of Jesus."

I added, as if it were a well-known fact, that Jesus was killed by Catalonians.

"No, no, that isn't so. The Jews killed him," someone said very excitedly.

I feigned the calm of an adult:

"Don't you know that Pontius Pilate was governor of Tarragona before being governor of Judaea? Well, if you don't know your history, it's not my fault. But you can look it up in the encyclopedia."

Tarragona was very close to Reus. Not over an hour by train and it was an established fact that the Romans had been there. This disarmed the future priests somewhat. As for the encyclopedia, I knew that they would be unable to consult it.

"You know," I told them, "that the Romans got their soldiers from the colonies and that the best soldiers in those times were the Catalonians from the banks of the Llobegat River."

"That's where I come from," said one.

"And since they were such good soldiers Pilate took them to Jerusalem. A hundred soldiers and one centurion. The centurion was from Arenys de Mar and was always swearing: 'redeu, redeu, filldeput'—'God, God, God, sons-of-bitches.' He's the one who caught Jesus, nailed him on the cross and gambled away his clothing. His Catalonian name was Lonchinat—Longinus—and he was also the one who smote Jesus with his spear. That's why Catalonians have to prove their 'Catalaunum purity' before they can be priests. For fifty-two generations. Many papers are required for this. A great many papers. And coats-of-arms, and genealogical trees."

"How do you know that?" Tarsicio asked.

In need of some authorized guarantee I said that the lay brother had told me so. To reassure them, I added:

"Now then, if you have a genealogical tree, it's much simpler."

The boys listened, perplexed. That last word—genealogical—their Catalonian larynxes could not pronounce easily. Finally, one declared that his family had Catalaunum purity because they had a nun in the family, and he supposed that the investigations had been made for her. Ervigio arrived while I was talking, and listened in silence. But when he heard about the nun he interrupted:

"No, that doesn't count. There is another law for nuns. The law of the Cuaternary Oblates of Trent."

Then we broke up, leaving the boys bewildered and confused. Speaking of the lay brother's miracles, Ervigio, who had to make fun of everything, said that the lay friar would die in the odor of sanctity, and that he already had a little of that odor in advance. He made the remark with his usual gesture, wrinkling up his nose. He did not mean that the lay brother smelled, but that his clothing reeked of varnish and paint. I was then getting along well with Ervigio, who told me about a plan he and Prat had to annoy Father Lucas. This priest was to be in charge of the Good Friday sermon and something had to be done to keep the service from being a brilliant success. Ventós, the boy who looked like a Hindu, was strolling near by and joined us. Ervigio interrupted his confidences. Ventós had apparently been taking lessons from Ervigio and was beginning to stand on his own feet, or, as we say, stick his feet out of the basket. Watching the organist, a rather sickly type, go by, he said:

"There he goes. The poor guy doesn't have a single whole organ left."

Ervigio went on explaining the trick they were going to play on Father

Lucas. He and Prat were in league and the two of them had christened
it the "correlative yawn," which they found very fancy and cultivated.
The day of the sermon we would all show our boredom in church by
yawning together, in rows.

Everything went as planned. Prat coughed twice, alerting us. Then
once more (this was the prompting signal) and, just as in gymnastic
exercises, at the second signal the twenty or thirty pupils in the first row
feigned a long yawn all together, putting their open hands over their
mouths and throwing their heads back. When the first row finished the
second followed suit, then the third and so on until the last. Father
Lucas stopped in the middle of a long quotation from St. Jerome, was
silent for a moment, took a deep breath through his nose, looked at us,
and at the choir as if asking the Father Superior for help, then started
hemming and hawing—Prat called it cackling—until he finally decided
to finish the sermon, raising his eyes and quoting again from St. Jerome.

The priests questioned us, but we all insisted it had been pure coincidence and that yawns are always contagious. I had noticed the lay
brother kneeling motionless at one end of the chancel, hearing Mass on
his knees, and wearing a look of discreet humility. But since finding him
unconscious on the floor, I frequently imagined him in that same position. Dead. And imagining him dead I thought about the "odor of
sanctity" mentioned by Ervigio. And I really thought I saw the halo
behind his head sometimes. I was amazed that the other friars had not
found out about the carbon monoxide accident, for the boys were talking
about it and giving it fantastic interpretations. No one believed that
the lay brother could perform miracles, but thanks to repetition, an
atmosphere of magic was growing up around the friar.

‡ 11 ‡

I wrote a letter to Valentina telling her about the correlative yawn, the
unicorn that still fascinated me, and how she could not go with me to
hunt it since her name was Valentina and she was therefore not a virgin.
I also said other and equally daring things. That I had an anarchist
friend, that some day perhaps the workers would attack the convent,
that my friend the lay brother had died and revived, and finally I copied
some lines of mystical love for her—the only kind I could find at school—
where swooning (bliss) was mentioned. That swooning business—bliss—

struck me as a euphemism of kiss. Bliss was a kiss on the lips. The proof of real love, then, must be a kiss on the lips. The idea of kissing anybody on the lips was repugnant to me. Just to imagine such a kiss turned my stomach. One could kiss a pretty girl without any need to be in love with her. On her cheeks, forehead, neck. But to kiss her on the lips—that seemed to me rather dirty. One would really have to be in love. Nevertheless, whenever I thought about kissing Valentina on the lips, it did not repel me at all but on the contrary appealed to me as pleasant. I loved Valentina so much, I was thinking then, that I could even kiss her on the lips. Even if they were wet with saliva. That must be what bliss meant. I did not tell her precisely these things, but something similar.

Fortunately when I addressed the envelope of this extravagant letter the pen was too full of ink and made a blot. Intending to change the envelope I left the letter in my desk. Happily it was never mailed. I can imagine what would have happened if Don Arturo, Valentina's father, had seen it. For in the P.S. I repeated that she could not go hunting the unicorn with me since she was not a virgin.

I went to see the lay brother, who received me with a falsely sour expression.

"Here comes the one of the chapel yawns," he said.

I swore that it had not been my idea. He believed me and did not ask the name of the culprit. Then he said:

"You are all unjust to Father Lucas. He is good and loves you. Besides, he is a very well-read, very cultured priest."

"We love him too, brother."

"I know."

"Then . . ."

"That's what I say. Then why make life impossible for him?"

Just to see Father Lucas was to feel like doing something to him and no one could help it. I insisted that we were fond of all the priests and brothers in the school except Father Ferrer. The lay brother listened to me with one ear while polishing a piece of wood carved into a twisted column:

"You are also fond of Father Ferrer," he commented.

"Who? Me?"

"Yes, you. You would like him if Father Ferrer were to say to you: 'Pepe, you are an excellent boy and the best actor we ever had in this school.' If he told you that, you would consider yourself the happiest boy in the world. I am sure. But you feel that he does not esteem you as highly as you deserve. Don't deny it, because you know that I can see everything that goes on inside of you. But little brother, Father Ferrer cannot always be flattering his students. He deals with many and has to be firm, fair and cold."

I said nothing. The lay brother concluded:

"Do you know what, little brother? There always has to be someone who carries the burden of discipline on his shoulders. Father Ferrer is the simplest and most cordial man in the community. But he is the one who works hardest with the students. Haven't you noticed how he is always with you in the patio, refectory, church, classes? Try to see him as he is and you will understand that when you all speak ill of him you are unfair."

"All right," I said, changing the subject. "And you, how do you feel?"

"I? Well, thank God. Why?"

"You haven't . . . fallen down dead any more?"

"No, brother. Before lighting the charcoal burner I open the windows."

He smelled of oil, turpentine, varnish. I wondered if this might be the odor of sanctity. I asked him other questions:

"And your father? Hasn't he died yet?"

He looked startled and stood with the brush poised in mid-air, hesitating. Then he said:

"No. How you do talk!"

The marble head was over at one side. The lay brother did not seem very talkative that day. I told him—to get into his good graces—that if he gave me the hammer I would smash the statue. I was ready to close my eyes and deal a smart blow. The lay brother said no, and noticing a hammer within reach he put it further away to avoid temptation, maybe. He was preparing a canvas. A small Murillo print, which he was evidently planning to copy, lay on the table. He paid no attention to me that day. Seeing that I was getting ready to leave he suddenly laid the brush aside, came toward me and put his hands on my shoulders:

"Forgive me, little brother. I have no time today. And you are thinking that I am not giving you the attention you deserve and are leaving in an angry mood. Don't be angry with anyone, but especially with me. Above all right now when the school year is coming to a close, and therefore the day for you to leave us. I am painting a Purissima Concepción for the convent of Tortosa and I must hurry. But I know that you will come some other day. The only thing I ask of you is not to talk about me too much. Don't say that I died and you saw me come back to life, don't say that I am this or that. If the fathers hear of it such gossip will not sit with them very well. Do you know something? There is a good and a bad halo. A gold one and a tin one. When we speak lightly of others we steal the gold from their halo to put in our own. That's what you're doing to Father Lucas. His halo lost its gold. Now it is shabby, dented tin. I don't mind what you do to me. I've always had a tin halo and don't deserve any other. But if you go ahead speaking lightly of me I will be hurt because I'll think that you bear me ill will. I consider you my friend. Aren't you a friend of mine?"

I was moved and delayed answering. Finally I declared:

"You are the only friend I've ever had."

And looking at him solemnly, I added:

"Some day I will prove my friendship to you, brother."

He seemed alarmed.

"No, highness. Don't try to prove anything to me. I am seeing you now as you were on the stage. Promising, threatening. Real feelings do not have to be proved. You don't have to prove anything to me. You know that I have a liquid soul and that I can perceive everything . . . well, everything related to your feelings. But please, don't try to prove anything to me, little brother."

It looked as if he had taken my promise as a threat. I walked away slowly. In the doorway I turned to look at him again. The poor man had a fearful expression, of anguish. He knew that all the boys were talking about him and he was afraid. He did not keep me out of the shop because he loved me, and also for fear my violent friendship would change to resentment and hate, if he shut me out. Knowing how much I cared for him, he could not help being grateful for my feelings, even though they only meant more troubles and misunderstandings for him. The scandal about his saintliness. The misunderstanding about his ecstasies. The danger of our halos. He knew that all the boys, after having told about his being a dog lifting up a leg beside the wall, now talked about his raptures and ecstasies and miraculous deeds. The poor man must have regretted ever having let me inside his studio. Life is bitter and friendship is a consolation creating in turn its own discomforts and new problems. "Jacob's ladder" it was, an infinite ladder of light and shadow, and light and shadow and light and shadow, with demons carved in red mahogany, painted purple, in the interstices. Or angels—cherubs—which from a distance did not look very different from the demons. I must have been a disturbing element for him and at the same time a kind of open window onto the gay confusions of the world.

With spring examinations near—the private examinations of the school, preparatory to the final examination with the professors from the provincial institute—we were rather busy. Aside from Father Miró, whose goodness was stimulating, the others never succeeded in making us work. We pretended to work in study hall, although what we actually did was "illuminate the programs," putting initials, half-words, and other very small cabalistic signs on the margins of the study outlines to help us out in class. I drew little figures representing the lay brother with his halo—the real one, of gold—with heavy, yellow lines. Others read Calleja's tales which, being small leaflets, were easily hidden inside their textbooks.

We were quite unprepared for the examinations and had no intention of improving, if it meant any kind of effort. The situation was beginning to look threatening and one evening as we were talking about it, Planibell said:

"Not even the lay brother could perform the miracle of making me pass. If only I would get sick! Oh, for a good case of tonsillitis or glanders!"

Prat was also with us. He said that glanders was a horse and cow disease. Ervigio seemed to be dreaming. Planibell added:

"Do you know what? If we could only work up a good jaundice like my cousin had in military camp to get out of maneuvers!"

"I prefer the examinations," said little Ventós, always reasonable.

"Shut up, you," ordered Planibell, who would not let Ventós speak in front of him. "My cousin conveniently got sick the day before maneuvers and was sent to the hospital. A good trick."

Lowering his voice, he added:

"If I had a little saffron you would all see if I got out of being examined or not. But here in this school we are all still sucking our thumbs."

He explained that his cousin had turned as yellow as if he had jaundice, by taking a little saffron on an empty stomach. He spent a very comfortable week in bed, reading and smoking.

Thinking of the steward, I offered to be responsible for getting some saffron. The whole group was suddenly filled with hope and we agreed that I should go after it. It was kept in a rather large jar with *Bubus irideus* printed on it in the same Gothic letters as those used in the

Visigothic codes. But it was too near the steward's work-table for me to steal it unseen, so I went back upstairs to tell Ervigio to call Don Genitive on the telephone to get him away from the spot.

He did and I was able to reach the jar. The Latinist was still on the telephone when I left the pantry with my pockets stuffed with saffron.

The next day before breakfast I divided up the saffron between Prat, Ervigio, Caresse, Planibell, the brothers Pere and Pau, and little Ventós, keeping a bigger dose for myself, since I had stolen it. Prat asked for more because, as he said, he was taller than the rest of us.

We took it on empty stomachs and drank three glasses of water. We were not sure that the trick would work, but it did. By mid-afternoon we were all as yellow as lemons and Brother Pedro was alarmed, fearing an epidemic.

We were taken to the infirmary and the next day examinations began. So far so good. Nothing hurt us, although we said we had vague pains, to make it all more plausible. Some complained of a sore throat, others of a pain in the side, and almost everybody of a headache. Fearful that they would leave him without food for too long Prat complained of his foot—the organ farthest from his stomach—which really puzzled the physician.

But the adventure was proving to have its dangerous side, as we realized when we saw the doctor take out his hypodermic needle and mysterious ampoules. Prat, so presumptuously brave, screamed like a pig when stuck. When we had each had our injection and the doctor had left, we started wondering if it was really worth the price. Realizing that we were weakening we all took a solemn oath not to confess or squeal, no matter what happened.

Seeing how afraid some of them were (the brothers Pere and Pau, however, in spite of their delicacy, faced up to the hypodermic needle very well), I tried to frighten Prat: he should be careful about saying his foot hurt him, because there were cases of jaundice when they amputated legs. I also told how they were about to cut off my right arm once, back in the village, then decided to let it go till later since the doctor had no anesthesia.

"What's anesthesia?" Prat asked.

"That's something to keep the sound of the saw on the bone from setting your teeth on edge."

Prat was livid. I went on talking about surgeons cutting off feet and arms, telling—because I had heard it—how they kept on hurting after being amputated. The boys listened twice yellow: with saffron and with fear.

At the end of my long dissertation Prat, who had gotten up to go to the bathroom, was limping slightly.

Prat's bed was beside a window. Mine was at one end of the room, Pere's and Pau's on each side of the door, the others in the midle. Pere and Pau were almost albinos and their color was lamentable. When the doctor was attending Prat or me, he would turn to look at Pere and Pau again, astonished by their ripe-lemon color. He took our temperature and when he found we had no fever and that our bodily functions were normal, he was perplexed. The other boys did not come up to see us, but with so many of us in the infirmary we were not bored. To make everything turn out just right Father Salvá, who was the nurse and had the reputation of being strict and stern, did not take care of us as he himself was in the community infirmary with a severe cold. The lay brother, however, came to see us—to see me, that is. I had told my friends that this little friar discovered everything the rest of us felt and thought. Caresse called that prestidigitation, confusing it with telepathy, examples of which he had seen at the circus. I did not tell them about the "liquid soul" because I knew they would not understand and also because I knew that I could not explain it well enough. As soon as the lay brother appeared I thought: "He is going to discover our trick." He set some large cardboard boxes on the floor, looked at all of us, and asked:

"How do all you little brothers feel?"

Ventós, depressed by the injections, asked him to pray for us. The lay brother made no comment. I suspected that he realized something was amiss; otherwise he would have offered to pray. Silently he looked at Ventós, Prat, and me. He did not say if he would pray or not. Prat was impertinent:

"You are looking at us as if you had some doubts about our being sick. Why do you look at us like that? Or are you going to perform a miracle?"

I blushed, or turned yellower still.

"If you are going to perform miracles, you can begin with Pepe Garcés."

"Come now," the friar said, "I see that you are irritable."

"As far as I'm concerned," said Ervigio, "I don't give a hang whether you come see us or not."

Planibell added:

"And I don't give half a hang."

I wanted to insult everybody, but I saw that the lay brother had not taken offense. He had come—I was thinking—to see me, not the others. No sooner had I said this to myself than the friar was aware of it, or so it seemed to me. This always happened.

"I have come to see you," he said, "all of you, young friends. Not only Pepe, but everybody. But I can see that my visit is displeasing you."

He pulled a handful of candies out of his pocket and gave each of us two. When he was near the odor of varnish—sanctity—was noticeable. The friar had come to entertain us, tell us an interesting story perhaps. But he was ready to leave. His liquid soul told him that we did not want him. As a matter of fact we were all afraid of his "miracles," that he would discover our trick. Ervigio asked him why, being a painter, he was the one who "painted" least—that is, made the least splash—in all the school. The others laughed and the friar commented:

"Not only in the school. Everywhere. I don't paint a single thing, or make any splash at all. On the other hand, all by yourselves you paint yourselves as big as life for every occasion."

A breeze of alarm ran through the room. The little friar smiled:

"But don't worry. I won't tell a thing. What I know or what I don't know. Silence."

Then he told us the story of a very clever fox that was finally trapped and punished. But the punishment was gentle. We all listened trying to find hidden and indirect meanings in the friar's words. Naturally, we could not discover any. Soon afterward he left, wishing us patience and good humor, and without so much as a word about our health. The boxes he had left on the floor contained games—checkers, a little Chinese billiard game, and chess. While we were setting up the boards Pere flattered Prat, saying that he had done very well by the friar, and Prat swaggered:

"If there's one thing I can't stand, it's hypocrisy."

I did not know how to play chess and I heard Prat and Caresse quarreling about whether somebody was cheating or not. Caresse was a very original player. When Prat checkmated him, Caresse became indignant, saying it was impossible. Disdainfully Prat stood up:

"Where are you going to move the king?"

"Here," said Caresse.

"I'll take him there with my knight."

"That's a lie. You can't take the king."

With Caresse, then, the game would never end.

While our jackets were hanging in a clothes closet Ervigio committed a petty theft. He snitched Prat's address book. But he did not stop at trifles, and jotted down the address of Prat's cousin Ines. On Sunday they brought us writing materials, in case we wanted to write home, and Ervigio wrote the girl a letter on the sly. This was bound to have serious consequences, because when it came to the signature he hesitated and finally decided to use my name. He wrote, then, a declaration of love to Ines, boldly signed Pepe Garcés.

For a day or two he looked quite worried. Ignorant of the real cause of his trouble I attributed it to the fear everyone had of the doctor. He took me aside now and then to say:

"Don't you think that Ines, Prat's sweetheart, is very pretty?"

"Yes," I would answer, "but not as pretty as mine."

"What's her name?"

I looked at him haughtily, refusing to answer. Ervigio prepared to make some remark about my sweetheart, but sensing something ominous in the air, he decided against it. Then he asked:

"After due consideration, don't you believe that Prat is really unworthy of Ines?"

"Maybe so," I said, enigmatically.

"She ought to have a more refined sweetheart. And one her own age. Prat's too old for her."

"Maybe so," I repeated.

My sarcasm annoyed Ervigio.

It occurred to me that Prat, two years older than I, ought to know something about virginity. I told him what the dictionary said about the unicorn. Prat beat about the bush. He was clearly as ignorant as I, but unwilling to admit it. Ervigio repeated his theory about the Marys and at the far end of the infirmary the smallest boy, Ventós, was heard to remark:

"Nonsense. All women who have not had babies are virgins."

After a pause Planibell broke the silence with a really authorized quotation: "Whence it cometh that the Virgin Mary was a virgin before giving birth, during birth, and after birth." I decided that Ventós must be right, although "after birth" did sound contradictory to me. I decided to tear up my previous letter to Valentina and write another. I was glad that Valentina, being a virgin, could now come with me and subdue the unicorn. There were several differing opinions about that animal, however. Planibell did not believe it existed at all, but to clinch the argument I told them that it was on the coat-of-arms of the kings of England, as I had seen in the dictionary.

As bed neighbors, Planibell and I sometimes talked for hours on end. We criticized the education methods of the school, no less. Prat eyed us from a distance, jealous of the high tone of our conversation.

"Nothing I study interests me," complained Planibell.

I said, "Latin interests me."

"Latin? What good is Latin? Will you tell me?"

"For saying Mass," Caresse suggested.

Planibell insisted that the only valuable thing to be learned from the study of Latin was boredom. For we would probably have to be bored many times in our lives.

"This Planibell comes out with some very pithy arguments," said Caresse, laughing.

I said that Latin was useful for reading old documents and I told them what I had read in the book on love, written by André, the French king's chaplain. I recited several sentences that I remembered which stated that true lovers should never marry.

"That sure is good," commented Caresse. "That's the first time I ever heard such a thing. That's like the gypsies when they get together and say: 'Do you love me? I love you. I'll smash a cooking-pot.' And they toss an earthen pot up in the air which smashes to smithereens. Then they dance and they're married."

From his bed Planibell would look at Caresse and say: "From a distance you look like a red sea-bream. Now, painted yellow, you look like a sea-bream covered with mayonnaise." Furious, the boy said nothing, although he did occasionally throw a pillow at him.

We wandered around the infirmary all day long until someone gave the alarm, when we would scamper back into bed and stay until the sound of footsteps died away down the corridor. Then we would form our groups again to play or fight. Some of the boys wore bathrobes, others did not. Those who had none wrapped themselves up in sheets and looked like Roman senators.

Prat had proved to be the biggest coward as far as medicine was concerned. When someone told him so, he said very seriously:

"They can cut my head off. I don't care. But when they stick a fellow with a steel needle this long . . ."—and he indicated one fully six times as long as the actual needle—"that gives me the shivers in the coccyx and I feel like throwing up."

Ventós was usually silent although once in a while, thinking that he was really ill, he would talk about his family in a doleful voice, and how his mother would bring him good toast and honey if she were there. As for Ervigio, after each injection he would make a wry face and growl:

"That went clear to the bone."

Ervigio's face seemed smaller after turning yellow and his head looked like a very funny canary head. He took me aside now and then to ask in a solemn tone I could not understand:

"You, what would *you* say about Ines if you talked about her?"

"Nothing. I never talk about her. What for?"

The hypodermics took quite a while because first the doctor put rubber tubes around our arms to make the veins stand out, then he stuck us and injected the medicine. Meanwhile the infirmary was quiet as the tomb and from Prat's bed came a rhythmical little sound. It was the rosary cross at the head of his bed striking against the iron bedpost with the hero's every heartbeat.

The physician was a kind old man who once said something about "toxins." About the *dirty toxins*. Instead of *toxinas* the Catalonians understood *tosinas*, or *tocinas*—female pigs. Pere, yellow up to his ears, said that he could feel the piglets stirring in his blood. The strange thing about all this was their being feminine. Why female pigs? No one could understand what kind of pigs the doctor meant. When Pau talked about the pigs running around inside of him we listened terrified. "I don't feel anything," said Caresse. Yet that's what the doctor said when giving Pau his hypodermic. Prat seemed to have some hope as far as his own case was concerned. One day he timidly asked the doctor if he also had *tocinas* in his blood. The doctor understood *toxinas* and answered:

"Of course, little man. You all have them."

He explained that the injections were to keep them from multiplying and help the organism destroy them. This seemed to explain the sex of our pigs. That's why they were females. Then the physician left us utterly bewildered. No one questioned it any longer. Only Ervigio was skeptical of the doctor's wisdom and he immediately started calling him in a grotesque way—"*mérdico*" instead of "*médico*." Caresse was trying to explain the mystery to himself:

"It's because the saffron was full of bugs," he said turning toward me. "I saw them."

"And they grow inside the veins?" Prat asked with a nauseated gesture.

"Naturally," answered Caresse making the most of Prat's fear.

Ervigio imitated the pig's grunt. He said that he could hear that grunt inside his body and that it was a piglet dying in his veins, after the injection.

To tell the truth, we all felt the pigs in our blood and the whole affair was becoming uncomfortable. Yet Ventós, the farm boy, had his doubts: "How can pigs come out of saffron? Nothing but plant lice come out of plants, for I have seen them."

The examinations had been over for four days and we were still in bed. Boredom was making us ill-humored. I considered all the boys inferior except Prat, because of his size, and Planibell, because of his intelligence. Ervigio, who was playing dull practical jokes on Pere and Pau, did not dare go very far with me. The only thing he did to me was put a brush on the electric switch, in the dark, so that when I turned on the light from my bed my hand was pricked by the bristles.

We spent the day looking at ourselves in the bathroom mirror, to see if the yellow was disappearing or not. Ervigio said that we should drink a lot of water, but then there was the danger of making frogs grow. Would it be better to have frogs than pigs?

Ventós talked about writing home to say that I had poisoned them all. Planibell defended me, although rather timidly.

Prat asked me once, looking out of the corner of his eye, if poisoners were hanged. I felt my heart turn over. The adventure was becoming terrible. Everybody felt ill. We were beginning to believe that the saffron on the one hand, and the injections on the other, could really kill us. For the moment those *tocinas*—female piglets—in our bodies were repugnant and menacing.

Prat, who seemed to be the most serene, concluded:

"Now we belong to the yellow race."

There were days of great depression. At night an owl hooted on the roof. Ventós trembled between the sheets and said that the owls were coming. According to him, they only came to places where some dead person lay, to pick out his eyes. Pere talked about going to confession, but if he confessed he would have to tell about the saffron trick. Planibell and I protested. We had sworn to die without confession and face the eternal fires. Nevertheless, we sometimes thought that the examinations, all things considered, were not so terrible.

Amidst such doubts the *tocinas* continued stirring in our blood.

Our forced living together was making us more and more irritable and one morning Prat gave Ervigio two resounding slaps. Ervigio did not fight back or do anything except try to tyrannize Pau, whom I defended. Then Ervigio, seeing himself threatened from two sides—by Prat and Prat's adversary, me—realized that he was lost. To show that he was not afraid of us, however, he exaggerated his clowning. Using a sheet like a Roman toga, he danced: the flunking dance. The dance of Father Chaveta. But the most successful was the dance of the agonizing *tocinas*. Little Pere and Pau laughed and Prat chewed his nails with rage.

Ervigio found some pincers in the bathroom and came in leaping about and making ludicrous gestures as if he were pulling out his teeth. Pere and Pau who always felt obliged to flatter someone older or stronger, guffawed. Ventós looked Ervigio over from head to toe and said, in Catalonian:

"*Tontu*—You fool."

Ervigio started over to settle his score with Ventós but Planibell yelled from his bed that if he so much as touched Ventós he would have to settle matters with him. Ervigio hesitated a moment, finally climbed back in bed resignedly and said: "What an outrage! Everybody here has his whipping master. And you, Pepe? Who's protecting you?" I told him I didn't need anybody's protection because I could lick him myself. He was pensive for an instant, undoubtedly thinking about the possible consequences of the letter he had written Ines. Then he was excessively nice to me, almost flattering.

Pau hummed:

"*'What will we give to the little shepherdess . . .'*"

Planibell said that Ervigio was the little shepherdess—and so the ignominious nickname was fastened on him then and there. Seeing that he was getting nowhere, Ervigio began to imitate the pig again. He really did it very well.

Finally one day the doctor announced that we were well and could leave the infirmary. It was a great relief for everyone. I went to see the lay brother. He welcomed me without either surprise or joy.

"Are you all right now?" he asked, I don't know if seriously or not.

In view of his slightly joking tone, however, I did not answer. The lay brother had finished the Murillo picture and was varnishing it. The Virgin had a half-moon under her foot.

"That, it's not so," I said, as ready to criticize as ever. "That half-moon is not true, because there is never a half-moon in the sky, but a whole one."

"All right, it's an illusion. But there are also people who believe they are sick and everybody accepts it. And they give them hypodermics and say pater nosters for them. Besides, in this case it is not a lie. It is only art. But who knows if what we call a lie may not be more true for God than what we call the truth. We don't know. Only God knows what truth and falsehood are, little brother."

The friar looked around for the marble head. Then his eyes fell on the hammer on the carpenter's bench. He looked at me as if asking my advice. The same old question, maybe. In the last few days I had changed my mind about that arduous task. Would I be capable of smashing the marble head? Would I do it for him? I shook my head and continued looking at the Immaculate Conception. The face was very beautiful but what fascinated me was the night sky in the background, with its little stars. There were no clouds. The blue—clear and dark in spots—was so fluid and diaphanous that, as I stared at it, I thought I discovered new stars where there were none. I asked him if he had fainted recently and he said no. He thanked me for my interest, but he always opened the windows when lighting the burner. That stupid accident would not happen to him again. The cat, naturally, took advantage of the open windows to run away, hunting. Since it was springtime and the birds were building their nests, the cat went hunting baby birds to eat. As the friar spoke the cat listened, kindly, purring with friendliness. No one looking at the animal could possibly attribute such uncivil acts to it.

We worked. As I helped the lay brother sandpaper a board he told me that the marble head had so upset him that he could not sleep. He would be grateful to me for smashing it. I told him that my liquid soul enabled me to see that if I did smash it he would be sorry. "That's so," said the friar, "but I would also be glad. Sorry and glad at the same time." The lay brother was afraid of the head. I gazed at it as I would at a third person in the shop.

When I heard the dinner bell I left at a run.

It was Thursday, and raining, and since there was no recess we were permitted to write home. I wrote Valentina telling her about the saffron and *tocinas,* saying that everyone had had them but me. Again I explained about swooning and bliss.

‡ 12 ‡

Now that the real final examinations were near—given by teachers who were not priests and whom we had never seen—something unexpected happened in the city: a strike. It did not look very threatening at first, but then it grew and finally spread into a general strike with parades in the streets and distant shots. The monks were somewhat uneasy. I felt myself entering the heroic stage that I had been waiting for since *Life Is a Dream.*

I went to Planchat, who told me:

"My father is afraid because the strikes cost him a lot of money. I'm glad. And it's not for nothing, either. I really love my father, who is very good in his own way. But that doesn't keep him from being a filthy bourgeois."

I knew nothing about social conflicts. He explained to me that a general strike was a very serious affair. It began with shots in the streets and the third day the strikers attacked the convents. Ours was in no danger, since the workers would be electrocuted if they came close enough to touch the iron gratings. In spite of his anarchistic ideas, this did not really calm him. Planchat thought that all convents should be burned, except ours. When they burned them, the fire always began in the confessionals in the chapels. Planchat added other details, equally sensational.

I also found a propitious aspect to the revolution:

"Then, there won't be any examinations?"

"No. That studying business is always suppressed in revolutions. What's the use? We'll all be equal and if anyone doesn't want to be . . ."

Planchat made a strange guttural sound and at the same time acted as if he were slicing off his head with his open hand.

It seemed all right to me, on condition that I would be one of those directing the incendiaries. At night from my cell I listened to the city noises and, since we had a power plant beside us that was under guard, I could also hear the hooves of the horses of the Civil Guard. The next day Planchat, who was paying close attention to what was going on, said to me:

"Haven't you noticed that the monks are afraid? Especially Father Ferrer."

The supposed fear of Father Ferrer made Planchat very happy. Looking out of the corner of his eye to make sure that Father Ferrer was out of hearing, he added as he nudged me with his elbow:

"The high-tension wires won't do them any good, because there are more workers than soldiers and police. What is electric current beside the knife and the gasoline can? Ah!"

Planchat had a fiendish joy. I repeated his words to Pere and Pau. My knowledge of the situation—which came to me from Planchat—increased my prestige with them. Planibell also came to ask if the revolution would strike before the examinations. We were all more or less hoping to be saved by the revolution. But the workers would have to hurry because examination day was near. I could not understand why they were so slow.

Another letter came from Valentina. I was sure that the revolution would not affect the villages, only the cities. Valentina agreed to go unicorn hunting with me but said that she did not understand about the saffron. To be like me, however, she was going to eat a little and see what happened.

I wrote her by return mail telling her on no account to eat saffron. Then I added: "We are on a volcano." I had heard Father Miró use the expression. "There is sand in the streets to keep the horses from falling during battle." That day my letter was rather long and went on to say: "They might attack the school, since it is a convent and cloister in addition to being a school. But in *Life Is a Dream* I learned what to do with conspirators. It would not surprise me at all if all the monks except the Superior and Brother Pedro were killed. I don't know what will happen to the lay brother in the workshop who makes saints and has ecstasies. He is not a real priest and almost never wears a cassock. He wants to be a martyr, but I don't know if martyrs are used any more in these times.

"I know where the switch that electrifies the iron gratings is, and when this letter *reaches your hands*"—this sentence sounded very grown-up to me—"I will already have turned off the current. You will see. It will be easier to go unicorn hunting now, when I get out of school, with all the disturbances.

"When the workers come in I will tell them that I turned off the electricity in the gratings and they will cry 'Hurrah!' and I will say:

> On the mighty world's great stage,
> 'mid the admiring nations' cheer,
> valor mine, that has no peer,

enter thou; the slave so shunned
now shall reign Prince Segismund.
And Valentina's sire his wrath shall fear."

I had made up the last line. In the P.S. I added: "Don't mention this to anyone because your father will get angry and Pilar will make fun of us. Furthermore, lovers have secrets and such is life. *Vale."*

The high-tension cables and switch-boxes had to be somewhere in the building and I was determined to find out where, so that I could shut off the current at the crucial moment. I began wondering if I would need an accomplice among the servants. But they were unreliable. Some of them looked too cynical to me. Others too pious. Whatever I had to do, I would do alone and unaided. Then all the glory would be for me.

I added a second P.S. to the letter:

"When the convent friars are dead we will go after those who are to blame and that is where these lines will come in very apropos:

Fortune, we go forth to reign;
wake me not if this is vision,
let me sleep not if 'tis true.
But which ever of them is it,
to act right is what imports me.
If 'tis true, because it is so;
if 'tis not, that when I waken
friends may welcome and forgive me.

"And when everything is burned up and sacked I will fetch you and we will go unicorn hunting and start living together and practicing free love. *Vale."*

During those days I was unconsciously identifying the unicorn, and the search for it, with the revolution Planchat was talking about so constantly.

I began looking for the electric switches. It took me two days to locate them. Beside the gatekeeper's lodge was a dark and windowless room that had a row of large switches with white porcelain handles on the wall. The certainty of having discovered what I was looking for calmed me down greatly. I now knew my main objective. In some way I believe that this dark room had become the place of the unicorn for me, and that it was a kind of electric horse, blue like lightning flashes.

When I heard galloping horses I wondered if the moment had arrived. But there was no shooting or shouting. I went to see the lay brother who continued working tranquilly.

"Brother," I asked, "don't you know there's a revolution on?"

"There always is," he replied, without changing a hair or interrupting his work. "There always is. With violence or without it."

"They tell me Father Ferrer is very afraid."

"No, little brother. No one is afraid except the one who talks about it. Don't you know that? And I only feel sorry. Sorry for the workers. See? The marble head on one side. Jesus on the other, just as in the street and in the revolution. Yonder"—and he pointed to the archangel St. Michael—"is the Civil Guard. Don't think for a moment that I like it. I don't even like a sword in the hands of an archangel. Violence—what for? Don't we all have violence enough in our own souls? Why more? But people suffer and sometimes lose their reason and want to suffer more or make others suffer."

"Do you believe," I asked him, "that the school is defended, safe from attack?"

"Why not? Man's innocence is a defense."

"And also," I added, "the high-tension cables."

The brother stopped working to look at me:

"What cables?"

"Some connected with the iron fences of the gardens and the window gratings."

"What for?"

"To kill workers."

"Come, come, Pepe. That's a criminal lie."

I dared not continue. Finally I said:

"You are innocent and you are right. Innocence does protect you. And so will I. But the others? Ah, that's what we ought to look into."

I was thinking about Father Ferrer and what Planchat had told me about strikes and revolutions. And I asked:

"Don't you believe in anarchists? I've heard about them and about other things, brother. There are socialists, too."

The names of these political groups rang out like shots in the workshop. The lay brother said:

"For me there are only human beings. Some more unfortunate than others. Some lose their heads and want strange things—to be more unfortunate, or luckier, than the rest. And to be seen and heard. And they shout. In the end, it all amounts to nothing. None of that destroys the harmony of God. What do you think, *tontito*—little fool? Do you believe that we can do anything against Him, against God?"

"I don't say that."

We were silent for a moment. Then I told him that he had no reason at all to be afraid, like Father Ferrer. I don't know how to describe it, but the lay brother looked at me as if smiling with his whole being: with his eyes, lips, hands caressing my shoulder. As I left for the dining hall I thought, somewhat disappointed: "No, the lay brother is not afraid. Surely Planchat, with all his boasting and threats, is more afraid."

One night, probably an hour after I had gone to bed, three or four shots—or supposed shots—were heard on the other side of the power plant, and someone shouted something. It was neither a shout of protest nor pain, just someone calling somebody else. There was also the sound of trotting horses on the stone pavement. Half-dressed and barefooted I slipped out of my room and down to the gatekeeper's lodge, pausing in front of the door to the dark room. The unicorn. I was afraid to go in, and also of being found there at such an hour. Finally I went in and stood in front of the switches, hesitating. All those white handles had their own secrets. I decided that it would be best to change the position of all of them. If the gratings had been electrified, the current would naturally be cut off. Without further hesitation I raised the handles that were down, pulled down those that were up, then ran for my room, satisfied with my work. All the building was glowing like a golden ember.

The fact that the plan was mine alone gave it a certain secret and immense conspiratory value. I thought about the lay brother and said to myself: "Surely this saving of the workers' lives will please him, for they are, after all, only human beings."

I had done well to go barefooted because the corridors were lighted up and everything looked as if there were some kind of celebration going on. When I reached the third floor, out of breath, I heard sounds coming from the convent cloister where the monks lived. I had evidently shut off the lights in the cloister and turned on the others, with my manipulation of the switches. Later I found out that I had left the friars in the dark in the middle of their nocturnal prayers, and had turned on the lights in the chapel, corridors and gardens, as well as the special lights installed for the Constantine centennial. The friars were indeed surprised and nonplussed.

Before entering my cell I heard steps and voices on the lower floor.

It was the monks. Their shoes did not sound like ours. Bother Pedro was saying: "We must go down to the laundry to shut off the current." At that instant more horses were heard in the street. I went to my cell and finished dressing, waiting for developments. I had not the slightest doubt that the moment of attack had arrived. I held my breath listening from time to time, but all I could hear was the sound of the cavalry patrols more or less near.

I did not sleep until daybreak. Tired, toward dawn, I decided that my foresight had been in vain. The daylight brought me back to reality. Later I was often to discover how simple the most difficult things appear at night. And that the daylight makes them vanish, revealing our own extravagance to us.

In the early morning light I saw that life was unchanged. My hopes that the workers would attack the convent struck me as quite illogical. But thinking about my letter to Valentina made me glad that I had changed the position of the electric switches. For I had told her I would do it, and I should not lie to Valentina.

The priests and brother seemed a little uneasy the next day. In French class Father Miró appeared distrait. In Latin I looked at Father Chaveta and said to myself: "I don't know why he should worry. In all probability nothing would happen to him." Later, in geometry class, I gazed at Father Ferrer, recalling Life Is a Dream.

When classes were over I looked up Planchat. But he was the one coming toward me with news:

"Did you hear the shots last night?"

"Yes. Near the power plant."

"No. They were farther away. A real battle. It must have been at the mine pool. My people, the anarchists, know what they're doing and the monks are afraid. The worst, well, the best of all, well, that depends on how you look at it, is that the servants are in cahoots with the strikers because last night there was sabotage inside the convent. They turned off the lights in the cloister and turned them on in the garden."

I did not know what sabotage was, and Planchat explained. But I did not tell him that the sabotage was mine. I made a mental note of that new word, however, to write it to Valentina. I suspected fear and distrust in Planchat. Maybe he was not as brave as he pretended. And he explained to me about the lights, just as if I knew nothing:

"They turned off the electricity, carrying out secret orders from outside. The convent servants. I saw those orders."

He repeated that within a week the revolution would have triumphed in the whole country. We would not even have to think about examinations. He had thrown his study outlines down the toilet. And he intended to throw his books in the sea at Salou, the beach nearest Reus. As he talked he kept looking out of the corner of his eye, to be sure no monks were about. Planchat, however, was losing his prestige with me. I could not help looking at him with a skeptical air. In the afternoon, during recess, I slipped away to the workshop on the sly.

And I had a sensational encounter on the way. Looking furious, Prat came up and planted himself in front of me, obstructing my path, then asking through clenched teeth:

"If I wrote a letter to your sweetheart, what would you do?"

"I don't know, but you'd better not try."

"Why not?"

"Just in case."

I answered him clenching my teeth also and pronouncing each syllable with care. Prat drew a letter out of his pocket and showed it to me. It was the one Ervigio had written Ines and began with the old familiar phrase: "Señorita, Since I first laid eyes on you . . ." I told him that this letter, even though signed with my name, had been written by Ervigio. I recognized the handwriting. I added that if I had written it I would not deny it, and that then it would only be a question of our killing each other in a duel. Prat gave me a poisonous smile:

"That's just what I was thinking. But if you're telling the truth I'll have to see La Pastoreta about this. I'm sorry. I'd rather fight with you, Castellá."

"It wouldn't be the first time," I retorted, recalling the blow given him by Providence shortly after my arrival at the school.

Prat said that he was going to demand an accounting of Ervigio, but I asked him to wait before challenging him to a duel, because I wanted to beat him up to punish him for using my name. This struck him as reasonable and he agreed to wait. Prat waved the letter in his hand, exclaiming:

"This is what is called an outrage."

He left and I went on to the shop absolutely convinced that Prat had good reason to kill La Pastoreta. Spring was in the air and any form of violence seemed more natural than at other times of the year.

In his workshop the lay brother was working on the marble head. He was rubbing the forehead and cheeks so hard that he was breathing fast with the effort. When he saw me he smiled, as always. I told him that I was worried about the dangers surrounding us, and he looked at me with mocking eyes:

"There is no danger at all, little brother."

"What do you think? Are the workers good or bad?"

"Neither good nor bad. They are men like you and me," he replied, rubbing the ear of the statue energetically. "The bad thing is that the poor do not hope for the justice of the Lord, little brother."

I was surprised by the lay brother's calm and I wanted to push the matter further:

"Even so, they could set fire to the convent. It's very possible. I believe they'll burn it some day."

The lay brother looked at me with a frown:

"Eh, little brother, that's what you want to happen."

"I do?"

"Yes. You want them to set fire to it."

I dissembled. I had forgotten the lay brother's "liquid soul." The friar went on:

"Who's going to set fire to the convent? The workers are people like you and me. Would you like to burn the convent?"

I looked away. Avoiding his eyes, I still went on arguing with him:

"Workers don't pray. You say they are like you, but they don't pray."

The lay brother glanced toward the door with that movement of distrust I knew so well and added:

"They pray better than we do. There are many ways to pray, little brother. When they are together and talk, they get excited with words because the sadness of one is added to the poverty of another. All right, who hasn't been violent some time in his life? But when they are alone in their homes at night and think about the simple miracles of living, who can say if they believe in God or not? Ah, brother, it's all much more complicated than it seems. Even if they did not believe, which would be lamentable indeed, the truth is that God believes in them. Don't you think that God believes in them just as in you or me? Maybe more, little brother. The workers are more deserving than you and I. And they pray. Well, don't they have to pray?"

He added other things. Many other things. The lay brother was eloquent. When a worker could not buy shoes for his child, for instance, he felt pain and sadness. His sadness was a prayer. When he wanted to reply harshly to an unjust boss and said nothing, he could not help feeling sad and anxious. His anxiety was a prayer. When he wanted to give his wife better living conditions and had no money, he despaired. His despair was pain in his soul, good as a prayer. During those days of the strike there was no fire or bread or hope in many homes. That also was a way of acquiring merits. Everyone who suffers acquires merits. And in one way or another we all suffer.

Somewhat bewildered I asked:

"Do you mean to say that the general strike is good for acquiring merits and going to heaven?"

The lay brother burst out laughing:

"Don't be stupid, little brother. Living is a prayer in itself. Life is so complicated and no one can help praying to God our Lord. We are like insects who come and go without ever knowing what for. We weep and laugh and sleep and love without ever knowing what for. Only God knows. And, in the end, we can only do what He desires."

He kept on, rubbing the head briskly. And he added, letting his voice fall to a whisper:

"Last night rather strange things happened. Some monks were uneasy perhaps and slept badly. In that case their uneasiness is a prayer. Do you understand? But don't repeat what I am saying outside this room, little brother. They would not understand you. That is, they would not want to understand you."

As on previous occasions the lay brother spoke easily with me, in spite of the disappointments I had caused him.

"And why were those friars afraid?" I asked. "Because of the shots?"

"I did not say they were afraid. They were uneasy because someone turned out some lights and turned on others. Nothing of any consequence, but they were all wondering who could have done such a thing and why. Turning off the lights in the cloister. Turning on the others. What for?"

I told him about the high-tension cables connected with the iron gratings and fences, speaking of this as established and unquestionable fact.

"Old wives' tales, little brother. There's nothing to it. Such things have never existed."

"But I've heard it said."

"I don't doubt it."

"And it could be," I added, "that someone with good intentions got up last night and went to the switch-box room to shut off the current."

The lay brother looked at me astonished:

"Ay, little brother, don't say another word."

Now he was rubbing the tip of the nose hard, which was rather comical. And thinking. Finally he raised his head and looked at me, with a kind of surprise in his eyes which I had never noticed before:

"I see, brother, little donkey."

"What do you see?"

Neither of us said a word. The cat stared at us with his tail curled over his front paws to keep them warm. The friar had understood what happened the night before. And he looked at me in silence.

"If the workers came in," I said, "they would kill you. Unless," I added condescendingly, "someone took a hand in your behalf. But in the first moment of confusion they wouldn't have any time for little courtesies. The knife and gasoline can," I concluded, recalling Planchat, "are no joke."

"Bah, there you're mistaken. No. They would not kill me. And if in the confusion, as you say, they were to kill me, I would be sorry for them. Not for myself. As far as I'm concerned, I don't care, little brother. All right, listen to me. I like living, but I am so simple that I find happiness in everything, even when it seems impossible. I am happy living. If they killed me, I also believe that I would be happy dying."

"That's what you say, but one who is murdered has to suffer tremendous pain. Horrible pain."

"No, little brother. God is merciful. When pain is unbearable, man loses consciousness. Did you ever have a toothache? Well, it's no worse than that. Maybe not even as bad. And what is that? Nothing. God knows what he is doing, little brother. God does not want us to suffer more than we can bear."

"And if they burned you? Ah, burning one alive, that's no joke. But even if that should happen, someone might act in your behalf."

The lay brother was now gazing at me without any astonishment. But he held to his own opinion:

"Apparently only the first burn hurts. Then, as the nerves are destroyed, one does not suffer. But," and here the lay brother frankly laughed, "who is going to burn me?"

He went on rubbing the neck of the marble head, happy, maybe, in the thought of his own death. He guessed my secret reflections, but I also believed that I understood his, realizing that no kind of real unhappiness was possible for him. He was happy if they burned him and also if they despised him. Happier still if they insulted him and called him evil names. And if they did murder him some day, when he felt the knife in his flesh, he would undoubtedly enjoy that also. (If they burned him, better still.) He looked at me, smiled with his eyes and, still rubbing the marble, said:

"Death is not a misfortune, little brother. The moment the soul leaves its poor body must be such a glorious moment that no human being can imagine it."

He went on talking. He was beginning, as at other times, to feel somewhat intoxicated:

"Turning the electricity off the gratings could be good or bad, little brother. It would be good if you did it for love of the workers. Bad, if hatred of Father Ferrer or the Latin teacher, or who knows whom, prompted you to do it. Maybe there was neither hatred nor love in you, but a desire for notoriety. Ay, brother, that would be still worse. Hating is not so bad because it carries its own unhappiness along with it and one suffers the consequences. But the bad thing is feeling superior to others, because even when they punish us with humiliation we think they are wrong and unjust. Vanity, little brother. That's a wicked thing."

Then he added, returning to his favorite theme:

"I don't know what God is going to do with me. I'm good for nothing. I can only pray with my lips and imagination. Everybody else prays with his whole life. Everybody. Even . . ."—and here he looked toward the door again and dropped his voice—"even the workers when they burn convents. Do you know why? Because they themselves fear the police, their conscience, their hands. They're not sure of being right, of doing what they should. Their hesitation is a prayer. And they have their halo. Their own, just like Father Ferrer's and mine. Their halo is cleaner, brighter than mine, because they suffer and I do not. Poor people, in addition to their natural sufferings, are afraid of danger, jail, bullets, death, and of leaving their loved ones—children, wife—alone and in a difficult plight. They suffer, little brother, and willingly or unwillingly they pray with their grief. But I . . . what do I do? Imbecile that I am. I pray with the only thing I have: my foolish happiness. Is that praying? Listen, brother, to what I'm going to tell you. Sometimes I envy those violent men who suffer distress in their bodies and souls and in those of their dear ones. I don't envy, and may God forgive me, your Benedicto José, who was as happy as I am, or other saints since they enjoy God on earth. Ah, highness, to enjoy God on earth. That really frightens me. Isn't it too much? Couldn't that become, in certain cases, sin? We have come here to pray with our bodies and soul, senses and faculties. And

I do not pray. I am always happy, I rejoice. And if your workers come in here and tie a rope around my neck and drag me around, the pain in my neck and the blows on the stones will be like a chain of miraculous and wonderful things. I am such a dog and so miserable that seeing the miracle of my martyrdom, thanks to which I would be able to pray like other people, would ease my pain. And I would be happy. Without pain there is no prayer, little brother. That's why I sometimes think that I am the vilest of living creatures. Do you see that cat? Well, I can't look at it, it seems so superior to me. It is precise and intelligent and enjoys and suffers, like anybody else. I have very little intelligence. I only have love for persons, animals and trees, and even rocks. Sometimes when no one is looking I kneel and kiss the ground and the wall. No, I'm not crazy. Thank God it is not madness, but folly. And the horrible thing is that in my foolishness I am also happy. Little brother, as you see, I am hope-less. No matter how we look at it, there is no salvation for me. My only hope is that when I die God will keep me suffering for years and years in Purgatory. But without my knowing what the express will of God is, for then I will see the miracle and also be foolishly happy. What do you say, little brother? I see that the same thing would happen to you in this life, but perhaps you do everything without love, only for . . ."

I was going to protest, but he thought he understood and said:

"No, I don't say that you do things out of vanity. No, little brother."

"That isn't what I was going to say."

"What then?"

"That if everybody prays in his own way and has his own halo, churches aren't necessary."

"Ah, that's another question, brother. Too grave a question for us, who don't know or have not studied enough. But what I was saying is that you don't do things out of vanity. You do them out of pride. And pride is stronger than you yourself. But that doesn't matter. Life will punish you and punishment will be your prayer. The bad thing is that the pun-ishment could be so terrible that it would rob you of the last shadow of joy, and that distresses me. For you. Try to be humble, if you can. Just a little, brother. I know that you have tried to be. Tell me the truth. Weren't you happy when you refused to accuse Planibell when you hurt your knee? Tell me the truth. Weren't you happier?"

"No," I answered.

"Well, it doesn't matter. Go ahead with your defects. You will pray. You will be more devout than I, because others will wound your pride and you will suffer and strike back in self-defense, and that will hurt

you. And you will love others for themselves and not for God, and you
will have disappointments and sorrow. You will pray, little brother,
whether you want to or not. You will be much better than I because all
your life will be a prayer. No matter. Before I blamed you for your pride.
Now I think better of it. God illumines me and makes me see that your
pride will become prayer."

He glanced around, and at the cat as if the animal could understand
him—the cat immediately started purring—and added:

"I am a monster, little brother, because I am incapable of suffering
even if the greatest misfortunes in the world befell me. I cannot mix
with the fathers and other brothers, students or anybody, because I have
no talent for suffering, that talent, gift, which in some way has made
them men worthy of God. I am only a fool who laughs and sometimes
cries without either grief or pain. And I am in my corner hammering
away and ashamed of the look of the cat. Have you noticed what beautiful eyes the cat has? Only one thing saddens me at times: the idea that
the other fathers and brothers might become aware of my happiness and
believe me to be more of an imbecile than I really am, and put me out
in the street. They might throw me out. Well, little brother, I am talking
too much, but that's because you will be leaving in a few weeks and you
are the only student who comes to see me. I am grateful to you. And if
we don't see each other again . . . Well, yes, we will see each other.
You will see. Now your family is going to live in Zaragoza. You will find
many schools there as good or better than this. Maybe you won't be back.
Well then, I would like your advice, little brother. Nothing important.
The advice of a friend. Your pride doesn't bother me any longer. Be
proud if you cannot be otherwise, and you will serve God with your pride.
Here is the advice I ask of you, little brother. What do you think I ought
to do with this marble head? I really do like it. I like the others, of the
Virgin, Jesus, San Felipe, in God. But this one pleases me for itself and
sometimes, God forgive me, I like it best. And it is a pagan head. With
it I pray to myself. I asked you to smash it and you refused. It must be
for some good reason. What do you think I ought to do?"

I looked at the lay brother, then at the head which had a rare
diaphanous quality here and there. I looked at the cat:

"The best thing," I answered, "would be for you to give it to me when
I go home."

"Give it to you? And what will you do with it?"

"I'll put it somewhere, with your name on the base."

"No, not my name," he protested, blushing slightly. "And where would you put it?"

"In a little meadow, in the Pardinas."

"On a column? On top of a little gray stone column? Gray would be better than white."

"Yes, if you like."

"Ay, little brother, I think that is a very nice idea, and may God forgive me."

Repeating his own words, I said:

"If it is vanity, that doesn't matter. You would probably like to be the best sculptor in the world and cannot be. When you see you cannot . . . you will be very unhappy. And so you will pray. Isn't that what you want?"

The lay brother looked at me with shining eyes:

"You are giving me back my lesson, and you say it very seriously, very sure of yourself. I wonder if you are right, if we are right? Well then, this very instant when you are talking with the sincerity of innocence I ought to kneel at your feet and kiss your shoes. Yes, my son. I like that statue, indeed I do. I want to make statues and not only for the devout to venerate because of what they represent, no. I want to hew out of the stone and wood forms that I alone have seen in my solitude. Will I do it? I don't know. Take away that head and put it wherever you like. I will think of it there now and then. But I will not put my name on the base, no, not that."

"Why not?"

"No, don't insist. It is useless, little brother."

He was rubbing the marble head again and for a moment I forgot these preoccupations and thought about Ervigio's letter to Prat's sweetheart. I felt flattered by two things: that the lay brother had asked for my opinion as to what he should do with the statue, and that Prat should think of fighting a duel with me before discovering that I was not the guilty party. I racked my brain for ideas and words heard at home that could have some bearing on the lay brother and his problems. I remembered a certain Father Villegas, a Jesuit, professor of the school in Salamanca, who sometimes came to see us. My father called him a saint. One day at table, when discussing problems brought up by my father, Father Villegas remarked that God wanted men to possess things—to acquire properties or natural attributes—fully, solidly and joyfully. Not very sure of repeating the idea accurately, I said to the lay brother:

"You should sign your name, because God wants everyone to possess things thoroughly and completely."

The lay brother looked at me, hesitating. Then quite dramatically he said:

"That's not your idea. You heard somebody else say that. If you had thought it up, I would believe you, little brother. And I would follow your advice. But that idea is not yours. All right, no matter. Going back to what we were discussing before, how will you carry the marble head when you go home?"

Seeing that I did not know what to say, he promised to make as light a box as possible, for me to carry on the train. As I prepared to leave the shop, the friar asked:

"And your studies?"

He surmised that they were going badly and told me to take advantage of the time left before the examinations. I promised him I would, and in return asked him to keep the secret about the electric switches. He nodded with a sigh. I also told him about Ervigio and Prat, and immediately regretted it, for the lay brother's alarm warned me that he might tell the other friars so that they could protect the culprit. I had described the affair as an insult to Prat deserving punishment.

‡ 13 ‡

When I left, the lay brother was hurriedly putting on his cassock. He was surely going to find Father Ferrer. I did not know whether to be sorry or not. As a matter of fact I felt no preference for either Ervigio or Prat, and they could both go to Hell together as far as I was concerned.

I thought of the need to put to good use those three weeks reviewing my books, although the idea of flunking all my courses and annoying my father rather appealed to me. If that made my father suffer, however, and contributed to the salvation of his soul, that was not so appealing. All day long I mulled over these things. There was no escaping the uncomfortable experience of the examinations, for not only did the revolution not materialize, but the strike had been settled. Thinking about this and Valentina and the lay brother, whose words had quite confused me, I set to work that very day. Not only did I study during "vigils," but took my books to my room—which was not allowed—and since there was no light in the cell, I went to the toilet where I read for hours on end. It was somewhat more uncomfortable to read those books than Salgari's novels, even though the conditions were similar.

Ervigio was constantly trailing some friar and was on the alert around Prat, from whom he feared something. Then one afternoon Prat and I trapped him in the recreation storeroom. No one else was about and we shut the door. On the wall was a rack with foils used by the older boys in their fencing lessons. They all had blunt points sheathed with leather. Prat and I each took one. Ervigio thought that we were going to fight as a joke and that he was not concerned. He was terrified when Prat struck him on the legs and said:

"Your hour has come, Pastoreta."

I struck him on the arm. With no points or cutting edge the foils could do him no harm, but the blows must have been more painful than those struck with a stick. I restrained Prat with a gesture and saying: "My turn first. Then you can kill him, if you like." I struck Ervigio a sharp blow on the knees and asked:

"Why did you write Ines a love letter signed with my name?"

I struck him again. And again, but Ervigio screamed when looking at Prat, whose mute threat terrified him. Maybe he was expecting Prat to kill him. He screamed so loud and so shamelessly that they heard him outside. Several boys opened the door and Prat and I then started fencing as if playing. Behind the boys came Brother Pedro. As soon as he saw him, Ervigio shouted:

"Brother, Prat says he's going to kill me."

His legs bore the marks of our foils—especially mine—but he was only worried about Prat. Seeing the brother near and that Prat was busy with me, Ervigio picked up another foil from the floor and holding it by the hilt struck Prat a hard blow on the back. As he turned around Prat received another and harder blow across his face, which made his nose bleed and almost cost him an eye. Brother Pedro stepped between them. I had dropped my foil and Ervigio was in the doorway and shouting, beside himself:

"Look at yourself in the mirror. Go ahead, have a picture made and send it to Ines."

Then he started singing like one possessed:

"Ines, Ines, Inesita, Ines,
Ines, Ines, qué bonita es . . ."

Prat looked at his blood-covered hand. From the cloister Ervigio screamed as he tried to escape from Brother Pedro's iron grasp:

"I'll write Ines again, I will, and sign my own name. And I'll ask her for a picture. And when you come to beat me up I'll make the sign of the cross on you again with the foil. Or cut your head off."

"Silence!" the brother commanded in vain.

And again Ervigio chanted in his hoarse voice:

"Ines, Ines, Inesita, Ines . . ."

Prat was on his way to the infirmary and did not hear. Does a lion heed the yelping of a fox? No. He can kill him with one stroke of his paw, but not fight. This is what we were all thinking as we saw Prat walk tranquilly away while Brother Pedro was still restraining Ervigio.

When Prat returned from the infirmary with his face bandaged he told the group of boys around me:

"This coming summer I'll grab La Pastoreta in the street some day and you'll read about it in the papers."

The examinations were held a few days later. I did well only in Latin, although they passed me in all my courses because of the consideration the professors have for the friars. I went to say goodbye to the lay brother, who was so moved he could scarcely speak. He showed me the box he had made and then the statue itself which was luminous and did not look like marble but coral recently taken out of the sea.

"Where have you finally decided to put it?" he asked.

I was thinking about a place the peasants called *El Mas,* and also the the Pardinas. Mosén Joaquín had told me that this name—Pardinas—came from the Latin *parietinae* and referred to some old walls and a Roman arch that stood near the road. There was also a shrine there, in ruins, and a pool.

"Is there really a pool?"

"Yes, with a stone causeway at one side. And the statue will face the road, for everyone to see. In the chapel is an incomplete inscription in Latin that says . . . *magna nominis umbra* . . ."

"Go ahead, go ahead. What else?"

"They also say there's a lamia's haunt in the chapel. But I haven't seen any. And many swallow nests. Those yes, you can see. And beehives."

I went on recollecting.

"The clouds there are real."

"What do you mean?"

"Well, genuine. And there is a caretaker and keeper of images and saints—even though there aren't any saints—who knows romances and recites one that goes like this:

Virgin of the Beautiful Love,
sovereign Holy Christ,
with the crown of thorns
and a partridge in his hand . . ."

"A partridge?" asked the lay brother. "What for?"

"He's the patron of the hunters. They bless the retrievers there every year when the hunting season opens. They also bless the vineyards."

"And is that where you will put the statue?"

"Yes. On a little column."

"No, no, brother. A thick column."

He told me how thick the column should be and wrote down the dimensions for me.

"Do you have storks there in the summertime?" he went on asking with childish curiosity.

"There used to be a nest and every summer the same pair would return. They have not come for several years now and Tía Ignacia says they both are dead, or at least one of them."

The lay brother seemed to be seeing the things I described:

"And what kind of people pass by there?" he asked.

"In the morning hunters with their dogs. And sometimes the judge or notary, or a swineherd or civil guard. And the wife of the tenant farmer with a cow or two with a tinkling little bell. And her daughter with a line of geese that go swimming in the pool every day, a little pool where there are tadpoles. There at one side is a great big hill covered with thousands of grapevines with a special kind of long yellow grapes they call *uvas de muslo de dama*—ladies' thighs. Once my father had to throw out some young boys who went there serenading with their *bandurrias* on the day lots were being drawn for military service. One of them was drunk and sang a 'pernicious' song that I remember very well."

"How did it go?" the lay brother asked.

"Like this:

Undressing I asked her
to take off my socks:
yes, she said, then she said nix,
giggling with her bag of tricks."

"Why do you call it pernicious?"

"That's what my father said. I think it must be because it's about *piernas*—legs. Pernicious comes from *piernas*."

The lay brother roared with laughter. I added:

"And sometimes tramps go by who are angels in disguise like Benedicto José."

We were silent for a moment, then the friar said:

"Well, little brother. I give you this head which will live longer than you and longer than I. Try to be like it, tranquil and firm. And if you have the courage for living that I lack, live fearlessly, my son. Your wounded pride will be your prayer. And maybe your salvation."

On the square base of the statue the friar had carved, in small but very neat letters: *Fray Blas S.F. fecit.* He laughed loud and somewhat abashed when he realized that I had seen it, and gave me his hand.

"Sometimes, depending on how the sun falls on it," he said, "this head will have its halo too."

He laid his hand on my shoulder and walked to the door with me:

"That will remind you of the halos all men have and will help you to appreciate them in their greatness and in their wretchedness. Yes, little brother, in their wretchedness. It is through their wretchedness that they resemble us. And your mania to be different and unique makes you resemble all the rest.

"Don't forget that I know. You wanted the workers to attack the convent and kill the monks so that you could stand up for me and show me your real feelings of friendship by saving my life. But it was not necessary. It will never be necessary. Not because the workers would not like to come, but because even if they did come some day and went quite mad and tried to kill me, martyrdom would really give me joy. Yes, little brother. That stupid contentment makes it impossible for me to be a true martyr. I am useless even as a martyr. But I thank you for your good will and your help, just as if it had all really happened."

Once again I perceived the lay brother's liquid soul with which he divined my intentions so well hidden that I myself had been unconscious of them until that very moment.

And half-grieving and half-contented, I departed.

‡ ‡ ‡

III

The Villa Julieta

translated from the Spanish

by FLORENCE HALL SENDER

‡1‡

I TRAVELED ALONE from Reus to Zaragoza, by train. This was a journey lasting over eight hours, a real man's adventure for me.

In one of the wayside stations I caught a glimpse of Planibell walking up and down the platform carrying a valise and packages, still wearing his schoolboy's cap. He boarded the same train two or three coaches ahead of mine. I do not know if he saw me or not. In any case I did not see him again until Zaragoza, since the train was an old-fashioned one with coaches that did not communicate.

We met on the station platform in Zaragoza. Between civilian life and boarding school, distances were fabulous and in some way equivalent to eons of time. I looked at Planibell as if I had not seen him for years.

A boy about sixteen years old came to meet my friend. They greeted each other like old acquaintances, although without familiarity. Planibell explained to me that he was going to spend the summer with the Biescas family, who were business associates of his father. The newcomer was, or appeared to be, a little shy, and hastened to explain:

"Well, not exactly, not really business partners. Mr. Planibell is a factory owner while we are only small merchants. Felipe Biescas, at your service."

Planibell glanced at me with satisfaction, as if to say: "Well, what do you think of that? Who is important around here?" At this point my mother and sister Concha arrived. I introduced Planibell, whose archangelic beauty made quite an impression on my sister, although ordinarily she looked down on boys under twenty years of age.

Planibell introduced Felipe Biescas, who took off his hat and repeated

that he was not a big wholesale industrialist like Mr. Planibell. Biescas'
humility had nothing affected about it. In any case, it was pleasant.
Everything about him seemed honest and simple. So much so that I had
some doubts—later—about his sincerity.

Planibell was not going to stay in Zaragoza. He was on his way to the
country, to the Pyrenees Mountains. Since Planibell's parents were
spending the summer in Portugal, they had given him permission to
spend his vacation in Aragón. Felipe Biescas explained:

"Monflorite is where my father was born and we still have a farmhouse
there."

Planibell turned toward me to say belligerently: "Know where I'm
going?"

"No," I replied.

"I'm going bear hunting."

Biescas arched his brows in amazement. My sister looked at him out
of the corner of her eye, skeptically. But I believed him in spite of his
reputation as a liar. And I said to him, "Watch out; remember Favila."

"There are bears near Monflorite, that's a fact," Felipe prudently
remarked.

Then with a great show of reverence and respect, the two boys said
goodbye to my mother and sister.

I started talking to them about Planibell, favorably, as was natural, to
show my importance as his friend. My sister listened absent-mindedly,
my mother carefully. My mother liked Felipe Biescas' humility. "He
looks like a good-hearted boy." Of Planibell she said, "He must come
from a very rich family."

I was somewhat surprised to find both my mother and sister dressed
up as they only dressed to go to Mass on holidays in the village. Aware
of my surprise, Concha explained that in the city people dressed up just
as if every day were Sunday. I was quick to add that it was just the
same in Reus. Then my mother looked at me with astonishment and
exclaimed:

"My goodness, you have a terrible Catalonian accent."

I was carrying a good deal of luggage—a bunch of books tied with
straps, the marble head in the wooden box prepared by the lay brother,
as well as a suitcase with my clothes—so we took a cab. As the cabdriver
picked up the box and noticed how heavy it was, he asked jokingly:

"What's this? A bomb?"

Since bombs were then the fashion in Barcelona, and my train came from that city, I said yes. In spite of her good sense my sister Concha—and she was the most sensible of my sisters—was not completely reassured and looked at the box with misgivings. My mother was explaining that life was different in Zaragoza and that I would have to live in a civilized way. They both agreed that I had grown a lot.

I was wearing my gray suit with double-breasted jacket, short trousers, and my school uniform cap, like those worn by naval officers, blue in winter, white in summer, with a patent-leather visor and shield in front. As we waited somewhere in the crowded traffic, another open cab carrying a priest passed by. The priest looked at me and I tipped my cap. The priest hastened to answer my greeting and took off his hat. My mother asked:

"Do you know that priest?"

"No, but Brother Pedro told us we ought to greet all the priests we pass in the street."

This struck my mother as a nice idea. My sister was a little shocked. "How strange!" she said. Brother Pedro surely could not imagine how many priests there were in Zaragoza. It was not that I was ready to carry out all the suggestions and regulations of the friars, but I wanted to make the experiment to see what would happen, and I liked it. For three or four days, then, I continued obeying Brother Pedro, but I soon began to realize that it was a little silly and forgot it. "The friars," I thought, "are always shut up inside their convent and don't know what goes on outside. They can't imagine, as Concha says, how many priests there are in this city."

Brother Pedro and the lay brother in the workshop were all I remembered of the school. The rest could go to the devil, especially Father Ferrer. As usual, my decision not to greet the priests drove me to the opposite extreme. I felt rather anticlerical in my own way, not as a matter of principle, but in imitation of the terrible Planchat.

My father had rented the first floor of the Marquis de M.'s house, at 15, Don Juan de Aragón Street. The Marquis and his family lived on the second floor. The house had an immense porch—porte-cochère—and a patio paved with small, compact round stones. Remembering this house in later years I related it, without knowing why, to heroes' houses in old novels, the house of Calixto and Melibea, for instance. But ours had no garden, only three small inner patios serving to light the inside rooms.

Even though only two stories high the house had a broad façade, with *rejas* and balconies and overhanging eaves, and was so deep that the back rooms faced the distant Plaza of the Kings, a vast, rectangular and always deserted square with stone arcades and the faded air of a medieval manuscript. Sometimes I felt as if I were still in the castle of Sancho Abarca.

My father was not acquainted with the Marquis and his family. Our only relation was that of tenants to landlord. Above the stoop next to ours I saw the great portal of carved wood at the entrance to their dwelling. Around the Marquis everything was grave, silent, and dark in tone. His two sons were young men already, much older than I, who sometimes passed by us without speaking. And almost without looking.

Our apartment had so many rooms that we children could change and choose another if we did not like the one assigned to us. There were at least twenty-five bedrooms, half of them empty. In one large room the girls had their piano. There Maruja spent the morning seated on the piano stool playing scales and arpeggios. The house was so large that in some rooms the piano could not be heard. Luisa would sometimes get lost and start screaming. We would have to go to her rescue, for she was afraid. Luisa was always afraid.

The Marquis' family rarely left home. They must have lived in the back part of the house, prudently withdrawn with their relatives and devotions. We, going to the movies and schools, fighting at home or pounding the piano, must have represented—or so it seems to me now—the ascending middle class and they the decadent aristocracy. Or declining, perhaps I should say.

We lived in the oldest section of the city. The dark, narrow street of Don Juan de Aragón began at the Magdalena Church, an old pagan temple dating from the era of Augustus, upon which a mosque and minaret had been built in the time of the Arabs, later consecrated as a Christian temple. Bats flew out of the arched Moorish windows at dusk. At the other end of the street was the Arch of the Dean, which was no arch at all but a stone tunnel over twenty yards long and the really grandiose entrance to La Seo. La Seo was the true cathedral of Zaragoza, with its Roman mosaic floor, Mudejar decoration, and Gothic arches. The choir carvings were Renaissance and altogether there was an impressive sobriety and grandeur about the place. The parish priest of La Seo was a relative of ours, Don Orencio. Mosén Orencio. His surname—Borrell—was also that of Wilfredo el Velloso and it was my maternal grandmother's. Borrell. That branch of my family was of Visigothic origin. Those ridiculous preoccupations with lineage now seem to me—

in memory—to have a certain poetry. My father was fond of recalling the origins of my mother's family, not out of aristocratic snobbishness, however, but because that same poetic quality added something to the personality of his wife with whom he was in love.

We usually went to Mass at La Seo. My father every day. At eight o'clock in the morning, and sometimes before, we would hear him returning home and shouting "Everybody still in bed!" in a scandalized tone.

Then he would have his breakfast, which was invariably a bunch of grapes and a glass of water. Afterward he smoked a cigarette, scolding all the while, and left. When we heard the door close behind him we would all heave a sigh of relief and turn over in our beds.

My father was very busy at the time. He had sold over half the landed property, mortgaged the other half, and with the capital was trying his hand at various kinds of business. For the moment he had become co-owner of a rather large printing establishment and bindery whose owner was in financial straits. Whenever my father was asked what kind of person this owner was—he was a small man, dressed in mourning, with the face of a fox—he would say, raising his head with great solemnity: "A daily communicant."

I visited the press and bindery occasionally. There all my school exercises were bound, with my name printed in gold on the cover.

But the owner, even if he did go to church every day, did not strike me as a man to be trusted. He was too humble, and a certain rigidity between his shoulders, neck and head almost always kept him from moving with natural gestures. Children's instinct is very reliable. Later I decided that my father had not read Molière's *Tartuffe*. As a matter of fact, he only read legal or religious books. All the rest seemed to him to be a rather indecent way of wasting one's time. This was the period when my father was trying to register as a licensed real-estate broker and every day he had *very important* interviews. One might get the impression from what I am saying that my father was stupid, but nothing could be farther from the truth. He was merely trusting, noble and inexperienced.

Living in this house and section of the city was not like being in Zaragoza. I had the impression of having returned to the castle. Going from my house to the city was an adventure. The city was El Coso, Independence Plaza with its promenade of the same name, Alfonso Street and Pilar Plaza. The famous and grandiose Pilar Church was modern and decorated almost like a luxurious hotel or bank. The entire

Pilar neighborhood, with the exception of San Juan de los Panetes—a church apparently dating from the thirteenth century—was modern. My parents venerated the Virgen del Pilar although they did not think much of the temple.

As for the southeastern part of the city from the Plaza del Justicia Lanuza to Torrero and Buena Vista heights, this was the modern section where prosperous merchants and people of independent income lived in houses with gardens, central heating, and private swimming pools. Here the future lay.

I was a great walker, as one can imagine, and within a few days I had covered the entire city from one end to the other. Just as in the village, I had to know what was going on in every neighborhood every hour of the day so as to feel comfortably at home. Besides, I was making up for my confinement in the Reus boarding school with these walks. And I was seeking adventure. Surprises, that is, like all boys.

I discovered that at seven in the morning in the asphalt-surfaced Coso the street cleaners with long hoses swept the pavement with streams of water, iridescent in the sun. At that hour there used to be a wolfhound playing with the water and the streetcleaner would give it terrific shower baths. The dog liked them and would go to meet the streetcleaner with open mouth. The streetcleaner told me that the dog was very intelligent and that all his—the animal's—relatives were on the stage. By which he meant that they worked in the theatre or circus.

A little further down Cerdan Street was the market where thousands of buyers and sellers attended to their daily business in fruits, vegetables, meat and fish, protected from the sun by an immense roof of metal and cement, as complicated as the Cretan labyrinth. The most varied odors mingled inside, where a sensation of damp freshness prevailed. Down the middle of the brick pavement were little streams of running water, as in the Moorish *alcazars*. This struck me as a terribly exotic place. From one stand to the other the women argued, especially the fruit and vegetable vendors, and called each other the most shameless names I had ever heard in my life. Some of them stopped talking when they saw me, as if embarrassed.

Right here at the market place began the street I found the most historic in Zaragoza. Predicadores Street—or the Street of the Preachers—where the jail was located. Here Antonio Pérez, the favorite of Phillip the Second, had been imprisoned before his escape to France. This was a broad street with tall buildings with that half-topaz and rose patina

given by the centuries to residential buildings, while the stone of
cathedrals and palaces takes on a darker hue of stained iron. On Predicadores Street I occasionally found a soldier sitting on the curb and eating
a melon he sliced with his knife. There were also little carts shaded with
awnings selling American *galletas*—a kind of vanilla ice-cream sandwich.
They cost about three cents and I ate my full share.

Beyond the north side of Predicadores Street one could see the Ebro
River with its three great bridges. One for the trains, then the classical
stone bridge with Roman pillars, very wide, with both streetcar tracks
from the suburbs and the North Station running across it. Further still,
the bridge with cement arches which must have been the one used by
cart drivers and farm hands from the agricultural part of the city, near
the mouth of the Gallego River.

I explored the rest of the city on succeeding excursions, prompted by
curiosity. I only wanted to see. And not a single detail escaped me.

Zaragoza was much larger than Reus, and they were just as different
as an industrial and an ancient, traditional, agricultural city can be.
Zaragoza had its aristocratic districts, its plutocratic districts, its central
section of professional people and merchants, its military districts, its
neighborhoods of artisans, its ignoble and also extensive slums, like
those in the vicinity of San Pablo Street where modest people lived.
Reus was merely a city of businessmen, with factory chimneys and banks
everywhere.

Reus, however, seemed more romantic to me. For me romanticism was
not to be found in castles or Gothic palaces, but in the wide streets of the
modern sections flanked by shops with broad show-windows where, on
rainy days, the rubber-tired coaches were reflected as they passed by,
silent except for the clopping of the horses' hooves. The coachmen's legs
were covered with waterproof oilcloth.

For me, who came from feudal country, the automobile, movie theatre
and fashionable restaurant were romantic. Of course I changed my mind
later on. But then I was dazzled by civilization, or what appeared to be
civilization. I can still remember some evenings at the Ambos Mundos
Café where, from seven to nine, girls dressed as pages fired rifles at a
target from a red platform. Not daring to venture in, I watched from the
outside, through the enormous plate-glass windows.

Naturally, the marble head had caused surprise and confusion in my
family, and finally became the butt of laughter and jokes. At first they
thought it was a gift of some kind. A person returning from a long

journey usually does bring gifts. Even Maruja, who had no right to expect anything from me, thought for a moment that it was a present for her. When I uncovered the head, my father, who at that particular time was constantly repeating that school had made a new person out of me, asked in surprise:

"Where in the world did you get that? Steal it from some museum?"

Briefly I explained about the statue. My father asked:

"And you say that it is to be set up out on the Pardinas farm? But why Pardinas?"

"That's what I told the lay brother."

My father shook his head, pained:

"Too late. The Pardinas farm doesn't belong to us any more."

He had sold it to invest the money in his business ventures in Zaragoza. I was puzzled. I did not have the slightest idea about what advantage there could be to owning a pond and a shrine in ruins, but the idea of having no place for the statue disconcerted me. My father must have been aware of this and asked:

"Must you set it up somewhere? Take it to the county museum. I know the secretary. Although it might be better in a church, for it must be a saint. But what saint can it be?"

"No," I said dryly. "It's no saint. And I won't put it in a church or museum."

My father kept looking at me as if thinking that maybe the school's influence had not been so beneficial after all. He thought that I had changed a great deal in Reus. But he was the one, as a matter of fact, who was changing character in Zaragoza.

The statue suffered the strangest and most contradictory fortunes. Concha put it on top of a bookcase in the room which, with more optimism than justice, we called the study. There my father had a work table, two or three armchairs, and some books. But he never used this room. The table lamp, which was broken and did not work, was never fixed in all the time we lived in this house. My father had a horror of rooms filled with books, inkstands and armchairs inviting reflection.

‡2‡

Sensational things happened that summer. Some in connection with the family, others unrelated. The most important outside event was the declaration of the First World War. The most remarkable family development was that my sister Concha was beginning—as she put it—to like boys. The enthusiasm with which she admitted it, without anyone's asking, revealed the innocence of that natural inclination. But this same innocence also led her to risk more than was prudent. Concha was becoming a specialist in curtain and window flirtation. Her capacity to dissemble was immense but she only made use of it with my parents. With me she was sincere and natural. I saw her one day in an inside window smiling, looking up, down, and smiling again, very conscious of being contemplated. Man in sight, I fancied. Taking the necessary precautions and changing my vantage point I discovered, in another window, one of the Marquis' sons winking at her and blowing her kisses. At first I felt offended by the ease with which the Marquis' son was sharing the intimacy of our home, even though from a distance and in a trivial way. Then I thought of Valentina. My sister Concha could be the Valentina of the Marquis' son. This was worthy of respect.

I was my sister's confidant in these intrigues. I did not question her being interested in the Marquis' son. He was a handsome man, dark-skinned and fair-haired, with that kind of dull, gilded-silver blondness typical of a part of the old aristocracy. He was tall, athletic, with at the same time a stylized refinement in his vigor. I did not oppose my sister's inclination.

But Concha's love affairs were the most peculiar things in the world. She fell in love through the windows and through the windows she became disillusioned, without ever having exchanged a word with her gallant or even reading one of his letters. For the Marquis' son sent her billets-doux which did not reach my sister's hands, or if they did, were torn up or returned unopened. Before tearing them up Concha would become very nervous and say to me:

"Do you think it's decent for him to write to me?"

Then under her breath she added:

"If Father finds out, he'll break my neck."

Concha was then a ripe fifteen years of age. Sometimes I had my doubts. I did not know whether to take the part of offended brother or accomplice.

We had a cook and a housemaid, both from our village. Or perhaps I should say that the cook came from the village next to ours. It was the housemaid who opened the door and who more than once had received notes from the Marquis' son. My sister made her return them and I laughed at all these contradictions, although sometimes I felt a little uneasy.

When the Marquis' son saw that his letters were being returned unopened, he stopped writing. But this began to worry my sister. "I wonder if he isn't interested in me any more," she asked me. "Or maybe the maid refuses to receive them?" She asked me to find out because she did not want the maid to think she cared too much. I asked the maid and she told me:

"He wanted to give me other letters but I refused to accept them. The señorita gets mad."

This calmed my sister. She did not want to read love letters but she wanted them to be written to her. I told her:

"If you smile at him through the windows and spend your leisure hours winking at each other, isn't it absurd for you to refuse to receive a letter? What's the difference?"

She shook her head. A letter was a serious matter. And she was shocked that I, her brother, who should admonish her, would be so lenient.

When Concha had to leave the house she dared not go alone. If she went out in the afternoon she was accompanied by the maid, if in the morning—when the maid was working—she asked me to go along. She was afraid the Marquis' son might approach her. When I accompanied her she obliged me to wear long trousers and she would take my arm. In the street my sister treated me with a great deference and gentleness, as if I were her sweetheart. Then at home we frequently fought, perhaps because I tried to abuse the authority given me by the window secret. One day, when I threatened to tell our mother, Concha put her hands on her hips and said:

"Do you think I'm afraid? Mamma is a woman, too, and knows that windows are for looking at men and that a look or a smile are natural things that don't harm anything or anybody. Do you think Mamma will say anything to me? She knows you have to get married, and if I don't look at men, who am I going to marry?"

She was probably right. The slightest liberty in matters of behavior was so far from my sister's imagination, and certainly my mother's, that for them all of this could only be the innocent road to the church and sacraments. I was getting bored, however, and decided to pay no more attention and leave my sister alone. Definitely, I thought, Concha wanted to be a Marquesa. This seemed to me ridiculous as well as impossible.

But maybe I am unfair to my sister because she never cared in the least about forms of social splendor.

Another of my father's investments had been to buy German securities. When the war began, German propaganda was intense and many Germanophiles, especially my father and a group of his friends, bought war bonds. When they met in the streets they exchanged looks of satisfaction and pointed to the folded newspapers in their hands as if saying: "These German rascals have already taken Charleroi and are advancing on Amiens. They are almost in Paris. We are going to make a killing." No one had any doubts about the Germans winning the war.

If I had been like my sister I, too, could have flirted in the windows of my room because from there one could see the rear of the school of Pauline nuns where there were novices as well as boarding pupils. They peered out the windows sometimes and tried to provoke me with winks or some sweet word which I took as a real insult, since I suspected that because of my age or for some other reason they were teasing me.

Meanwhile the statue had been removed from my father's study, although not by him—he had not even realized it was there—but by my mother who eyed it with distrust now and then and said:

"Isn't it Nero? It must be Nero, my son."

Then she went closer to see the signature in the small pedestal where the lay brother's name and the Latin *fecit* were carved. And she added:

"I couldn't sleep a wink with that head in my room."

My mother did not like it. Nevertheless I looked at the statue thinking, "I would certainly love to be like him when I grow up." Then I would run my hand over the head from back to front, feeling its baldness.

There were conflicting opinions about the bust. My sister Luisa stupidly said that I had stolen it from a cemetery and that I should take it back where I found it, because it was the soul of a *margarito*. For Luisa, suitors who waited under balconies were *margaritos*. So were the young men she saw in the street with their heads glued to *rejas*. When she saw a couple in love walking along arm in arm, she said they were a *Margarita* and a *margarito*. All sweethearts for her were called *Margarita*, and even though the masculine form of this name did not exist, she applied it to all suitors, which was quite ridiculous. She was about to reveal the innocent flirt that Concha was when she said:

"Concha has her *margarito*, too."

But no one took that irresponsible observation seriously and Concha bought the child's silence with candies.

Everything had a natural and logical explanation, even Luisa's foolishness. Near our home, in the same street, there was a flowering *reja* where
about mid-afternoon in the summertime a tall, slender, elegantly dressed
suitor, with his cane, and a flower in his buttonhole, would appear. His
sweetheart's name was Margarita. This young man was a local writer who
edited a weekly review with literary pretentions named *Cosmos*. The
magazine was printed in my father's shops—or rather, in those in which
he had invested. My father had met this writer in the printing office and
they had become friends. When he called at the house Luisa would be
the one to run ahead to announce him, crying out:

"It's the *margarito* from *Cosmos!*"

One day a cavalryman, covered with gold braid and wearing a long
saber, came to see us. His name was Baltasar and he was from our village.
My father treated him with a certain paternal air. This soldier, who was
a big-hearted, candid, kind and timid soul, became a friend of mine.
Sometimes he came to the house looking for me and without entering
would say to the *doncella*: "Tell Master Pepe that Baltasar is here." I
would go out and together we would take a stroll, to the market, sometimes to the Almozara grove where we had a snack. We would buy a
well-chilled watermelon or a couple of dozen peaches and sit down to eat
them beside a stream. The soldier would tell me about military life and
then sigh and say, "Only three more months to go."

"Do you want to go back to the village?" I asked him.

"Oh, I sure do."

"What for?"

"Well, if only to hear the little birds singing in the orchards."

I repeated this to my father and he made very curious observations. For
instance:

"Bah, Baltasar is a blusterer and talks just to be talking. In his whole
life he has never eaten as well as he is eating now."

My father seemed unjust to me. Maybe Baltasar was eating better in
the barracks, but his yearning *to hear the little birds singing in the
orchards* was legitimate and I understood it. The truth is that my father
felt veneration toward the army and traditional institutions in general.
Baltasar's nostalgia annoyed him.

On certain summer days Concha and I would go out seeking adventure. We would get up at six in the morning and take the Torrero streetcar to the Pignatelli Canal where we rented a boat and rowed around for
an hour or two. My sister Concha would wear my sailor's cap, which was

quite becoming to her. And if some young man who appealed to her passed by, she would start her coaxing ways and say sweet things to me, as if I were her lover. It must have been quite absurd for I was too young, and surely no one fell for it. Whenever I heard Concha saying something sweet to me I thought, "Gallant approaching." I never missed. If I became angry she started talking to me about Valentina:

"Don't I help you with her? Well then, you have to help me now. That's what brothers are for."

If memories of Valentina were not enough to win me over she would say I looked like Hugo, the hero of a film serial called *La Moneda Rota* —The Broken Coin—that was appearing at the Emma Victoria Theatre, where I could go for the moderate sum of twenty céntimos, or four cents. This Hugo was an athlete who dealt out a formidable number of punches to rescue the heroine, whose name was Lucille Love, from perilous situations. In this movie theatre, which opened early in the afternoon and ran until one in the morning, there was an *explicator* to explain to the illiterate peasants what was happening on the screen. It seems to me that I can still hear that good man walking up and down the main aisle and crying out in a sing-song tone:

"Lucille was crossing the desert . . ."

The accented syllables of each word he recited in a much higher tone. Sometimes they also showed Chaplin's short films which were all the rage among young and old alike.

I went to the movies because I was following *La Moneda Rota*. Although my father objected strongly to modern forms of entertainment, he did not disapprove of my going. Yet he never gave me any money. I did not need it either, since I was in the habit of filching any loose change I found lying around on tables as long as it was less than two pesetas, which seemed like a sizable sum to me. Oftentimes I found a peseta and a few copper coins on a table or chair which I pocketed without the slightest qualm. When the cook said: "I left a peseta eighty here and can't find it," my mother took for granted that I had helped myself to it. None of my brothers or sisters ever did such a thing. And I did it without greediness. So long as I had a peseta in my pocket I never touched any more, even if I saw money scattered around everywhere. But once it was spent, and with nothing left, I grabbed the first I saw.

On one of those early morning excursions with my sister, in search of adventure, we went quite a distance up the canal and discovered a boat much larger than mine, white all over and shaped like a swan. It would hold some twenty people and was drawn by a white horse walking along the green bank.

The swan's neck rose like a question mark in the prow and between its wings were two parallel rows of comfortable seats for the excursionists. I gazed at it, fascinated, and Concha, who had been in Zaragoza longer and was better informed, said:

"This must be the gondola that takes people to the Villa Julieta. I've heard about it."

But still I did not understand:

"What's the Villa Julieta?"

My sister, giving a caressing tone to her voice, said:

"Don't you know? It's a paradise-like place. A real little corner of heaven."

"All right, but is it public?"

"Naturally."

"And what do they have there?"

"Well, what do you expect? Walks, circles, lawn, romantic summer-houses, bowers, rose gardens. A paradise, I'm telling you. And it is public. That is, you pay a peseta for the trip in the gondola and entrance fee altogether."

"Is it far?"

"An hour, more or less, they say, by boat. The maid goes there every Sunday with her sweetheart."

I was calculating: one hour to go, another to return, two inside the Villa Julieta. It would take the entire morning. What would they say at home?

"We might be able to go," I said.

She took off my cap, which she had been wearing, tucked into a strap a flower she found floating on the water, put it back on and said:

"I don't believe we ought to go today. It's time to go home. But we can go some other day."

Then she looked at me dreamily and added:

"Every time I look at your Petronius I remember the Villa Julieta."

Concha was reading *Quo Vadis?* at the time and Petronius seemed to her distinguished and handsome. *Arbiter elegantiarum*, she would repeat, as if she knew Latin.

Nero, or Petronius, continued making the rounds of our house. The day before, I had taken it out of the kitchen where the cook was sharpening a knife on it. I put it in my room, on the small study table where I had my books, even though it occupied over half of it. I did not want to leave it on the floor because that seemed irreverent. I became impatient thinking about the Villa Julieta and it occurred to me that if I found no other place, I could go there some day and leave Nero. In secret, of course.

"Are there any truncated columns there?" I asked.

"It's got everything, I told you. But I don't know for sure. I've never been there."

"If you've never been there, how can you know so much about it?"

"Well, one hears talk. One isn't deaf. I know what the sea is like, too, even though I've never seen it. What I can tell you is that the Villa Julieta is an ideal spot for lovers like you and Valentina, *queridito*."

That *queridito* reminded me that some gallant must be lurking around on shore. And sure enough there was. He was a jovial young man who greeted us with a smile and a military salute. I made a light, grazing stroke with one of the oars and sent a spray of water his way that must have soaked his shoes. The young man jumped back and, still laughing, asked:

"Don't you remember me? Felipe Biescas, Planibell's friend." And saluting again, he added: "At your service."

"What are you doing here?"

"Looking at your boat and its precious cargo."

My sister laughed without pleasure. I rowed the boat ashore. The swan-shaped gondola was still close by. Felipe withdrew slightly, not quite sure of himself. I asked him:

"Do you intend to go to the Villa Julieta?"

"Yes, I do. The owner is a relative of mine. Well, the real owner is somebody else and my relative is the manager."

"Really?"

"Sure, people usually have relatives. That's my case. My uncle pays so much and exploits the Villa Julieta."

Again my sister laughed mockingly. She wanted to give the impression she despised Felipe—but why? Maybe because he did not yet shave.

"When does the gondola leave?" I asked.

"The first trip at seven-thirty sharp."

"Not very early."

"No. Nobody gets up early here but you and I. Well, and my people."

"What people?" I asked.

"Friends," he replied in the military way. "There they are. Don't you see them?"

Some girls could be seen laughing and skipping the rope among the trees. The boy went on loquaciously:

"You make too much of an effort rowing and get needlessly tired. I'm more accustomed to it. Let me show you."

He jumped in the boat. I sat down on the bottom, leaning against my sister's legs, and Biescas started rowing with all his might, but with a slower rhythm than mine, not with his arms but throwing all the weight of his body backward. He was larger and stronger than I, in spite of which he treated me as an equal, although with a certain manly and friendly hostility. My sister eyed him suspiciously. Could this be proper? She got along with men very well from window to window, and perhaps from one side of the canal to the other. But the two of them in a boat, even with me in between . . . As he rowed, the newcomer finished introducing himself:

"I am, as you now know, Felipe Biescas and I live in Escuelas Pías Street. My father has a dry-goods store and I work there in the afternoons. I like to get up early, at dawn, winter and summer. And go out into the country. In winter, when there's snow, it's very nice. Looks like a polar landscape. I return home at noon. In the afternoon I work in the shop. I only live, what you call really living, in the mornings. At twelve, with the last peal of Pilar's bell, it's all over. To the store. Then the struggle for a livelihood begins. A yard of percale, three of velvet, seven of calico for countrymen's shirts, two bolts of muslin. Remnants at half-price. Well, the whole repertory. Now you see. My father knows nothing but buying and selling. Not even a grain of this"—he tapped his forehead and started rowing again. "A good person, sure enough. He doesn't bite, I mean. Even though he does kick sometimes. I say bad things about him, but don't get me wrong, I respect him and obey him. I realize he's not to blame. He does what he's seen done. He says I'm a fool. But it's not so. I look like a fool sometimes, but I'm deceptive. To get ahead in life one's got to be two-faced."

Felipe's way of talking irritated my sister, who kept looking at him as she would at a dog that knows how to stand on its hind feet. Felipe continued:

"My father thinks he's got the right to break my bones with the yard-stick. Does your father have those ideas too?"

He talked like a phonograph and I listened trustingly and contentedly. But I did not answer his impertinent question. He became still more talkative:

"I only enjoy myself in the shop when peasants come in. Especially if they wear old fashioned knee-breeches. Lots of them come because our store has special materials of velvet and velveteen, corduroy and braids and bindings, all those things used only by peasants who wear knee-breeches. My father doesn't like them because they're a bother and stingy, but I get along with them very well. A country bumpkin with full skirts and white wool stockings comes in and I say to her: 'What do you want?' —'Some cloth.' 'What kind of cloth?'—'A cloth good for outside skirts.' 'What kind of skirts?'—'Something for us countrywomen but that looks good.' 'About how much do you want to spend?'—'Well, whatever is right among us poor folks.' 'Where are you from?'—'From Zuera, at your service.' 'Are you Aunt Benita?'—'No, sir, Aunt Benita's older than me, and no disrespect meant. I am Señora Vicenta, the Cripple's wife.' Then I keep quiet for a moment, thinking, and say: 'Now I know what you want.' And I say to my clerk: 'Fetch some good skirt cloth like Señora Vicenta, the Cripple's wife from Zuera, wears, something for country folks but good-looking.' And the clerk brings out any old kind of percale and the countrywoman buys it without a murmur. Two-faced. One's got to be two-faced in business. I get along with them very well because almost every Sunday I go on an excursion to some village or other and I know what they wear."

"And what do you do in those villages?" I asked, thinking that I was more of an expert in village life than he.

"I take part in the young men's games. Some places I play *pelota*. Others, bowling. In others, if it's fair time, I enter the foot races."

"Do you ever win?"

"No. But even if I could win I wouldn't want to, because I do believe for a fact that the young fellows would kill a foreigner before letting him win. You've got to be careful."

Although a good girl, my sister had the gift of laughing at strangers in an irritating way, sometimes without saying a word. She had returned my cap to me and was listening, but gave the impression that she was thinking of something else. I knew what she was thinking about: about that stranger climbing into our boat. The unknown son of a shopkeeper on Escuelas Pías Street, near the market, who talked like a parrot to make himself agreeable to my sister. To my father and grandfather, a shopkeeper was a man who lived without working. My grandfather used to say—when he was still alive—that they were all thieves. My father, more reasonable, said only that they were venal. They felt a natural contempt for shopkeepers with which my sister and I were contaminated. At first I could not believe there were so many merchants in Zaragoza. Since I did not know there were houses with several floors to be rented to different families, and could not imagine such a thing, I assumed that the merchant of the shop underneath occupied the whole house. So the entire center of the city looked to me as if inhabited by merchants. Some time passed before I realized my mistake. At first the fact that two families lived in the Marquis de M's. house seemed to me a sign of lamentable poverty for them as well as for us. And there was Felipe—a merchant—rowing and talking. Seeing that we were moving far away from the place where we had met him, I asked:

"And your people? Your girlfriends, I mean."

"They aren't girlfriends. They're my cousins. I don't care about them. My cousins are daughters of the gondola owner and they go to the Villa Julieta every week."

"And you? Don't you go with them?"

He was silent for a moment and for the first time gloomy:

"Once in a while," he said. "But I give them the slip whenever I can and stand them up. Just like today. I'm a better friend of yours than of my family. Those girls, aside from being relatives, and one can't help that, don't appeal to me. They only want to . . ."

He glanced at my sister and realized that he should go no further. I egged him on:

"What do they want?"

"Nothing. They only want to go on a spree, as they say. That leaves me cold. I'd rather be with you and row. Well, I talk a lot, but that usually happens when I'm with strangers I like. Then when we get acquainted, things will change. That's what happens. Well, here we are at the pier. The owner of the boats is a friend of mine. Eh, Uncle Nicanor, these young people will come some other day, won't you? They've been out twenty minutes over time. Don't charge them anything extra. They're friends of mine. Let's go. Now we'll take the streetcar and go wherever you like. Planibell's friends are my friends. It's still early. The sun doesn't burn. Here's the streetcar. All aboard. Well, everyone on his own, French way, no courtesies here. All right?"

My sister did not say a word.

Felipe was older than I. Three years? Four? He had a round face. He was fair-skinned and black-haired, with fine features, but quite manly

in appearance. It was evident that others did not greatly concern him
and yet he lived for others, always on the surface.

"How do you happen to know Planibell?" I asked him.

"Business."

"He's a two-timer also."

"I can't tell you anything about that."

"Some people," I added aggressively, "believe that all merchants are
thieves."

"You're right," he answered, without changing his expression. "I'm a
big thief, too, because I steal a five-peseta coin from my father every week.
In the shop. Saturdays after making a sale I go to the cash register and
open it: cling! But I ring up a *duro* less than I have in my hand, and then
I keep that *duro* instead of depositing it. It's always a *duro* in one piece so
it won't jingle in my pocket, because then my father would be suspicious.
You know how fathers are. Mine thinks fathers have a right to break
their sons' backs with one whack. Backward ideas. But look, here is last
week's *duro*, still unbroken. All in one piece. A Republican coin.
You're not Republicans, are you? Neither am I. What for? Republicans
are people who say, mine, mine. And yours, mine. That's what they say.
Life for them is keeping what they have and stealing what they can.
What do you all think of that? Social distribution. No, I don't like Republicans. The only thing I like about them is their *duro*. See? Spanish
Republic: 1873. And this matron sitting on her throne with a little laurel
branch in her hand. It's the only thing about the Republicans I like.
Depending on how you look at it, then, I am a thief. I steal from my
father. Good enough. That's the least a fellow can do to his father. Fleece
him a little."

"But why?"

"Well, because he brought me to life. I think about things a lot, although it may not look like it. They didn't consult me to find out if I
wanted to be born or not. And once here I'm not going to be a dunce.
I'm telling you. Later on, for example, I'll go for a swim at Doña Pilar's
house. And things like that cost money."

"Swim in a house?"

"Well, Doña Pilar's bathhouse. And it costs a quarter. You see. A
quarter. And where am I going to get a quarter if not out of my father's
cash register?"

My sister was staring out the streetcar window, to show him she was not listening. I was sitting between her and Felipe. It was one of those old-fashioned streetcars with two long benches facing each other from end to end, and an aisle in the middle. We were the only passengers. The streetcar was damp and clean and smelled of disinfectants, freshly swept and scrubbed. Felipe continued:

"I'm going swimming at Doña Pilar's. With this summer heat what can you do? I go in the late morning, around noon, because in the afternoon the water is thick and warm as soup, with the filth of everybody that's bathed in it. Yes indeed. You've got to go there early. I'm young, sure enough. But I know how to sail through life."

My sister looked at him with contempt. Sail through life. What a way to talk. He was so fine now because a moment ago he had been so vulgar talking about people's filth, and he wanted to make up for it. I also looked at him with a certain disdain. Sail through life, bah. Aware of it, he said:

"Well, pardon me. I'm sorry I talk so much. From the very first moment I thought we were going to be good friends. Ever since that day at the station when Planibell came and I first met you. Well now, maybe we're not going to get along. In that case I'll just vamoose and so long. I don't say this because of you, Pepe, but your sister. In any case, so long. Not just yet, of course. I may not belong to your class, but at least I know I'm very inferior to Planibell."

I was impressed by his humility. My sister took my watch out of my pocket to see the time. It was time for her window session with the Marquis' son. As we got off the streetcar in Constitution Square I had what seemed to me a good idea:

"You," I said to my sister, "go along home and I'll stay with Felipe."

She was startled:

"With whom? With a man who steals every Saturday?"

Then Felipe, who did not appear offended by my sister, took her side:

"I am a thief with my father, that's right. Only with my father. But your sister is right. You should take her home. But we don't have to separate because of that. I'll go with you, if you don't mind. You must go with her. With some other girl, that would be different. Like my cousins. I leave them there. Let lightning strike them. All right, I beg your pardon, señorita. That's just a way of talking. I mean that I don't care what happens to them, because being all together they are safe. Do I make myself clear? But your case is different, allow me to say so."

"Your case is also different," said Concha dryly. "And to tell the truth, I don't like it."

"I knew it," Felipe admitted humbly. "But there is something you all can't deny. I'm sincere."

I took his side:

"That's so. Felipe is sincere."

My defense made such an impression on Felipe that he decided to *tutearme*—to use the familiar form of address with me. I accepted this, also. Concha's treating him so badly annoyed me, it seemed unjust to me, and I wanted to make up for it.

We ambled along, through Don Jaime Street, the post office street, Argensola Plaza, Main Street, and it took us quite a while to reach the old Plaza of Don Juan de Aragón and our home. For our house faced a deserted little plaza, square, small, with moss and grass growing between the stones, and always deserted, into which one entered by a narrow passage from the Main Street. Felipe said:

"I'd like to live this way, too, on a secluded street, without any shops. This street is like Tenorio's, where Don Gonzalo de Ulloa lived. Don't you know who Don Gonzalo is? The one who says, with his face covered with his cloak"—and Felipe raised his bent arm to the height of his nose, as if he were covering his face with a cape:—" 'Villain, you have touched my face with your hand!' That's the Comendador. A terrible man."

Felipe laughed. Only Felipe, it's true. He came in the house with us and started climbing the stairs. My sister was indignant. We reached the top and the three of us entered our apartment. In a distant room Luisa's piano scales and arpeggios could be heard. She had made an early start. Felipe listened and exclaimed:

"*Hombre!* You have a piano! What luck! I know how to play a little. It's been my hobby since I was a boy, but my father never wanted to buy me a piano. He says that's something for young ladies. But I know how to play something. I can give you a little concert, if you like. Nothing much, of course. And you? Doesn't music interest you?"

My sister had disappeared, as one can easily imagine. I made a gesture of indifference. My friend—now I could call him that—asked me if it would be too early to play in the house, and promised to play only one piece.

"Which one?"

"The Waltz of the Fleas."

What a strange name for a waltz. We went to the piano. Luisa did not want to give up her place, but as soon as she saw a stranger she changed her mind. Felipe sat down, gazed at the ceiling dreamily, and suddenly began a ratty piece of music such as gypsies play on harmonicas when making the rounds of the fairs with a monkey. So vulgar and wretched that my sister Concha came in, closed the piano—almost nipping Felipe's fingers—and said calmly:

"Stop. That's enough for now. Excuse me"—and she repeated—"but that's quite enough for now."

Felipe did not know what to make of it.

"That's all right," I said to him. "Now you see that your music annoys my sister. Let's go to my room."

He noticed the statue on my table as we entered and asked:

"Is that your grandfather?"

"No."

After the "Waltz of the Fleas" I felt that he was unworthy to hear about the lay brother. But Felipe was an insatiable talker and again started telling me about his family. I interrupted:

"But what's the Villa Julieta like?"

This broke the thread of his conversation, but only for a moment:

"It's nice. A beautiful spot, like a place for poets. I only go when it's closed to the public. One day a week they close it to clean, sweep, prune the trees, sprinkle and cut the grass. Since the overseer is my uncle, I can do as I please. But you'll see what happens in my family. My father's very strict, though I don't know why. Maybe money drives him crazy. Money doesn't matter much to me. With Saturday's *duro*, I get along."

Again he remarked that he did not work in the shop in the mornings. His family thought he had a weak chest and ought to breathe fresh air. "That's my mother's idea. Mothers are more humanitarian, you know."

"What day of the week is the Villa closed?" I insisted.

"Tuesdays. I invite you to come Tuesday of next week, if you like. Free. Everything paid. Not a red cent to spend, as they say. The gondola free, too. And that gondola is something, no doubt about it. Really something. My mother says an opera called *Lohengrin* was written about it. Being in that gondola with a beautiful girl in the moonlight must really be bewitching."

"I'll take my sweetheart some day."

"Do you have a sweetheart?"

"Sure."

Felipe was thoughtful:

"And how good looking she must be!"

"She is."

Again he mused:

"That's great, really. A sweetheart. In the moonlight. My congratulations."

I thanked him curtly and Felipe changed the subject. He started telling me that the gondola was not the only boat in Zaragoza. Between the railroad bridge and the stone bridge over the Ebro there was a boat attached to a cable for travelers who did not want to walk the stone bridge. Crossing in the boat they saved three-quarters of an hour. Watch in hand he had verified it when he went to the groves of Almozara Park. The best thing to do, then, was to take Uncle Toni's boat. He was a great friend of Uncle Toni's and often went for a chat with him, and if it rained they would go in the tunnel in the stone battlement. A mysterious tunnel, quite large and deep like the places where pirates buried treasure. Long ago, of course.

"The owner of this boat is your uncle, too?"

"No. That's his name: Uncle Toni. Everybody calls him Uncle Toni. He fishes for barbels and says that all the fish in this part of the river between the train bridge and the mouth of the Gallego have a little bone in their head with the face of the Virgin del Pilar on it. I didn't believe it but he showed me one and it's true. I know what the Pilar Virgin looks like because they took me to the *camarín*—her niche—in the sacristy when I was little. My mother is very pious. Children seven years old or younger are taken to the *camarín*, you know. They climb up a little silver stair, fifteen or twenty steps of solid repoussé silver that's worth a fortune. And at the top I saw the big niche. In the middle, at the back, is a marble column and on top an image of I don't know what material. Alabaster, I believe. Black gold, others say. I have my doubts about that. Is there such a thing as black gold? Quite dark. That's where they get the song that says the Virgin del Pilar is a brunette. Once up there, with an acolyte wearing a red cassock and rochet, you genuflect"—Felipe did so—"and kiss the center of the Virgin's mantle. Don't you know that the Virgin's treasures are worth hundreds of millions? And they are in the sacristy and I have seen them, too, for I'm a friend of the verger's, the fellow who goes around with a long green silk cape-cloak dragging on the ground and a white wig and a silver staff. I am a friend of his. I have lots of friends. Know something? At night they turn several huge mastiff dogs loose in the temple. Like lions. We'll see who's a brave enough thief to go in there and steal. Each one of those dogs eats over seven pounds of raw meat a day. I know because they buy it in the butcher-shop next door to my store. In Escuelas Pías Street. You'll probably say I talk a lot. That always happens when I meet somebody new. Then when we are really friends, I control myself."

He paused. Suddenly he stared hard at me and said:

"What you need is a friend like me to open your eyes. Because you come from school quite a hick. Well, understand me, for city ways, I mean. In everything else you and your sister are way ahead of me. I saw that from the very first. And Planibell said to me: This Pepe Garcés will go far. I think so, too. That Planibell is a queer guy. All the time he was at home he spent talking about his rifle with a telescopic sight. That's a kind of telescope they put on top of the barrel, you know. Well, I didn't see the telescopic sight anywhere. It's a mystery, I'm telling you. Changing the subject, do you know that I go to the Emma Victoria Theatre whenever I want to?"

"Also free?"

"Yes, of course. The *explicator* is a friend of mine. He comes to our store shopping and I give him the stuff at half-price."

"How do you have so many friends? Do you sell cloth at half-price to all of them?"

"Oh, no, that's not necessary. It's very easy to have friends. All you have to do is make yourself little and insignificant beside them. Everybody's looking for people who belittle themselves. And when they find them, that's it, friends forever. I'm that way. But I have my own ideas. I look insignificant but I have my own ideas. Well, when you're as old as I am you'll have your own ideas too, naturally. Or maybe you have already. My idea is to flatter my mother and fool my father. So I get along fine at home."

Felipe stayed all morning and I was amazed that he did not invite himself to dinner. Finally he left. I accepted his invitation to go to the Villa Julieta on Tuesday of the following week. I intended to place the marble bust there—somewhere—and afterward write the news to the lay brother. But first I would have to do a little reconnoitering.

‡ 3 ‡

About this time someone invited us to the little Catholic Social Action theatre in Espoz y Mina Street. My sister and I went. The actors were good, but the theatre was small and crowded. They were performing a one-act play: "Corporal Pérez." It was unbearably hot. My sister did not flirt with anybody. That was a relief, because her flirting in public outraged my sense of dignity.

In the same building with the Social Action theatre was a library with a periodical room. I used to go there to see, among others, a magazine devoted to mountain climbing and exploration. The only thing that really interested me, however, was a serialized cartoon, a little adventure story about two English explorers.

The magazine reached the library on Thursday. And every Thursday at three in the afternoon I headed there with a voluptuous impatience such as I have never again felt regarding books or printed matter. I went up the steps panting and sweating with emotion. And opening those pages and seeing the little pictures with the new adventures was a rare delight. I came to dote upon it so that at home I drew more episodes of my own invention. Concha said that they were very good.

In those days my sister was exchanging letters with Doña Julia, Valentina's mother, who was sending me news of my sweetheart. I had the vague suspicion that my letters never reached her hands. I had written, telling her what life was like in Zaragoza, but saying less about love, because this struck me as a bit affected, or false, "especially at our age." My sister told me I was wrong about this and that true love is never false. It cannot be. Love is natural. How can anything as natural as love be false? She added that the only false thing was to talk about gondolas in the moonlight, the way my friend Felipe did.

Consequently I decided to write about love again in my letters to Valentina. But, I insist, someone was intercepting them.

My sister was wearing a little bunch of violets with the green stems turned up at her throat. This meant—I know for I heard her say so herself—that she was in love. Maybe she wore the violets for the Marquis' son to see. Just then all women with their mania for love seemed ridiculous to me, with the exception of Valentina, whom I found sublime. Those violets of Concha's put a distance between us. Woman's world was different and incomprehensible.

Another family from my town had come to the city with three daughters, all young and unmarried. In the village they had lived in a palace with a salon full of lances and helmets, but in the city they lived in a rather shabby third-floor rented apartment on the main street. They belonged to the nobility, but the father, whose name was Lucas Ramírez, did not work for a living. He spent his days searching for specialties in the grocery shops, for he was a great gourmet. And when he found them he would start home with his packages, telling all the acquaintances he met what he had bought, where, how much it had cost, and how the cook was going to prepare it under his immediate supervision. Reaching his house he would sit in the porter's lodge to rest before climbing the stairs. He was always pale and sweating. Meanwhile he showed the *portera* the three pounds of fresh salmon and told her that he was going to bake it as they do in Bilbao, so that it would be so-and-so, exquisite. Then looking at the stairs with melancholy he would say:

"Climbing three floors, in addition to the mezzanine and ground floor, is agony for me. Five floors. I have wondered if we couldn't rig up a large basket with a block and tackle that I could climb into. What do you think, *señora portera?* Would you be strong enough to hoist me up?"

He was serious and spoke in all sincerity. She told him that he could rent a lower apartment or move to a building with an elevator. She said this with irony, although he was unaware of it and answered solemnly:

"I have thought about it, but the elevator frightens me. People have been known to be left hanging between two floors all night long. I am afraid of it."

This family came to see us frequently and my father laughed at them. Don Lucas was so naïve that he was always praising my father to the skies and extoling his practical sense. Don Lucas' ancestors were among those who had crowned kings and gone to ransom the Holy Sepulchre with Godfrey de Bouillon.

Life in the city was a little more animated for us than in the village, but not much. Don Lucas Ramírez' daughters, who were a little older than I, came sometimes and we played lotto. If I happened to be wearing long trousers at the time, the second of the daughters, whose name was Vicenta, flirted with me. Her boldest coquetry consisted of choosing the cards and always giving me the violet-colored ones. The color of love, as everyone knows. If I was wearing short trousers, she paid no attention to me.

They were coming that afternoon but this was the day I had promised to meet Felipe at two at the Arch of Cinegio. Felipe did not work in his shop on Tuesdays. He worked Sundays instead.

When I arrived he was already waiting for me. We set out at a fast pace.

"You're fifteen minutes late," Felipe complained. "If I were like my

father I'd tell you that you had to pay for this in some way or other.
That's his mania."

"What is."

"What he calls 'impunity' drives him crazy. He says everybody's got
to do his duty or take his punishment. He with his impunity and I with
my duplicity, to see who can hold out the longest. You can just imagine
how careful I am. My mother saves me occasionally. But we have an
apprentice in the shop who's jealous of me for being the boss's son and
he goes tattling to my father. Some day I'm going to give him such a
drubbing you'll hear his screams clear to Calatayud. Well, to change the
subject, let's go to Doña Pilar's baths."

"Didn't you say you can go only in the morning?"

"Yes, but it isn't late yet. Until three the water's all right."

Doña Pilar's baths consisted of a pool some sixty feet square. Admission
was two reales. You could stay in the pool an hour.

The sun glared. All around were small terraces and compartments
closed with wire screen where on working days laundresses hung out
their clothes.

When I entered I had quite a shock. Some ten or twelve men and boys
were swimming around, all as naked as the day they were born. Felipe
stripped in an instant and plunged into the pool headfirst. He swam
around the pool once dog-fashion, paddling forward with both hands and
feet. Reaching my side he said, out of breath:

"Don't you swim? The water's stupendous."

For the first time I heard that word. *Stupendous*. I would have to remember that one and use it, too. Meanwhile I was looking at those naked
people and could not understand. Everything repelled me.

"No," I said. "I don't swim here, with all these people."

My friend frolicked in the water, swimming back and forth contentedly. He was really getting his quarter's worth. I felt like insulting
everybody. Or running away. But I stayed on, thinking: They're right.
What they're doing is natural and doesn't mean a thing.

Doña Pilar was a gray-haired matron, large and broad, with cold, pene-
trating eyes. She herself ran her business and kept an eye on the customers. Neither she nor the bathers seemed to attach the slightest
importance to the men's immodest nudity. Doña Pilar had a notebook
and pencil. Also a small watch hanging around her neck on a string of
jet beads. She was apparently jotting down on the stub the hour each

one had entered, so that she knew how much time they still had left. She came out of her little office and went to the water's edge:

"You," she called to one who was doing the dead man's float, "come, come, it's ten minutes overtime for you now."

She handed him what looked like a bunch of rags. He grumbled and she cut him short, imperiously:

"No loitering now, we know each other well and I see that you're a rascal. So be quick about it and out into the street. There are your clothes."

He climbed out of the pool, looking like an enormous frog. Doña Pilar passed by me talking to herself:

"You've got to be sharper than a tack in this business, sharper than Lepe, Lepijo and his son."

She went back to her office while the bather dressed slowly, muttering. I could not understand. For the first time in my life I wondered if maybe people exaggerated when speaking of modesty, the shame of nakedness, and the like. Dressed among all these people, I was beginning to feel different and uncomfortably odd.

Other customers arrived. The pool was soon full. More human flesh than water was visible. My friend Felipe came out, saying:

"This is what I call Doña Pilar's soup. From now on the water is dirty and warm and so thick you could cut it like jelly. But I see now. You don't like to swim. One must come before noon, as I told you."

He started dressing, first his shirt, then socks. Next his shorts and trousers together. And he was chattering happily:

"How I needed that swim!" he said.

We left, silently.

"You've got something on your mind. What's wrong?" he asked.

"I thought," I answered, "that the bathers wore swimming trunks."

"Now I see what shocked you," he said seriously. "But what difference does it make? Don't you see we're all men? Well, there's Doña Pilar, but then she's like a mother."

I was surprised to see that my not wanting to strip the way they did gave me a certain prestige with Felipe. When I said that the swimming pool looked like a frog pond he burst out laughing:

"With a few *samarugos* here and there."

In Zaragoza fools are called *samarugos*. The *samarugo* is the fat-headed tadpole that later on turns into a frog. It struck me as funny. Very well. Now I had seen Doña Pilar's baths where people bathed utterly naked like the Romans in ancient times. And the next Tuesday I would get to see the Villa Julieta. The name sounded strange to me. Why Julieta? It also sounded like the name of a pleasure villa in Roman times. Then the city was called *Caesaraugusta*. That's where the name Zaragoza comes from.

I still felt a certain aversion toward my father even though he did seem much more human than in the village, probably because of his being in an atmosphere like that of Zaragoza where we were nobody. My enmity manifested itself only in small secret attitudes. For instance, I favored the French in the war. In other and less important matters the same thing was true. I would always take the opposite side. My father did not especially care for Mosén Orencio, the parish priest of La Seo, because he was my mother's cousin. He was jealous of him. *Nice* jealousy, of course. Not erotic jealousy. My mother admired her cousin and that was enough to make my father unable to bear the sight of him. I decided then and there to go to him for confession whenever my father reminded us that everyone had to receive communion, usually once a month at least. And if not with Mosén Orencio I would not go to confession. I did not refuse just to annoy my father. I really liked this confessor with his solemnity and paternal gentleness. If my father asked:

"But what kind of a mania is this for Don Orencio? One should not confess to relatives."

I answered, feigning surprise:

"Well, a priest is a priest. And one's just as good as another. I began with Don Orencio and I'll go on with him because he understands me better than the rest."

But the main reason was to annoy him. My father clacked his tongue and went out, slamming the door.

The parish priest Don Orencio was fat, vulgar, not very spiritual and not at all intelligent. He had a splendid library, which he had inherited from Gracián y Lastanosa, and he did not feel the slightest curiosity about it. My father criticized and ridiculed all my mother's relatives. Mosén Orencio deserved the censure, for sure. He was a quite materialistic priest who understood wines better than books. A wine merchant of French origin named Labatut had told my father that Mosén Orencio was one of his best customers.

My uncle Orencio had a broad face, reddish like a new potato. You could see his blood through every pore of his skin—a tiny red dot, ready to spurt out.

My sister Concha's adventure stayed in its primitive state, neither progressing nor worsening. The only possible progress, of course, would be for the Marquis' son to formalize the courtship by asking permission to call. Since this did not happen, and my sister, being very young, did not expect it, they continued winking at each other from the windows of an inside patio where doubtless many gallants and many virgins had been winking at each other since the time of Ferdinand and Isabella, and who knows if not from before the time of the Arabian King Marsilio. Don Juan de Aragón Street was a constant reminder of the Arabic world of mosques, alcazars, orchards, and strong castles. My sister with her ivory, oval face and large eyes dark as night must have looked like a *fatima* in her arched Moorish window.

But the gallant, doubtless to make a favorable impression on my sister, appeared at daybreak in one of the small square patios with riding clothes, whip, and shining boots. From somewhere he produced a bay horse that almost filled the patio. Before getting up I heard the cries of the rider hushing the brute, the sound of the impatient horse's hooves, and more horseman's cries in a low, grave and affected tone:

"Boha, Babieca . . . sooo."

I don't know if the horse was anything like Babieca or not, but the little Marquis was certainly a far cry from the Cid. The horse whinneyed, sometimes reared, making a thud when falling on all fours again. I could not imagine what the young man was doing with that horse in such a small space. I never saw him ride. Nor did I know the house had stables, either. I had the impression that it was a horse kept in some cupboard for purposes of heraldic chivalry. And the boy showed it off before my sister one hour every day. It was a very handsome horse, to be sure.

We did not live in that somber palace on Don Juan de Aragón Street for very long. We moved suddenly from the historical end of the city to the most modern section, which seemed romantic to me then, as I mentioned before.

The rest of the family fortune—of the usable capital, I mean—my father invested as a bank guarantee for some work he had been given. Quite good work as agent for all Aragón of an important company: "National Insurance and Union." It sounded more like a political slogan than the name of a corporation.

The company had its offices at Number 3 Coso Street, with a large jasper sign on the balconies. It was in the very heart of the city. There were the houses of finance, de luxe shops, fashionable cafés with famous concert performers. In short, the exact opposite of Don Juan de Aragón Street. The building was an old six-story house and the second floor was given us by the company for our residence. It was on the corner of the Callejón de la Audiencia—the Court of Justice—but as Coso Street jogged there toward Cerdan Street, the windows and balconies facing the narrow street of the Court of Justice were practically overlooking the Coso itself. A really beautiful place to live. I was elated. I felt like a modern, civilized and cosmopolitan man.

The house next to ours was the palace of the Lunas, a large old Renaissance building visited and photographed by tourists. It had an immense porte-cochère with two stone giants, one on either side, supporting the frieze and threatening hypothetical enemies with enormous stone maces. Here the provincial Court of Justice was housed. Going in and out of my house I always looked over there with respect.

My father had the weakness to link this palace with the history of my mother's family. "In the mountains of Aragón," he would say, "the Garcés and Luna families have always been related." My mother paid no attention. She never thought about anything concerning ancestry, nobility or *hidalgo* rights.

When we moved to Number 3 Coso, we lost one of our servants: the cook. My mother did not replace her. This left us with only one servant for everything, the one who formerly had been housemaid. My sisters would now have to lend a hand.

I realized that something was going badly, economically. My father sighed with a sad, hermetic expression and spoke harshly of his printer associate. At such times my mother grew pensive and melancholic.

Nonetheless the house was unusually bright and gay. In my father's office there were three employees, besides a boy who opened the door. My father called him a *meritorio*—an unpaid employee.

This side of the Coso was the most beautiful and quiet part of the main artery of the city. Since here there were no streetcars, and cars for hire were still non-existent, our street was like a silent backwater in the bustle of the commercial section of the city.

At the very corner of our house, facing the door, and occupying little space on the broad sidewalk, a tall man with a large drooping moustache sometimes set up his stand. He wore dark clothes. He carried with him a small square table about breast high. A yellow silk fringe hung around the edge of the little table.

He was a French charlatan, or pretended to be French, at any rate. After setting up his little stand he would open a suitcase and take out small objects. He sold fountain pens. Although a charlatan, oddly enough he chattered very little.

Solemnly he would bring out a bodkin and two perforated discs. He put one disc on each side of his nose. Then he placed the bodkin threaded with red twine in the hole of one of the discs. It looked as if he were punching a hole through his nose with the bodkin. At the same time he moved his tongue and made sounds like mucous membranes being violently pressed. I could not help laughing. Then he drew the end of the string out of the little disc on the other side of his nose and pulled it back and forth through his perforated nose. I could not understand how he did it. The man looked at me with a clownish familiarity.

But this was only to attract the attention of the little ones. When he had eight or ten boys around he produced a small machine with two rubber inking-rollers. By turning a little crank he made the rollers revolve against each other. Then he inserted a sheet of blank paper on one side, turned the crank, and it came out on the other side changed into a real one hundred peseta bank note.

The blank paper remained inside one of the rollers, while a real, new bank note came out of the other. We were not only impressed by the trick, but even more by the fact that a poor traveling quack could have so much money.

When enough people had gathered he set to work. He took out a fountain pen. As he showed it off he said:

"*Délicate, parfaite,* a gem for the fine penmanship of the modern man."

He removed the cap, showed the gold point, then suddenly jabbed it in the table top as if he wished to nail it there. The nib of the pen was lamentably twisted. Then with his fingers he straightened it and wrote on a pad. He showed the audience the pad and said in a loud voice:

"*La plume fine, la plume élégante.* Impossible *gompé.*"

This man was one of the types I hung around most. Others who interested me were the open-air painters who made little sketches in pastels and then raffled them off to the public.

‡4‡

I continued my explorations around the city. Sometimes I went by our old house on Don Juan de Aragón Street, recalling the recent time we had lived there as if it had been thirty years ago. I pitied the Marquis and his family for still being there when we had moved to the neighborhood of the luxury shops. I really believed that I was a privileged being. We no longer went to Mass at La Seo—too far away—but to the church of San Felipe Neri, in a square behind our house. I remembered how that saint had gone over the world with a tiny little monkey tied with a thick rope and I couldn't take him seriously.

Our moving changed my plans and I had to telephone Felipe to postpone our date and the excursion to the Villa Julieta. The merchant was delighted that we were now living near his house. We agreed to meet the following Tuesday, at the Arch of Cinegio.

It could not have been after seven when I arrived and since I was there ahead of my friend I amused myself watching how the streetcleaners sprinkled the Plaza de la Constitución. I hoped to see the wolfhound that played with the water from the hose, but he did not show up that day.

When my friend arrived he was glad to find me alone, without my sister. "You know," he said, "your sister is already a señorita. That's the trouble with women. At sixteen they are young ladies. While we fellows at sixteen are nothing. Only tadpoles. How old are you?"

"Fourteen," I lied.

"You see now, fourteen, nothing. I sixteen, nothing. But I don't care. You see what I do. Instead of going around with the big boys I go with the younger ones. That way we both feel good. What do the big ones talk about? Women. All right. We can talk about women too. Or business. I'm a businessman. You have to come to my house so my parents can get to know you. I've told them all about your family and about you. I told them . . . Well, my father is an imbecile like all or almost all fathers. He has the mania to punish *impunity*. My father . . ."

We were in the streetcar. The car went up Sagasta Drive with fresh breezes blowing through the open windows. Felipe kept on talking and although he said very complimentary things to me, he said them naturally and without the slightest tendency toward flattery.

"I told my parents about you," he continued, "and I said: a boy of merit who is studying to be engineer of roads, canals and ports, in Catalonia. My father is an imbecile and my mother a saint. I'm sure glad you've come to live nearer my house. My father wants me to be a traveling salesman. Me. A traveling salesman. What for? To sell wholesale. But it's just as I tell him. Only the manufacturer sells wholesale. Only a manufacturer can do business with wholesalers. Do you know what he told me? Well, he goes and says: who told you I'm not going to manu-facture textiles some day? And sooner than some people think. Maybe my father will manufacture textiles. That's why he's dealing with Planibell's father, because he wants to buy second-hand machinery. By the way, I have a letter here from Planibell in Monflorite. He says something about you. You'll see. He says . . .: 'If you see Garcés tell him that Prat met up with Ervigio in Salou and gave him such a beating that, according to indirect information, he'll have to stay in bed for two weeks. That's what he deserves for having outraged his feelings.'" I confirmed Planibell's words. That's what Ervigio deserved.

In his letter Planibell praised me to the skies but with a protective air which annoyed me a little. I asked Felipe if his father was really going to set up a factory.

"That's what I'm telling you. It's a question of money and my father's got it. He's rotten rich. But to tell you the truth, I don't feel like working in that or anything else. If he expects me to go running around the world with a suitcase full of samples, well, he is utterly mistaken. It's just as my cousin Juan says: living is living. One gets up, goes out into the street with a *duro* in his pocket and to live. That's what I want. To live. And with my time to kick the bucket never to come"—another expression that I was hearing for the first time. "That's what my cousin Juan thinks and I praise him for his taste. He works as a gardener in the Villa Julieta. You'll meet him. For I want you to know all my family."

I was thinking: this boy has a high opinion of me in spite of his being older than I am. What will I do to keep from disappointing him? Nat-urally I dared not tell him that I was not studying to be an engineer of roads, canals and ports, because perhaps—I thought—he was basing his respect for me on that. And I watched my words.

We finally reached the end of the line and got off. We walked toward the canal. I looked at the water with the eyes of a canal expert. I realized that Felipe was treating me as if I were a man. In reality I could not understand it, although dressed in long trousers I could very easily be taken for a young man of fifteen or more. Everybody at home said that I had grown a great deal. My father, who normally never seemed to notice me, had said a couple of times while eyeing me attentively:

"You won't grow any more now. Now you will broaden out at the shoulders."

Since I was already as tall as he, evidently he did not want me to keep on growing.

The gondola was tied up alongside the bank of the canal. No one seemed to be around. The white horse was munching grass. My friend harnessed it to the gondola and the two of us climbed in. The horse started off. Considering that vehicle too grand for two boys, I said:

"We could have walked."

"What for? To waste shoe leather and energy? No. In summer one must move as little as possible. When you're as old as I am you'll realize this. If my uncle comes and finds no gondola, he will say: my nephew took it away. Or he may say: Micho's son, because my father has a micho's, or cat's, face. We are common people and you know how that goes. My grandfather came from Monflorite, from the Mountain. He was the one who set up the shop. The people from Monflorite are not bad. Taken one by one they are honest and hardworking. Good friends and noble. But all together . . . That's the trouble with villages. You've got to understand them. They said my grandfather set up the shop with stolen money. Because one night a moneylender in the next town was killed and robbed of seven hundred ounces in gold. They never found the criminal and when they saw my grandfather setting up that shop, well, you know what: Micho here, Micho there. That's why my father can't stand the village folk. I don't know if there could be any truth in that seven hundred gold ounce business or not. What do you think?"

"That depends. Was the victim a moneylender?"

"Yes."

"Then well done. Let us take for granted that it was your grandfather. So what? Usurers are the scum of the earth."

Felipe went on to say:

"A worse usurer than my father does not exist, that's the truth."

"Who knows?" I commented with equanimity.

I had realized that it would be better for me to appear laconic and reserved, in view of Felipe's loquacity. At boarding school, I remembered, the one who talked little, even if he were stupid, was held in greater esteem than the one who talked a great deal, even if he were intelligent. That's why, as well as to keep from disappointing Felipe, I was silent. Again my friend spoke:

"My cousin Juan speaks Esperanto and thinks the same way you do about some things. With the difference years make, for he is a man. Of course sometimes there are men like children, and children like men, and I say this because of you. You're taciturn. One might even say sullen."

I could not understand how Felipe could treat me with such deference and consider my expression so important, but naturally I liked it all.

We had left the Torrero section of the city far behind us and were gliding along the water in silence. My friend remarked:

"My cousin is not very talkative either. But that's because he thinks a lot. He thinks so much that my uncle in charge of the Villa Julieta, who is a brother of the one who owns the gondola, says to him sometimes: you'll never live to be old, always imagining something or other, and that dries up your insides."

He clicked his tongue to admonish the horse which was stopping to eat and the animal, with a little grass in his muzzle, started off again. I said that it would be better to let the animal eat in peace since we were in no hurry. My friend shook his head, grinning from ear to ear:

"No, the horse isn't hungry. He does that because he knows I'm in the gondola. That I'm alone or with a friend. When the gondola's full of people, and especially when he hears my uncle's voice, he doesn't stop for even a second. He does this as a vice. My cousin Juan wants the animals to eat in peace too. He has queer ideas, my cousin does. Sometimes I wonder if he isn't a little cracked. He believes that plants see and hear and understand men just the same as we understand them. He doesn't eat meat, either. Only fruits and vegetables. Not even fish. One day he quarreled with me because he caught me fishing. He said then, says he: how would you like it if someone caught you with a big steel hook in your throat or back of the palate and dragged you around in the water until you suffocated to death. Because that's what we do with fish. We pull the fish out on land with a hook and they suffocate. There's something to it. I haven't fished since then. Thinking it over slowly, the business does have its mystery. Don't you agree? My cousin's a deep thinker."

I was silent. Had not Felipe just said that his cousin was laconic? I kept still, to be like him. I envied Felipe for many reasons. One, his many uncles. Felipe was a kind of universal nephew.

I, on the other hand, had only one uncle, Mosén Orencio, to whom I went for confession.

The Villa Julieta could be seen a little over a quarter of a mile away. One could see walls, the top of which sparkled in the sun, encrusted, evidently, with those jagged pieces of glass often set in adobe walls. Blooming trees on the other side and, further still, buildings with gray stone columns and whitewashed walls.

In a moment we were stopping in front of the Villa entrance. A mature-looking young man with broad shoulders and blue shadows on his shaven face came up carrying a horse's feed bag half-full of oats.

"Hello, Felipe and company," he called, without looking at us.

He put the feed bag on the horse and gently stroked its ears. Then without another word he went away.

The Villa Julieta was everything I had imagined it would be. Green, yellow flowerbeds, arches of climbing roses which in some places formed real tunnels. As we went along a brick-paved avenue with grass growing in the cracks, I was beginning to understand that here was an atmosphere of privilege, a celestial and supernatural aura. I was deeply moved, but managed to conceal my emotion. It looked as if all this belonged to no one. It seemed to be mine. And it was, in my imagination. When a place, a palace, a park appealed to me, I appropriated them and no one in the world could have convinced me they were not mine. Looking around I thought: this is the right place for Valentina and me. Everything is love. Flowers, pools and swans. I would like to work here always and live with Valentina until we are both old and then both of us die the same day. All is love here. And the people must be good, like angels.

Turning a corner—there were avenues formed by box hedges or climbing roses—I saw a broad stretch of closely clipped lawn. It looked like a carpet. In the center stood a small white column with a fat angel on top, a chubby cherub of pink marble. I kept thinking: what a wonderful place for the lay brother's statue, if I could just get that fat angel that looks like a sausage off there! Then I saw that the sausage was Eros, god of love, and I was terribly repentant.

Curiosity, however, left me no time to ponder. I kept taking in everything voraciously.

We went to a *glorieta*—a small circular garden—where four paths came together, the four with columns and small statues at the sides. The *glorieta*, covered with honeysuckle with trailing, delicate yellow flowers, was in the shade. Marble benches formed a circle open only at the corners to give access to the avenues. We sat down. Some time passed in silence and suddenly I heard a voice above our heads. A human voice that seemed to come down from heaven and repeated a single word:

"Hello."

I looked up and saw no one. A man could not have been in the honeysuckle. The same voice again said:

"Hello."

Seeing my amazement, my friend explained:

"It's a crow. That's all it knows how to say, but it says it just like a person. He's very gentle, the creature. Since no one has ever done him any harm, he's not afraid."

At that very moment the crow's voice again descended from the honeysuckle:

"Hello."

We got up and started walking. Suddenly animated, my friend suggested:

"Let's go to the nurseries. See that glass house covered with green blinds? That's where the nurseries are. My cousin Juan could have a job in a bank or government office. He's very smart. He's always reading some book. I'm not praising his taste in that. I don't read books. I've never cracked a book since Cato. What for? It doesn't mean a thing, you know that. I think it's fine for others to read them. But all I want to do is get up and go out in the street and see the people. I don't need to know anything else. And do you know what?—Women pay more attention to somebody selling materials than they do to somebody who studies. A surgeon, for instance."

I wondered: why a surgeon? He could have said a professor or engineer. But that place was paradise for someone in love, like me. How happy people must be there! Sweet odors were everywhere and to look— only to look—was a delight. I thought of Valentina as I walked along beside Felipe. We reached the nurseries and went in. Inside the air was moist and dank. Shadows of branches were swaying on the panes of glass. My friend went over to where two young men were working.

"Monflorite!" he called.

"That's my name," a calm voice answered. "Ah, it's you? And your company? How good."

This affable man who was in his shirt sleeves and working in a seed-bed gave me his hand. My friend explained:

"His name isn't Monflorite, but we call him that because he comes from the same town as my father and grandfather. The other one working over there is Pascual."

In the door we heard:

"Hello."

The crow had followed us. The other workman, hairy and sullen-looking, came over. Facing Felipe he suddenly exclaimed:

"You're a good fellow, but you have your bad blood, too."

Felipe, without looking at him, tried to teach him a lesson:

"First you say good morning, Pascual."

But Pascual was not listening:

"You," he cried, shouting as if Felipe were deaf, "you are the boss's nephew. All right. What I need to know is who's the boss here, in the nurseries. Understand?"

The affable Monflorite withdrew and started working among some carnation slips.

"I don't know a thing," said Felipe absent-mindedly. "I suppose you ought to ask my uncle about that."

It was evident that these two workmen had recently had a fight. Felipe said to the affable workman:

"Come along with us."

"Wait until I take these cuttings out of the pail," Monflorite replied with affected calm.

He took out a few handfuls of carnation slips. Fifteen steps further on, the grim-faced workman came and went with a wheelbarrow. Monflorite began whistling a waltz just to show us how calm he was, when suddenly Pascual's sharp voice rang out:

"Shut up once for all or I'll ram this wedge down your throat."

He was holding a kind of rusty iron wedge in his hand. Monflorite kept prudently still. He finished with the carnations and left with us. Again we went to sit in the crow's *glorieta*, leaving Pascual alone with his rage.

As soon as we left the greenhouse, poor Monflorite started grumbling:

"All the trouble comes from the same old thing," he said, "from my treating him like an equal in spite of being his boss. But that's the way I am. For some reason or other your uncle put me in charge of the nurseries. I haven't told Pascual yet. But he realizes it by the way the work's organized. He realizes, I say, that I'm his boss. Is it my fault? So that's why . . . If I sing he gets furious. If I whistle he says he's going to ram a wedge down my throat. If I laugh he thinks I'm making fun of him."

Without really understanding what was going on I interrupted and advised Felipe to put them at different jobs. Felipe answered:

"I'm not the one who decides such things. I'm only my uncle's nephew."

Monflorite, with the taut expression of the frightened man, added:

"I'm not afraid, it's not that, but Pascual does go around with the pruning knife in his hand and he's a man who fast loses control of himself. It's not fear, but I have heard he killed someone in Tudela."

Ah, this was something else. Amidst the honeysuckle the crow repeated:

"Hello."

Monflorite was biting a carnation stem, pensively:

"I don't know that it's so, but that's what they say. A decision will have to be made. In a pleasant way, but something must be done. Not because I'm his boss, but for other reasons. Trifles. If you made him boss of the nurseries and me his helper, things would be just the same, that's what I think. He's all burnt up."

"Would you accept him as boss?" I asked him.

Monflorite looked at me as at a child whose words are meaningless. Felipe repeated my question and Monflorite answered:

"Why, frankly no. The way things are now I'd rather starve to death than accept such a situation. But suppose I do accept. Nothing would be settled. I'm telling you that nothing would be settled."

I was terribly impressed by the possibility that Pascual might have committed a crime in Tudela. I asked if it was true and Felipe said:

"Gossip."

I was amazed to find such problems in so beautiful a spot as the Villa Julieta. I could not understand. And meanwhile Monflorite was insisting:

"No, those aren't things to be taken lightly. When you can hear the river it means it's full of water. Besides, even if he hasn't done anything yet, he still could some day. It's the gospel truth that a week ago when I was selecting seeds in the cupboards he came up behind my back, for I saw his reflection in the glass. I could only jump aside when he came at me. Well, he saw that I had discovered his intention and then he said: 'It looks like you know me. If you want to find out more, go to Tudela and ask about me. They'll tell you, there.' And he did not laugh. He never laughs."

Felipe spoke again:

"Pascual comes from a family of honest farmers. He probably had some kind of a fight. And a drunk man can sometimes swing a bottle around, but he doesn't get blood on himself."

My amazement was growing steadily. I listened, with my eyes, ears and mouth. Monflorite went on:

"No, but he doesn't drink. I've never even seen him take a glass of anisette. His vice is women. Which is why . . ."

"You, what do you think?" Felipe asked me.

"Who, me?" And sure of my own importance, I added: "They are both right and both wrong. In their own way, of course."

I was repeating what I had sometimes heard Brother Pedro say after separating two boys who were fighting. Then Monflorite looked at me surprised, maybe, to see me so reasonable, and continued:

"Not over two days ago I told him: 'Get going, dig around the edges of that parterre and prepare the ground now that the weather is right.' Well, one is a gardener and knows something about what people in Madrid and Barcelona do at this job. That's why I said to him: 'Go ahead and dig around the edges of the parterre.'"

"And he didn't understand what you meant by parterre?"

"No. What can that dope understand?"

I did not understand either, which was quite humiliating for me. But Monflorite continued:

"'The parterre,' I told him. And he said he'd never heard the word. 'Well, I don't know any other,' I insisted, 'and what I order you to do I order you to do, as is right. Go to the parterre.' Then he looked at me with murder in his eye and said: 'If you say that word to me again I'll throw the pruning shears at your head.' And that's the bad thing about it, he always has something that cuts or jabs in his hand. I said to him: 'Come and I'll show you what a parterre is.' And I explained all about it. Then he said I didn't know my job because that was not a parterre but a border, and that what I was calling the edge of the parterre was *platabanda* or the border. Well, I know those words, but a parterre is something different according to the style of Madrid and then . . . well, as an ignoramus Pascual is an ignoramus. That goes without saying. But now you know. I am responsible for the work to your uncle. So he obeys or he doesn't. Well, since the parterre business he's been calling me *Uncle Partegre*, for he can't even pronounce the word. Still if he would only say it laughing . . . but no. He never laughs. And I laugh a lot because my conscience is clear. Now you've seen what's wrong," he added, turning to me. "Every time I laugh, his blood starts boiling. If I say a word to him that he doesn't know, he begins to swallow hard. If I laugh to myself, he starts throwing his tools around, or kicking the wheelbarrow. If I whistle a song, he begins insulting me and if I sing . . . well, I don't dare any more because one day when I was singing he jumped on top of me like a tiger. I told you about that before. Thank heavens I saw him in the shadows and got out of the way. That's what I was telling you before."

Felipe listened solemn-eyed and asked:

"What were you singing that day? The day he jumped on you."

"A very innocent *jota*. A *jota* sung by dung-gatherers that I heard in my town."

"And how does that *jota* go?"

"Well, the words say: *I am called the silly fool — the silly fool of my home town — while they all live by working — without a lick of work I'm living.* It's true that I sang it when he was sitting down to smoke a cigarette. The same old story. I don't use the weed. But all the time he's trying to get a light for his cigarette. And he doesn't even work when he smokes. He has to sit down on the ground and blow long breaths through his nose until he looks like a locomotive. Well, you all should have seen how he took on. If my song . . . or some such . . . whenever he wants . . . in short, the same old story."

From the honeysuckle bower the crow repeated:

"Hello."

And Monflorite said:

"The crow also reminds me of the day this Pascual said, says he: 'I've got that crow stuck down in the pit of my stomach. It isn't right for an animal to talk like a person.' 'Why not? And what difference does it make whether he talks or not?' I said to him, and he answered: 'I don't like things I can't understand.' I said to him, says I: 'Well, I understand it. That crow is probably the son of a she-crow and a little parrot.' Just see how innocent that is. Anybody else would have laughed. Well, the joke got his goat and he went on to tell me that no one made fun of him, not even his own mother who bore him. We were friends to begin with and used to go out together on Sundays to the grove or suburbs, with our girlfriends. Well, the same old story. My sweetheart's mine. And she loves me, as she should. His sent him out to weed the onion-beds. Those were her very words: 'Go out and weed the onion-beds.' The next day we were working and finishing up that border when I said to him, forgetting what had happened the day before: 'Pascual, go out and weed those onion-beds.' Then he started mentioning my mother again. That's it."

"But you did it on purpose," I said.

"*Gachó*—man—that's the best thing that's been said around here this morning. You've put your finger on the sore spot."

What I liked best was that expression *gachó* which I had only heard gypsies with Andalusian or Madrid accent say in front of taverns. Then Felipe looked at Monflorite, who was somewhat nervous, and asked:

"How are you going to answer my friend?"

Monflorite began to explain the incident in the suburbs in greater detail:

"When his sweetheart sent him away from her and Pascual started off, he turned around after eight or ten steps and asked me: 'Aren't you coming?' I did not answer. My girl said a little impudently: 'It looks like he's lost his hearing in a cold draught.' And we all laughed. Then the girl who had sent him out to weed the onion-beds said: 'He isn't decent, that fellow. He only wants to touch me. And I say, let him go touch a lamppost of the public light company.' Then all three of us laughed. He was mumbling bad words as he walked away and finally disappeared. The next day some lampposts in the *glorieta* were newly painted and I said to him, says I: 'Go touch that lamppost to see if it is dry.' He acted like a poisonous snake. You know how he is. And I didn't do it with evil intentions, only it looks as if fate comes to whisper in my ear the words most likely to poison his blood. As I say, I am careful, but when I want to beware, the words have already slipped out and it can't be helped. Too late."

Felipe looked dubious:

"Then what can be done?"

After a long pause Monflorite continued:

"I say it could still be fixed up. We would only need to call him here right now, for example. The three of us sitting here on this bench, your cousin Juan, too, I say. The four present. And don't mince words with him. Tell him that I'm a man as one must be, and come from an honest family, and that the father of this fellow here, Mr. Biescas, knows it very well, and that he has to bow his head and obey all my orders without a murmur. But we must call him here, in front of the four of us sitting like a court, and he with his cap in his hand. And tell him that if I laugh it's because my conscience is clear, and if I whistle a tune or sing it's because I have a right to, and I don't waste anything except my own wind and voice and don't have to give an accounting to anybody. But it's not easy, I know. It's not easy, I mean, to get Juan here to form a court with the three of us. Because he likes to fix everything up in a nice way, and with Pascual nice ways are no good. You still don't know what that guy is really like."

At that moment the bell of the entrance gate rang. Felipe's uncle was arriving. He was a reddish-haired man about fifty years old. Monflorite went back to work while Felipe explained to me:

"Today is a bad day for going to my uncle with problems of this kind. He's in a bad humor on Tuesdays because the park is closed to the public and besides he has to pay extra wages if he needs day laborers. He not only earns nothing, I mean to say, but also spends. He doesn't like that. And today he's in a worse humor than usual. I can see it from here. I think that instead of bothering him with that nursery dispute it would be better to go on having a look around the Villa. Way off yonder is the house. Some call it a palace. I wouldn't go that far. It's only a house or, let's say, to make it sound a little better, a kind of mansion. Your house is a mansion, too. Where I live, it's a house. Not even a house, just a dwelling."

We had changed our course and instead of heading for the entrance gate were making for the interior of the park. The nephew was afraid of his uncle.

I was becoming aware that this place of delights was also, or could become, a hell. Felipe was still talking about palaces, mansions and dwellings. And walking beside me and looking at the borders with their graceful designs of flowers and shrubs, he added:

"My house is a hut, really, with its front covered with big painted letters and advertisements."

We passed near Juan who, without stopping working, asked us:

"What are you two talking about?"

"Well, about the house," Felipe answered, "the palace, I mean, of the Villa. And I was saying it's more than a house and less than a palace. What should we say? Mansion?"

Juan roared with laughter. "It's a country house," he said, adding: "What difference does it make? Some day everybody will live in houses like it and gardens like these. But first we need a lot of rain. A great deal of rain has to fall."

Felipe did not pay much attention to what Juan said. We went on walking. We were beside a round and rather deep pool where small fish were swimming. The edge of the pool was mosaic, decorated with figures of the Middle Ages: the Cid, a Moorish king, the Virgen del Pilar. Next to the pool's rim and at equal distances were green *majolica* frogs spouting water from their mouths. This water must have been cooler, for dozens of tiny fish were flocking beneath each jet to enjoy it. My friend went to a hydrant concealed behind some boards and opened it full force. The streams of water from the frogs' mouths stretched out and rose in the air, meeting in the center of the pool and forming a liquid cupola. The sun fell on it slantingly and a perfect rainbow was visible. I shivered with emotion and at the same time thought: Will the workmen in the nurseries have killed each other by now? I would have liked them to kill each other and be buried at the foot of some beautiful tree which they would then fertilize. The men—so ugly—would then be tributaries of the trees—so beautiful.

My friend turned off the water and we went on. The morning was enchanting, in spite of the workmen in the nurseries. The best of all had been Juan's affirmation: some day everybody will live in places like this, although first *a lot of rain will have to fall*. I did not understand the connection between rain and universal happiness. But I had just made a discovery. Inside the pool and rising above the water was a column ending in a rather rough capital. It was quite thick and had nothing on top. It looked exactly like the right place for the lay brother's bust, or head, I should say. I told my friend and he answered:

"Some day when my uncle's not here we'll come and put it there, just like that. But don't tell a soul."

"Why not?"

"My uncle will think it has some hidden meaning."

"Shall we tell Juan?"

"If he says anything when he sees the statue already set up, we'll tell him."

"And Monflorite? Pascual?"

"They're a couple of blockheads. I call people who don't notice things 'blockheads.' Do you think they'll see the marble head? They haven't even noticed that column and they'd have to be passing the statue every day for forty years before they'd see it. They're really blockheads. They don't think about anything but eating and women. I'm more than you and you less than me, and so forth. You must come to my house. You'll see that even my parents are rather dumb too, but good people. I can't get very enthusiastic about my father because he's given me so many drubbings my hair stands on end just to think about it. But I respect him. Naturally. Don't I have to respect him? We, you and I, are human beings. My mother too, although she's a little on the simple side. My father, no. He's always harping on how he hates impunity. But he's my father. We, you and I, says I, are different. Real human beings."

"And Juan?" I asked. "What would you say about Juan?"

My friend looked around cautiously and whispered:

"Are we alone?"

"Yes," I said nervously.

"My cousin Juan is a gangster."

At that time there was talk of gangsters in Barcelona who settled trade union affairs with shooting.

"But he must have some other trade or profession," I said.

It did not seem right to me for Juan to be a gangster-gardener. It was a ridiculous combination.

"You're right," said Felipe. "In Barcelona he did work at something else. As a tailor's cutter, I think."

And I had one more disillusionment. A tailor's cutter, bah!

"And he earned as much as he wanted to. You should see him sometimes when he wears a tie; he looks like a gentleman. But now I believe he's half-hiding out. He doesn't want any trouble with anybody, my uncle or those guys in the nurseries, because he knows he's in a difficult situation and if someone informs on him they can put him in jail. Or who knows what might happen to him. My uncle thinks that I don't know anything, but I'm no fool! I see apparent things and hidden things, too. I can be a dunce in some things, because they say I take after my mother, but I'm plenty sharp. My uncle wants Juan to kick those fellows in the nurseries around. He says that if Monflorite and Pascual have a boss they can get furious at, they'll settle down and get to work. Common people have to hate someone, he says. That's the only way they can get along. That's why you've got to have foremen. It's a rather queer idea but then I guess he may be right."

To show him I wasn't in the thumb-sucking stage either, I said:

"I don't think Juan's capable of kicking those two fellows in the nurseries around, as your uncle evidently wants him to do."

"Who knows? For Juan those nursery men aren't human beings. He's quite capable of beating them up and insulting them. You don't know what Juan's like. He treats a dog better than some people when he thinks they don't deserve it."

After a pause I asked:

"And what could Juan have done as a gangster in Barcelona?"

"Oh, I don't know. And no one asks him because it's better not to talk about such things. But do you think it could have been a crime?" And before I had time to answer, he added:

"Well, there are crimes and crimes. He can be a saint and . . . A man who splints the twisted twig of a bush and carries little handfuls of special manure around to certain plants every week, well a man like that . . ."

He left his sentence unfinished with a meditative silence. I was indeed having experiences and adventures far outstripping all those I had had in my village as well as in boarding school. Yet I remembered Prat with admiration, Planibell with a reverent distrust, Brother Pedro and the lay friar in the studio with friendliness. And I continued hating Ervigio, whom I remembered disheveled, with features contracted like a girl's when she is having a fight with another girl, striking Prat on the head with the foil. I intended to write all my friends except Ervigio, and tell them what I had seen in the Villa Julieta. I wouldn't mention Juan, just in case. If he was in hiding, one should be careful because sometimes the police open letters and read them. I was no longer in boarding school. Outside in the world it was serious business. There were watchmen and police and jails and scaffolds. It was not a matter of performing plays like *Life Is a Dream.*

I looked at Juan from a distance as he bent over some borders working. I was dubious about this man's being a gangster. Sometimes I believed what Felipe said and sometimes I was not sure. I felt especially inclined to believe him when I heard the still unbroken *duro* stolen from his father the previous Saturday tinkling in his pocket. As we were leaving the Villa Julieta to return to the city I told him:

"Your coin's jingling in your pocket and if your father hears it . . ."

Felipe declared this was because he had a small key in the same pocket, but that he would put the key in his left pocket before reaching home. And on going out into the street he would put the key and the *duro* in the same pocket again.

"That little sound," he said, "makes me *more of a man* with people, you understand."

Then he added:
"Women, especially."

‡ 5 ‡

When we separated I hurried home without seeing anybody. My friendship with a gangster was making me grow in my own estimation. I was not sure that Juan was one, but I liked believing it just to feel more important. And I said to myself: If my father only knew what kind of friends I have . . . I was not worried about my mother. My mother was the kind of person always ready to explain, accept, and understand everything. If I said to her: I have a friend who is hiding from the police, she would ask me for further details without becoming in the least frightened. I do not think that my mother knew much about society or its laws. She had married on leaving boarding school. A school run by the Pauline nuns, the same order that had a boarding school near our old home on Don Juan de Aragón Street. And before she knew what love was, perhaps, her first child was born. For her, life meant saying amen to those she loved. She loved everybody in one way or another, I believe. It has sometimes occurred to me that her mind had not developed beyond the eleven- or twelve-year-old level of intelligence, and that it was entirely devoid of any kind of resistance. I don't know how to explain it, but maybe for that very reason my father did nothing to urge social life upon her. My mother had no social life at all, or at least in Zaragoza. My father never took her anywhere.

My mother was, I believe, an example of a certain type of femininity so common in Spain, of those women born to be wives and mothers. Without any ideas about the world and without resistance, because in them everything was love. In matters of love and maternity she had the wisdom of the instincts. This explains why, if I asked her some question, she always had a wise answer. When, years before, in the village, for instance, I had asked her if I was a handsome man, she unhesitatingly said no, and that I never would be handsome, but that I was the kind of man all women like. A discreet reply. There was certainly something fundamental, instinctive, wise and barbarously feminine in my mother.

My mother was very pleased with me that summer because I had received an "A" in French (only just passing in everything else, and grateful for it) and I owed this "A" to her. It was like this. My mother

still knew by heart some of the things she had learned in boarding school
—everybody at that time had to memorize—and sometimes she would
repeat these things to us when we were children. One was the grammatical analysis of the preposition *à*—to—which went something like this:
*à denotes the complement of the action of the verb without grammatical
accidence, being an invariable part of the sentence.* We used to repeat
this definition as a joke, to prove we knew any lesson well, whatever
it might be. In the French examination I was asked to analyze a sentence
and on reaching the *à* I repeated the phrase, adding at the end: *and it is
distinguished from the verb 'a' by the accent.* This so pleased the professors that if I had said anything reasonable in the rest of the examination they would have given me the highest mark. I told my mother about
it and we laughed. Maruja, who was growing up fast and liked to show
off, had found out about the trick and wanted to learn the phrase by
heart. She could not. She called it "the little tune of the 'A'," picking up
the expression from my imprudent lips that had used it once. She thought
that by memorizing it she would get an "A" in any examination in any
subject. Even astronomy or arithmetic.

My mother had several relatives in Zaragoza, besides the parish priest
of La Seo, of whom my father was not very fond. There was a half-
relative, a nun who had been my nurse when I was very small, Sister
Adela, who used to call on us. She had had a brilliant career in her order
of the Sisters of Charity and was now abbess or Mother Superior of a
nunnery right there in Zaragoza. This nun felt a kind of maternal adora-
tion toward me and when she came to see us she never took her eyes off
my face, and would pinch my cheeks or arms, always putting the thin
veil of her consecrated habit between her fingers and my poor person.
Between pinches she would say to me:

"Shameless rascal, how many sweethearts do you have?"

I hastened to say only one: Valentina. Then she would give me a
little cartridge-shaped, tissue-wrapped packet tied with blue ribbon, containing fifteen or twenty half-peseta silver coins. I loved Sister Adela like
my mother. Maybe a trifle more. Not because of the coins but the
pinches, and what Concha had told me about her. According to my
sister, when this very pretty nun was a girl working in our home, I was
one or two years old. And she played mother with me. The girl fell in
love with my father. She was platonically in love with him, but when
my mother became aware of this, without violence of any kind and
understanding that all this was natural and inevitable, she helped her to

enter a convent. And Sister Adela, who was very alert, in ten or twelve years had the positions of greatest responsibility in her order. I do not know if her love for my father had really existed or if it was all Concha's imagination. Both things are equally possible. Concha saw love everywhere.

My mother had another relative, an old maid in her forties, thin and dried-up, whose stringy hands I detested. Concha said that her hands were dead and I thought to myself: not quite, but they are the *bloodless* hands poets talk about. This woman, whose name was Rita, came to see us at least once a month and she and my mother chatted for hours on end. When she saw me wearing long trousers, Cousin Rita would say:

"Doesn't it shock you a little to have your legs covered?"

"Yes, it does."

Then, since that woman had solutions for every problem, she told my mother that in her place she would order my trousers gradually cut a little longer and longer, so that without realizing it and in a progressive way I would one day find myself in men's trousers. I could just see myself wearing trousers half-covering my legs, ridiculous and laughable, and I looked at my cousin with aversion. She, I repeat, had solutions for everything. Except her spinsterhood. When speaking of some man, she would say that he was *very suggestive.* For one reason or another all men were very suggestive. It so happened that she always met them in the bank where she went to clip the coupons of her small capital.

My father sometimes said to my mother: "That cousin of yours, Rita, is going to commit some grave folly some day." And my mother would shake her head, saying: "Don't you believe it. She might if a man really fell in love with her. But that isn't likely and she has a fine nose and knows it. Don't think for a minute she's such a fool." My mother was right. In such matters she was always more intelligent than anyone else because she did not think with her reason but with her instinct or temperament. My father would have liked to take a hand in Cousin Rita's finances, to make her invest her money in his own business, but he did not dare. He understood—in those things my father was very prudent— that to make her risk her means of livelihood would have been criminal. And he would look at her now and then with a little melancholy, as at a propitiatory victim he had renounced out of gentlemanliness.

The marble head was still in my room. Again I was beginning to see in it the mysteries of the lay brother's workshop—vague mysteries which occasionally became specific and made me uneasy. I wrote a letter to the lay brother saying that I had found a better place for his statue and explaining where and how we were going to put it. If he came to Zaragoza he would be able to see it. I did not say whether it was a public or private place. On rereading the letter I realized that the lay brother could think the Villa Julieta was a property belonging to my family. Although I had not done so purposely, I did not mind the confusion. I talked about the canal and the white swan, but said nothing about the horse that drew it. The poor lay brother must have thought that I was telling him a dream. Several days later I received a letter from him on that crested paper I knew so well.

With a cross and religious sentence as heading, it read:

"Dear brother in Jesus: On receipt of this favor I trust that you will be enjoying the benefits of health in the company of your kind parents and brothers and sisters. As for me, and even though I do not deserve it, God keeps me in a propitious condition for His holy service. So be it.

"Regarding the statue, I thank you for the information and the good will you show for my poor handiwork, and since it seems to me that it will probably be a long time before I can go thereto, I will deem it a special favor if you will take a photograph of the place where the afore-mentioned work is installed and send it to me. In case this occasions you some expense, I enclose a peseta in postage stamps.

"I beg you to greet your virtuous parents in my name and assure them, as well as you yourself can rest assured, that I will not forget any of you in my daily prayers.

"Yours very affectionately in Jesus . . ."

The letter had a postscript saying that Father Ferrer was ill and was to have an operation. This news gave me great joy. Children are easily cruel. But as I read and reread the letter I asked myself if this could be the same friar I had known. He spoke of his "poor work" and then asked me for pictures of it so he could see where it was. The plaintive and humble tone of the letter sounded like him, yet he told me about Father Ferrer without saying a word in praise of him, as if he knew that the news of his operation would please me. Later on I realized that the lay brother, like many other intelligent people, was lost with a pen in his hand. He did not know what to say, and to avoid saying more or less than he wanted to say, he took refuge in clichés and formulas.

It was not one peseta but one peseta and five céntimos, or seven fifteen-céntimo stamps. I kept them thinking that I would use them on my letters to Valentina. As for the photograph, I could ask Concha to lend me her little camera, a cheap box camera which she called a mousetrap. We had no really decent photographic apparatus at home. Maybe my friend Felipe would have a better camera. All merchants have good cameras. But first I would have to put the statue in the Villa Julieta. When? Next Tuesday. Felipe was to let me know.

Concha wanted to go to the Villa but under no consideration was she disposed to have anything to do with young men like Felipe, who did not yet shave and who stole money from their fathers. I told her that we could go to the Villa some day when it was open to the public. She asked:

"And that Juan who, you say, committed so many murders in Barcelona, what is he like?"

"I don't know. If you're afraid, don't go." But she wanted to see the Villa, and one day we went there together.

My sister liked the trip in the gondola. Inside the Villa we went to the pool with the green frogs. I turned on the water and Juan came over when he saw the fountain playing. He recognized me at once and asked if I was going to the nurseries to see Monflorite. I said no and he understood that the very idea displeased me.

"Your sweetheart?" he asked, looking at my sister.

My sister Concha laughed as she always did when we were taken for sweethearts. She had laughed even more on an outing with my father when someone said "your señora . . ." referring to Concha. She had a good time in an absurd way that sometimes slightly shocked people. Concha's reaction to Juan was very different from her reaction to Felipe. She seemed to be thinking: "This is something else, even if he has murdered someone in Barcelona." Concha respected the rights of the imagination among us children. One could believe anything we said, on condition to believe nothing, if required to prove it. She saw Juan and decided his was not a murderer's face. So my words were meaningless. If she had found herself before a sinister-looking man, things would have been different. And she looked at him with friendliness and respect. Perhaps, I think, with reservations of pleasant fear.

Juan behaved very well. He did not flirt with Concha or entertain her more than courtesy demands. When Concha asked him about the column rising out of the water, Juan told her a series of very strange things.

"A year ago they had a faun with goat's feet, a flageolet and two little horns on its head, there. And something terrible happened. A two-year-old child fell in and drowned. An accident. The child slipped on the edge. The judge came, the coroner and also a priest. When the formalities were over the priest told the manager that it would be better to remove the faun from the column, since it was a pagan image. I believe it's authentic, from before the Christian era. And he took it away. As he was looking at the statue the manager said: 'And he does look like a demon for sure!' Silly superstitions. Since then there has been no accident, true. Coincidences, I say. This pool is quite deep. Four hands over my head. So one must be careful."

Later on, when my sister and I were alone, we went to the *mansion*, as Felipe called it. On a porch at the side, where stables had formerly been, were some marble objects. Half Venuses, a broken angel . . . I immediately remembered the lay brother's studio. In one corner was the little faun, less than two feet high, short-legged and full-bearded.

"It really does look like a devil," Concha remarked.

"And it is."

"Why do you think so?"

Until recently my sister had gone to nuns' schools where the girls were only taught how to write with pointed letters—a specialty of the school—with no attention to spelling, since a few mistakes are attractive in a woman's letter. And to sing in chorus. They also had calisthenics and general and religious history. And they read and discussed Fray Luis de León's *Perfecta casada* which contained many things understood neither by the students or nuns. "Worldly things," said the teachers somewhat scandalized, in spite of the author's having been a monk.

My sister looked upon me as learned, in comparison with herself, and sometimes when I made some comment that sounded like something new and unheard of, she gazed at me in astonishment. One day I told her that every hair on our head is a tube with a liquid inside and she was dumbfounded, exclaiming: "Chico, you're a magician. A real wizard." That day in the Villa Julieta I explained to her what a faun was, telling her the Greek tradition of the terrible god Pan and the origin of the word 'panic' which I had read a few days before. My sister was really amazed.

"You study too much," she said, "and I don't think anything good can come from it. Imagine, Greek customs. How many centuries ago?"

"Twenty-five or more."

"*Qué barbaridad!*"

Furthermore, everything Greek seemed quite indecent to her. There were statues . . . well, well.

I wanted to take her to the nurseries and show her that I had other friends but I was afraid they would quarrel in front of her. When we came to the marble *glorieta* the crow, as usual, said:

"Hello."

Concha was ready to leave then and there.

"Let's get out of here," she said. "This *glorieta* looks haunted to me."

We walked through the rest of the park. My sister wanted me to take her picture everywhere, leaning against columns, her face beside clumps of roses, fountains. But the crow followed us everywhere:

"Hello."

The crow finally drove her out of the park. She looked at it out of the corner of her eye and said:

"Come on. Let's go."

We finally left. Outside she said to me: "What an ideal spot for two people in love!" She must have been thinking about herself and the Marquis, but she added generously: "Like you and Valentina." I was thinking: "And the crow?" But my sister realized that this was not a serious objection.

"They could put that bird in a cage," she said after long reflection.

At the park gate we saw Juan again who came up to say goodbye, very politely.

On the way home Concha told me that she had broken with the Marquis's son because one day, when she was out with the maid, he was strolling down Coso Street and had approached her. My sister was terrified.

"What can he have been thinking of?" she asked.

"Then you haven't talked to him?"

"No. That would be the last straw!"

"Haven't you written each other letters either?"

"No. Not I. Who do you think I am, anyway? A nobody?"

I was tempted to tell her what I thought about free love, but realizing that this was not good for everybody, I kept still. My sister was impressed by Juan.

"And you say he's just a worker?"

"Yes; in Barcelona he was a tailor's cutter, they say."

What a mean trade. Concha seemed disconcerted. She said:

"I don't know what's happening nowadays. There are common men, workers or the like, who have a wonderful appearance. This must be peculiar to cities. In the village a worker is a worker and a gentleman a gentleman. Here they all look like important people."

Then we talked about the war. Concha was not a partisan of either the Allies or Germans. She wanted the war to end and for there to be no other. I preferred the Allies, although without great enthusiasm, but when they suffered heavy casualties I was inclined to feel admiration for the Germans, like my father. This, however, struck me as unworthy of a self-esteeming son. And I decided to think no more about it.

When the newspaper "ABC" arrived from Madrid, every evening at dusk, and dozens of vendors started running down Coso Street and shouting, I would go down and buy it always from a withered, nervous little old woman who carried such an enormous bundle under her arm that she could hardly walk.

My father was a Germanophile not only out of devotion but self-interest. He continued to buy German bonds and had invested over thirty thousand pesetas in them. If he lost, it would be a rude blow because at that time the sum was a real fortune.

My sister and I often talked about the Villa Julieta and especially the pool where they said a child had drowned.

‡6‡

Felipe took me to the Casino Mercantil one day where he had to go with a *matraco*—a country hick, that's what he called him—from Monflorite. The peasant, a friend of his father's, was a shepherd who had come down to Zaragoza "to bargain his wool." And the Biescas family was entertaining him. According to Felipe, his father played the great and generous gentleman with the people of Monflorite whom he hated with all his soul. In spite of his own duplicity, Felipe could not understand this. I told him that his father wanted to be on the good side of them to sell them goods and squeeze their pennies out of them, and then Felipe said something that surprised me:

"That's no way to talk because, well, my father is my father. I can say he's stingy, even an imbecile. And it's the absolute truth. But if someone else says so, I have to stick up for him and defend him."

I hesitated a moment before saying finally:

"I'm sorry."

Felipe seemed satisfied and, as if to prove it, he added:

"That doesn't mean that you're not right about what you say against my father. But since I am his son," he repeated, admiring his own loyalty, "I'm obliged to stick up for him."

Suddenly I thought I understood what my friend meant when talking about his own duplicity, and that kind of duplicity in connection with his father really struck me as plausible, in spite of everything.

I had never been inside the Casino Mercantil, although I had noticed the luxurious modern building with its liveried porter when passing by. Felipe invited the shepherd and me to have a cold drink in the Casino café. Near by, on the other side of a glass door, the sound of coins and cards could be heard. "That's the gambling room," said Felipe. Gambling had not yet been banned in Spain. We went in. Since the shepherd seemed interested in the roulette game and asked Felipe questions, Felipe said to him: "Put a coin on a number and see what happens." He put it on the black eleven and immediately the croupier sang out: *Black eleven, impair, manque*, and tossed him thirty-six coins through the air. The shepherd was completely taken aback. Felipe told him: *"They're yours."* Finally the shepherd picked them up, very slowly, and prepared to leave. Felipe asked:

"Aren't you going to play any more?"

"No," he answered, and looking around suspiciously, added: *"They give too much."*

We left. After that Felipe, mocking the suspiciousness of peasants in the city, used to say: "They give too much."

As was bound to happen sooner or later, my sister Concha discovered that from the balcony of my room she could see, across the very narrow Callejón of the Palace of Justice, the interior of an office where the walls were lined with files and bundles of papers tied with red tape. Near the window was a large table where sometimes a man, well along in years, worked. But frequently a very elegant young man would come to that table. He wore a summer topcoat—if the sky was overcast—with silk lapels. He looked like a tailor's figurine, which did not displease my sister. He had a long lean face, aquiline nose and small moustache. He was like the manikins in the de luxe tailoring shops. He wore a derby hat.

Before long he and Concha were exchanging glances and smiles. This was beginning to annoy me, really.

"This is my room," I told her, "and from here I won't allow you to go on with such foolishness."

Then she became terribly offended. She refused to speak to me for several days. But since I was in my room very little and could not lock the door, she went on with her pranks. Convinced that everything was futile, I finally became her confidant once more. She said to me:

"That young man must be a judge or something like that. Or a district attorney. Or a defense attorney. He dresses like a judge, always in black."

In our new house we had a janitress with a daughter nine or ten years old who was very stuck-up and always showing off around me. Through this girl a letter reached Concha one day. Since the janitress sometimes had mail for us, Concha was not surprised to receive it. As soon as she read it she handed it over to me. It was a declaration of love copied, perhaps, from a manual. But it had an autobiographical part which was original and genuine. The gallant's name was Santiago Martínez and he was a circus acrobat. He was, in fact, one of a pair called *the kings of the flying trapeze* in the advertisements. With the S of Santiago and the first four letters of his surname they had formed an English name: *Smart*. The *Smart Brothers*, kings of the flying trapeze. I was too astonished to have any opinion at all.

My sister's heart fell. First because of the boldness of the letter. Then because of the vulgar and pedestrian manner in which it was written. Finally because of the gallant's profession. And my sister, with a faraway look in her eyes, said to me:

"But what in Heaven's name is a circus acrobat doing in the offices of the Court of Justice every day?"

This incident helped her to curb her window romanticism somewhat. For a long time I knew of no other adventure. But even though I said nothing to her she would sometimes try to defend herself and to defend the king of the flying trapeze, saying:

"Well, an acrobat is someone. Something like an ancient hero."

I said nothing. With Felipe I had learned that my silences gave me authority. But I never again found her in my room or at any other window in the house. Furthermore, I had really frightened her one day when I said: "Through those windows of the Court of Justice you'll start flirting with the hangman himself some day when you least expect it." I insisted that the executioner went there every day, precisely to that office facing my room.

I used to go to my father's offices when I wanted to write a letter. In the clerks' room there was a table occupied by a retired sergeant of the Civil Guard, a tall, gray-haired man with an enormous moustache. He had been the commandant of the post in my village, and upon retiring had come to Zaragoza to live with his children who were quite prosperous wholesalers of cereals. My father had given him some work and every day on the dot he arrived, greeted the one opening the door for him, went to his place where he stayed writing until time to leave. He was as regular as a clock, and courteous, calm, impersonal. He smoked very strong tobacco in cigarettes which he himself made at home and which he always carried in a very ornate, tooled-leather case. He never spoke except to say something necessary and unavoidable.

I would sit down on the opposite side of his table and start writing my letters. We never said a word. The other employees moved about silently. The only sound was the scratching of the sergeant's pen on the paper, and his huge hand looked larger still on the table. From time to time, however, the good man cleared his throat—a smoker's habit—and waves of cold tobacco, catarrh and old age would blow my way. Fortunately his was a healthy old age. But fifty years of smoking twenty or thirty cigarettes a day had given his breath the stench of old pipes.

I admired him very much. Everyone who knew him admired him. He was a big strong man, obliging and honest. When I thought about the sergeant I could not believe in the cruelties attributed to the Civil Guards.

In another room the walls were covered to the ceiling with bookcases which appeared to be full of books—hundreds of books—bound in quarto, the size of writing paper. But they were not books. They were wooden boxes resembling books, which opened, and each one contained the complete file of a client insured against fire. This was the only kind of insurance sold by the company, I believe. I liked to gaze at those four walls lined with false books.

About that time I received a letter from Planibell, which said: "From Monflorite on such and such a day of the year of grace so and so. Esteemed friend: I hereby inform you that within a few days I will appear personally in your city for a week with our common friend Felipe Biescas and his worthy family. It will therefore be opportune for you to bear in mind my journey to the heroic city of the sieges so that we may be reunited in due time.

"With nothing more for today, and hoping that all your family is well (mine in good health, praise the Lord), I beg you to put me at the feet of your beautiful sister and gracious mother. Your friend, Planibell. P. S. My arrival in that capital will be, God willing, the 8th. *Vale*."

Planibell was also fond of postscripts.

This was precisely when I had the opportunity to go with my father and sister Concha to the village. The worst of it was that the date we were to leave for the village coincided with Planibell's arrival. It was too bad. But there was no doubt about my preferring to see Valentina.

First, however, I had to go to the Villa Julieta and leave the marble head on the column in the pool. I told Felipe. He agreed. We would go two days later, Tuesday, at six in the morning, before Felipe's uncle arrived. We had technical details to discuss, for the pool was very deep and we would have to invent some sure means of reaching the column which was three yards or so from the edge.

Felipe started telling me that this pool had been haunted since a child fell in and drowned, and that he was not sure if my choice was sensible or not. There were other places in the Villa. I did not want to explain that my decision had something to do with the liquid soul the lay brother had talked about. Besides, if the pool was haunted, the friar's work would perhaps take away the evil spell. On the other hand, I could not understand why the pool should be under a curse because a child had died there.

Then Felipe became confidential once again:

"The fact of the matter is . . . I wonder if you know that what happened there was a crime? The crime of a crazy woman. A widowed mother threw her child in the water so he would drown. And he did. Of course he drowned. I wasn't there but they told me about it. The mother is very young and beautiful. The thing happened on one of those Sundays in the summertime. Still daylight but the moon was out. I say this because the moon casts an evil spell sometimes, especially on women. Her husband had been a machinist on the cruiser *Reina Regente* and drowned. Her father and grandfather had been sailors and died at sea. She was afraid of the sea, had a horror of the sea, and left El Ferrol, for that was where they were living. When her husband died she was pregnant and she came inland because she did not want her son to see the ocean and like it and want to become a sailor. So she came to Zaragoza. The boy was born here. The woman used to come to the Villa almost every Sunday with her child. But she did queer things. That's why I say she was crazy. She would go up to two strangers who were talking and act as if she were going to kiss their hands, but spit on them instead. 'Just spittle,' she would say with an apologetic smile. This was her only madness then. One day she saw that her son wanted a boat others were playing with in the pool. And she said to him: 'No, son. Leave the boat alone. What a mania for boats! Let's go to the mountains. We'll go to Jaca to live where there is no river or sea or lake. Where there are no little boats, real ones or play ones.' But the boy kept on screeching and wanting the boat and suddenly the mother let him go, set him free. And the boy went to the edge, slipped on the green tiles and fell in. That's what happened. Others say they saw her push the child into the water, saying: 'All right, go with your father and grandfather.' Anything's possible since she was a little crazy. They arrested her. Then they set her free and she spent her time drawing pictures of the child, on paper, on embroidered cloth, and even in the sand of the avenues in the Villa. When I told her the sketch was good, she answered: 'Byzantium is illuminating me.' Who can Byzantium be, I wonder? Now she's in a hospital. Well, in an insane asylum, under observation, they say."

Impressed, I said:

"It's incredible that such things could happen in a beautiful place like this."

"Yes, that's right," he said. "That's the way it always is."

I had money because Sister Adela had come to call and given me the little roll of coins when she said goodbye. A small fortune: seven pesetas. When Sister Adela came it was always in the morning and she herself looked as if she had just stepped out of the depths of the early morning light. She appeared blushing, fresh and plump in her wimple and habit. Not too plump, but round, with the fragrance of a Maiden Blush apple, and joyous as a sleighbell. She came in smiling and happy, always inquiring for me. Whoever saw her first would start shouting and repeating her name, and at once my mother would hasten to welcome her.

In spite of what my sister had said about the little nun's platonic love for my father, my mother never had the slightest jealousy or any reservations. She was happier than anyone else when Sister Adela came to call and was the first to embrace her. Then she would kiss the copper crucifix half-hidden in the fold of the nun's scapular. The little nun's wimple was bluish in its dazzling whiteness. Underneath her veil her eyes were also blue as turquoises. Sister Adela's skin was like mother-of-pearl and she looked—as Concha said—like a rose in the snow.

My mother chatted with the nun for hours. Sometimes I heard her say:

"How wise you have been, Sister Adela, choosing the cloister!"

The nun smiled and said nothing. I understand now that in those so sincere words of my mother there was an unconscious double meaning of provocation and victory. Because everything in my mother had the primary honesty of instinctive life. And she repeated:

"What you left behind with the world is worth nothing."

The little nun replied:

"Oh, one cannot speak so positively. Secular life also has its charms, its legitimate satisfactions."

Sister Adela looked at me and at my sisters. Sons and daughters. We were sons and daughters. Wasn't it enough for a woman to have children like us? Once she said this to my mother who looked at us and, smiling with melancholy, said:

"Do you think children belong to the mother? No, Adela. That is another illusion."

She was right. Later on I discovered that sons do not belong to their parents. Children, once they outgrow childhood, belong to their own potential sons. To the children of tomorrow. To a future in which their own sons are already clamoring for them.

After the nun's visits, Concha always repeated, with a secret and delightfully scandalous air:

"I think she's still in love with Papa. In her own way, of course."

She meant: not like a woman, but like an angel. Everything related to love was all right with my sister.

I was planning a surprise for Concha. Having noticed that her window flirting had ended, I thought that it would be a wonderful joke to take her to the circus. First I made sure that the Smart Brothers were on the program. It was a little expensive for me (almost a *duro* for the two of us) but I was very fond of the circus. And my sister, who was going to the village with me and was a kind of fairy godmother to my love affair with Valentina, deserved it.

We went to the circus, in Santa Engracia Park, opposite the temple and gardens. The canvas tent, with the national flag flying above it, was very large. Clowns were playing on their flutes and trumpets at the entrance. And an animal-tamer with his whip was showing off his chest covered with decorations. To avoid being recognized, my sister had tucked her hair under a green cap. She was wearing a sleeveless middy blouse. And as a precaution, to disfigure herself, if necessary, some old lady's steel-rimmed glasses with pinkish oval lenses. She did not wear the glasses. They were in my pocket ready for an emergency.

Since my parents did not allow my sister to use make-up, she had to put it on when going down the stairs, almost in the dark, on her way out. This time she put on her powder and rouge at the circus entrance, while I was buying the tickets.

The tent was full. I have always liked the light cast by circus canvas during the day. That afternoon you could also see the shadows of pigeons flying back and forth above the canvas top.

At first my sister did not care very much for the circus. The clowns with their swollen red noses and enormous starched collars frightened her. At times she could not bear to look at them and bowed her head.

Finally came the Smart Brothers' act, after an imposing introduction. The lights went out, a distant waltz was heard, and a purple beam of light from somewhere fell on the edge of the ring. There the two acrobats were, beside each other. They were wearing red and black capes wrapped around them, and a kind of cap or calotte stuck tight to their skulls, revealing the shape of their heads. It was curious: they were exactly alike. A little moved, my sister said:

"Well, they really are brothers."

The spectator beside her turned to remark: "Not only brothers, but twins." And he showed her the program.

They had removed their capes and were now climbing up the ropes, each one on an opposite side of the ring. Two reflectors crossed, forming an X and illuminating the acrobats. My sister looked from one to the other, unable to tell which was the one with the derby hat and summer topcoat. Then she decided to make herself known. She loosened her hair and refused the glasses I offered her, saying:

"I need to know which one he is. I think that when the one it is sees me, he'll do something. A gesture, a smile. Something. Then I'll know. Don't you think so? It's just to find out."

Those two young men were really athletic. Their fine virile figures had an elastic and harmonious perfection of proportion. Without looking at my sister I could see her rapt profile full of admiration.

Now they were at the top. Each one had reached a platform suspended from the canvas top. The base of the platform was covered with purple velvet, studded with stars underneath. Their tights, with a silver S and B on the chest, were also purple. The spotlights, purple. The trapezes painted purple, that is to say violet (the color of love). Then I realized that my sister was wearing a little bouquet of violets with the green stems turned up at her throat. I felt slightly uncomfortable.

And one of the Smart Brothers looked around, as he wiped his hands on a handkerchief. Lean, in their tights every muscle was perceptible at the least movement. One of them, as I say, looked down. And he saw my sister. He did not smile. He gave no sign. But several times he turned to look at her. Now we knew which one he was.

They started swinging on the flying trapezes. Suddenly they leaped through the air and exchanged trapezes, passing each other in mid-air. Now my sister no longer knew on which trapeze her gallant was and I had to tell her.

They really performed very dangerous feats and more that day than ordinarily, as if they wished to shine in front of Concha. Meanwhile I was asking:

"What do you think of it?"

She answered with great conviction:

"Well, aside from the nonsense people say, one man's as good as another, and this one is an artist. But what in the devil is he doing in the Court of Justice?"

I told her that the Court of Justice is a public office, adding:

"If you marry him you'll have to learn to do these acrobatic stunts and then there'll be three of you and the advertisements will say: THE SMART BROTHERS AND THE FLYING ROSE. The Rose will be you. Don't you have the heart for it? Don't you want to be a flying rose?"

She pinched my arm until it hurt. Silently she watched. The acrobats were doing extraordinary things. One, head down, grabbed the other as he flew through the air. All with miraculous ease and litheness and following the rhythm of the music, besides. My sister stammered:

"Thanks a lot for bringing me. I would say, like Cousin Rita, that both men are very suggestive."

They had the place of honor on the program and were evidently real stars. This made Concha proud. She must have been in love with both of them at the moment, since they were alike. I was thinking: 'I don't believe I'll ever bring Valentina to the circus, especially if there are trapeze performers like these.' Without looking at me, my sister said in an undertone:

"Do *you* think I ought to answer his letter?"

She was referring to the gymnast's declaration of love. Many days had passed since she received it and she had not intended to answer, but now, looking at the heights dreamily she said:

"I believe I ought to answer, if only to refuse him."

I was thinking that it would not be a bad thing to have one of these men for a brother-in-law. At least I would get in the circus free. But I said:

"Of course, to refuse him."

"But," she added, still gazing high in the air, "letting him know that I esteem him as a person and admire him as an artist."

"No. Artist, no. As a gymnast, say."

"But he is an artist. What a pedant school has made of you. What's the difference? Come along, look, it's like they have wings. Where is he now? Which one is he? The one on the left? Clap your hands, Pepe, clap."

I applauded. So did my sister. She said:

"Let's leave when this number's over. I don't want him to come by here to greet us. Do you think he'll come? It's very possible. Not that, no. I say no."

"Well then, why did you smile at him? Don't you know that a smile is a sign of friendship and an invitation? Still more, with those violets you're wearing."

"An invitation to what?"

"To come over. And to ask for your hand and marry."

She was pensive:

"If a girl smiled at you, would you go up to her?"

"Naturally, if I weren't in love with Valentina."

Concha looked at me with alarm. But now she was attentive to the last and most dangerous feat. The music had stopped. You could have heard a pin drop. The acrobats were way up high and behind them the canvas cupola was illumined by the setting sun. Fugitive shadows flitted by on the canvas—doves—and in that great silence an insistent and voluptuous cooing was heard.

My sister sighed and said:

"We're not living."

"No? Then what are we doing?"

"Talking. We talk and they live."

Was she referring to the acrobats? What did acrobacy have to do with life? Sometimes, depending on the direction of the light, a dove's wing would cast an enormous shadow on the canvas. They looked like giant birds instead of doves. Or angels.

Finally one of the acrobats leaped from his trapeze without seeing the other, who was concealed from him by a large paper-covered hoop. Plunging through the paper headfirst, he caught hold of his brother's hands at the precise moment the other reached the spot hanging by his knees on his trapeze. In order to synchronize their movements the one who leaped through the paper-covered hoop could only be guided by the other's voice. It was a diabolically alarming business, especially without nets, and when they met and caught hold of each other's hands in mid-air the audience uttered a long ah, relieved. My sister applauded. So did I. Now in the ring the acrobats were bowing together. One of them was smiling at us. Then they made their exit running, but returned twice to acknowledge the applause.

My sister got up somewhat distressed:

"Let's get out of here."

I wanted to see the rest of the program, but she insisted:

"Let's go right now."

"What do you care? Wait a little longer."

She was annoyed and said, as she took her seat:

"All right, but I swear to you that if that man comes over here, I'll go off with him all over the world making flying leaps."

She was quite capable of it. I got up and we left. At the entrance she said to me, smiling:

"What would happen if I did go away with the Smart Brothers?"

"Well, the police would bring you back."

"Why? That's no crime. Ah, because I'm not of age. It's a mess to be a minor. Don't you agree?"

I realized on that day that man's and woman's attractiveness to each other is governed by very strange laws.

My sister and I were walking along arm in arm—I was wearing long trousers—and she said:

"Do you know what? You're a clever fellow."

"Why?"

"You have your sweetheart already. You know now whom you have to marry. Could you marry anybody else but Valentina? And isn't it glorious for her to have her husband already, her sweetheart, I mean? You do make a good couple, you really do. Did you know? She's grown, too. She is very tall and slim, with a waistline like a willow. And almost as tall as you."

I took for granted that her father would oppose the match when the time came. My sister could not imagine such a thing. Why should he oppose it? I asked her:

"Haven't you noticed that her father is getting richer and richer?"

"Well, so what?"

"While we are getting poorer and poorer every day."

She was not frightened, far from it. I told her that I had heard my father talking to a stranger in his office, saying: "I am ruined. In the end, between all of them, they're going to steal even my shirt. Is there no good faith left in the world?" My sister said that she did not understand how people made or lost money. I explained to her—by conjecture only—that all our father's business was going badly. He evidently lacked the character of a businessman. He needed duplicity. And we were living on the meager salary from the insurance company. Concha was thoughtful for a moment; then she said, suddenly:

"Well, the sooner the better. Let him be ruined as soon as possible and then I'll marry the Smart Brother."

She said this seriously. On the other hand, if I were poor and could not have a brilliant career, I would never marry Valentina, as long as her father Don Arturo lived, at any rate. That was the difference. Nevertheless, just like Concha, I was seeing myself alone, poor, and without a profession or fortune, with a certain romantic admiration. Many roads would still be open to me. And I thought of Juan in the Villa Julieta. It seemed to me that to have nothing in the world but day and night—and a pistol in my pocket—and to live in the Villa Julieta, was just as good as being a millionaire. I was not ambitious. I had enough with the indispensable, that is to say, with what I had at the time: a bed, a table on which to eat, a suit. The pistol was only to make me feel secure. That would be like being master of the world. But I would have to give up Valentina and that was inconceivable. My sister consoled me:

"Do you know what? Valentina is in love with you and you've always had her mother on your side."

Near home my sister asked very seriously when ruin—catastrophe—would strike. I was thinking: if I say soon she will write a letter to the Smart Brother this very night. I did not know how to answer her. Finally I made her promise she would not write and only when she swore, crossing her heart and saying she hoped to die if she lied, did I answer:

"Ruin will come any day. For the moment I still find money scattered around on top of the furniture."

"What, the money you steal?"

"I don't steal it. It's mine, it's family money. But one day there won't be any money lying around any more. And then what?"

In that matter my sister was more reasonable than I was. She said that maybe there would not be money for schools and travel and carriages, but that money for shopping, clothes and household expenses would never be lacking.

Concha did not write to the acrobat or flirt with him again, not from my balcony at any rate. She was very reasonable, as most women usually are, as long as they are single. She knew that she ought to think about another kind of possible husband. She had said to me one day:

"Do you think I'm crazy? No, son. If I fell in love with a man unsuitable for me, I would bite my tongue before I'd accept him. I'm not such a fool. Matrimony is serious business."

‡ 7 ‡

Some days later the cavalry soldier, good old Baltasar, came to see me and I went out for a walk with him. This soldier looked up to my father as a kind of god capable of making and unmaking the world. I realized that a part of Baltasar's friendship for me was due to the extravagant idea he had of my father. He generally came to see us on important holidays, such as St. James' Day, for instance. And he would come all dressed up with his white straps on his blue uniform, his leggings and tinkling spurs. I liked being treated as the equal of a man with so many leather straps and shining pieces of metal.

We strolled along the Paseo Independencia under the arcades flanked by handsome shops. We talked about the war. Baltasar thought the Germans would win, although he was not a partisan of either side. From the subject of the war we went on to something much more sensational. Assuming that I knew all the details, he suddenly blurted out that the cook we had had on Don Juan de Aragón Street had come to a bad end. And he added:

"When she left your house she was pregnant."

This took my breath away.

"That's impossible. She wasn't married."

"All right, Pepe. It's wrong, but people being what they are, are like that, and sometimes worse. Your mother fired her and she did the right thing."

"What's that? It's not so. She left, but nobody threw her out."

"Oh, really? Then she didn't want to wait until she would be fired. She's in a house of ill fame now."

This was scandalously unpleasant news. The scandal was all I thought of. A person who had lived with us, under our roof, was now a prostitute. Nothing could be uglier, more abject. Baltasar the soldier looked upon it only as something natural and inevitable, since he knew all about it. And he went on:

"She comes from a town next to ours and I know her sweetheart. The father is not her sweetheart, however, but a soldier from my regiment who is married and has two children. Ah, I don't know what will happen when the girl's sweetheart finds out. That's a bitter pill for anybody to swallow. I don't know what will happen. One never knows what goes on deep inside a man. She's afraid, and she has a right to be."

I was not concerned by what might happen to the poor girl. Being where she was, and what she was, I found it very natural for her to be insulted, mistreated, even murdered. That is, for the scandal to go on to the logical end. But the idea of a woman who had lived in our home now being in a house of prostitution horrified me. And this, in addition to the danger of my father's economic ruin, truly alarmed me. I was afraid even to remember those words of the soldier Baltasar, which had to be true like everything else he said.

Baltasar realized that he had made a tremendous impression on me.

A few days later my friend Felipe and I went to the Villa Julieta. We took along the marble head in the cage the lay brother had built for it. It was quite heavy. My friend was ingenious and made a lasso out of heavy rope. Through the knot he put a small stick and so we carried it suspended between the two of us.

When we reached the Villa we saw that Felipe's uncle had not yet arrived. Only Juan and the nursery workmen were there. They went on with their tasks.

Juan helped us place a plank beside the pool, with one of the ends extending over the water. He had chosen the widest to make the maneuvering easier. Before allowing me to walk out on that plank with the bust in my arms he asked if I knew how to swim. When I said yes rather

hesitantly, he asked me for the statue and with it in his arms he went
up the plank while Felipe and I stood on the opposite end.

"Is it all right like this?" Juan asked.

"No, don't put its back to the public. Or facing, either."

"Like this? Sidewise?"

"That's right."

Then Juan came down and we withdrew the plank. The pink bust
on the gray column was very effective. It was reflected quivering in
the water when the breeze rippled the surface. Without taking his eyes
off it, Juan asked:

"Who is it?"

Felipe hastened to say:

"Nero."

Juan shook his head. It could not be Nero. Nero was fat and had a
degenerate and stupid expression.

"Then who is it?" Felipe asked, looking at me.

Remembering the lay friar, I said:

"San Benedicto José Labré. A saint who was a tramp."

Juan burst out laughing, came over to me, and seeing that his laughter wounded me, became serious and said:

"This is the head of a Greek or Roman sage. Don't you know? At that
time all wise men were Stoics. I was laughing because of what you said
about tramp. No. Stoicism was a doctrine for aristocrats. This is one of
those nobles who were beheaded in a corner of their gardens by the men
of Spartacus. Beautiful head, really."

They were all agreed that the pool looked much better. I kept thinking
of the lay brother. If only he could see the statue there, above the surface
of the green-blue pool! The head looked as if it were made out of some
diaphanous stuff.

Again Felipe mentioned the drowned child and Juan nodded, but told
the story in another way: "It was not the child's mother who threw the
child into the water, but her lover. She was in love with a man who did
not want the child. This man wore a gray gabardine coat with a mourning band on the sleeve, and he used to hang around here. He loved the
widow, but not the child. Everybody knew that. Some men can't tolerate
the child of another father. One day he gave the child a shove, when
he was playing on the green tiles, and knocked him into the pool. Then
the mother told her story and they believed her, even though they say

she is a little mad. Sometimes when I was digging around in the carnations she would come up and spit on my hand. It was not repugnant.
And the girl's madness is not surprising. The poor woman's father was an
alcoholic, her grandfather too. They were all sailors and drank too much.
And as far as the lover, or sweetheart, is concerned, what he did . . ."

"Is a crime," said Felipe, getting ahead of Juan.

"Sure, it's a crime, but I won't be the one to turn him in."

"And if we do, saying we heard you say so?" Felipe threatened.

"But you won't." Then Juan looked us over from head to toe and
added:

"If you do, you'll be a couple of swine. And I would be surprised at
you, Pepe, that's a fact."

We said nothing and Juan roared with laughter. I suspected that this
man knew more about the child drowned in the pool and refused to talk.
Maybe the mad mother who spat on his hand was his mistress and went
to the Villa Julieta to see him. For a moment I found Juan dangerous
and disagreeable. Baltasar with his stories of prostitutes, too. And Felipe
going to swim in Doña Pilar's baths. I was different. Valentina and I
were different. I could not explain it to myself. She and I together and
alone in the world, eating on silver dishes or living on roots and sleeping
in a cave, were different. She and I alone knew what life was like. Everybody else talked about life—as Concha had said—but Valentina and I
lived. I sought refuge in that secret and felt stronger and better.

Besides, I was going to see her soon. The idea of my father taking me
with him just so I could see Valentina was very moving.

Felipe and I had intended going to the nurseries, but Juan said:

"Better not go. Let's leave the dog and cat alone in there."

"But they can't let each other alone," said Felipe.

"Then let them kill each other. One to the cemetery and the other
to the gallows. We'll all be better off."

And he laughed. I did not like that. Juan seemed to me too hard and
rude that day. As we were about to leave, the overseer arrived. On Tuesdays he always came between eight and nine. He glanced at us with
that expression which looked disdainful while still meaning to be cordial.

"Hello," he said.

He said it exactly like the crow. The bird doubtless imitated him.

"So you two are early risers, I see," he remarked. "At your age one is
an early riser only to get into some kind of mischief somewhere."

Juan said:

"This time no, they have done no mischief." And he told about the statue, adding that it was ancient and very valuable. The overseer must have been in his fifties, with a firm, slightly rigid heaviness of limb that reveals oncoming old age.

When we were beside the statue he said, looking at the bust's reflection in the water:

"The saint's handsome there."

Juan winked at me as if to say it was lucky the old man thought it was a saint.

"The saint's handsome," the overseer insisted. "All right, I don't have any objections. This pool needed a saint after what happened."

Then he began to tell the tragedy of the drowned child. The boy was playing on the very edge of the pool. He was trying to stick his finger in the mouth of one of the green frogs which spouted water. He called his mother with a single sound: *Ma!* And the mother, who was standing beside the overseer on the other side of the pool, said to him: *Come.* This was an idea of the devil's because of the pool which was between the mother and child. And the boy, obeying his mother, ran toward her and fell into the water. Just like that. Fast as they ran to save him, the child went to the bottom. They had to drain the pool to get him out. The mother did not do it on purpose. She called the child, expecting him to go around the pool. But the boy wanted to walk on the water.

Then the overseer said that he was going to see if Pascual and Monflorite had finished planting the new borders. "Because those fellows," he added, "are having themselves a fine time while they do or don't kill each other."

Juan sent greetings to my sister and walked with us toward the gate. Before saying goodbye he warned:

"What the old man says about the child's accident isn't so. I was there that day and saw it."

I could not leave without asking him another question:

"Felipe told me that you believe flowers and plants see and hear us."

Juan threw both arms up in the air:

"Ah, that would take a long time to explain. I did not think that up. An eighteenth century Aragonese naturalist, Feliz de Azara, discovered it on the frontiers of Brazil. If the subject really interests you, go to the University library and ask for his *Journeys through South America.*

When you have read the book, then we'll talk, if you like. And when you come back I'll tell you something else about the boy's mother, with her little spitting habit. Crazy or not, she's a swell female."

I did not know what he meant by "swell female," but I refused to show off my ignorance by asking Felipe.

Outside the Villa Felipe said he was sorry about my going to the village, but he promised to hold on to Planibell until I returned. Not that I cared much about seeing Planibell, but I did have the vague hope of making him talk against Prat, something I had never succeeded in doing in boarding school where they could disagree and even fight, but before the rest of us defended each other with the devotion of members of an ancient clan.

‡ 8 ‡

Finally came the moment to leave for the village. My father said that Concha and I would go. We would be in our old country house for two or three days and then return. I wanted to wear long trousers, but my father and sister agreed that we should all go dressed for the country. I put my watch in my breast pocket, the chain quite visible with a small compass attached, in case I should get lost in a virgin forest or desert.

The day we left I was thinking of the Villa Julieta. It no longer seemed to me merely a place of delights, but also of dangers. When I said so to my sister, she agreed with me:

"For Heaven's sake, *chico*. That old bird's saying *hello* is just as unpleasant as it can be."

I was thinking: "If you only knew . . ." And I was remembering the fights of the nursery workmen, the tragedy at the pool. I suspected that life would always be like this: beautiful things, with misery or horror underneath. My sister had a copy of the magazine *Cosmos* in her hand, from which she read aloud a little poem about a girl who was going to smell a rose, but in the rose there was a wasp that stung her on the lips. That poem cleared up many things for me in a twinkling. I would have copied it for Valentina if I could have found the word *love* somewhere in its eight lines.

I grew impatient as we approached the town. And I forgot all about the adult world of Juan and Felipe, and the soldier Baltasar with his horrible story about the cook, and felt again as I used to when we lived in the village. Still I was not the same. I thought seriously about how I had traveled, been around, studied in distant schools far from the familiar scene. And I felt important. My sister Concha, pensive, had left *Cosmos* on the seat, and suddenly she said to me while our father was peering out the window:

"Do you know something? I'm sure glad you lost that Catalonian accent. For it would have shocked Valentina, honestly."

What had happened was that Concha had caught my accent, so she had it too, although both of us less than when I first came home from Reus.

As we approached the village I was beginning to turn a fixed idea over in my head: the nuisance that Don Arturo was in my relations with his daughter. And after considering possibilities I came to the last resort of thinking of the pool in the Villa Julieta into which someone had made the child fall. I thought of the voluminous Don Arturo floating in the water of the pool and refusing to sink. Floating like a buoy. It would certainly be difficult to make Don Arturo disappear. Then I was ashamed of these ideas, not because of their criminality but their extravagance.

We were slowing down for the town. Escanilla, the old coachman, would be at the station to meet us. Although he was no longer coachman or in our employ, he would come for the pleasure of seeing us and also— everything must be taken into account—receiving a tip from my father.

There were many stories about Escanilla, as, for instance, the day he was going to ford the river when it was swollen and turbulent. In the middle he found himself in grave difficulties. The current was stronger than he had expected. And with the greatest show of devotion he said, gazing heavenward:

"Holy Virgin del Pilar, get me across, for I'm from Aragón."

As everyone knows, the Virgin del Pilar is the patron saint of Aragón. And several times he repeated: "Get me across, for I'm from Aragón." When he finally reached the other side he took off his wet clothes, spread them out in the sun, and a half-hour later dressed again and went ahead very happily, muttering to himself:

"Go ahead and get mad, little Virgin del Pilar. I'm from Navarre!"

My father's humor always changed when he took a trip. He was contented. He was going to sign some papers in the notary office of Don Arturo, who had drawn up the sales contracts when a part—the biggest part—of our estate was liquidated. I had noticed that he was losing some of his intolerable arrogance as he disposed of our land. This, plus living in the city where he was nobody, were making him almost agreeable. Although in the city he found everything wrong. He criticized every single detail. When he bought fruit he liked to pick it out himself in the shop. And in spite of always buying the dearest and best he would say, as he paid for it:

"You call this exquisite, yet we would feed it to the pigs in the village."

Then he explained that this melon or those pears had ripened in packing boxes instead of on the tree or vine.

Finally we reached the station. No one was there to meet us but Escanilla with the old carriage we used to call *zolleta*, or little pig-sty. This seemed to disappoint my father somewhat. My heart fell when I saw Valentina was not there. Aware of my disappointment, Concha said:

"That's natural, *hombre*. How could you expect her to be alone on the road for two hours in the stylet?"

"She could have come with her mother."

My father installed us in the carriage and asked Escanilla:

"Why didn't you bring the other carriage?"

"The new one, you mean? That one, they say, says they, your honor sold it, Don José."

"Couldn't you have borrowed it?"

"Well, to tell the truth, Don José, I don't have any dealings with the one who bought it. Because a nephew of mine had something to do with his daughter and then the daughter went to Barcelona. And there's plenty of gossip. One listens and says nothing, but I don't know what they say she's doing there. The girl, I mean. And then I said, says I: well, a few buckets of water on the *zolleta* and she's still okay for the road, and no sooner said than done."

We took the road back to town. I sat beside Escanilla on the coach-box, hoping he would let me hold the reins. I said to him:

"It looks like the horse didn't recognize me."

"No. Horses ain't very bright. Some folks think a horse has more sense than a Christian, no disrespect meant, but t'aint so. A horse has no brain. They're very forgetful."

Concha was listening from behind. And she asked:

"You, Escanilla, who do you think's the smartest? Among the animals, I mean."

Escanilla hesitated. Finally he said:

"I wouldn't want to mention that animal here in front of your honorable father."

"Why not?"

"Because it's not a decent name."

"You may say it, Escanilla," my father said.

"Well then, the smartest is the pig, and excuse my saying so."

"Is it possible?" My father asked, even though his mind was on something else.

"Just as I say, Don José, sir. The pig, and said with no disrespect. While . . . well, don't you see, sir? All the names of that animal are bad words. Begging your pardon, the smartest is the pig, I mean to say, but only when . . . well, if the pig, I mean, and please excuse me, is whole with all its parts."

I asked, also thinking about something else:

"And after that, which one?"

"Well, the cow, I'd say. And then the cat and after that it's likely to be the goat."

"And the dog?" Concha asked.

Escanilla looked skeptical:

"The dog only understands two or three things, eating and defending the house. But the cat understands man's most hidden thought. And if a man wants to beat a cat, before he grabs the stick the little animal's on the roof and catch him if you can. A cat can get through where no man can."

"And after the goat?" My father asked.

"After that, Señor Don José, comes woman, I believe, present company excepted, and said with no disrespect. And allowing for my ignorance."

Concha protested, indignant, and the coachman added:

"I said, no disrespect meant, señorita. I've only known my wife, praise the Lord, and what I say is because of her. My wife attends to the cat and goat before serving me. And what I say's because of her, says I. That's why I think she must have more or less the same idea of me, of my sense, says I. I wouldn't be shocked, and that's a fact. The cat, wherever he is, sure knows how to become the master. And no one can fool a goat."

We were all silent. The coachman added, as he urged on the horse:

"That's the way God wanted things to be in this world."

I was thinking about the Egyptians worshiping cats. And about the goat and devil being identified not only by witches, but by painters and poets. I had read about it in school in Reus. I was about to tell Escanilla, but kept still, thinking of Valentina. Would she be waiting at our house? If not, my disappointment would be painful.

Escanilla still felt obliged to explain his previous judgments further:

"I was not talking about all women. Miss Concha, here present, is something else again, but my wife, as I said before, Don José, after the goat."

The closer we came to the village the more I was beginning to feel just the same as before, as if I had never been away in Reus or Zaragoza.

The coachman hesitated to ask questions, but he was full of curiosity.

"It looks, Don José, like you've gone to live in the capital forever," he observed. "Around here they say, says I, you're selling everything. The house, too?"

My father told him briefly about which farms he had sold. As he was talking the coachman turned his head to one side slightly, to hear better. Before, when he talked of other things, the old coachman never turned his head. I realized how great Escanilla's curiosity was. And he had dared to ask, which was very bold indeed.

I could not believe that the pig was the most intelligent animal. But after much caviling I recalled that the pig belongs to the same family as the elephant, which has the reputation of a mental giant. Escanilla was probably right.

We entered the village. My first impression was that the houses were smaller. And the streets. And plazas. Concha was still not satisfied:

"Your wife," she said to the coachman, "knows how to read, and if she doesn't know she can take lessons and learn in a little while. A goat or cat couldn't learn how to read."

"That's where the señorita is mistaken. My wife could never learn."

Concha was confused. She insisted:

"But if they gave her good teachers she could learn."

"That's quite possible," said Escanilla, "but I'm not talking about those things. What good would it do my wife to know how to read? I, señorita, am talking about the reason that's good for earning a living, defending oneself from hunger and cold, finding out the intentions of others and so on respectively. Furthermore, looking at things as the señorita wishes, my wife could not learn how to hunt rats with her fingernails either, or how to walk along cliffs and ravines."

Knowing how to read seemed like nonsense to the coachman, but he dissembled. And for that nonsense of studies and schools we had left the village. Apparently no one in the village could understand it.

We went to our house. Valentina and her mother were there. Valentina was quite grown-up, and her eyes had also grown. On the other hand, her mouth and face looked the same. And so did her braids which came together on top of her head, their ends fastened with a little barette of artificial flowers. And the little gold chain which on her neck had the same color as her skin. I looked at her. Doña Julia said:

"Give her a kiss, Pepe. Don't begin acting like a grownup."

Valentina and I kissed each other on both cheeks. Then she caught my hand. We entered our old house. The mastiff was not there. Everywhere it smelled stuffy, of having been closed. Voices had an echo.

From the porch my father called:

"Where are those children going? Pepe, you have to go see Mosén Joaquín!"

Then he told Doña Julia that he was going to see her husband at once because the business he had in hand could not wait. Without listening to my father Doña Julia followed her daughter and me with a loving glance. Concha and Pilar—who had just arrived with Tía Ignacia—were chattering incessantly without listening to each other. The coachman had gone to the back of the house with the carriage and suitcases. Again I felt as if I had never left the village. The fact that Maruja was not around seemed wonderful. Pilar was striving to give the impression that she was unaware of my presence.

Tía Ignacia looked at Concha and my father and wept, without saying a word. With her tears she was saying: what a pity they went away. I am an old woman now and won't see them any more. She did not say so. She looked at us and big tears rolled down her cheeks. That was all.

Valentina asked her mother if she could go with me to see Mosén Joaquín and Doña Julia hesitated a moment and then, noticing my expression, hastened to consent. Concha asked her to let Valentina stay for dinner with us.

It must have been around noon then. A whole afternoon lay ahead of us. One of those afternoons in the country, much longer and more profound than those in the city.

Everything still looked smaller to me. Everything except Valentina. She started telling me about how most of my letters never reached her hands, the last two, for instance. Pilar had these and refused to give them to her. Her mother had taken a hand and told her that mail was sacred and that if she insisted on keeping the letters she would commit one of the vilest and most reproachable acts of her life. Valentina remembered her mother's words very well: *vile and reproachable*. She stammered as she pronounced the last one. Then Pilar gave the letters to her father.

"Do you know something?" Valentina asked. "Pilar and Father are against us."

As if I didn't know. I told her that it did not matter if she and I loved each other. I had never used that expression about *loving each other* before. I had only used the verb *love* in writing, but now I repeated: if we love each other, what does the rest of the world matter? With their saying no and our saying yes, who would win? They weren't going to cut off our heads, said I. Valentina was delighted with my assurances. And we sauntered along the Callejón de Santa Clara talking animatedly. On her little balcony Clara, with her carnation in her white hair, was laughing like a parrot:

"Look at the little gentleman and lady together, the little maiden and her suitor."

And again she laughed, like a magpie. Valentina looked at the balcony out of the corner of her eye, fearfully:

"She's a witch, they say," she whispered a little frightened.

Then she stumbled and almost fell. This frequently happened to Valentina who, because she was looking me in the face as we walked along, or at Clara or somewhere else, would stumble. Her legs were growing too fast and she did not have perfect control of them. I told her that all women who had passed the marrying age without getting married gradually turned into witches. That's what I had read in the book *On Love* by the Chaplain André (the chaplain of the French king) at boarding school. Valentina told me that at first she had thought her father's book could be a good one for us, but then she had never been able to read over four lines. "I don't understand a thing," she said. Incredulous, she added that her sister Pilar insisted she herself understood everything. It was eagerness to flatter her father, for even her mother Doña Julia had to confess there were pages where she only understood every third line. "And I," Valentina insisted, "one in thirty." Once again she added that Pilar was smarter than she was, but she doubted that she was any smarter than her mother.

Certainly Pilar would never marry because she was a girl without charm and one who did not know how to "keep friends." That's what her mother had said. Keep friends. Then gradually she would turn into a witch and spend the whole day on her balcony with a carnation in her hair laughing mockingly at couples going down the street. Nevertheless

Pilar deserved better luck, according to Valentina. Yes indeed. She was very smart.

As we reached the Santa Clara Convent, Valentina was still talking about Pilar and how she antagonized the people around her. Their characters were very different. Valentina, who was a brunette, was very much like her mother, who was blonde. While Pilar, very blonde, took after Don Arturo, who was dark-skinned.

The priest's housekeeper received us with the greatest show of surprise and sympathy in spite of her dried-up, sullen and resentful look. And behind her, limping slightly, Mosén Joaquín appeared:

"Pepe? Great Heavens, what a surprise!"

And it was true. Surprise was written all over his face, all over his adult person. I made Valentina go in first, but Mosén Joaquín had eyes only for me.

We went in the same room where I used to recite my lessons. There was the little round table covered with a light cloth—a dark one in winter. A pack of cigarettes on top. Beside it a tray full of stubs and a silver lighter. It looked like the same pack, the same lighter and the same ashtray as always.

Mosén Joaquín asked me questions. If I had finished the course, received good marks, who my teachers were and many other things. On hearing that my grades were not as good as when I studied with him, he concealed a certain contentment. I told him about the "A" and the "little tune" of the prepositions. Mosén Joaquín laughed at that trick which he had heard about. On the whole things had been quite mediocre in Reus. But I did not come right out and say so, naturally. I did not want to humiliate myself in front of Valentina.

We were both convinced that it would have been better for me to go on studying with him.

Valentina behaved with a really admirable gravity and self-assurance when with strangers. She had kissed Mosén Joaquín's hand when we entered, but after this reverential act, which the priest had acknowledged by patting Valentina's cheek, she gazed straight at Mosén Joaquín, alert and bright, and answered his questions with authority and aplomb. Too much aplomb, maybe, because when for some reason Valentina raised her head slightly the gesture could have appeared arrogant. I noticed that her feet now reached the floor, as she sat on her chair, and this had not happened before. She was wearing patent-leather shoes and white socks. One of the socks had a dirty spot, perhaps caused by the shoe on the other foot when she scratched her leg with it. For the mosquitoes pursued her. They evidently liked her blood better than that of anybody else in her family. Sometimes the mosquitoes bit her through her sock, she said astonished. And even through her dress. That's why her mother had her rub her arms and legs with eau de cologne before she left the house. Mosquitoes didn't like the odor of eau de cologne.

Valentina explained this sometimes when she realized that someone had noticed the perfume. That's what she did when she saw Mosén Joaquín looking at her and rubbing his nose with his index finger. Valentina told him she wore perfume to ward off the mosquitoes. Mosén Joaquín laughed without saying anything. That odor against the mosquitoes—to which I was already accustomed in previous years—seemed charming and exclusively Valentina's to me. I confess that when I noticed the same fragrance on others in Zaragoza it moved me somewhat, and if it was a girl in the street, I hurried to pass her by to see if she was pretty. Valentina listened to the priest and to me. He was also shocked by my father's selling most of our estate.

"At least," he said, "so long as you don't sell the house, I suppose you will come back here once in a while."

"They're selling that too," said Valentina, "and Papa wants to buy it, but I don't know if he will. I would like to live in that house, because it's bigger than ours. And ours is not bought but rented. Because Papa's family comes from Zaragoza and Mama's from Borja, and although we were born here, Papa doesn't know if we'll be here for long or not. In Papa's profession one never knows."

Valentina was much more grown-up than before. She spoke with grownups without curtness, as with equals, reasonably and logically.

Meanwhile my father and Concha were at Don Arturo's house. Concha told me later what had happened during the interview. As always my father wanted little things which represented small extravagances in the business world. He wanted Don Arturo to ask the buyer of one of his farms to make the second payment now. This was not to have been paid until the following spring. Don Arturo took out a pencil and began figuring. Then he looked up, glanced at my father gravely, threw the pencil on the table, took a deep breath and said:

"I don't advise it. You will lose two thousand, four hundred pesetas."

Don Arturo looked like a Buddha, always fat, motionless, sure of himself. My father asked:

"Two thousand, four hundred? But why?"

"The thing's as plain as day." Don Arturo frequently used the expression about things being plain as day or having meridian clarity. "If the buyer pays you now, he will deduct the amount of the annual twelve percent interest."

"A bank would do it for less. But I don't want to ask a bank for it because I know myself."

The notary looked at him as if to say: I know you, too, and I know that you are a very disorganized man. Nevertheless in that look there was a certain respect. It was as if he were telling him: you are careless and generous. You would spend the bank's money as well as the rest. You were born to be rich and the money is running out and is not enough. There has never been enough money for any generous man.

Then my father offered to sell the house to Don Arturo, but when the notary saw my father's haste he offered him half of what he had formerly said it was worth. This offended my father so that he could not control himself and he made two or three impertinent remarks. Don Arturo answered with his fat man's, and also businessman's, calm. All this acted on my father's nerves, but he concealed it as best he could, stood up and, with friendly coldness, said:

"Don't bother about any negotiation. I will wait for the installment according to the terms of the contract."

"That's the best thing you can do."

He had also risen and was again talking about the meridian clarity of the affair. They went out into the garden where Don Arturo, exaggerating his affability, showed him his flower beds and also the breeding pigeons which he had bought in Zaragoza. They were carriers and he wanted to experiment with some of them by taking them to Zaragoza and seeing if they would return to the dovecot when set free. My father said:

"I don't think they'll return. Why should they?"

Don Arturo showed him some cages which he had ready. My father said that they were too small. Don Arturo called a pigeon with a little corn in his hand, caught it and showed him its foot with the aluminum band. In that band the message was placed in a little celluloid tube which he also showed him. My father said that it was clever but that nothing larger than a rolled-up cigarette paper would fit into that small celluloid tube. The notary assured him that it would hold a large sheet of onionskin paper properly folded. My father was incredulous. He was still upset and found fault with everything.

My father and Concha left. Out in the street my father growled: "I

need money, but not as badly as they think." And he went on down the
street talking like that to himself. An ugly word slipped out, something
unusual in him. Concha exclaimed:

"But Papa!"

Meanwhile Valentina and I were leaving the convent with a handful
of sweets Mosén Joaquín's housekeeper had given us. He watched us
from the little terrace balcony smiling, smoking his eternal cigarette,
bent and losing its shape in his fingers.

I said to Valentina:

"As soon as I finish school, we'll get married."

Valentina could not understand why I should want to marry now,
after having written from boarding school that I was an enemy of matrimony. I told her that we had to think of Mosén Joaquín, who would insist
upon officiating at our wedding. I would not like to deprive a man like
Mosén Joaquín of that pleasure. Valentina agreed, as always, after thinking things over and seeing that I had all the reason in the world on my
side. We agreed that we were partisans of free love but would marry to
please Mosén Joaquín.

Valentina stayed for dinner with us. She told me all about Pilar's new
outrages. Concha told about what had happened at Don Arturo's. I felt
that behind my father's attitude toward Valentina's father there was
something humiliating for me as sweetheart and future husband. I also
told my sister that Pilar was intercepting my letters and that from now
on I would write Valentina in code. I had already thought of this several
times. I decided to teach Valentina how to use a code. In an adventure
story I had read that the surest and most undecipherable code, as well
as the simplest, consisted in using any book—in this case we could use
Don Arturo's thesis on love—referring to each letter with numbers. For
example: 7-3-8 meant the letter corresponding to page seven, line three,
the eighth letter. Nobody in the world could decipher that.

It seemed to me that my father's sudden enmity toward Don Arturo
was due not only to business but to their political differences, since the
notary was a furious partisan of France. After dinner, which was quite
gloomy because my father was in a bad humor and talked only of returning to Zaragoza, I carefully instructed Valentina. She would have to get
hold of a copy of her father's book, which would be easy, and keep it
with her. If her father found out she would say that she was reading it,
which could not fail to gratify him.

But there was another difficulty. If Pilar continued to steal her letters, what difference would it make if they were written in code or not? Even if she could not read them, she would go on stealing them just the same. They would not reach Valentina's hands.

Concha had told me about the carrier pigeons and a new idea was stirring in my imagination. It was absurd, but at that time the most absurd thing always struck me as the best.

My father had gone off on other errands. Tía Ignacia was moving about quietly and sometimes looking at Concha or me and crying, her big face looking rather comical.

I finally mentioned the carrier pigeons to Concha. If I took one with me to Zaragoza I would send it to Valentina with the first love message, in cipher. Don Arturo would not take the trouble to look at his pigeons every day, much less count them. Concha called Valentina. As always when I took the initiative, Valentina's eyes began to shine with impatience. The difficulty or incongruence did not matter. As usually happens with children, the practical end of my initiative was surrounded by baroque and absurd circumstances. Valentina said to me: "You can take one pigeon. Or two. Once in Zaragoza you set one loose with the message on its foot. And another day, the other. And I will be on the lookout and catch them and take off the little paper and go up to my room with Papa's book and start digging out the letters one by one." Hearing her talk revealed how she was going to relish the voluptuous pleasure of digging out those letters one by one. Concha listened, moved. She sighed and said:

"Just see what people in love can think of!"

Then she said that we were very lucky to have loved each other since we were so little and that once again anyone could see how futile it was to try to put *obstacles in the way of love.*

The problem was how to get hold of the pigeons. But Valentina said she would be responsible for everything. When she wanted to do something so that no one would find out about it, she only had to get up early. No one got up early at her house; no one left his room until half-past eight. She would put two pigeons in a small cage her father had, she would wrap the cage in newspapers, tie it up with string, and bring it the next day before we left. Fortunately pigeons would not screech the way hens do. No one would be the wiser.

Concha offered to be an accomplice. Concha would call for her at seven o'clock on the pretext of attending Mass at Santa Clara. Valentina would tell her mother the night before. Concha had her doubts:

"Don't say anything. Secrecy is most important in matters of love. Besides, supposing Pilar finds out?"

Valentina did not think she would.

"Pilar's the last one up. That's why father says she's *lymphatic*."

We agreed, then, that at seven-fifteen Concha and Valentina would come with the little cage wrapped in papers and the two pigeons inside. I kept on thinking of the future. We would need more pigeons, and Valentina said:

"Whenever somebody we know goes to Zaragoza I can send you a pigeon or two. What trouble would that be? Just to go to your house with a small package and say: 'This comes from Don Arturo.' That way we'll use his pigeons to carry the message, his book to write it in code, and it will be like a punishment from Providence."

Noticing my sister's pensive mood I asked her what was wrong. She said:

"I think I must be lymphatic too, even if I am a brunette."

Late in the afternoon my father returned with a peasant and Mosén Joaquín. He was more taciturn than ever and repeating:

"Everybody in this town is getting a ridiculous idea of me."

He had tried to sell the house, it seems, and they offered him a fourth of what it was worth. Even Don Arturo offered only half. There was no longer any doubt about the fact that the family's rôle was in decline. Concha was beginning to be really frightened. And she thought of the Smart Brothers.

We spent the evening together, Concha, Valentina and I. My sister said to us:

"You two are ideal sweethearts, but Pepe is stern and never says sweet things to you or pays you compliments, Valentina. Really, I can't conceive of a sweetheart who doesn't say sweet things. Why don't you, Pepe? You can call her *my darling,* and also *adorable, beloved, precious, madness of my heart.*"

Valentina's face was radiant as she listened, but I felt ashamed.

"I don't believe anybody says such things," I said.

"Pepe writes them to me in letters," Valentina said.

"Yes, but spoken," I added, "nobody says them any more. Because they sound silly."

Tía Ignacia's face appeared in the kitchen door, that big, wrinkled, *carnival face* we all loved so much. Concha asked her:

"What did your husband say to you when you were sweethearts?"

According to Concha, Tía Ignacia's husband was the handsomest man in town. Tía Ignacia asked:

"What did he say to me? But when, why?"

"What did he say when he was courting you and saying sweet nothings to you? What sweet names did he call you?"

"Me?"

Valentina and I listened very attentively. And finally Tía Ignacia said very seriously:

"*Milorcheta.*"

"What? What's that?"

"He called me *milorcheta*, I said."

My sister looked disappointed. How was I going to call Valentina *milorcheta*? And what did Tía Ignacia have to do with a *milorcha*, or kite? Tía Ignacia went on:

"He called me *cardelina*—goldfinch, too."

Concha was somewhat more convinced but still unsatisfied:

"Nothing more?"

"Well, he also called me sugar-kitten and stream of gold."

We burst out laughing. Concha repeated: *milorcheta, goldfinch, sugar-kitten, stream of gold.*

"It may sound a little queer," she added, very serious, "but it shows they were in love. That's what I would like: to see you two fall in love some time."

Night finally came, and the following day. Not wanting to be lymphatic, Concha was up and out by six. At seven she and Valentina were back. They had the little cage wrapped in newspapers and tied with string. I made two little holes in the paper, so the pigeons could breathe. Concha said: "This Pepe doesn't miss a thing."

My father, who had gone to Mass at Santa Clara, returned shortly. We had breakfast and as we were finishing Escanilla appeared, greeted us, and went to the kitchen where Tía Ignacia served him breakfast, too. This consisted of two glasses of spirits while a large chop broiled on the coals. After the chop a couple of eggs with sausage. He came out wiping his lips with the back of his hand. My father asked him what he had eaten and when Escanilla told him my father arched his brows in surprise:

"But didn't you eat any supper last night?"

"Yes sir. To sleep I've got to have my innards—and excuse me for saying so—good and full. Then I get up just like nothing was there."

"But how can you eat all that so early?"

"Well, Don José, just by pushing it down with bread."

He said it naïvely. Then he added that we should be on our way, to catch the train.

We left, taking Valentina home first. My father was sitting on the coach-box with Escanilla, which made our conspiracies easier. The box with the pigeons was at the back of the carriage, covered with my father's duster. Because when traveling my father always carried a greenish canvas duster and a cap with a visor. Before saying goodbye at the notary's door I learned from Valentina's mother that she and my sweetheart were coming to Zaragoza the first of October for the fiestas. They would stay for two weeks. This revelation filled me with a secret confidence in destiny. Valentina was so happy she was speechless.

At the station I took charge of the box and duster. We boarded the train and I put everything in a corner. My father had inquired on seeing the box:

"What's that?"

But frequently he asked questions without waiting for an answer. When I answered *an errand*, I am certain that he was already thinking about something else. Escanilla had gone off very happily with his five pesetas in his pocket. From the train we saw the carriage returning along the highway at a trot between two rows of poplars. My father sighed and said:

"Nothing like country life."

Concha dared ask him why we had moved to Zaragoza.

"And you ask? We went to give all of you a suitable education. What do you want to do, stay in the village and marry someday like Tía Ignacia?"

My sister concealed her desire to laugh. But thinking about the Smart Brothers I could not hold in and burst out laughing. At that moment my father heard pigeons cooing. Maybe we had a male and female in the cage.

"What's that?" he asked.

Casually Concha answered that it was a couple of pigeons to return to the shop where Don Arturo had bought them. They had sent him the wrong kind. My father asked:

"What kind of pigeons did Don Arturo want?"

Concha was in a tight spot. I helped her out:

"*Polainudas.*"

Since Don Arturo wore *polainas*—leggings—almost every day, even though he did not go hunting, this sounded natural. I had not the faintest idea that there was such a thing as *polainuda* pigeons in the world. Neither did my father. He unfolded the newspaper and started to read. Suddenly he said:

"I have the impression the conductor won't permit pigeons in the coach. The regulations are posted up there and I think traveling with animals is forbidden."

I stood on my knees in the seat and read the regulations on the wall, framed and covered with glass. When I finished reading I sat down again.

"What does it say?" my father asked.

"Nothing. Only that traveling with dogs and cats is forbidden. So if one comes with two pigeons or a goat or crocodile they can't say anything."

My father gave me a sympathetic glance, smiled and said:

"You ought to study law."

The conductor did not see the pigeons. We reached Zaragoza before noon. The other two sisters were waiting for us impatiently. Maruja, who was always expecting presents, walked around the cage eyeing it covetously.

‡9‡

Naturally we decided to go to the Villa Julieta to set the first pigeon free. But first I had to write the letter to my sweetheart and this chore took me two days, during which I forgot all about Felipe Biescas, Plani-bell and everybody else. My letter, written on onionskin paper on the typewriter in my father's office, was a succession of numbers: 7-2-5/4-9-6/ 2-6-1/5-9-4/ and so on, covering the entire page. My signature was also in code.

Then we decided to turn the letter-carrying pigeon loose on the sum-mit of Buena Vista. But on the way there Concha convinced me that we should have gone to the Villa Julieta. She said to me: "Setting the white pigeon with a love letter free there, beside the pool, would be like a poem of Bécquer's." And she went on to say that the pigeon would go to Don Arturo's house and knock, as in Bécquer's poem, "with its wing on the windowpanes." Although Bécquer was not talking about white pigeons, but "dark swallows." For Concha, however, it was all the same. And saying so, she sighed.

I do not remember the letter but it contained all the tender expressions that the most demanding lover (Concha, for example) could desire. I called Valentina delight of my soul, joy of my solitude, dream, dear heart, angel of my life, and many other things besides. I insulted Don Arturo a little, but not too much.

We decided, then, to go to the Villa Julieta. What finally convinced me was that it was higher there than the summit of Buena Vista and commanded a vaster horizon. It would be easier for the pigeon to get its bearings.

Curiously, we found Planibell and Felipe there. Felipe hastened to tell me that Planibell had arrived two days before and that he would be around for another week. My sister was quick to see that Planibell with all his masculine beauty was younger than she. So she promptly struck him off her list of curiosities and left us, strolling hither and yon as if she were alone. Planibell wasn't interested either. Women, bah!

Although this was a day when the park was open to the public there were few people around and most of them had gone to the mansion and to visit the *palacete* behind it. Without explaining anything to anybody I took my box to the side of the pool in whose calm waters the marble bust was reflected. My sister came running when she saw me fooling around with the cage.

"That friend of yours," she said, meaning Planibell, "is a stuck-up snotty brat."

"You're right. But at school he wasn't so bad."

I opened the cage—which I had left on the ground—and the pigeon walked out. It walked for a couple of yards and turned around to look at me. Its shadow on the sand was very black, making a violent contrast with the whiteness of its feathers. Suddenly it started flying. It rose almost vertically and began flying in circles above our heads. Then it took a northwesterly course. I had been studying the map to see what direction the pigeon should take to reach the village. And in the Villa I had found my bearings with my little compass. The bird flew precisely in the foreseen direction. Concha was in ecstasy watching the horizon, even after the pigeon had disappeared. Then she said with a sigh:

"Did you ever see anything so beautiful?"

There were tears in her eyes.

Planibell and Felipe who had witnessed the proceedings from a distance came over. Felipe was full of curiosity but Planibell looked peevish
and bored, repeatedly commenting on the smallness of the Villa Julieta
in comparison with the park in Reus. Finally Planibell asked:

"What kind of pigeon was that? A carrier? Bah, I have carrier pigeons
at home, too. Anybody can have them. And why were you releasing it?"

"To carry a message."

"What kind of message?"

"A love letter."

"To whom?"

"My sweetheart."

Planibell acted as if he were in the habit of seeing people send off
pigeons with love messages to everybody every day. He looked unim-
pressible and indifferent. Finally he said:

"I would never do a thing like that. If the pigeon falls into strange
hands they will read the letter and discover everything."

"They won't discover a thing. The letter's in code."

Felipe pounded his right fist in the palm of his left hand:

"I told you, Planibell, this Pepe Garcés can't be beat. You'll never trip
him up unawares."

Assuming a tolerant air Planibell said:

"Codes can be deciphered. There are people for that. And you, Pepe,
don't argue with me."

Then he started telling what he had done in Monflorite. He had not
killed deer or bears or wild boars.

"Those wild boars," interrupted Felipe, deferent and shy, "that's in
the wintertime."

But Planibell had killed over forty rabbits and a fox. He intended to
have the fox skin tanned to keep as a trophy. I had never had a real
grown-up person's shotgun. But then Planibell was older than I, although
younger than Prat. At any rate I curbed my envy to the best of my ability
and went on listening.

Planibell said that he had to return home soon so that he could go to
France with his uncle and aunt before the first of October, when he
would have to be back at school in Reus.

"Do you remember the lay brother in the workshop?" I asked him.
"Well then, take a good look at the statue in the pool. He made it. Look
at the pool carefully, and at the height of the column and the color of
the water, which is almost green. Look at everything hard, so you can

tell the friar all about it when you see him. Because that statue was made by him. Note carefully the sunlight and the reflections on the water. And tell him all about it just as you see it. Tell him that the marble looks like crystal and looks like human flesh and looks like air."

"Bah, how silly. You can't see air. And who put it there?"

"I did.

Planibell snorted with laughter.

"This Pepe Garcés never changes. He sends carrier pigeons, puts statues in lakes. Always meddling in other people's business. I never meddle in other people's business, do I, Felipe?"

Felipe made a vague gesture. I realized that he did not care for Planibell. Planibell added:

"At school we put on a play and I was Pepe's father."

Again he laughed. That laugh reconciled me with him somewhat. We started walking toward the nurseries. My sister Concha was heading for the mansion with a group of rustics. I watched her from a distance, thinking: she despises Felipe and Planibell because they're too young. I approved of her contempt even though it did seem unfair. After all, what does age have to do with it?

Planibell and Felipe stayed in the *glorieta* with the marble benches while I went to the nurseries. Nothing could be heard inside, nothing, that is, except someone whistling a waltz. "It's Monflorite," I thought, "and he must be alone. For if Pascual were there, he wouldn't dare whistle a waltz."

When Monflorite saw me he stopped whistling and said:

"The statue looks nice in the pool. Looks something like the Patria's husband. Haven't you noticed the marble Patria crowned with laurel farther on? Well, this looks like her husband."

Then he went on to tell what had happened at the pool the day the child fell in and drowned. "Do you want to know who threw the boy in the water? Felipe's uncle, the overseer. Well, I'm laughing, but don't get me wrong, it wasn't funny. For a crime is a crime. Yes sir, the overseer threw the boy in the pool. Don't you breathe it to a soul. That bad-tempered old man would be capable of cutting off my head. I know he did it because someone who saw him told me. I won't mention any names. I'm not a man to turn informer. My silence means freedom and almost life itself for the boss, because just imagine what might happen if the law found out."

"But why?" I asked. "Why did he throw him in the water?"

"Because he's in love with the little widow who spits."

"And what does the one thing have to do with the other?" I was thinking. I did not believe it. But hearing so many versions of the death of the child who fell in the pool was beginning to make me feel dizzy. I wondered who was telling the truth.

I told him that Felipe's uncle was not a man to kill a two-year-old child. An older man, in a quarrel, maybe, that would be a different matter.

"That man is capable of anything," said Monflorite. "What can you expect of a guy who knows he has a murderer like Pascual around, and still doesn't fire him?"

Pascual arrived shortly in an ugly frame of mind.

"When I come in you two stop talking. Are you talking about me? For I tell people who talk about me to keep their tongues where they belong."

This was the first time a stranger had ever insulted me in such a way. Pascual must have noticed something in my expression, for he hastened to say:

"I don't mean you, my friend."

Monflorite explained:

"This time we were talking about what happened at the pool. About the boy's unfortunate accident."

"You? And what can you say, liar, if you weren't there?"

Monflorite said nothing and started working. Pascual continued:

"I drained the pool and pulled out the boy who was down in one corner fuller of water than a sponge and deader than my grandmother. And the mother was outside and holding her head between her hands and saying: 'He's not his father's son but he took after him.' That's what she said. Then she gave a scream that must have been heard all over the whole park."

Monflorite insisted:

"No person in his right mind can believe that. How could she say the child was not his father's son?"

Pascual sprang toward him. His right hand, with which he was gesticulating, trembled:

"You have to believe it because I say so. Hear? I say so and that's the last word. It's as plain as these five fingers on my hand. Hear? Say that it's true. Come on, you bawling tramp, say it once for all. Say that you're hearing the woman's cry in the air."

I decided that I should interrupt:

"Don't take it that way, Pascual. He's not saying you're a liar but that you don't know."

Monflorite stepped aside and went on working as if he were alone. And he talked to himself, although addressing me:

"It's just that he's burned up. He's always burned up, around me."

A knife lay on the ground between them. I picked it up casually and as I reached the door heard Pascual's voice:

"Leave that knife here just in case I get it in my head to slit the throat of this shameless good-for-nothing."

Beside the door the crow was repeating, excitedly:

"Hello, hello, hello."

I left and went to the *glorieta* where Planibell was sitting, alone, on a bench. I sat down beside him and started drawing with my finger in the sand.

"What's that?" asked Planibell.

I went on drawing figures and explained: "This is an animal. And this"—half a yard to the left—"its shadow." Planibell laughed mockingly:

"The shadow," he said, "is attached to the body. Always. Without fail. You go, come, lie down, get up, and always your shadow sticks to your body."

"That isn't so."

"How come?"

"Maybe it's so with persons, but not all animals. And it's not so with people either."

Planibell laughed so hard he had to hold his stomach with his hands to keep from exploding. When he was able to speak again, he said:

"In that we're all the same. Animals, persons, trees. Everybody and everything."

"That's not so."

"How come?" and Planibell went on laughing.

The crow was walking around the avenue. I asked my friend:

"Do you see that crow?"

"Yes, sir, with its shadow sticking to its feet, like everybody and everything."

"Okay, you'll see."

I got up and the bird flew leisurely to a branch nearby. As it took off flying its shadow left it and started moving in the opposite direction. I looked at Planibell:

"What do you have to say?"

I had seen this shortly before when the white pigeon, above its black shadow, started flying. The black shadow flew in the opposite direction to the white pigeon. That had been a great discovery for me. One of those discoveries I kept for great occasions. I had wanted to dazzle Planibell and with that purpose in mind I had begun drawing in the sand "innocently." And Planibell had taken the bait.

"I would never have believed it if I hadn't seen it with my own eyes," he said.

But still he did not want to admit he was licked:

"That happens with birds, but not with people."

"People too. Look."

I walked out in the middle of the avenue, in the sun. The morning light was coming down obliquely. I jumped. As I went up in the air my shadow took off in the opposite direction over fifteen yards away. Planibell could not believe it. He jumped, I jumped. The shadows moved away from us to return to our feet as we touched ground. Planibell was still astonished, and I took advantage of that moment of confusion to tell him that I did not believe he had killed any fox in Monflorite. The fox runs so fast you can't aim at it. Besides, foxes know more than many men.

"I'll never believe that," he said.

"You won't? When a fox is full of fleas it doesn't kill them one by one the way men do. What the fox does is pick up a little stick in its teeth and slowly back into the river. As it enters the water the fleas move on to the dry part of its body. And the fox goes in deeper and deeper. When only its head is above water the fleas move on to the stick and when most of them are on it the fox ducks for a moment. All the fleas then jump onto the stick. And the fox drops the stick in the water and comes out on shore as clean as a whistle. When have men done a thing like that?"

Planibell listened concealing his surprise. Finally, and to have the last word, he insisted:

"All right, I saw the fox in the water with the stick between his teeth. Since he was still, I could take aim."

"That's a lie. Foxes can smell a hunter over half a mile away."

"I was that far away."

"You can't see a fox from that distance."

"I had a telescopic sight on the barrel of my rifle."

I knew Planibell and that he had to come out on top regardless. Very well. I refused to argue. Planibell again started jumping as high as he could to verify what I had said about the shadow. At that moment my sister appeared. Ashamed, Planibell began to dissemble and set about tying his shoe.

If Planibell and I had been such friends at school, why shouldn't we go on being so outside? But Planibell wanted to impress me with the pre-eminence and superiority he was enjoying around Felipe, abusing the respect that the poor dry-goods merchant had for the rich Catalonian manufacturer. I couldn't let Planibell get away with that. Either we were friends or we were not. I recalled Brother Pedro when he said to Planibell with distrust:

"You're a mystifying scoundrel."

My sister and I left without paying any attention to Planibell. Since Felipe was not around, we did not tell him goodbye.

On our way home my sister and I talked about the pigeon, and whether or not it could have arrived. I thought it could have. Because the pigeon took off like an arrow toward the northwest. I showed Concha the compass and the direction in which it had flown. She said:

"It couldn't have arrived yet. It takes us four hours on the train and two in the carriage."

"Yes, but we zigzagged, going around mountains and picking up passengers at stations along the way. Pigeons travel in a straight line."

And I explained to her how pigeons fly.

"You know a lot, Pepe. No one can get ahead of you."

Once again she looked at me as at a superior being, and insisted:

"You know more than all the boys your age. You scare me sometimes."

Then she said that Planibell had whispered a compliment in her ear and this was why she had gone off to the *palacete* and left him alone. Then she saw Juan, the gardener, who treated her in an attentive and courteous way. Suddenly she said:

"Really, father's ruin doesn't worry me. You'll be . . . what will you be? Whatever you like. With that compass and everything you know and your love for Valentina you can go all over the world and do whatever you like. Ah, if only I had been born a man. Well, I'll go to work too, if necessary. But what kind of work? My spelling's not good enough for secretarial work. I wouldn't like office work either. To be half working-girl and half lady? That would sure be funny. All or nothing, don't you think so? I'd rather be a seamstress going back and forth from the workshop. My sweetheart would wait for me on the corner and I'd go out and take him by the arm and off we'd go. For there are workers

who are very nice. Juan, for instance. That's why I say that if Father has
to be ruined, the sooner the better."

I was thinking about the pigeon again.

"Now it has arrived," I said, very sure of myself.

The following days were unbearable. Every time the bell rang I ran
to the door thinking it was the mailman.

In the afternoons I went to the University library to read the book by
Feliz de Azara that Juan had recommended. It took me some time to find
that curious passage which said: "I have observed many times in Para-
guay and in territories on the Brazilian border that wherever man builds
a hut or house a few weeks later plants appear around it. Plants which
had never been seen before except many leagues away and which spread
to the point of choking out all other plants. It is enough for man to cross
one of the new roads opened up in uninhabited places for these same
plants to appear on both sides. And these testify to the fact that man has
influence over the vegetable kingdom and produces a kind of mutation
and change . . . It seems then that man's presence brings about a
change in nature, destroying some plants that grew naturally and making
other new ones grow."

Other things in that book attracted my attention and I was eager to
see the Catalonian gardener to find out what he thought about these
important matters. For the time being I went around looking at the
flowers and plants in the public gardens as if they were sensitive beings
that could hear me and have opinions of their own. I talked to them
occasionally about my sweetheart, when I was sure nobody was around
either to hear or see me.

Finally a letter came from Valentina. It said: "Unforgettable Pepe:
The pigeon arrived and father was waiting because he had noticed the
white and the mottled ones were missing" (the mottled one was the
second pigeon which was still at home all alone in its cage) "and father
said: It has a paper on its foot. And he took it off and could not read a
single word and called us all together and said that this pigeon was not
his but another that came from the war, because carrier pigeons are used
in the war, and it was in code and he was going to send it to Paris to the
generals in command. This kept him very busy day and night. He showed
the letter to the mayor and many people. The mayor has written to the
governor and to Madrid and other places and has sent the letter to be
decoded by the French. Father says that quite probably the victory of
the French depends on this letter and that they will give him a medal

which he will wear on his coat. And so on. Now you see. So time lost. But about the French winning the war thanks to your letter, I don't know what to think. Although it would not surprise me. Tell me what you think.

"Now send me the second pigeon and I will be on the alert and catch it before father gets home. The trouble was that the white one arrived just when father was feeding them, at nine o'clock. Send it so that it will arrive earlier, when everybody is still in bed." Then she called me *cielo* —heaven—writing distinctly the *i* as well as the *e*. Valentina always called me *mi cielo*, and it is the sweetest expression I have ever known, even though the memory of Ervigio's jokes somewhat marred the pleasure of it for me.

I was half-disappointed and half-gloating with pride. My letter had gone to the General Staff of the Allied Armies. Would they decipher it? How? Was it possible without having Don Arturo's book at hand? I was calm about this. Nevertheless I deplored my bad luck and above all the possibility of Don Arturo's getting a decoration because of it.

A month later the mayor received a letter from the French embassy in Madrid thanking him and saying that the message was in a code based on a book. They added that it was a love letter of no consequence.

Don Arturo could not understand. A love letter? I nursed my wounded pride. Of no consequence?

A few days later I sent the next pigeon and Valentina caught it before her father saw it. She deciphered my letter very well and enjoyed doing it so much that she promised to send me more pigeons to Zaragoza.

This, however, was not easy.

Good old Baltasar came to see me occasionally. His visits were only for me, since I was the only member of the family who paid any attention to him. Again he talked to me about our former cook and I listened to him with shame.

‡ 10 ‡

Felipe took advantage of Planibell's stay in his house to invite me to dinner and introduce me to his parents. Felipe lived on Escuelas Pías Street, you may remember my saying, a narrow street lined with shops leading down to the market. The school of the Escolapians was also there, one of the oldest in the city, where the friars had the reputation of beating the boys.

Most of Felipe's house was a textile shop. On the front, between the balconies, hung huge letters spelling out the proprietor's name vertically. Felipe's mother appeared stupid at first. She smiled and stared and said nothing. His father impressed me as a markedly unreliable fellow, and I judged him to be very stingy. Amidst such people Planibell acted like a rajah. They all waited on him. He considered himself superior to his surroundings and let himself be cared for as if this treatment were his due. "What Planibell's doing is indecent," I said to myself. And I remembered Brother Pedro's words.

As I suspected, Planibell's rifle had no telescopic sight. This made me quite indignant. Behind Planibell's back I said to Felipe:

"Go on, take that stuck-up fellow down a notch or two."

"Planibell? No. My father would lick me. My father worships that boy's father and wants to buy secondhand machinery from him to set up a factory of his own. And if my father becomes a manufacturer, I'm lost. That's the gospel truth."

Felipe was biting his nails and commented philosophically:

"The only thing I need is for my mother to live many years."

At one o'clock we sat down to dinner. Planibell was given—what a shame!—the place of honor. Don Marcos plumped down in his seat, repeating:

"That's right. That's right."

A small Chinese figure of porcelain on the dresser moved its head, smiling. The father, respectfully called Don Marcos by his employees, suddenly asked Planibell:

"Pardon my curiosity, but your papa wouldn't let himself be hanged, if he could get out of it for a million pesetas, would he?"

Planibell, understanding Don Marcos' weakness, replied:

"That's exactly what the 'Bella Leonor' cost him."

The mother frowned, wrinkled up her little rat-like snout and looked at me suspiciously and asked, lowering her voice:

"Who is the beautiful Leonor? A dancer?"

The woman was treating me as an adult, thinking that I knew everything a man of the world can be expected to know. Don Marcos, listening to Planibell with one ear and to his wife with the other, parried:

"*Mujer*, the beautiful Leonor is a boat, a small amusement boat."

Then he thought: "a million," and slammed his fist down on the table, because he liked to make a show of energy once in a while, and the blow was transmitted to the table pedestal and from there to another console where a *majolica* elephant started wagging its head, surprised and wondering. I did not look at the elephant because if I did I would also begin moving mine.

It did not take Planibell long to see where he stood. For he had a scheme. One of his mystifications, as Brother Pedro would say. In spite of everything, he said, his father was very stingy with him. Don Marcos snatched at this golden opportunity and even though he was small and fat, he fairly swaggered in his chair:

"It's not stinginess, son. It's just that everything must be taken into account, and the pro and con of things must be considered from the point of view of the youth of today."

Don Marcos had the gift of speaking with great firmness and conviction, but rarely saying anything concrete. Planibell went on with his scheme while beneath us, in the shop, we could hear the doorbell ring whenever anyone entered or left.

"For example," said Planibell, "it cost me God knows what and then some to get him to give me a telescopic sight for the barrel of my gun, and finally he bought it for my last birthday. But how I had to fight to get it. And I took my telescopic sight with me to Monflorite."

I was thinking: "I don't believe it." And I bided my time to reveal my skepticism, which was rather heroic, since the entire family was seeing through the eyes of Planibell. But he went on, allowing no one to have a single word:

"And now I lost the sight in Monflorite. How can I go home without my father's gift? That's what I keep saying to myself. And I get goose flesh whenever I think about it."

"Did you have the town crier proclaim it through the town?" asked Don Marcos' wife.

"Yes, but nobody there knows what a telescopic sight is. You understand."

Don Marcos was meditating. He did not know either, but he got in his word after wiping off his eyes, nose and lips with his napkin:

"Then this is what I say. Right or wrong, what was lost was lost, and nothing one can do to get it back will do any good. Right or wrong. Isn't that so, young heir of the firm PLANIBELL AND SONS?"

With fork in one hand and knife in the other, Planibell repeated:

"But how can I go home without that telescopic sight?"

Don Marcos sighed to show how sorry he was and then stuck his fork into a pork chop. Felipe tapped my knee by way of asking me to pay attention and said:

"When Planibell arrived here his rifle had no telescopic sight whatsoever. I saw him open his suitcase and the sight was not inside either. Who has seen that famous telescopic sight of Planibell's, anyway?"

"I didn't see it either," I said curtly.

Somewhat heartened, Felipe added:

"It's very possible that he is now hunting the way to make us come through with a telescopic sight. As for me, I'd do it gladly if I had the money . . . But a gadget like that costs a lot of money."

Planibell decided that this was the moment to make some show of supreme dignity. Dropping his napkin on the table he got up, pushing back his chair. The father also left the table and laid a hand on his shoulder. So many and such energetic movements shook the dresser and the elephant nodded its head, full of wonder. Don Marcos said:

"Sit down and pay no attention to these ragamuffins. Scorn them."

Then I jumped to my feet, offended. On a corner stand I saw another porcelain Chinaman with his hands tucked in his sleeves. But his head was stationary and did not move. While holding on to my sleeve, Felipe said to his father:

"You are insulting my friend. Look here, Pepe. My father did not mean to offend you." I sat down. "He just talks without rhyme or reason sometimes."

Don Marcos with his napkin knotted around his neck repeated:

"It's not a bad word: ragamuffin. But one talks, others listen, and what happens happens. It is not a bad word, I insist. Inside the family it's actually affectionate. We can, however, buy a telescopic sight for the boy, as a token of esteem. Money is round so it can roll. How much would a good secondhand telescopic sight cost? In good condition, I say."

I interrupted:

"Do you know if Planibell's father would approve of his son's having a telescopic sight?"

"Do you know the father of this one here?" Don Marcos asked.

The mother smiled at her son, her lips shining with grease. Felipe said:

"One moment, father. Do you know what a telescopic sight is used for? For long-distance killing, and just try and find out who hit you. Our friend's father is very rich and he could have bought him the tele-

scopic sight a long time ago. And ten more telescopic sights. And a whole
battery of artillery. If he doesn't buy them it's because he doesn't want his
son to fool around with such dangerous things. So if you give him a
telescopic sight, his father will never forgive you."

Don Marcos looked at his son, at Planibell and at me. Finally he said:
"And that could certainly be so."

Planibell was livid with rage. He glanced over us and made so bold
as to say:

"I wouldn't accept a secondhand telescopic sight either."

Don Marcos began explaining, playing around with a fork as he did
so. One elbow was resting on the table and every time he shook the fork
to emphasize some statement the vinegar and oil cruets struck each other
with a delicate little sound.

"And it could certainly be true! A gadget for long-distance killing.
That's what I say. The father out of love for his son buys him a death-
dealing machine. And then what happens? Destiny. Fatality. Let me
tell you, Mr. Planibell, that I hesitate. My good will is on your side but
at this moment a doubt assails me and I don't know what to say."

The mother nudged me with her elbow and wiped off her lips. In a
low voice, but loud enough for all to hear, she said:

"As a matter of fact, he doesn't want to buy the telescope at all. For
he's stingy." Then she added, raising her voice and addressing her
husband:

"What Mr. Planibell Jr. is saying is that he does not want a secondhand, but a new one. Boys today know what they're angling for better
than you do."

Don Marcos pretended not to hear and followed the thread of his
interrupted discourse, touching his lips and then his left ear with his
napkin:

"Long-distance killing. What for? Ah, holy Heaven, the times we
live in. No. I won't buy a rifle with a telescopic sight for my own son here
present either, even though some day he will be successor to the firm the
same as you with your respective father. And if I do buy it for him, since
money was made round to circulate, and my son kills another human
being from a distance, willingly or unwillingly, I will be the first to
inform the judge. Yes, sir. Here is my son. Jail, dishonor, the gallows.
Anything but impunity. In the times we live in the worst thing for the
social order is lack of responsibility. Throw the stone and hide one's
hand? No, no. Let each mast support its sail."

He pounded the table with his open fist and the ceiling lamp gently swayed. The house seemed fragile and unsteady as a ship.

"The trouble is," the woman repeated, "that my husband's tighter than bark on a hickory tree. I know him by heart after forty years."

The merchant raised his round head with its little nose in the middle and added:

"It's like what happened to the son of Perico Zajones, from Monflorite. The son had had a sweeheart since childhood. And the sweetheart came to the city to learn to be a seamstress. That's what hapepns. And if so and so, yack-yack, or so and so, yack-yack, the girl did wrong and willy-nilly woke up in the hospital one day. Gossip was rampant in the town and the boys laughed at the son of Perico Zajones. I don't know what ailed his sweetheart. I believe it was that new sickness they call the *siphilosis*. Anyway, when the girl got well she went to a wh . . . whore house. Just what she deserved. The one who takes a wrong step falls. That's the natural law."

He drank a glass of water, the way orators do, to clear his voice. I was thinking about our old cook and felt guilty, as if I were to blame for what had happened to her. Again Felipe's mother nudged me:

"Now he'll tell the complete and true story of Perico Zajones. For three years he's been harping on that, always the same old thing."

Don Marcos looked daggers at his wife and continued:

"Some neighbors from Monflorite came here on business to see about wool, hides, fillies. A cousin of Perico's who couldn't get along at all with the family came down here to buy sheep. A ram for breeding. Fifty *duros* it cost him; the seed must be good, you know. And here he came, as I said, to Zaragoza. And as usually happens, out of curiosity or because of the gossip, he went to the house of ill-fame and saw the girl. Since some human beings are made for evil and that's the way people's instincts are, this cousin of Perico's returned home and went all over town proclaiming that if the sweetheart of so-and-so and he had had more or less what man and woman have between them . . . Then Perico's son came to Zaragoza without saying a word to anybody and went from the station straight to the wh . . . house. Well, blah-blah here and blah-blah there, but they wouldn't let him in and when the girl found out who it was, still less chance did he have. And then the blabbing mistress upstairs and the blabbing mistress downstairs, and was he a handsome young fellow, and did he look like a gentleman, and whether with one explanation or another, they finally let him in, anyway, and as soon as

Perico's son saw his former sweetheart he pulled out a fifteen caliber double-barreled pistol and bing, bang bang . . ."

Felipe raised his hand:

"Excuse me, Father. Only bing-bang. If it had two barrels, only bing-bang."

I burst out laughing. The wife enveloped her son in a look of sympathy and the father growled:

"Silence, *samarugo*. What I'm telling Mr. Planibell Junior is that he shot her twice at very close range. The poor girl fell without confession. One bullet here, the other there. Dead as a doornail, that's what she was."

"Finally," his wife said, "you'll get around to saying you're not going to buy him the telescope, so why so many speeches?"

"Hush up, woman of the devil. Bing-bang. Stone dead. And the police came and arrested Perico's son. It was in a house behind the Arch of San Ildefonso on the left hand side. Well, judging by what they say, which is what I . . . by references only. To jail with him. And in the trial he got a death sentence. I didn't go see him, and didn't want to either, because a criminal is a criminal and God deliver us, but I did write to his father saying as how sorry I was about his bad luck. And the father answered saying the guilty must pay, and that he wanted to come down for his son's execution and would I let him know about things. He wanted to see him at least the day before the performance in the Predicadores Jail, where he was. He also asked me to send him six yards of corduroy and two of braid for a new suit, by messenger, so he could be decent the day of the execution. The Pericos have always been well-dressed people, so in that case it is understandable, because the newspapers had talked a lot about the affair and the father, well, he was the father and knew that people were going to be staring at him. So I said to him: 'Come when you like and my home is yours.' And here my wife will not let me lie. Three days before the execution he came wearing his new suit. And he slept in there, in the room now occupied by Mr. Planibell Junior. And I said to him: 'Have you asked for a pardon?' And the father answered: 'That's up to the lawyer. He will know if it's proper or not.' Then, the day before he told me that I must go to the jail and talk to his son about as how he ought to sign a paper. Because he had sold a piece of land without his son's consent. And since this land was part of the legitim of his mother, well, Perico could not sell it. It was against the law. So the father said that I had to go with the paper

for the son to sign. And I said to him: 'You are the one who has to go.'
The father already had the paper written which only had to be signed.
And the father said: 'Well, but you and your wife must come as
witnesses.'"

"That's true," said Don Marcos' wife, "he's not lying about that."

She said this as she served more wine to Planibell and me. Don
Marcos continued:

"That's the way things are. You give an inch and they take a mile. I
offered him a sleeping-room and he asked me to be a witness. I agreed
to be a witness and then it turns out that we all signed a paper dated a
year before, before the calamity. When I realized it, it was too late. At
the jail the son was very bullheaded and said: 'The only thing I regret
is not having also killed the swine who had been with her.' And the
father said to him: 'Don't you realize that this is the last day of your
life?' And the son said, says he: 'My life is mine, and with it I am paying.'
And when we left Perico said to me, as he put the paper away in his
pocket, satisfied: 'I had another son who was even more hotheaded than
this one. They killed him in Morocco, in the war. If not, he would have
gone to prison, too. You can't imagine what that boy was like.' Well, to
make a long story short, he needed the boy's signature because the one
who had bought the piece of land found out that they had sold it without
the son's authorization and wanted to bring suit, for he had not yet made
the last payment and he hoped to get it lowered with his threat. I didn't
find out about it until after signing. That signature of mine was worth
more than three hundred *duros* to him."

Felipe looked in my direction and winked. The father looked daggers
at him. Then he looked at Planibell apologetically and continued, picking
up crumbs from the tablecloth with his knife as he talked:

"I said to him: 'Perico, didn't your son notice in the signing, the date
on the paper, I mean?' 'No, Marcos. That's why I waited until the last
day. No human being could notice such trifles on such a calamitous
occasion.' 'Come, come, I say it because . . . what you're doing isn't
right.' 'Well,' said he, 'but I'm his father and I do it with a good intention.' And afterward he came and told me that everybody was treating
him and welcoming him as the father of his son and that they had taken
pictures of him for the newspapers. The plain, unvarnished truth is that
Perico didn't spend a penny on the burial. He had not sold the farm to
pay for his son's expenses but had already collected and spent it,

squandering it on himself. Because he's a spendthrift, that's what he is. But not on me. He still owes me for the cloth he bought from me. And my signature had been worth three hundred *duros* to him, yes sir."

"Mine too," said the wife, "for I also signed. But I don't say a word. All those stories are water under the bridge now."

She served Planibell and me some more wine. Don Marcos said:

"I don't care. I received Perico Zajones in my house because he had the guts to face calamity and because he did not like impunity. I don't either. And that's how it is. We were from the same town, that's the trouble. After all, a *paisano* is a *paisano*."

The wife, wetting a finger with saliva and smoothing her eyebrow, added:

"All the truth must be told. Perico had never been in Zaragoza. To Huesca, yes, he went every November for the cattle fair, but not here. And he took advantage of the opportunity. He was sorry about the death of his son. But it looked as if he were showing off with his misfortune. I told him . . . because I call a spade a spade, I told him: 'Now without children you're going to really enjoy your wife's legitim.' And Perico said: 'Well, now that the house is on fire, let's warm up!' "

Don Marcos picked up the bottle, held it against the light, saw that it was empty, and put it down again saying:

"The Zajones were always conceited. Perico went to see the executioner to thank him for having treated his son well. What he wanted was to get to know new people and make contacts. One never knows what may happen tomorrow, and even in hell it's a good idea to have friends. And the hangman came here to return his call. These people here were present, and would not let me lie. He was very conceited, Perico was. When he went back to his home town he was puffed up and strutted like a peacock. It seemed a little strange to me for him to act like such a braggart after what had happened, but if society is to march on, each one must face up and pay when his luck is poor at cards. And for the boat to navigate, each mast must support its own sail. Isn't that so? For these as well as other reasons I do not mention I believe, Mr. Planibell, that I must not do more than your own father would do for you, since otherwise I can incur his ill-will and break our precious friendship. You," he said to his wife, "bring another bottle."

She did not move from her chair. Planibell was ashamed, but he kept face:

"I've only told what happened to my telescopic sight in Monflorite. And besides, I don't intend to kill anybody either at close range or far away. And above everything else take note that I'm not asking for anything."

I pushed my chair back and said:

"You're lying. You're lying like a trooper. You haven't done a thing but ask for it since you started talking."

Planibell and I had drunk the bottle of wine between us. It was the first time that I had ever taken so much wine. And I repeated:

"You're lying like a trooper, Planibell."

He looked at me with watery eyes and asked:

"Who? Me?"

He was not in the least offended but calmly started explaining to Don Marcos:

"This friend says I'm lying because he's envious. He doesn't have a telescopic sight, not even a rifle. He spends his time writing letters in code and sending them by carrier pigeons to his different sweethearts."

"I only have one sweetheart," I answered him threateningly.

The wine was making me aggressive and Planibell prudent. We had contrary temperaments. Planibell said:

"Well, your sweetheart. I certainly do have a telescopic sight. I had it, that is. Do you know how long your carrier pigeon would last in the air if I were down below with my telescopic sight? Less than a flash. But I've lost the sight. I'm not asking you to buy me another, especially a secondhand one. What I'm saying is that I lost it or it was stolen in Monflorite, your town. And you are partly responsible. And then you refuse to understand. And you, Pepe, excuse me, but you're not holding any candle at this funeral so you keep out of this. Shut up. Scram. Go on and send a pigeon to the beautiful Coquito."

I gave him a kick under the table and hit him smack in the middle of the shin. Planibell stifled a cry of pain, then said three or four very ugly French words and started groaning. He was drunk, of course. Between sighs and gasping for breath, he said:

"I have no choice but to tell my father, Don Marcos."

Looking at Planibell the wife said:

"Poor dear. He looks like a little child."

Planibell went right on, never losing sight of his interests in spite of everything:

"I'll tell my father. I will tell him that you invited me to dinner to give me kicks under the table"—he was evidently unaware that it was I who had kicked him—"and that I have slept in the same room as the father who came to see how they hanged his son. I'll also say that the hangman comes to call on you."

Suddenly he became calm, looked at me out of the corner of his eye and said in French: *merde*. Then *salaud*. He did not sound as drunk in French as in Spanish.

"Just once," said Don Marcos sliding his chair back and getting to his feet with such violence that the elephant began to nod its head again. "The hangman came just once and he didn't come to see us, but Perico Zajones. I respect the laws of hospitality. If he came to see Perico I could not shut the door in his face. But don't say anything about this to your father. I realize such things don't sound well. Aside from this, what kind of telescopic sight do you prefer?"

Planibell calmed down instantly.

"Zeiss," he said, "and new."

Don Marcos laid his hand on his chest, over his napkin:

"You'll have it this very afternoon," he promised.

That afternoon—true to the merchant's word—Planibell had a magnificent Zeiss telescopic sight which he fitted on the barrel of his rifle. I was thinking: "What he's doing is ignoble and he would not have done it if he had not been drunk." Planibell told me later that he had gotten drunk purposely, to have the courage to be so bold. I was scandalized. Everything scandalized me in those days and this, certainly, with no less reason. I saw only irregular things around me, terrible things, incongruous things. Valentina alone seemed all right to me. And she was far away and I had no more pigeons to send her. I was beginning to find the entire city suspect and little worthy of Valentina and me.

Planibell had left by now and gradually my contempt and feeling of shock turned into admiration and even envy.

‡ 11 ‡

On Saturdays and Sundays no one worked in my father's offices and the balconies along Coso Street belonged exclusively to my sister and me. Especially to her, since she had inspected very carefully and one by one all the houses in front and knew who lived there, what they did, and whether they were bachelors or married.

Across from our house in an *entresol* apartment lived the impresario of the bull ring, a former *novillero* named Villa, or Villita. He had a very beautiful daughter. A girl as slender as a reed, lithe and delicate, with an air of old aristocracy. Concha tried to interest me in her and when I told her that I could only love Valentina, she sighed deeply and said:

"How lucky some women are!"

Then she confessed that if she had talked to me about Villa's daughter it was only to try me out to see how far the fidelity or perfidy of men would go.

On those Sunday afternoons the main balcony looked like a presidential box in an ancient circus. At that spot the Coso was broad, clean, quiet. Couples in their Sunday-best passed by, automobiles, carriages with snow-white wheels. There were already quite a few cars in Zaragoza. The Marqués de Urrea, an acquaintance of my father's, had a Hispano, I remember, with the license number 105. Still, there were no cars for hire. At the cab stands there were only horse-drawn carriages. And toward mid-afternoon strolling musicians would appear playing and singing, and selling small pink sheets of paper printed with the words of the songs. The people gathered into a great motionless crowd around them and the voices of the singers found a holiday echo on the stone façade of the Palace of Justice:

> *Goodbye Ninon,*
> *gentle Ninon,*
> *the jewels I won*
> *I have stolen*
> *to adorn you*
> *But woe is me,*
> *how mad could I be,*
> *so mad for your beauty*
> *I'm going to lose my head*
> *because of you.*

My sister sighed and said: "I don't know what it is about those songs that sometimes almost makes me cry." This, despite the fact she understood perfectly how wretched they were.

On certain Sundays at dusk great crowds would pour through the

Arch of San Roque from the direction of the Escolapian School on the way home from the bullfights. Newsboys appeared crying out a weekly paper devoted to bullfighting: *Pitos y Palmas*—Boos and Cheers—with the account of Belmonte's goring or maybe the triumph of Florentino Ballesteros, an Aragonese matador. Admist that sudden clamor the musicians' voices grew faint but did not entirely fade away:

Adiós Ninón,
gentil Ninón . . .

That summer I suddenly had an important revelation: women. It was very odd. Before then I could not conceive of men kissing women on the lips. It seemed repugnant to me. And I had come to base the strength of my affection for Valentina on the following picturesque and absurd reflection:

"I love her so much that the idea of kissing her on the lips is not repugnant to me."

Well then, suddenly that summer I understood that the lips of women were not repugnant. But quite the contrary. An important part in the revelation was played by a newspaper stand facing the Emma Victoria movie theatre. All four sides were covered with daily papers, magazines and cheap books in bright-colored jackets. Always some really stimulating photograph stood out above everything else. I used to go there to buy the magazine *Blanco y Negro* for my mother. And while there I looked and stared. What things I saw! On one side a magazine opened in the middle displayed a double-page photograph of an "artistic nude"—a woman reclining voluptuously and revealing her plump thighs. I could not look at it without my head swimming, round and round. "Good Heavens" I thought, "how much beauty there is in the world!" Those quick glances at love magazines awakened my puberty.

And I began to understand that woman, any woman, was an exquisite promise. But it was a clandestine and vicious promise. When I thought of Valentina I felt no promise at all. Valentina was something else and my feelings toward her were very different. The idea of kissing her on the lips seemed all right to me, but those thighs and rumps in the love magazines must belong to another world. Yet they were charming. There was no need to identify voluptuous pleasure with love. And it took me quite a while to realize that they should be the same thing.

I was going through great periods of melancholy when a letter from

Valentina made me snap out of them. She said that she and her mother were coming, as she had promised, for the Pilar festivities on the twelfth of October. This was still several weeks off, but I began counting the days. I thought that they would stay with us but Concha said no, that Doña Julia had relatives who lived on the other side of Coso Street near the San Roque Arch. Doña Julia had visited there with her daughter Pilar the year before.

About the pigeons, not a word. I wondered if there might be some way to train them and make them come flying to my house just as they flew to Valentina's, but I was soon convinced that this was a ridiculous illusion. So Valentina had only received one letter of mine, in code.

I still found money on top of the tables and I took it as long as it was less than two pesetas. In those days two pesetas was a lot of money. For twenty céntimos (four cents) I could go to the movies. Coffee on a terrace cost the same amount and an immense glass of orange drink at the *Espumosos*—soda fountains—in the arcades of the Paseo de la Independencia, three cents. Two pesetas—forty cents—sometimes lasted three weeks.

At that time many Germans from the African Cameroons, which had been taken over by the Allies, were passing through Zaragoza. The city was full of fat Germans with shaved heads wearing broad-brimmed hats turned up on the sides. Whenever they met they waved their hats at each other with such extravagant gestures and bowed in such a Versaillesque way that people could not keep from laughing.

Then tragedy struck at the *Espumosos*. When a waitress went to serve a group of Germans seated around a table, one of them grabbed her around the waist. The girl raised a siphon she was carrying and struck him over the head with it. The German fell dead at her feet. The next day the waitress was still at her post, just as if nothing had happened. The judge had released her after an interrogation with witnesses.

The German's burial, attended by all the Cameroon refugees, seemed like public affirmation of the scandal. Everybody was sorry about it, but the judge let the waitress go free, as I mentioned before, after a brief discourse on the rights of feminine modesty in general, and Spanish modesty in particular. After that whenever I went to the *Espumosos* and saw her I thought of those double-page photographs in the love magazines and said to myself: the German risked his life, and lost it, for an irresistible desire. I also felt capable of such irresistible desires. And even understood how someone could risk his life and lose it. I thought that it was worthwhile. I was awakening to the life of the senses, to puberty, I mean to say, with a vigor I could never have suspected in myself. It was like a torrent sweeping me along with it.

Meanwhile my father had quarreled with the owner of the press and bindery. The collateral for the loan was evidently not executory, so my father could not threaten him with reprisals, and his industrial partner was behaving like a swine, to use my father's words. If he shouted at him he would fold his hands and tilt his head to one side and sigh. If my father called him a thief, he would sigh again, blush slightly, but never come through with any money. If my father were to beat him—naturally it never came to this—the man would undoubtedly wail but not let go of a single penny either. The only method that might have produced some results—my father said—was the rack of the Inquisition. But in Aragón— he added comically—it could not be applied, for it had been pro- hibited by law since the Middle Ages. And not even the tribunals of the king could torture anybody in the fifteenth or in the twentieth century. That's why criminals used to say: "Deny, deny, for you're in Aragón." And now it was my father's turn to sigh.

These prohibitions in Aragón made me feel a certain pride, but my father received no benefits from them nor did he recover his capital. German bank notes were not quoted on the stock exchange any more and the war was dragging on and on. Nor was it certain that the Germans were going to win. My father felt at times as if there were a universal plot against his money and he reacted with a universal rancor. When his desperation bordered on catastrophe he would sigh, go to church and receive communion. Then he was tranquil for a couple of days.

I felt the mystery of voluptuousness all around me, as I was saying. I told Don Orencio, the confessor of La Seo, and he laid his hand on my shoulder as he said:

"My son, you are entering adolescence and no human misery will be spared you. Especially, being who you are. For I know your family. The Garcés have always been so."

Then he gave me advice, not only religious but hygienic. I should get physical exercise, play football or something else, go to bed at night exhausted, and not lie in bed in the morning once awake. Nor look at sinful magazines (those newsstands, he said, should in fact be set on fire), and above all else be a frequent communicant. He warned me against many dangers as an older brother might have done, and I left these inter- views strong and toned-up, following all his advice except for being a frequent communicant. At the same time I was developing a certain erotic-mystical tendency. I saw feminine thighs in the iridescent nimbuses, in the Gregorian music and in the clouds of incense. I don't know by what chance I heard several other persons say that the newsstands with love magazines should be burned. And I do not know if what I am saying now is the unreal materialization of a desire in my memory or if it was true, but I believe that one day I did try to set fire to the kiosk in front of the Emma Victoria, and that the wind blew out the last of my three matches before I could succeed. I felt drawn to those pictures which my conscience condemned. But my inner fire was stronger than any other stimulus. I would have risked my life like the German in the *Espumosos*; I would have killed like the son of Perico, of Monflorite. I did not know what was happening to me. It was like a strong wind from the sea uprooting me from the earth.

My love for Valentina was not enough. That affection was on a different plane and irrelevant to the great problem.

Nevertheless when she came and as long as she was in Zaragoza, I felt free of that torture. I had saved up money from my petty thefts, and Doña Julia let us go to the fair, alone. Naturally this place of wonders was just the spot for me to show off my lover's generosity. Everywhere carrousels, side shows, shooting galleries, candy stands (of a thousand different kinds and colors), "Russian Mountains" (roller coasters), mills, big spinning stars and besides all that, the old familiar circus where I did not want to take Valentina for three reasons: first, because of two things which frightened her—the lions and the clowns. And second, because I did not want her to see the Smart Brothers, or look at them, rather, with the same reverent expression as my sister had done. Finally, because the day I was debating whether or not to buy tickets, I saw Felipe and his cousins at the entrance. I did not want Valentina to be around those people. Not because Felipe's father had received and lodged in his house the parents of hanged men, but because I remembered Felipe at Doña Pilar's bathhouse, and it gave me an uncomfortable feeling to associate him with Valentina. In any case, for some days the erotic torture greatly decreased.

Valentina liked the roller coaster best of all. She screamed like a lost soul when the little cars hurtled down an almost vertical ramp over forty yards high to enter a tunnel at the top of which it felt as if we were leaving our heads behind us. My heart was in my mouth and I felt as if

I were turning into some kind of projectile. As far as I was concerned, I would never have returned to that fiendish labyrinth of anguish, but Valentina never had enough and I did not want to confess my fear. Being with me, she said, kept her from being afraid.

So we spent our time between a shooting gallery, where I shot with a .22 at a little rubber ball floating in a jet of water, and the cursed "Russian Mountains." In the shooting gallery I won almost every prize, including a magnificent doll for Valentina, who was radiant with joy.

My vanity placed me in grave danger, however. We paused in front of a kind of low bench on which a man was pounding with a mallet, trying to make a leaden ball climb a post marked off in meters. If struck hard enough for the ball to reach the top a bell would ring, a light come on, and a parasol open. The poor man was sweating and vainly trying to do it. Finally he gave up. The one exploiting this concession must have been a real rogue for he winked at me, as he said to his client:

"You'll have to eat more heartily, my friend."

I walked up and asked him for the mallet. It was a long-handled hammer and the head must have weighed six or seven pounds. The man looked at me with sympathy and began to shout: "World championship of muscular strength! The blow that hits square in the groove and sends the ball clean up to the sky!" After two unsuccessful attempts, aware that for me it was a question of life or death, the man manipulated something so that the third time the ball went to the top, the bell rang, the light came on and the parasol opened. The barker cried:

"Champion of muscular strength of both Castiles, Priorato and Upper Rioja! Here is your well-earned medal, gentleman. My congratulations to the gentleman and his fiancée."

And he winked at me again.

Valentina and I marched off haughtily, Valentina prouder than I, however, since she did not share the sad secret of my victory.

We also went on the most luxurious carrousel—full of mirrors—where they had not only horses but pigs, burros, dogs, and even wooden deer. And they all moved in three directions: forward, up and down, and with a rocking movement back and forth. Valentina never tired. Her cheeks glowed with excitement and her eyes sparkled. I had heard the music of the carrousel before, with my sister. There were two or three tunes that we especially liked and since we were good customers the lady-manager had them played often. Our favorite was the *pasodoble* "Moors and Christians." On a small platform in the center of the merry-go-round there were at least thirty dolls with their musical instruments and a conductor who waved his baton and moved his head energetically.

Whirling around in the carrousel full of mirrors beside Valentina I really felt transported and fancied strange things. "The carrousel is spinning like a real galaxy." Everything was mobile and shifting. Once, at the end when we came to a stop, Valentina was left too high in the air to get off her horse alone. She did not know how to dismount. Her left thigh—half nude—was beside my face and it was just as beautiful as those I had seen in the double pages of the love magazines. I touched it, to help her get off, but she did not want to dismount yet. "Once more," she said laughing. And I climbed back on my horse, still feeling the warmth of that contact in my hand.

When it began to grow dark and all the lights in the park were turned on I took Valentina home and left her in the arms of Doña Julia who did not allow her to be out after dark. Valentina told her one by one—and with a prodigious memory—all the things that we had done, especially those which reflected glory on me. When I left I kissed her and we both hesitated an instant several times as we sought each other's cheek and our lips touched lightly. I felt an unknown and new emotion. My nerves twitched. She seemed just the same as ever, friendly, sweet and in-different at the same time. And I felt the lights of the carrousel whirling around me, like the unknown worlds my astronomy textbook talked about. I was beginning to identify voluptuousness with Valentina's body.

Several afternoons I returned to the fair alone. To hear the "Moors and Christians" *pasodoble* and not have Valentina beside me caused me a kind of adult melancholy. And I liked it. One evening I ran across Felipe again and we talked about the incident with Planibell. My friend was still astonished and repeated:

"He's a tramp. Well," he corrected himself, "my father says he'll be a businessman. A shark, a financial wizard, that's what the fellow will be."

Then he told me that the mother of the boy who died in the pool in the Villa Julieta had been released from the insane asylum. Apparently she was not insane or considered guilty, either. He asked for my opinion, but I continued to guard my discretion:

"What do you want me to say? Especially when I've never seen her."

One of those days Valentina, who could not keep a secret from her mother, told her what we had done with the pigeons. Doña Julia wanted to laugh, but she pretended dismay:

"My child, you know what confusion the first pigeon with its message caused at home. The letter in code went to Madrid, Paris. Why didn't you mention it then?"

Valentina said she had not told her because they were in the village at the time and her father would have found out. Now it was different, since they were in Zaragoza.

During those festival days there were public celebrations that looked magnificent to us. Among them a review of cavalry troops in front of the Palace of Justice beside our house. The whole bugle corps was there, in gala uniform and mounted. Also that same day there was a cavalcade with enormous floats decorated with flowers and symbolical figures. And after every three or four floats, a band. One of the floats, I recall, simulated the ruins of a Greek temple. There were two very tall columns, one complete with its capital and the other broken. An Apollo. A fountain. A Venus. The proportions and spaces gave great beauty to it all. This float stopped right in front of my house. Near Valentina's a band was playing. I was looking at Valentina through opera glasses. On other days Valentina and her mother had come to our house, but that afternoon they had to stay with their relatives. I saw Valentina who was looking at my balcony, talking to her mother and looking at my balcony, as always hanging on to me. All at one time I saw the Greek ruins—which seemed to me like an allusion to the Villa Julieta—and felt myself being watched by Valentina, and heard in the calm of the golden afternoon that music—the municipal band—playing the chorus of the *zarzuela* "Maruxa" where the peasants sing: "*Ay, golondrón, golondrina de amor.*" Well, since then whenever I hear that part of "Maruxa," emotion fills all my memory, my present, and my hope to overflowing. Much more effectively than the music of Bach or Mozart. One must have the courage to confess it. Nothing is more interesting for anyone than his own intimate world and art is the more valuable the more it means inside that inalienable world of one's own where nobody else can enter.

I have no desire to compare the two kinds of music, naturally. I understand the difference between pure intellectual invention and the repetition of familiar modulations and forms flattering or wounding our sensitive memories. But since I must tell everything, I do not wish to fail to note that detail. Listening to that music I again feel myself in the center of a brilliant whirling galaxy. And in the middle of it, Valentina's naked thigh.

We did many things in those brief days of Valentina's and her mother's visit to Zaragoza. As may be imagined, I took them to the Villa Julieta one day when it was open to the public. The gondola made such an impression on Valentina that she was speechless with emotion. She had never "embarked" before, to use her own words, and that means of locomotion seemed much better to her than the train. Furthermore she did not get seasick. Valentina thought that there must be gondolas like this in all the canals and that people could choose between the gondola or train when returning home.

In the park, as everywhere, we made two couples, Valentina and I, and Doña Julia and Concha. Naturally I introduced Juan to my sweetheart and the three of us started talking like old friends. I told Juan that I had read Felix de Azara's book on plants and he looked pleased:

"Ah," he said, "you know how to get at the roots of things."

So that Valentina would understand what all this was about, I asked Juan:

"Do you believe, like Azara, that plants can see and hear us?"

"Man," said Juan laughing, "Azara doesn't go that far. Come and I will show you."

He took us near the pool. He led us through the flower beds surrounding it on the north side. And he showed us some small wild plants with tiny pink and yellow heads.

"These plants have come here all by themselves," he explained. "They appear wherever I stay working over a week. Well, it's not that they come, maybe the seeds are already in the ground and only germinate when they receive the waves of my thought and nerves. Other flowers follow my uncle, the overseer, around. And I suppose there must be some for Monflorite and Pascual. They don't know it, of course. And I won't tell them, for they would think me crazy. They already say aplenty about me. Didn't they tell you I'm a gangster? Nonsense. I'm a journeyman tailor who comes to spend the summer here as a vacation and who happens to know something about gardening. I've got my own ideas, sure. I believe every fellow must do his own thinking. And that there are many things we don't have enough of in Spain, as well as others we have far too much of."

"What do we have too much of?"

"Some heads," he muttered, lowering his voice.

"I think so too," I declared, thinking of Don Arturo.

Autumn had come to the Villa Julieta and the air was beginning to have that metallic smell in the groves. In some places the leaves were turning yellow. The marble head had melted into the landscape and become a part of it. Juan went back to talking about the sensitive plants again, thinking, possibly, that superfluous heads was not a suitable topic for children.

"Haven't you noticed," he asked, "how plants and special flowers grow at the side of the roads which are not seen anywhere else? That's because they come up to offer themselves to the men passing by."

Valentina could not quite grasp this and commented:

"I see. Those are the plants the road repairmen set out."

With Valentina's camera I took several pictures of the pool to send to the friar in Reus who resembled—so I believed—Juan, only in reverse. One was a friar and perhaps a saint, while the other was an enemy of friars and, maybe, a burner of convents. Since Valentina was in the pictures, when I wrote the lay brother I begged him not to show them to anybody, especially Ervigio, who had the impertinent habit of falling in love with other people's sweethearts. I also promised Juan a picture, one without Valentina, of course.

I confess that when we left the park I felt calmer. I was beginning to be afraid of all that useless beauty, especially when with Valentina. I was afraid for her. Later on I learned the real danger there is in all true beauty. At that time I had only the presentiment.

My mother and Doña Julia had many long conversations together. Two seamstresses were busy making underclothes at home at the time. My parents never bought ready-made underclothing. Everything was made to measure. I can still remember how one of the seamstresses, the youngest, held her arms around me for a moment when she put the tape measure around my waist, to embarrass me perhaps, and then how she exchanged ironical glances with the other. I caught a glimpse of her curving breasts and felt a thrill.

Doña Julia discussed with my mother at great length the bother and impropriety of seamstresses. Doña Julia apparently felt her position to be awkward or less successful at times because of their living in the village while we were in Zaragoza. And she was on the defensive. After saying that she would never have seamstresses around her home to make under-clothing, behind my mother's back one day she asked the seamstresses how much they would charge to go to the village for two weeks during which time, naturally, they would live in her house.

Also she underhandedly asked them (which was what most annoyed

Concha) to lend her some patterns, those pieces of paper made before cutting the cloth. My sister and mother were quite amazed when they found out about this. My mother told my father, who paid no attention. My sister told me, but I did not care to look into the mattter either. Women's business. Besides, I adored my mother-in-law.

Valentina and I went to many of my favorite haunts about the city. She was enthusiastic or indifferent, depending on my own reactions. We sailed in Uncle Toni's boat, but she did not like it as well as the swan. In the middle of the river where the current was strong, Valentina was a little frightened. We went to the Pilar Cathedral and La Seo, and my father and Doña Julia argued over whether Valentina was too old or not to go through the *camarín*. They evidently consulted Mosén Orencio who decided that Valentina was already too old. This made me think ill of Mosén Orencio for some time.

‡ 12 ‡

And then I was alone in the city once more. Summer came to an end and autumn arrived with its cold north winds and mother-of-pearl clouds. The fair and all its installations disappeared and school opened in the Instituto where I had been matriculated. During the first weeks classes were dull. The other boys—new and indifferent faces—were not interesting either. There were so many in each class that I felt lost in the crowd and alone. It took me a long time to make friends.

On the other hand I became friendly at once with a vendor of peanuts and sweets, among them some coconut cakes I used to buy. He would set up his cart stand in front of the Instituto door. He did not seem to be much concerned about his business and devoted his attention to some mysterious notebooks which he would take from underneath the cart, and spread out on his knees to write upon. The first day I went up to look over his shoulder and saw that he was writing dialogue in verse with a good deal of agility and ease. At the left he wrote the name of the character who was speaking: Leonor, or Froilán, or Federica. They were all very select names. He told me that he was writing a classical tragedy in five acts and nine scenes.

We became good friends.

I still had not lost my summertime habits. But sometimes I went through long crises of sadness. When I was saddest one day the messenger boy from the village came to deliver a little cage with two pigeons and a letter from both Doña Julia and Valentina. They told me that I would not have to use any code and Doña Julia promised me that no one would set his sinful eyes on my writing. She only asked me to take note of the hour and minute, and if possible, the second, when the pigeons were set free and let her know on a post card. This detail made me think that Don Arturo was interested in repeating the experiments. On that account, maybe, he was willing to compromise with my love letter.

I ran over to see Felipe to plan an excursion to the Villa Julieta with him. I also told him that I needed a watch with a second hand and his father looked at me out of the corner of his eye, fearing probably a repetition of the Planibell affair. Feeling very sorry that he had no such thing Felipe also said that he could not go to the Villa with me because they were taking inventory in the shop and would not finish for another two weeks. During that time his father did nothing but shout and kick the furniture around, making the elephants and little Chinese figures on the consoles tremble. Felipe told me in passing what a lucky man I was and that my sweetheart would be the ideal companion. He had seen her from a distance one afternoon when we were at the fair together.

I went to the Villa alone. It was beginning to look desolate, some trees bare, others yellow, dry leaves on the avenues. The surface of the pool rippling with cold gusts of wind seemed to allude to oblivion and to the sadness of things that are ending. The overseer was ill. Juan came out wearing a red jersey and we chatted. He told me that he was leaving for Barcelona the next day and that I was bright to come today because then he could tell me goodbye. I asked him questions about the plants that are friendly to man, but Juan had other things on his mind.

"I'll bet you can't guess who was here yesterday? . . . The mother of the child who drowned in the pool. She showed me some sketches of her son, very well done, for a fact. Once again she said that Byzantium was illuminating her and that the marble head you put there is Byzantium. Precisely Byzantium. What a strange coincidence. I believe that the boy fell into the water all by himself and that everybody is making up stories to make someone pay for it. Everybody wants someone to be responsible. What for? That's what I say. There are plenty of superfluous heads in the world, but not the ones ordinary people imagine."

Juan led me to the side of the border, beside the pool. Yellow flowers were floating near the shore. He bent over and showed me a row of plants, some with rose and yellow buds. "Look," he said, "these little plants appeared three days after the child's death. They go wherever some calamity occurs. This little thistle with a yellow flower some call *amargones*—dandelions. No one pays any attention to it, except to pull it up as harmful. But it's healthful, good to eat"—so saying he put a leaf in his mouth—"and it appears wherever man is unfortunate. Don't laugh, for this is serious. I wouldn't say this to anyone else, and not to you either if you hadn't read Azara's book. It's the truth. And three days after the accident they appeared here. I know it very well because I come to work in this garden every summer, that's why. I am experimenting with plants. They appeared here three days afterward. I told the child's mother and she . . ."

"She's insane," I said.

"No. She's not insane."

"And her spitting?"

Juan wriggled in his jersey as if he were having the shivers and said:

"That's something passing. She'll soon get over that. Those things happen to women when they lose their man. Not to all of them, of course. Nervous derangements."

When they lose their man. Was it possible that the woman felt herself swept along by an inner hurricane the same as I? Women too? I wanted to run away from those suggestions.

"So she's not crazy?"

"No."

"Does what she says about Byzantium sound sane to you?"

We looked at the marble head and Juan said:

"Why not? Byzantium's a city instead of a man, but what difference does it make? Aren't there cities with people's names?"

Since that time I have called the statue Byzantium and so I wrote to the lay brother. He did not object to it, either.

([ ])

THE FOLLOWING POEM PROBABLY REFERS TO THAT AUTUMN IN THE
VILLA JULIETA AND IS ENTITLED *The Yellow Hours*.

On the water
the whirling leaf
weeps and dances.
I see you just as you are
alive in the center of Spain,
look at me just as I am
dead in distant lands
and keep if possible
your embalmed voices
in the yellowing laces
of that gala nakedness
so different at times
through the distant spaces.
Yellowing tapers
in the collegiate church
and in the blonde winds
of autumn
the whirling leaf
weeps and dances.
Gold of sun and wheat
and of the veil of my dwelling,
silence is yellow
in mid-morning,
mead in the meadows
is drunk by the harvesters,

the lost winds come
yellow with revenge
and the evening sun falls
on the golden slope.
    Yellowing
    the embroidery on the albs
    and on the altars
    of autumn
    the whirling leaf
    prays and dances.
With the running of the autumns
I keep all your words,
some in my rememberings,
others in your old letters
and yellow through the autumn wind
they fly away from me,
from the letters to memory
and later to those bland
nudities of the miracle
you spread throughout my soul.
    Yellowing
    your enchanted eyes
    and Byzantium
    in the pool
    sees the dance
    of the whirling leaf.
The thirst of our pacts
in my poor throat
is just the same as then,
illumined voice of the dream
multiplied in echoes
at the foot of our mountain.
With it I patch the space
between my body and your soul
oh, my beloved, memory
of light, yellow flame.
    Yellowing
    the arches of the windows
    and in the autumn wind

the whirling leaf
Moans and dances.
In my emigrant's dream
the terraces undress
and suns are caught
in your gala apron.
Oh, virgin of my devotion,
as in the golden shocks of grain
yellow I remember you,
golden and wheatlike in the window
though with your crown
of black hair almost blue.
 Yellowing
the marmoreal light
of the morning song
· and I say hello
just like the crow
in the solitary dawn,
hello to the wind
carrying me away from you
toward nothingness.

THE END